DUATERO

BR

PRAISE FOR DUATERO

"Combines power armoured soldiers from the pages of sci-fi pulps, a world as intriguing yet bleak as Mid-World from Stephen King's Dark Tower, *and an evil as terrifying and paranoia inducing as John Carpenter's* The Thing. *A descent into the darkness of a failing world and the brutal zealotry of its defenders."* -

Matt Moore, Aurora-winning author of
It's Not the End and Other Lies

"Brad C. Anderson delivers a darkly compelling tale of the battle between reason and tradition in a meticulously evoked alien world where abandoned human inhabitants battle for survival on a planet that does not want them."

Liz Westbrook-Trenholm,
Aurora Award-winning writer

"An intense and realistic envisioning of generational survival on an alien planet, complete with cultural strife, high stakes, engaging characters, and fight-for-your-life action. Highly recommended!"

Adria Laycraft, author of *Jumpship Hope*

DUATERO

BRAD C. ANDERSON

SHADOWPAW
PRESS *Premiere*

DUATERO
By Brad C. Anderson

Second Edition
Published 2022 by
Shadowpaw Press Reprise
Regina, Saskatchewan, Canada
www.shadowpawpress.com

First edition published 2019 by Bundoran Press

All characters and events in this book are fictitious.
Any resemblance to persons living or dead is coincidental.

Trade Paperback ISBN: 978-1-989398-39-5
Ebook ISBN: 978-1-989398-40-1

Cover art by Dan O'Driscoll
Cover and interior design by Shadowpaw Press
Created with Vellum

To my wife, Joelle Bradley.
The smiles in your eyes are my stars at night.

EPIGRAPH

"... even if there is no truth, man can be truthful, and even if there is no reliable certainty, man can be reliable. If there was salvation, it had to lie in man himself, and if there was a solution to the questions raised by doubting, it had to come from doubting."

HANNAH ARENDT, *THE HUMAN CONDITION*

ONE

TALIA GREW up in the Founder city of Xuanhe, and her birthright was the ability to cuss with the intense depravity of a drunken longshoreman. But she and I are falchilo, scythes of the Founders, and our words should be worthy of our ancestors, or so I believed. It took years, but I had rid her of the blue streak that could fire from her mouth like a sling bullet.

"Fuck."

Kind of. Leaning in close to her as we walked, I said, "We have future falchilo to mould." Behind us, the squad of young men and women still wearing the white armband of initiates marched in formation. "Mind your language."

"Sorry, Kredo," she said. "But . . ." She pointed down a field of stubble on our left under the gray sky.

Narrowing my eyes, I came to a stop, bringing the entire company behind me to a halt, the squelching of their feet in mud falling silent and giving way to the patter of rain. Far off, a dark figure surrounded by a hazy black cloud walked through the field. Talia had good eyes. Even when I was her age, I don't think I had eyes as good as hers.

The falchilo initiates following me had that look of youthful enthusiasm. Maybe some kid stuck on the farm with a head full of dreams of adventure might be awestruck at their appearance. They held falchilo weapons, their rods belted at the waist, shield packs attached to the left forearm, and they walked in tight, crisp formation. Each of them wore a kiraso, the black, mechanized body armour of the falchilo, each suit brought to Duatero by the Founders over two millennia ago and painstakingly maintained generation after generation. In this muddy, grey morning, they stood, a portrait of dark, avenging spirits. To some kid stuck on the farm, that is.

But they weren't falchilo, not yet. Their only challenges to date had been drills by day and studying by night, their only enemy the judging glare of instructors and their exacting examinations. This was their final test, their first live field experience, and somehow I had offended the Founders' spirits enough to be saddled with the job of leading them. I had only met them this morning, didn't know one of them by name. They arrived with a message that they were the only support the Tero Kreinto in Aaronsburg could supply to help Talia and me in our hunt.

Tiel estu, as they say. So be it.

Looking at the band of initiates, I asked, "Is there any one of you who can tell me why my second seems to think this is an occasion worth fouling the language the Founders gave us?" They avoided my gaze in awkward silence. Typical.

One of them, a young woman, green eyes, short brown hair plastered to her face by rain, raised her hand. "You," I said, nodding at her. "Tell me."

"That," she said, pointing to the figure still walking far away across the field, "is a dark wanderer, Majstro Falchilo." Tension washed across the initiates as they strained to see through the rain into the distance, confirming her assessment, and a couple more swears burbled forth that I glared into silence. "This morning, you told us we were hunting a stage three nest," she said. "A dark wanderer means it's advanced to stage four."

She had eyes as sharp as Talia's. "What's your name?" I asked.

"Esperanta Sagido."

My head bobbed back as the name struck me. It was familiar. Where had I heard it? "Esperanta. The name means hope in the tongue of the Classic Kronoj." No, that wasn't it.

"And Kredo means belief," she said, lowering her head.

Talia and I exchanged a glance, and she moved in close to speak privately with me. "Dead languages aside, the girl's right, Kredo. The nest's gone stage four. I'd maybe—maybe—trust these kids to change their diapers, but burning a stage four nest?"

"The floods'll be swamping the roads any day now. It'll be weeks before reinforcements arrive. If we don't cleanse it now, we'll lose this entire township, maybe more."

I remembered my first battle with a dark wanderer. I was terrified, though I'd never whisper a hint of that to Talia. But the terror of seeing every childhood horror story I'd ever heard made flesh and running wildly toward me was undeniable. I remembered Mihaelo yelling us into formation, and his second, Aprila, beside me. "Shield up, young buck," she'd said. "Do what you're told, when you're told, and you'll get through." She had been right. Frightful as they are, dark wanderers are mindless beasts that crash and thrash through their prey, spreading contamination with each scratch and with every thorn fired from between its scales that even grazes the flesh of its target. Stay calm, think, keep your shield up, and look for your opening to hit them with the rod —that's how you beat them.

Scanning their faces, I found one initiate who seemed more nervous than the others, his eyes a bit wider, his hand fidgeting a bit more by the rod strapped to his belt. "You," I said, pointing to him. "Run back to the pagoda in town. Tell the paisajista to sound the alarm for stage four quarantine. Then run hard to the Tero Kreinto in Aaronsburg and tell them we've got a stage four nest."

"I . . . I want to stay and fight with you," the kid replied.

I forced myself not to roll my eyes, staring hard at him instead until he lowered his gaze to the muddy road beneath his feet. "We've got people out preparing for the floods that'll come any day, and dark wanderers are stalking the fields," I said. "It's a half-hour's hard run to the pagoda with your kiraso at full power. If I don't hear the stage four quarantine alarm ringing within half an hour, if I discover you haven't gone to warn the Tero Kreinto, I will hunt you down, and by the Founders, I will find you guilty of collaborating with Malamiko, and I will cleanse you myself."

I had not thought it possible, but the boy's pale face blanched further. He bowed his head. "Yes, Majstro Falchilo. Right away." He turned and sped away, his kiraso propelling him to immense speed.

"Xinhua's eyes, Kredo," Talia said. "*He* might need help with his diapers after that. Was that what passes for your teacher's voice?"

"We haven't time for pissing about. See, here we go." The dark wanderer had spotted us, its aimless meanderings replaced with a focused sprint bearing straight our way, its long, loping legs eating up the muddy field as it picked up speed. Tension washed through the initiates.

"Shield wall," I ordered. They moved, their training taking over their bodies that moments ago shook with fear (and probably still did), and rods telescoped to their full length with a snick. Shield packs on their left forearms spiralled open, becoming body-sized, transparent barriers of polycrysteel, light as a pebble, sturdy as a castle wall. Their kiraso came to life, engulfing their heads and faces in a helmet, enclosing them in a hermetically sealed cocoon. The larger falchilo, mostly men, formed a front rank, shields inter-locking, and the rest of the group piled behind, leaning into them, bracing the entire pack for the dark wanderer's impending charge.

The dark wanderer had closed the distance, the slapping thump of its feet hitting the wet ground growing louder with each stride.

"Hold formation. Take the initial impact. Once its momen-tum's gone, take it down with your rods, and for the love of Donna, don't drop your shield. Talia—gun."

"On it," she said, spinning its crankshaft to charge the weapon. With a thought, my kiraso enveloped my head in its helmet, and my mind connected with my suit. The familiar sense of power surged through my body. My visor zoomed in on the incoming dark wanderer. It was once a man, and folds of scales hung from its body like black rags, finger-sized thorns projecting from the joints between each scale. A dark cloud formed by a combination of gases extruded from the body, and flakes of dead flesh trailed behind it as it raced toward us.

Both Talia and I took a position back from the rest where we could see the fight unfold. "I have fought these things for decades," I called out to the young initiates. "Obey my orders the moment I give them, and you'll see the sunset tonight."

"Probably," Talia said quietly so only I could hear.

A silence broken only by the rain's patter and slapping of the dark wanderer's feet fell over us. Fifty metres, thirty metres, twenty, the thing closed. Then, without warning, it stopped, feet sliding in the mud before it came to rest not more than five metres from us. The kiraso's helmet hid my shock, my mouth and eyes wide open. One moment passed, and another, it staring at us, we at it, the only sound that of the rain. "What's it doing?" a hushed voice whispered.

"Shut up," I said. I had never seen a dark wanderer do this. They always—always—charge blindly, like a blood-mad ox. They do not stop. Never.

Talia and I exchanged a glance. She shrugged. I signalled her; we would flank the formation of initiates to where Talia could take a shot at it. From the harness strapped to my back, I drew my flamjetilo—sacred weapon of the falchilo used for centuries to cleanse Malamiko contamination—and powered it on.

I made two, maybe three steps before I froze, my heart leaping into my throat and a cold pit settling in my stomach. The dark wanderer raised its arm, pointing at us. "Fa—" the slit that had once been a human mouth opened and closed as though working out stiff muscles or chewing dry meat. "Fa—Falchilo." It recognized us! It spoke. How could it *speak*? I'd never even heard one grunt before.

A young initiate in the front ranks lowered his shield, not by much, but enough to expose the top half of his head. "Shield!" I shouted, but the dark wanderer was faster. A thorn fired from its shoulder and struck the kid's head, knocking him back into the initiates behind him. He dropped on his butt, dazed, hand to his head where blood poured through his fingers.

The dark wanderer turned and ran away—another thing I had never seen them do. At that moment, every rule book I had read (and written), every tactic I had known, every trick I had learned through years of the hunt, they all meant nothing. "Talia, after it!"

Before I took a step, one of the initiates in the front line broke ranks, and, Founders guide me, I don't know where he got it from, but in his hands was a lumberjack's axe. Both hands on the handle, he swung it high and behind his head and then lobbed it forward, sending it cartwheeling through the air until it sunk into the dark wanderer's back. The force of the blow sent it stumbling forward, crashing on hands and knees in the mud.

I sprinted around the pack of falchilo. The dark wanderer rose to its feet, but another initiate, this time a woman, also broke ranks and sprinted ahead of us behind the cover of her polycrysteel shield.

What's with these kids? When I was an initiate, when your majstro told you to hold formation, you bloody well held formation until they told you to stop or you died from starvation. "You, axe-man, with me," I said to the axe-wielding falchilo as I ran by. I tossed him my flamjetilo. "Hang back. Cleanse it on my order." Talia and I raced after the female falchilo who was closing with the creature stumbling to its feet, the axe-man behind us.

Thorns fired from the dark wanderer's back, deflecting off the shield of the sprinting woman. As it got to its feet again, the initiate leaped, slamming into the creature shield first with the full momentum of her body. The dark wanderer spun, struggled to maintain its balance, but did not fall as the young woman slapped into the mud rolling.

Before the dark wanderer could fire thorns at her, the sizzling crack of Talia's gun sounded. A chunk of flesh tore from its body in a black spray and knocked it back to its knees. It sprung toward Talia from the ground, thorns firing, deflecting off her shield. Talia was short with a body of lean muscle, and she easily dodged the creature. She tried to bring her gun to bear, but the dark wanderer was too fast. It hammered her shield with a blow that knocked her through the air. She landed on her feet in a crouch.

I was on the creature and unleashed a flurry of blows with my rod, each hit blasting a charge of energy into the thing. I had it back on its knees before it punched my shield with such force I slid a metre back in the mud, arm bones aching from the hit. Another sizzling crack from Talia's gun, and the creature landed on its belly. I drove my rod through its back. The body shook with electricity. Joined by Talia and the female initiate, we shocked the creature.

"Enough," I said, stepping back, and the others followed. Legion were the stories of over-eager falchilo who drained the power pack of their kiraso shocking their prey too long. The creature lay prone on the ground, its body spent and beginning to dissolve into a putrefying black mass of flesh and liquid. I smacked the axe from its collapsing back with my rod.

"Axe-man," I signalled him forward and then pointed at the flamjetilo in his hands. "You know how to work that thing?"

"Absolutely," he said.

"Good. The flamjetilo in your hands is one of our oldest artifacts. It arrived on the *Percy James* in the year 57. It has cleansed thousands of contaminants. Today, you will use it to cleanse your first. Be ready." I turned to the collapsing blob that had been the dark wanderer and began the Rites. "To the human whose body this once was, your torment is at an end. Tonight, you dine with the Founders. To Malamiko who stole this body—burn."

With a click from the flamjetilo, waves of energy distorting the air sailed forward, expanding until it touched the stubs of grain in the field, and remains of the dark wanderer, erupting in a brilliant flash of flame. Sizzling pops sounded as the dark wanderer burned, and the rain hissed into steam as it fell near the flames.

I turned to the young woman and demanded, "Who are you?" The mask of her kiraso retracted; it was Esperanta, the girl with the eyes as good as Talia's. She stared straight ahead, nervous. "What were my orders?" She hesitated, and I dived into the silence. "My orders—what were they?"

"To hold formation, then strike with rods, Majstro."

"And did you hold formation?"

"No, Majstro."

"For the love of Donna, can you tell me why, after I ordered you to hold formation, you broke and charged the bloody thing?"

She looked up at me, her eyes were wide with fear of my anger, but by Founder's grace, she held eye contact with me. "It was running in that direction," she said, pointing. The building of a farmstead stood no more than two kilometres away. "If it had got to its feet and taken off at full speed, you wouldn't have caught up with it before it reached those buildings, even with your kiraso. If there were any people there, it would've infected them before we could cleanse it."

She was right, and I cursed myself for missing it. At that distance, dark wanderers could outpace a fully charged kiraso, and our battle would have taken place amid a farmer's family. Good eyes and a good tactical sense. She could *see*. Discipline, though . . .

"Get back in ranks."

"And you," Talia said, pushing the axe-man with both hands, sending him stumbling back. "Where'd you get a bloody axe, and where'd you learn to throw it?"

"I grew up in the lumber camps of Lu Guang, about a day west of Woodvalo," he said.

I walked over to his axe lying in the field and, picking it up, asked, "You are?"

His helmet receded from his head, revealing dark hair shaved close to his scalp, dark whiskers on his face, and dark eyes that looked like he'd spent more time scowling than laughing. "Jakopo Brunido, though most call me Jak."

I tossed the axe to him, and he snatched it from the air. "It's not regulation issue," I said, "but I think I'll let you keep it. Now, we have one last bit of business before we hunt down the nest. Give me the flamjetilo." I walked back to the other falchilo, moved through them to the young man who'd been winged in the head by the dark wanderer's thorn.

He sat on the ground, his kiraso's helmet retracted, hand on head, blood seeping through his fingers, leaving red trails through the rain soaking his face. None of the other falchilo came close to him; none offered aid.

I knelt in front of him. His big, white, terrified eyes stared out from behind a red mask of his blood. "Talia, get the GC," I said. A murmur of awe rippled through the gathered initiates. Only one functioning GC remained in all Duatero, and I had been given the honour of using it on the hunt. With it, I could detect Malamiko—the native life of this planet. Even if it was too small to be seen by the eye, I could follow their trail and root them out from their hiding spots. With it, I, and I alone, could detect stage one and two contamination with absolute certainty. Whereas other falchilo must rely on cruel, brutal techniques to detect early contamination, the GC allows me to cut it out with surgical precision.

As Talia went to where we dropped our packs to get the GC, I pointed at the engraving of bow and arrow on the breastplate of the boy's kiraso. "Your kiraso came on the *Artemis*."

He straightened, pride rising him up. "Yes, Majstro Falchilo. It was first worn by Founder Tseng Chun, Patrol Trooper."

"The Tseng Chun," I said, following the tracing on his chest piece with my hand. I now touched the design on my kiraso of a bird in flight carrying a twig in its beak. "My suit's from the *Jingwei*. Founder Tod C. Levitt, Trooper First Class, was the first to wear it."

He touched the engraving on my chest, wonder in his eyes as he whispered, "The Tod C. Levitt."

"Did you know my kiraso was at the Siege of Lu Guang? It was worn by the urbo falchilo who brokered the peace between Lu Guang and Aaronsburg."

"And it was worn by you at Eta Monteto," he said, looking me in the eye.

Eta Monteto. Of course, he'd have to remind me of that place now. So many parallels with today, events echoing through time. I closed my eyes, remembered another spring, another rain sucking my boots into the mud, another contaminated falchilo I had to cleanse—the first falchilo I had to cleanse. I tell people it gets easier.

"It's time," I said. "Take your kiraso off. One of the nearby pagodas will have the supplies we need to fix it. It will fight again."

His eyes widened in shock, then dropped in resignation, and he complied. Moments later, he stood, loose-fitting underwear his only protection against the cold spring rain, shivering. Talia handed me the GC, a boxy, golden-coloured, gun-shaped device with a nozzle at one end and a display screen facing the user. There was no need for the GC—everyone in Duatero knows what it means to be struck by a dark wanderer's thorn. For the morale of the initiates, though, each of whom had trained with this young man for four years, the certainty afforded by the GC would help them deal with what needed to happen.

I pressed the nozzle into the flesh of his arm, and he winced as it pierced him. It hummed quietly as it processed its sample, and then a blue indicator light blinked at the top of the display. Malamiko. Stage one infection.

All the initiates took a step back, the mass of them draped in soft murmuring. It struggled to hold back tears. I hate when contaminants cry. The other contaminated falchilo had cried that long-ago spring in the wilds surrounding Eta Monteto.

I placed a hand on its shoulder, turned it around, and led it away from the group. "What was your name?" I asked.

"Alek," it said.

I stopped some distance away from the others, turned it toward me, and with a hand on each of its shoulders, said, "Be strong, Alek. It's almost over." Many believed the human died the moment of contamination, leaving only Malamiko. I knew that wasn't true. Call it experience after decades of observation, or intuition, or what you will, but I knew it took time for the contamination to kill the human. I suppose that's what makes cleansing stage one contamination so hard and why so many adamantly choose to believe the human dies instantly.

I walked back to the rest of the initiates, scanning their faces as I did, their expressions ranging from disbelief to misery. This is what broke initiates. We'd find out right here, now, who was ready for fieldwork, and who'd end up in admin in some city or town. Esperanta stood with a group of other falchilo, the lines of her mouth set hard, her eyes sad, knowing what we had to do. There, several people over, Jak stood, arms crossed, a scowl on his face.

"Malamiko surrounds Duatero," I said. "It stares at us with envious hunger, seeking our ruin, seeking to pry us from this world that the Founders claimed as ours thousands of years ago. It has many weapons. Some are subtle: silent weeds that ruin our crops. Others, like the contamination, are horrors. Malamiko's greatest evil, though, is this. When our crops fail, it is we who must cull our old, our weak, and our sick. When the contamination infects us, it is we who must cleanse the bodies of our neighbours. Rather than strike us directly, it forces us to take our own."

Talia walked up beside me as I turned to face the body that once was Alek, standing alone, shivering in the dank cold. The human inside fought back the tears that would erode our morale. With head held high, that human called out to his former classmates. "This is how it has to be." Far in the distance, the stage four quarantine alarm sounded, immersing us in its mournful wail. "This is how it has to be. It's okay." See? That's how I knew the human didn't die right away.

"Let's get this bloody mess over with," Talia said, cranking the wheel of her gun to bring it to full power. "Mercy shot?"

"Yeah," I replied.

I turned to the contaminant standing in the road before us, rivers of rain cutting through the blood on its face. "To the human whose body this once was—Alek—your torment is over. Tonight, you dine with the Founders."

A sizzling crack sounded from Talia's gun, and her shot

slammed into Alek's body, lifting it off its feet, tearing open its torso, and driving it into the mud. The body flailed in its death throes, hands and feet slapping the tiny pools of water and blood forming in the road. "To Malamiko who has stolen this body—" I switched the flamjetilo's safety off. "—*burn*."

TWO

I LET the blinking lights of the GC guide us to the nest. It followed the foul off-gassing the dark wanderer had left in its wake, leading us to a farmstead sitting on top of a rise. With any other falchilo squad, it might have taken days, weeks even, to find the nest as they checked farm by farm. But the GC pointed like a finger of the Founders to the source of contamination.

Talia had launched her assault minutes ago, and the sizzling crack of her gun sounded in the distance. Her job was to draw the nest's sentinels away so I could search for the host. I wanted to run Esperanta and Jak through their paces, so I kept them with me. Talia had the rest of the initiates.

I poked my head around the corner of a mud-brick barn. "This isn't right," I said. All our helmets were engaged, encasing our heads in dark, featureless orbs. From inside the helmet, the rain sounded like a hollow drum roll. The black orbs covering Esperanta's and Jak's faces stared at me.

A human becomes infected by a dark wanderer, and a stage one nest begins. The primary contaminant becomes a host. They initially contaminate others in the same way a cold or the flu passes from person to person. But this is no flu. These new contaminants become the host's secondaries. During stage one, it is hard to detect contamination without a GC. As the contamination enters stage two, subtle behavioural changes give them away. Contaminants withdraw from the community to begin nesting. In stage three, they cocoon, secondaries transforming into shells, sentinels, and dark wanderers, the host metamorphosizing to its final form—the neural centre of the nest. In stage four, the nest replicates by sending its dark wanderers out, and when a series of nests begin coordinating activity, they enter stage five—the final stage, so far as we know.

Through my visor, the farmstead appeared plain: mud-brick buildings the colour of blanched almonds, beaten by years in the sun and rain, scattered across the yard with a spider web of paths cutting through the grass connecting them. A woman dressed in a grey tunic walked between the house and a barn. To a falchilo's eye, signs of a stage four nest abounded. The family whose home this was should be out preparing their farm for the floods coming any day. The yard was still, the pens for chickens and sheep empty. And the woman? It was a shell, a component of the nest that kept its human physiology and went through some rote routine, giving the illusion of normalcy. The shell here mindlessly paced back and forth from barn to house to barn again, a blank expression on its face. Dark craters pocked the yard where sentinels had burst forth and shambled down the hill to capture Talia and the other falchilo. To the eyes of an *experienced* falchilo, though, there was something more.

"There's one shell. No sentinels in sight," I said to Esperanta and Jak. "Have a look, tell me what you see." They peered around the corner while I stepped back. I could hear the distant yells of Talia's initiates and grunting of sentinels. "Quickly, now."

"There," Jak said, pointing to a mud-brick barn. A series of clay drains had been affixed to the edge of the roof to collect rainwater, channelling it to a spout that emptied into a clay basin dug into the ground that itself emptied into a pipe leading into the building. "The host's in there."

Normally, he'd be right. Hosts needed water and food. As contaminants built their nest, they modified the area to direct these resources to the host. The drainage of the barn was modified to direct water inside—a clear sign of a host. Until today. "Look closer," I said.

Both looked again. "The house is also set up like a host's den," Esperanta said.

"So is that other barn," Jak said. "And the tool shed."

Esper gasped. "Is there more than one host? Is this like Eta Monteto?"

"No, this isn't like Eta Monteto," I said. "Stage five hosts spread out over kilometres. Multiple hosts this close merge. They don't set up separate dens in one farmstead. I think they've set up decoy dens to try and mislead us."

"Decoys?" Jak said. "Damn trainers never taught us to look for decoys."

"You're not a lumberjack anymore, so choose words worthy of your station—and respect your teachers," I said. "You've never been taught to look for decoys because they've never done this before. This is new."

"So, what do we do?" Jak asked.

"We hunt," I said. "Building to building."

"Should we split up?" he asked.

"Don't be daft. You don't want to go one-on-one with a sentinel. Come on. We'll check the main house first."

"But . . ." Esperanta began before cutting herself off.

"What?"

"No, it's nothing. It doesn't make any sense."

"Out with it. Don't make me ask again."

"This nest's behaviour is unusual, right?"

"Cut to the point."

"The dark wanderer knew us as falchilo. It knew its enemy. If the rest of the nest has that kind of insight—enough to create decoys—it might set sentinels with each decoy. Maybe they're not decoys—maybe they're traps. Falchilo traps."

Until today, all the nests I'd known were mindless pathogens that operated on rote instinct, not premeditation. They didn't construct falchilo traps. But today, the rules had changed. And if a sentinel spotted us, even just one, the nest would know we're here, and it'd call every other sentinel within half a kilometre. If we hadn't found and cleansed the host by the time they arrived, they'd tear us apart. We had to find the host on the first try.

Ah, sweet Donna—what were we to do? For all the history of the falchilo, we'd believed stage four was the most advanced stage a nest got to. Eta Monteto showed us a fifth. Now this—falchilo traps. For thousands of years, everything was the same, and now, for the second time in my life, Malamiko had changed. *Think. And quickly!* I out-thought Malamiko at Eta Monteto. I could do it here, too.

"Either of you ever smell a host?" I asked. They shook their heads. Of course, they hadn't—none of us had, our kiraso filtered out every trace of the outside world when our helmets were engaged, and no falchilo's fool enough to walk into a nest without engaging their helmet. "The host feeds on livestock, or people, that the sentinels slaughter and bring to them. They'd reek like death. We'll sniff out the true den." I was guessing, but my reasoning seemed sound.

"But our helmets won't let us smell . . ." Jak said, trailing off.

"I'm withdrawing my helmet," I said.

"In a nest?"

"Only hosts and dark wanderers can contaminate you. Sentinels either kill or capture you, depending on if the host wants to eat or reproduce. The dark wanderers are out in the fields, so only sentinels will be here. As long as our helmets are up when we face the host, nobody'll get contaminated." That was a flimsy rationalization if I ever heard one, but we were winging it.

"All due respect, Majstro," Esperanta said, "if something happens to you, I don't think Jak or I will be getting out of this nest. My family raised livestock growing up, and I've seen plenty of animals butchered. I know the smell. I'll do it."

She was right. I didn't give good odds to raw initiates getting out of a stage four nest alone. "You're it," I said. "We'll do the house first." With my head bowed, I called on the Founders' favour: "Grace of the Founders be with us. May Donna, star of the fields, lead us to safe roads."

"*Tiel estu*," Esperanta and Jak answered.

I sprinted to the house, hopping a small fence and running across a neglected vegetable garden. The building was made of mud brick with a door and roof of thick reeds banded together. Its windows were small and high to keep out the heat in the summer.

Jak and I flanked the door while Esperanta retracted her helmet, wafted air from the space between the door and its frame, and smelled. "Nothing."

"Onto the barn—that one," I said, running across the yard, sidestepping the shell walking the other way. The farmstead was still. The silence of these buildings accentuated the distant screams of the other initiates and the orders shouted by Talia. The crackling boom of her gun sounded again, but none of that noise cracked this bubble of stillness.

At the barn doors, we repeated the process. "Smells of animals—chickens. It's strong, but I wouldn't say it's of carcasses."

The yard had so many buildings. "This way," I said and ran to the next.

"Wait," Esperanta called out when we were partway there. She backtracked a couple of steps, face jutting forward, probing the air, a mythical fox on the scent.

"Do you smell it?" I asked.

"I did, just a whiff of something rank. It's gone—oh," her head recoiled back. "Right here." A drainage ditch lined with clay tiles was cut into the turf, draining a tiny stream of water to a dark hole the size of my fist and into the ground.

"Helmet up," I said to her. "Now to figure out how to get in."

"I found the entrance," Jak said. "It's down this side of the hill."

A worn trail led to a door of bound reed recessed into the hill's side. "The family's mausoleum," Esperanta said.

"Founder Neil says it's bad luck to enter another family's mausoleum uninvited," Jak said.

My helmet kept him from seeing my eyes roll. I opened my shield and snapped my rod to full length. They both stared at me dumbly. "Ever fought a sentinel? A real one?" They both shook their heads. "Well, you're about to, so why don't you get your rods out?" They grabbed for their rods, hands shaking, and their shields spiralled open. "When it hits me, you jab it and shock it into submission."

"Hits you?" Esperanta asked, arms dropping slack at her sides.

"Shield first," I said, moving her shield into a defensive

block. I kicked the door, and the strength of my leg, augmented by the kiraso, sent it shattering inwards. A blur like a charging ox crashed into my shield, heaving me off my feet. I rolled down the hill on the wet grass. A sentinel. My shield arm burned with the intensity of white-hot coals, and my head reeled. Jak and Esperanta struggled to fend off the sentinel. "Sweet Donna, stop dancing! Shock the bloody thing!"

I've been at this game for a lot of years, and I still find sentinels wretched beasts. Knowing they were once human chills me. It loped on four legs, each one as powerful as a bull's. Out of its shoulders, two chitinous pincers extended that could crack a femur clean in two. Between the shoulders of its pincers hung the face, the human face, now nothing more than a vestigial organ, its gaunt, hollow eyes and slack mouth the stuff of night terrors that have torn more than one falchilo screaming out of a fitful sleep.

I scrambled up the muddy slope. Jak was pummelling the sentinel with his shield, using his rod to parry a pincer. The creature bucked its hind legs into Esperanta's shield, sending her sprawling in the mud and wet grass.

I drove my rod into the sentinel's flank. The dark creature convulsed, and Jak joined in with his rod. By the time Esperanta had staggered to her feet, the sentinel was insensate on the ground.

"Blast, those things take a lot of juice," Jak said. "My suit's down to half power already." Fully charged, a kiraso could last days if all you did was walk. Fight, though, and use your rod and shield, and the charge drained faster. The wise falchilo always kept an eye on their kiraso's power levels and charged up often.

"Ain't like training dummies, is it?" I rolled the sentinel away from the door and down the hill with a kick. "The nest knows we're here and will call all its sentinels back. No time to waste." I pulled the flamjetilo from its harness on my back, and it came to life with a cavernous groan as I entered the mausoleum.

Light from the door cut through the darkness smothering the room. Stone benches lined both walls where the family could lounge while they shared holiday feasts with their ancestors' spirits. Across from me was another door made of wood imported from the far-off foothills of Lu Guang. The family had polished and coated it in a preserving stain. Carved in each of three panels lining the door was the spiral symbol of the great Founder Donna, mother of agriculture, saviour of us all. Empty niches flanked the door, small shrines where the living could place food for the dead. Who would feed the spirits now that this family was gone?

Water splashed down through a hole in the roof—the hole Esperanta had found above—and into a rough basin dug in the floor, where it drained into a small, tile-lined ditch. The stream led straight underneath the door ahead. Beyond that door was the realm of the dead where the family buried the bodies of their ancestors—and, I hoped, the nest set up its host.

"If I fall, what do you do?" I asked.

Silence, save for the music of falling water.

I spoke over my shoulder at Esperanta and Jak. "You are falchilo. If I fall, what do you do?"

"Take the flamjetilo," Esperanta said. Her voice was all nerves: slight tremor, a hint of uncertainty, her tone rising at the end of her sentence as though asking a question rather than answering one. "Burn the host."

"Burn the host," I said. "That's all that matters."

I offered a quick prayer to the spirits of the mausoleum and opened the door. Another sentinel dominated the narrow passage. Alcoves lined the walls; bones littered the floor. Dark membranous sacks—cocoons in which the contamination was transforming once-humans into sentinels and dark wanderers —throbbed in the alcoves.

The sentinel charged, its slack, human face hanging like a rag off boney protuberances, its mouth hanging open in an eternal, silent scream. My kiraso propelled me forward, meeting the beast's charge. My shield rammed into it, barely budging it a centimetre. It beat my shield with its pincers, each blow a jarring thunderclap. It pushed me back with its powerful legs. Jak and Esperanta leaned into me with all their weight and kiraso-augmented strength; I angled my rod around my shield in the narrow hall to strike. I didn't have enough room to manoeuvre my weapon. Someone behind me lost their footing. The sentinel's weight pushed me over them, and I tripped. The beast clambered over, its weight crushing me, my kiraso the only thing saving my rib cage from snapping.

Someone struck a blow with their rod. For agonizing moments, the beast, the size of a large yak, shuddered and thrashed on top of my body. I tried to say, "Enough," but I couldn't fill my lungs with enough air.

Finally, the creature's seizure ceased. I gulped air while shifting it off me. Jak kneeled over me, heaving at the creature with his shoulder, but we didn't have enough space to roll it completely off.

"The flamjetilo," I managed to say. It was slung over my shoulder, pinned under my back. Jak immediately began to wedge it out and, after several tries, pulled it free. "The host," I gasped, but Jak was already clambering over the sentinel to get to the passage beyond, flamjetilo in hand. That kid was all business. I liked that.

It was Esperanta whom I had tripped over, and she and I

were alone now, pinned under the sentinel. We pushed and shimmied our way out from under its bulk, first me, then her.

"Get to—" I stopped as a new sentinel entered through the entrance into the mausoleum's dining chamber from the outside. And then another. And another.

Esperanta was on the side of the sentinel farthest from the entrance, the passage leading deeper into the mausoleum at her back, where Jak had disappeared. I was on the side of the fallen sentinel closest to the entrance where the new beasts were gathering. "Help Jak. Cleanse the host; I'll hold them off," I said. I clambered over the downed sentinel so that it would be between me and the others.

"You can't handle three on your own."

"No, *you* can't handle three. But me, I'll be—oh." A fourth sentinel entered the mausoleum, and they began pushing toward us. "Cleanse the host! Go!" She ran down the passage. I made it to the other side of the downed sentinel as the first of the new beasts climbed over the top of it, pincers clacking. I jabbed my rod into it, sending it into seizures, but the sentinels following pushed into it, driving the bodies of both fallen sentinels, along with me, sliding along the ground. The passageway turned a corner, and I was pushed into the wall of the bend, crushed beneath the weight of advancing monsters.

Screams came from further down the hall: Jak was swearing, Esperanta yelling at Jak to throw her the flamjetilo. They were young—had I ever been that young? I hoped they'd make it. If they didn't, I wouldn't either.

The vestigial face of a sentinel was pressed into my shield, its mouth tearing apart, leering at me through the transparent polycrysteel. The display of my HUD showed the strain my kiraso bore as it maintained the structural integrity needed to keep me alive against the immense force crushing me. An indicator on the periphery showed the energy drain from my power pack. The sentinels further back scrambled to get around, desperate to save their host from Jak and Esperanta. I struggled to keep my rod arm free to stab at any of the demons who made it past.

From down the hall, above the clatter of sentinels, the whump of ignition sounded and the crackle of flames, and then . . . stillness. I strained to look beyond the sentinel pressed into my shield, could barely see the other sentinels behind it standing with sheep-like docility.

Jak and Esperanta had done it. With the host cleansed, all parts of the nest, sentinels, shells, and dark wanderers, stopped, like an arm might drop once the heart stopped beating.

Jak and Esperanta came back down the passage, Jak leaning on Esperanta, limping badly.

"Are you okay, Majstro Falchilo?" Esperanta asked.

"Get these stupid beasts off me," I said, struggling to unpin myself from the mass of sentinels pressed against me.

Talia called from the direction of the mausoleum's entrance. "Kredo?"

I called out to her and then saw her nimbly slithering over the backs of the now dormant sentinels. She saw me and then counted the sentinels in the hall. "It only took five sentinels to pin you, Kredo." She stared at me, the angles of her face sharp, like a mythical wolf of earth, her eyes dark and intense —a predator's eyes. Then she smiled. "You're getting old."

"We've fought together a long time, but not long enough I won't find a farm with a stable for you to shovel out."

"Aw, you wouldn't do that," she said, dropping down to the ground and starting to shove the sentinel back so I could get out. "Wouldn't be right, considering I have a date tonight."

"Tonight? I don't think I've ever known you to plan your life so far in advance. Who's the unlucky soul whose heart you're going to break?"

"I don't know; I haven't met him yet," she said, offering me a hand and pulling me free. "I'm thinking a young farm-hand near town, someone strong, maybe a bit dumb." She noticed Jak and Esperanta behind her. "Hey, you guys are still alive. How 'bout that." She turned back to me. "Let's get out of here—it's bad luck being in another family's mausoleum uninvited."

We clambered our way past the sentinels and out onto the hillside. The rain was still coming down. "How many initiates did we lose?" I asked.

"Four, and one of them got her arm mangled pretty bad," Talia said. "So, are we going to talk about the obvious?"

"The obvious?"

"You ever saw a dark wanderer act like that one this morning`?"

"You know I haven't," I said. "Wait until you see the setup they have in the yard. They have decoy dens."

"Decoys? And a dark wanderer that talks, that runs away . . . Why haven't they done this before?"

"This is new; it's a change. Malamiko is changing." What other answer could I give?

"Think it's related to last year's crop failures?"

I shrugged. "Once the floods are over, we're travelling back to Firstsite. I want to consult the manlibroj at the Tero Kreinto there, see if they describe anything like this in the past."

Jak was laughing with a group of initiates, arms animated in the telling of a great tale of his heroics. Esperanta sat on the hill, apart from the others, head in her hands. Laughter drew my attention back to Jak. Talia saw me staring at him. "Aw, Kredo, let him have this. It's been a pissy day."

Ignoring her, I stepped toward Jak and the others celebrating. "Perhaps you think this is a victory?"

Their conversation stopped, their faces furrowed with uncertainty. It was Jak who spoke. "We cleansed a stage four nest today. That's a good thing, isn't it?"

"We encountered the dark wanderer a little under ten kilometres from the nest. We've no idea how many other wanderers were out there. And if a farmer stumbles upon one of their remains in the field and gets himself contaminated? You know the protocol for a stage four nest with dark wanderers in motion. We'll need to quarantine about, what, sixty hectares of land—good, productive farmland—for five years. That's land to feed a hundred, maybe a hundred-fifteen people a year. Who's going to feed them now? Last year's harvest was bad. We can't afford to lose productive farmland. Cleansing anything stage one through three is a victory. Stage four is damage control, nothing more."

THREE

I LIKE SPRING. Maybe it is the months of grey rain suffered during winter that make the colours of a blossoming world pop, be they the pinks of Judas trees or the brilliant scarlet of flame trees lining the Founder roads whose endless slabs of smooth stone, lined on either side by steel tracks, connect all the great cities.

"Will we meet the Kapo Falchilo?" Jak asked as we approached the walls of Firstsite. Brisk traffic of men and women hauling carts of seed going to and from the great city choked the road.

"The head of our order is a busy man," I said. I liked how Esperanta and Jak handled themselves during the cleansing of the nest, so I took them along with Talia to Firstsite to help me research the changes we'd observed in Malamiko.

Throughout the entire trip, Jak had been quiet. Now, suddenly, he spoke like an excited child. "Do you know him well?"

Esperanta rolled her eyes. "The Kapo Falchilo and Kredo

were the only two survivors of Eta Monteto. Of course they know each other well." I caught a glimpse of Jak glaring at her before turning his gaze forward, jaw grinding.

"We're passing through the market on the way to the Tero Kreinto, right?" Talia asked.

I remembered the crowded square, large as some small towns, crammed full of people, shoppers haggling, merchants shouting for attention, caged sheep and chickens screaming in bloody indignation. Thinking of it made my head ache. "No chance."

"Naw, it's the quickest way there."

"Not with you shopping."

"I'll be quick. You ever been to Firstsite, Esperanta?" she asked over her shoulder.

"No."

"Girl's never been to Firstsite, Kredo," she said. "And you know you haven't been to Firstsite if you haven't been to the Market. Lemme take her under my wing, show her how to haggle with big city shysters."

"What about Jak?" I asked.

"You like shopping, Jak?"

"No."

"Boy doesn't like shopping. Why don't you two go off and be dour or something? We'll meet you at Dorian's Gates in an hour."

I tried to be cross with her, but as we passed through the gates into Firstsite, I found I couldn't. Strange and wonderful Firstsite, where the Founders first set foot on Duatero. If I could call any place home in my adult life, this was it, and still, it bewildered the sensibilities of this old farm boy. Buildings, cliffs made of mud brick covered in plaster, flanked the road that cut through the city like a river running the length of a valley. Banners of brilliant reds and piercing blues covered walls. Homes and apartments stood one next to the other, leaving no space between them, save for the main streets. For most residents, the city was a landscape of rooftops. There, on top of buildings, high above the braying animals and dust, the life of the city was lived, stairs and ladders connecting different levels, openings leading down into personal dwellings pock-marking the roofscape. Everywhere, people moved, talked, and sung while they worked, sometimes accompanied by the rich, low tones of a four-stringed oud, the tinny rhythm of finger cymbals, or the beat of drums.

"An hour," I said. Talia winked at me in thanks and grabbed Esperanta's arm, and they pressed ahead into the crowds.

This left Jak and me to make our way through the new district of the city—new in that this portion of Firstsite was built after we lost contact with Earth, so some of these "new" areas were thousands of years old.

I sensed a nervous edge to the general hubbub. Everyone was skinny—gaunt, really, and groups of people clustered in doorways, having serious conversations with furrowed brows and animated hands. We'd had a string of bad harvests, the cause of which we were still unsure of, and the paisajista had scaled back the allotment. Everyone was hungry and, I imagined, wondering if we had enough food stored to raise the allotment soon.

But still, it was spring, a time of new hopes. Merchants hurried their wares to market, and farmers—men in simple reed skirts called a jupo with a loose shirt thrown over top, women in knee-length tunics—moved with bags of seeds slung over their shoulder and in carts they wheeled behind them. The floods had come and gone; it was a new year.

"So, what do you think of Firstsite?" I asked Jak.

He pushed his way through a group going the opposite direction, his brow furrowed. "There's a lot of people."

I smiled, remembering my first time in the city. I had thought within its walls must reside every human being alive. "What drew you to a life in the Tero Kreinto?"

"In Lu Guang, a son of a lumberjack grows up to be a lumberjack and the father of another. No way I'm following in my dad's footsteps. Figured this job'd be the way to do great things."

"All jobs have their place, from chopping trees to plowing fields. Each sustains us."

"Yeah, well, some jobs are crap."

I remembered hot summer days as a boy shovelling out the chicken coup and couldn't help but grunt in affirmation. We passed the time touring the streets, made offerings at a shrine to Founder Liam, the spirit of merchants and travellers, and then made our way to Dorian's Gate, the entryway to the old city—the Founder district.

Talia and Esper had beat us there. "Sweet Donna, you're on time," I said to Talia as we approached.

She jabbed her thumb over her shoulder at Esperanta. "This girl needs to learn how to relax. Xinhua's eyes, we hadn't been there ten minutes, and she starts freaking out about being late."

Esperanta blushed and bowed her head. "It was more like forty-five minutes."

"You," I said, pointing at Esperanta as I walked past her, "just qualified yourself for the job of keeping Talia out of trouble."

"Aw, Kredo," Talia said, "she could have such a bright future with the falchilo. Why you gotta set her up to fail like that?"

We passed through Dorian's Gates, a cyclopean portal in a wall made of Founder stone, and entered the old city—the city built by the Founders. We might as well have entered a different world, one where ships still flew between Earth and Duatero, and Founders raised buildings out of the ground. Grand edifices stretched into the sky, human-made mountains of Founder stone, seemingly immune to age. Roads were smooth and uncrowded. The sounds of the city faded into the background, and the trill of Firstsite's Babbling Brooks rose to the fore.

We passed a group of four kuracisto, the Tero Kreinto's order of healers, in their yellow, ankle-length robes, belted at the waist. "Should we switch into our formal wear to meet the kapo?" Esperanta asked, turning her attention from the kuracisto's robes to her kiraso covered in layers of dust and mud.

I grunted. "If we show up in our formal uniforms, Mihaelo will think we've gone soft and assign us to city admin." My nose caught the scent of something foreign. "Is that lavender? What's that smell?"

"I bought perfume," Talia said.

"What for?"

"I am going to break the heart of one of the Heroes of Eta Monteto before I die. Since you're boring as mud, I'm afraid the kapo's it."

"Good luck with that."

We rounded a corner, and Firstsite's Tero Kreinto complex came into sight. We passed through the southern gateway, a giant two-level pagoda structure, its base made of massive stone legs that we walked through. Members of the Tero Kreinto—thoughtful paisajista, dark and brooding falchilo, and serene kuracisto—went about their business. Here, the sounds of the city were almost absent, leaving only the breeze and the ever-present tinkling of running water.

Donna's Hall dominated the complex. It was a hundred-metre-high dual-level pagoda reached by a set of stairs easily the width of ten adults laid head-to-feet across. Back in the days of the Founders, and for centuries after, the Duaterano soil was conditioned deep in the bowels of Donna's Hall and transported by aŭtomato, great mechanical servants, to the surrounding fields, modifying the land so our crops could grow. Firstsite's Tero Kreinto was the first to fall silent as it ceased functioning, over a thousand years ago now. Even Donna's gifts were not immune to the passage of time. Now, the paisajista inhabit the Tero Kreinto, guarding the manlibroj and all the knowledge of the Founders they contain, guiding the spiritual life of Duatero, monitoring each year's harvest, calculating the allotment used to ration food, and ensuring each one of us is fed. We turned right off the main path before we got to Donna's Hall, making our way to the falchilo barracks. The road led through the Tero Kreinto's gardens, past pillars of stone, fountains, and gentle streams to the barrack's courtyard. There a single man, dressed in the uniform of the kapo falchilo, slim black pants secured by a golden belt and a trim black shirt with a golden sash, stood to greet us. Mihaelo, leader of the falchilo order.

He leaned heavily on a cane. Though physically, he still looked as hearty and hale as I remembered, age was beginning to wear deep creases on his face—more so than the last time I saw him. His hair was still long and dark, though now salted with traces of grey. Like all falchilo, he opted for a clean-shaven face, even though he no longer did fieldwork and so didn't need to worry about the kiraso helmet's ability to navigate a beard.

"You return in troubled times, Majstro Kredo," he said.

"A falchilo's time is always troubled, Kapo Mihaelo. Didn't you teach me that?" I replied.

A thin smile touched his lips. "It's reassuring you retain some of what I've taught you." His voice was quiet—he always spoke softly. His eyes flicked behind me. "And Talia, your affairs during your last visit to Firstsite led to considerable tension between the sons of the Sarida and Nikolaido houses. It took considerable efforts to soothe. They are both powerful kavaliroj families. Set your aim for less noteworthy trysts this time."

Talia looked at the kapo falchilo with a crooked smile. "I'm certain I don't know what you mean."

"I'm confident you'll figure it out." He turned to my two initiates. "Esperanta Sagido, I've heard much about you from your instructors in Aaronsburg."

Mihaelo had heard of her too? What was it she had done? I struggled to remember where I'd heard her name. "I'm honoured," Esperanta said, head lowered. I caught a glimpse of Jak, his jaw grinding and fist clenched, though he kept his eyes forward, standing at strict attention.

"It's a rare thing for a falchilo's research to gain approval for upload to the manlibroj," Mihaelo said. "Rarer still for the research to be performed by an initiate."

That was it! She had opted to perform a research thesis in her final year of training, and the Majstro Librarian accepted it for upload—an almost unheard-of event. Mihaelo and I had to discover that stage five nests existed, almost dying in the process, to earn a similar honour. I was impressed.

Mihaelo turned to me. "Strange you would choose someone so bookish as a companion. Not your style."

"I didn't choose her for her bookishness."

"Hmm. And Jak," Mihaelo said, turning his attention to him. "You still wear an initiate's white armband, and you've already cleansed a stage four nest. I'd worked in the field for five years as a full falchilo before I'd managed such an honour. Majstro Kredo has written me, asking permission for you two to join him in the field. I see no reason to deny such a request."

Jak's chest puffed up. "It would be an honour to learn at the feet of the Hero of Eta Monteto." I tried not to roll my eyes. What is it about young people? They're either hiding in a shell of self-consciousness or brash and loud, trying way too hard to impress. Still, I was glad for Mihaelo's approval. Talia and I could use the help while investigating the changes we'd observed in the contamination.

"Good," Mihaelo said. "Talia, could you see to the removal of their white armbands? I'd say it's time they graduated to full falchilo. Their kiraso look worn from the road. Show them our facilities so they can clean and repair them."

"Of course, Kapo Mihaelo," she said. With a small flourish, she stepped up to Mihaelo, produced a single purple flower from I don't know where, and planted it delicately in his golden sash. Mihaelo raised an eyebrow, and Talia flashed him a crooked smile.

"I believe I told you to set your sites on less noteworthy trysts," the kapo said.

"You're not the son of a powerful kavaliroj family, are you?" She winked, and then called over her shoulder to Esperanta and Jak, "This way, children," as she led them into the falchilo barracks.

"Walk with me," Mihaelo said once they'd left. He relied heavily on his cane, and I wondered if his limp had worsened since I'd last seen him. He led me past the falchilo's shrine and onto the paths of Donna's Garden, so named because legend says this was the first garden on Duatero, and Donna herself took solace amongst the blooms and trees growing here.

When we were some distance away, walking down a trail of crushed wood chips lined by flowers of every colour, trees bending overhead, allowing dapples of light to dance on the path, he spoke again. "I found the report of your stage four nest disturbing."

"Yes," I agreed. "Malamiko is changing."

He stopped to look at me and then continued walking. "So why are you here and not in the field rooting this new contamination out?"

The kapo had always been a man of action. "There are no reports of other nests to hunt down right now. I want to see if the manlibroj has anything to say about what I've seen before I face another one."

He replied with a noncommittal grunt. "I hear things, walking the halls of Firstsite's Tero Kreinto," he said as we crossed a stone bridge over a clear stream, lily pads drifting on the surface. It seemed to me that when the kapo spoke, the world stilled to give volume to his voice. "Last year's harvest was bad, and our food stores are stretched to their limits after the winter. The paisajista are scaling back the allotment even further."

"To what?"

"For active falchilo in the field, twenty allotment chips a day."

"Those are pre-Cull levels!" Twenty chips would leave me starving. If it was that bad for falchilo, it would be horrible for the poor farmers and traders who invariably got less.

"The paisajista aren't saying one way or the other, but I think they're going to Cull this year," he said.

"The last Cull was twelve years ago. That's nowhere near

long enough for our population to rebound and grow to exceed our carrying capacity."

"Our carrying capacity is decreasing." The words carried a tone of finality, and that they were spoken in such a soft voice amid the spring flowers of the gardens, that they were spoken by a man second in power only to the Unua Paisajista herself, made them all the more horrifying.

I imagined my feet treading ground where Donna herself walked and tried to imagine the problems weighing on her mind as she struggled to make a foreign world habitable for her people. Yawning chasms of time lay between then and now, and still the same problem vexes us: how to survive in a world that does not want us here.

We stopped in a small opening draped in the shade of trees, and Mihaelo sat down on a stone bench, massaging his thigh. "This leg, still giving me grief after all these years." I sat down beside him and watched tiny fish dart about in a pool that filled the clearing. A small island of rock and green foliage sat off-centre in the pond. "At any rate," he continued, "from the conversations I hear, they don't want to Cull until after Rendezvous this summer. They're hoping to draw out our food until then."

Rendezvous. Every nine years, the people of Duatero gather and wait, hoping this will be the Rendezvous when our progenitors from Earth re-establish contact with us. It's a time of hope. But for others to have hope, I must grind away in the real world. "What year it is has little to do with whether we have enough food to feed our people."

He smiled a thin smile, barely perceptible, more in his eyes than his lips. "I suspect there are those within the paisajista who hope this is the Rendezvous of Reunion, and we are saved."

"Bah," I said. "The heavens do not open up and save us. They never have. They never will."

WE HAD COME HERE to study the manlibroj for any clue that might explain the changes in Malamiko we had observed. Both Talia and Jak spent their nights in the taverns of Firstsite, though their purposes there differed. Whereas Talia would return early in the morning, a trail of broken hearts in her wake, Jak would come back with swollen knuckles and bruised face. Neither was well suited to research, so I set both of them to assist with the training of falchilo initiates. That left me alone with Esperanta for several days as we scoured the manlibroj in the cavernous libraries of the Tero Kreinto.

I have heard the librarians say that the collection of manlibroj is so vast that no one person could read them all. Indeed, the librarians have been transcribing them from their digital stores to paper for over two centuries so that we might retain their knowledge when the systems powering the manlibroj inevitably failed, and it would require another two centuries or more before they finished the job. Already, the library was packed floor to rafters with their tomes, their musty smell permeated the place, and vaults deep beneath the ground held even more. I preferred the older, digital readers to the transcripts written by generations of librarians. The readers allowed me to read the manlibroj the way the Founders had.

We did what we could, scouring the indices for every mention of the contamination recorded all the way back to the time of the Founders, trying to find some reference to contaminants that could talk and strategize. Nothing.

I tried to read Esperanta's thesis for a break to see what was so special it warranted inclusion in our holy tomes.

"You'll have to explain this to me," I said, dropping the digital reader open to her paper in front of her.

"You read it?" she said, a smile forming as she looked up from her desk. Her eyes, green as spring leaves, shone with her smile. She looked thin. Her black shirt and pants hung on her, and her belt was cinched tightly at the waist.

"Tried to." I picked up my reader. "Maybe you'd want to start with explaining the title. 'A Model for Threose-modified cysK Transfection of Terran-Incompatible *H. trespanes*: Resurrecting the Scholars of Port Donna'."

"Oh boy, how to say it." She thought for a moment, pushing away from the desk. "In Aaronsburg's Tero Kreinto, I stumbled on a cross-reference to a body of research recorded in the disc library that came from Port Donna."

"It was on disc? I didn't think Aaronsburg had a functioning disc reader."

"They don't. I spent my last summer at Shihbei."

"You've been to Shihbei?"

"Yes. And on those discs, I found fragments of research that were being carried out in Port Donna before the Black Cull. We can't eat native Duaterano plants—well, we can eat them, but it won't do us any good. For example, their proteins use the chemical selenium, whereas ours use sulphur. Our bodies can't use their proteins. This research was looking at ways to modify native plants to use sulphur so we can eat them."

"Eat native Duaterano plants? Were they doing this at Port Donna? It sounds . . . unnatural."

"Well, no. Think of it as purifying Malamiko."

"You did this?" I pulled up a nearby chair and sat down beside her.

"Oh, no. Not personally. I was only able to validate this was a legitimate branch of research, as well as build a model for how I think they were planning to do this purification. I'm not sure the original researchers were even successful in their attempts. I guess they weren't since we still can't eat native food."

"I'm surprised you chose the falchilo order. This type of research seems more what I'd expect from a paisajista."

"The paisajista are inward-looking. Their focus on food production is our foundation, but if we're ever going to expand again, it's going to be out into Malamiko lands, and it's the falchilo that knows Malamiko—not just the contamination, but all native plants."

Expansion. A young girl's dream. "Well, for now, we need to try to avoid another Cull."

"Speaking of that," Esperanta said as she turned back to what she had been working on, "I've been thinking. You had me try to investigate the link between the changes we've observed in the contamination's behaviour and our crop failures. What if they're not related? We could have two separate events happening. Here, I've pulled up the paisajista's records for food production." She picked up her reader and navigated through several screens to pull up a report. "Production's been declining for a long time. If you look at yields from centuries ago, we don't come close to touching them, even in our bumper years."

Our carrying capacity is decreasing. I thought about her comment a moment. "Centuries ago, we had more land to farm. Malamiko claimed all the fields around Port Donna when it fell. It's been advancing on Xuanhe to the west and pushing our northern borders back as well. Of course, our yields are down."

"I guess. Maybe that's it." She turned to look at her reader, brow furrowed.

We researched another day before Esperanta found something convincing me we were wasting our time.

I was taking a break by working in the garden, the sun warming my back, turning compost into the soil around a bush of Russian sage. Airy spires of violet blooms swayed as I worked around the plant's base.

"Kredo?" Esperanta called out.

"Here," I said. She appeared around a bend in the path, the colour of surrounding flowers catching the green in her eyes.

"Look at what I found," she said, dropping to her knees beside me in the dirt. She held her reader in front of me. The subject line read, "Centre for the Study of Selenophiles: A multidisciplinary approach to understanding Duaterano life forms." Underneath it was a list of papers and tomes. I scanned through them, my excitement rising, several of the titles catching my eye: *Morphological Changes in Duaterano Flora, Impact of Terran Soil on the Blue Leaf Lifecycle, Selection Pressures Caused by Human Encroachment on Selenophilic Lifeforms.*

But, as quickly as my excitement rose, it shattered. "Look at the source," I said, pointing to a column on the screen.

"I know," Esperanta said. "These were all stored on discs in Port Donna's Tero Kreinto awaiting upload to the manlibroj."

"Then they were lost when the sea rose up to claim the city centuries ago."

"But maybe the ruins of Port Donna still exist. The buildings of the Founders are indestructible—they might still stand."

"That land has been reclaimed by Malamiko. You know what that means."

Her shoulders drooped. To journey into Malamiko is to

invite death if you were lucky, contamination if you weren't. One of my earliest memories was of my brother, Paulo. I must have been four; he a bit younger. He'd found a wiggler in the yard—a small star-shaped Malamikan creature with five orange legs that wiggled as it walked. He had been poking at it with his finger, giggling. Even then, I knew you didn't touch Malamiko. The children's rhyme played in my head:

WHAT ARE *you not to do?*
  Don't touch the blue,
  Because if you do,
  Malamiko will get you too!

I HAD PULLED HIM AWAY, he cried, mom got angry at me, and so I had said nothing. A year later, he got jaundice and died. As a kid that age, I thought Malamiko killed him. Even now that I know better, I still feel guilt.

"It's so frustrating," Esperanta said, interrupting my thoughts. It was a child's complaint, and I remembered how young she was. It was easy to forget her youth. "Everything I need was destroyed with Port Donna. First in my research, now this."

"We lost much when it fell." The ocean swallowed port Donna, then Duatero faced a year without summer, driving two back-to-back Culls, which left a wound that still ached to this day. "Forget it. We don't even know if Port Donna's Tero Kreinto still stands. Let's focus on what we can control."

We walked back to the Tero Kreinto to renew our efforts, though our work here seemed in vain. Perhaps once in our halcyon days, we might have found the solution to this change in Malamiko in the tomes of wise sages, but not anymore. The heavens do not open to save us.

That afternoon, Mihaelo walked into the library, leaning on his cane, and sat down beside me. "I've received word from the town of Kubuto Falls, about a two-day kiraso-powered walk from here. Their paisajista writes their crops are collapsing—completely. No one knows why."

If the manlibroj held no answers, then facing our enemy where it struck might.

FOUR

AFTER PUSHING our power packs to the limits, we'd reached the city of Kolo in a day on our way to Kubuto Falls. We had left our kiraso at a pagoda where a nearby dam churned out enough power to light the temple lights and charge our suits. We had come to the tavern to eat, but it hadn't been long before the resonant rhythms of the oud had pulled Talia into the open space where people were dancing. Say what you wanted about Talia, but the woman could dance. The music tugged at her body, carried her, picked her up as though she were a leaf spiralling on the wind. Jak drank his beer while Esperanta laughed, clapping time to the music.

Talia circled by our table. "Come on, Esper," she said, grabbing Esperanta by the hand, pulling her up and into the mob of swaying bodies. Talia only gave nicknames to people she liked. Esperanta had been a mouthful, anyway.

I was alone with Jak. There are those who drink to have a good time; Jak was not one of them. He leaned over his cup, shoulders hunched, eyeing the tavern with a surly eye.

"I'm going to see if I can learn anything about our road

tomorrow," I said. As I got up, I said, "We're marching hard tomorrow. Easy on the drink." His eyes widened, perhaps in embarrassment, maybe anger. Either way, he nodded and pushed his drink away.

I invited myself to sit at a U-shaped bench filled with lounging men and women wearing brightly coloured travelling cloaks dulled by dust. Their faces were thin, and their cloaks hung off slight shoulders. "A blessing from the Majstro?" one of them asked, eying the red belt and sash that signified my rank.

"Of course," I said, and they bowed their heads. "*Mia korpo estas via shildo,*" I said, giving the ancient falchilo prayer. My body is your shield—my oath to my people.

"*Tiel estu,*" all gathered at the table said.

I lay on my side along one of their benches, as they were, propped on my elbow with a cushion under my arm.

A man, his hair greying, his face creased by years in the sun, offered to share their food, waving his hands in open invitation across large plates dotted with a few slices of bread and cheese along with a paltry scattering of raisins. I was famished and could have eaten every morsel and still not fill my hunger. "Our allotment chips don't buy as much food here as they should but let us share what we have," he said.

A strange comment. The chips were fixed to food's calories—the paisajista made sure of that. "No need, I've eaten," I lied, and my stomach screamed at me for it. The food, if spread evenly amongst them, wouldn't put a dent in any of their appetites. As falchilo, I was blessed with a higher allotment; if I was hungry, they'd be starving. I caught the eye of a server and ordered drinks and another plate of cheese and fruit for the group, eating further into my allotment.

Once the drinks arrived, I asked the man what brought them to Kolo. "We've pottery from Shihbei we're taking to

Lan Hu," he said. "We've been stopping along the way trying to trade, but it's been lean. The paisajista have cut back the allotment to pre-Cull levels, so if you ain't selling food, no one's buying."

"We're heading for Kubuto Falls tomorrow," I said. "Do you know of the road there?"

"Ah, I should have known a band of falchilo would be heading to Kubuto Falls," the old merchant said. "To anyone else, I'd tell 'em to stay away, but to a falchilo, I'd say get there as fast as you can."

"What can you tell me of it?"

"Me? Nothing. My business never takes me there. But I hear stories told by other merchants. The town's too close to Malamiko, you know. Oh, the people are good enough, but the land is poisoned. How many are you travelling with?"

"We're four."

His face scrunched up, and he pulled at his right ear. "I'd want more. Neither Lan Hu nor Aaronsburg patrols make it out there. Bad crops and no patrols mean bandits. My road's pretty safe from here on. I'd be willing to rent out my guards to you."

The danger of talking to merchants was the inevitable sales pitch. "I think we'll be fine." Tales of poisoned lands and bandits—I wondered how much of it was true and how much was oil to grease a sale.

"Sure, sure," he said. "Falchilo hold their own, and you'd have to be pretty far into the blue to attack someone of the Tero Kreinto. Still," he rubbed his chin with a leathery hand, "four people. Might be tough to see you're falchilo at night. The spirit of Liam's seen me prosper in my travels, so I'd give you a good price, seeing how you're a majstro falchilo and all."

As falchilo, I could, of course, commandeer his guards.

"How about I buy you and your crew another round of drinks instead." A lopsided smile crept up his face, and he agreed.

THE NEXT MORNING, we made offerings at the aŭtomato in Kolo's main square. Our sacrifice was a tiny statuette carved from wood that Jak had in his pack. The aŭtomato dotted Duatero. They were great machines, once. When the Tero Kreinto fell silent, the aŭtomato died. Some were as small as a baby goat, others the size of buildings that, legends say, had hovered above the tracks of Founder roads speeding from Shihbei to Port Donna in hours. They've since been converted to shrines. To my knowledge, no one has discovered a new aŭtomato in my lifetime. Finding a new one is the highest sign of the Founder's favour, and I admit a childish dream of discovering one of my own.

Kolo's is one of the largest I know—taller than a two-story building with a base of dilapidated wheels atop which sits a massive box that once carried soil from the Tero Kreinto to the edges of the fledgling colony. Trinkets and flowers littered the ground and piled up along the sides of it.

Our path took us away from the Founder's road, striking southeast along a dirt road. To our left ran the Jinhuang river, while green fields of wheat, turning to gold, lined our right. By early afternoon, the road took us into a forest that closed around us, blocking our sightlines. We weren't a hundred steps in before we could see something was wrong.

"These woods look . . . sick," Esper said, voicing my thoughts. The land was dying; even a child could see that. Bare and gnarled branches, reaching like aged, arthritic fingers, clasped and intertwined above our heads. The place reeked of wet, rotting mulch. A silence hung over it all, like a thick blanket draped over the treetops; only the sound of our feet crunching fallen sticks and dead leaves echoed through this ghost forest.

"Has there been a drought in these parts?" Jak asked.

"The soil's moist," Esper said. She was kneeling, working a fist full of dirt through her fingers.

"They wouldn't be sending us if it was a drought," I said. "The paisajista say we've everything we need for a bumper crop, but the crops fail."

"What could cause this?" Esper asked.

Talia grunted. "The only thing that gets falchilo out of bed in the morning: Malamiko."

She was right. "Let's settle this." I pulled the GC from my pack, walked up to a dead tree, placed the nozzle end against it, and waited for confirmation it had been infected.

Green light. No Malamiko.

"That can't be right," I said. I recalibrated and tested another tree. Green light.

"Try the roots," Talia suggested. I did. And the soil. Green light.

"Jak," I said. "Get your axe and chop this tree down."

I tested the exposed centre of the tree. Green light. Over the next hour, I tested other trees, both dead and alive, more soil, fallen leaves, everything I could see. Green light.

For thousands of years, falchilo had used the GC to detect Malamiko. The Founders had made their equipment to last, using feats of engineering and design long lost to us. The falchilo trained relentlessly in its maintenance and repair, scavenging parts from malfunctioning units to repair others, all the way down through time, culminating in the machine I held in my hands. It was the last working one on Duatero.

Has it stopped working? How would we defend ourselves from our enemy once we became blind to it?

No—it was detecting background threose nucleic acids and selenium-enriched amino acids in the air, hallmarks of Malamiko.

"It could be an earthly pathogen," Esper suggested. Earthly pathogens were rare but not unheard of. The GC was not set to test for such diseases, so we investigated by eye.

"I don't see a damn thing," Talia said after we'd searched a while.

"Talia," I said, a warning in my voice about her language.

"Apologies, Majstro. I'm not a fan of looking at dirt, is all."

"I'm not surprised there's no sign of pathogens," I said. "Look at this forest. There are dozens of different species of plant life, and they're all dead or dying. A disease attacks one species. This pattern of plant death suggests something affecting all plants: something in the soil or air. Or water."

"Maybe the soil's exhausted," Jak said.

"The ground's moist with a good cover of composting leaves," Talia said. "I may not have been top of my class, but I know good soil, and this soil's good. GC says it's not Malamiko. So what's killing this forest?"

"Malamiko's changed," I said. "We'll figure it out. Come on, we've lost a lot of the afternoon here and still have a long way to go. We'll have to camp out overnight. We can't make it to Kubuto Falls today." We marched through the dying woods the rest of the day and set camp as the sun set. After we ate meagre rations of dried fruit, nuts, and bread, Jak took out a piece of wood and a knife and started carving. Talia moved beside Jak. "Whatcha carving?"

"Founder Neil," he said.

"Really? How can you tell?"

Jak's voice hardened. "'Cause I know what I'm carving."

"You any good at wood carving?"

"Pretty good."

"Then why's that not look like Founder Neil?"

"I'm just *starting*."

I stepped away to look at what stars I could through the tangled branches.

"May I join you?" Esper said, coming up beside me.

"Of course." I indicated a patch of ground for her to sit. "I was seeing if I can spot Earth's sun, Terosuno, tonight."

"Can you?" she asked, taking a seat.

"Yes. There, you see the constellation of Aaron's Cross?"

"I see it."

"The star at the end of the cross's tail. Terosuno. And orbiting around it is Tero, our Earth; birthplace of us all. It is over three thousand light-years away. You know what that means?"

"It's far."

"Well, yeah. It's so far that the light from it hitting our eyes left Terosuno centuries before the first Founders boarded the *Spero* to cut across the voids of space to make their home here. Donna, Aaron, Xinhua, all the Founders, were not even born when this light left their sun; their grandparents weren't even born. Did that beam of light know what potential was blossoming within its very solar system? Did it know as it sped by Earth that its inhabitants would soon strike out into the galaxy to journey here where their distant kin, after thousands of years, would stare up into the night sky and see that same beam? When I was a child, after my chores were done and I'd finished getting my brother and sister put to bed, I'd stare out my window at that star and wonder what the human race was doing as that beam of light passed it."

"It sounds like you still do," Esper said, playing absent-mindedly with something in her hands.

"What's that you have there?"

"Oh, this," she said, embarrassed. "Is it my turn to tell you about my childhood?"

"Looks like it."

"Ah, boy. It's an almond seed from my family's farm."

"An almond seed? That's the tale of your childhood?

"Well, when I was a little girl, my father would gather my brothers and me together after dinner, and he'd hold out his hand like this," she said, extending her hand, her seed between index finger and thumb, "and he'd ask us what this is."

"An almond seed."

"Ah, that's what most people would say. Yes, it's a seed, but what is a seed? This is a collection of carbon, sugars, and fat. It feels like a tiny wooden pellet in my hand. Yet, if I were to bury it in good soil where the sun warms it, and moisture finds it, it will turn dirt and air into a stalk that pushes through the ground and into the sky; it will turn dirt and air into leaves that capture the sun and create flowers of beautiful colours. Other creatures will eat the plant it grows into, and other creatures will eat them, on and up the chain to men and women. Through this," she held the seed before my eyes, "life enters the universe. Can you imagine? Dirt and air turned into life by this little pellet. Through this process, humans are created and sustained, and through us, the universe gains awareness of itself. What is this?" She placed the seed in my palm. "It is a miracle."

I held it between forefinger and thumb, looking at its shape, its shell rough on my skin. "I think I'd have liked your father."

"He'd enjoy meeting you."

"He's still alive?"

"Yes."

"Why do you keep it?" I asked, giving the seed back to her.

She shrugged. "Well, I figure someday I'll find good soil and plant it. Turn dirt and air into life. Can you imagine a greater power? And to think, our farmers do it all the time."

I thought of my dad, beat down by the land he worked, thought of the ache in my stomach as gnarled branches swayed above me.

NEXT MORNING, the road took us out the other side of the woods, the river flowing on our left, fields stretching away on our right. We stared, dumbstruck at what we saw. This early in the season, the fields should be green, swaying in the breeze. As far as the eye could see lay rolling plains of brown with some sparse shoots of green. I was a farmer's son, and I knew these fields spelled ruin. The kind of ruin that kills.

"Kredo?" It was Esper, her voice small and afraid. "Is there going to be a Cull?"

On the far side of the wide, flowing currents of the Jinhuang River, Malamiko stretched to the Shandong mountains far in the distance. Plants with terracotta-coloured stalks reached knee-high, then erupted into wide fronds of blue, plate-shaped petals. The Malamikan field was spotted with copses of larger bushes stretching a little higher than an average man. Even at this distance, I could see the foliage was lush. Millions, billions of Malamiko thrived, the wind stirring them to movement, creating the illusion they waved at me, taunting me, taunting all of us. My stomach knotted in hunger as Esper's question hung in the air.

FIVE

"THEY'VE SPOTTED US," Talia said. Less than a kilometre out from Kubuto Falls, the sun swaddled us like a warm blanket. A figure poked above a short mud-brick wall surrounding the town, waved, and then turned to call others. Within moments, the pagoda bells rang. "Oh, I hope they don't sing for us," she added.

"Better than parades," I said.

She looked at me, head cocked. "Is it?"

Jak asked, "This is Kubuto Falls?" He sounded like a child disappointed with his gifts for the Dongzhi Festival.

"Yep," Talia said.

He horked and spat. "I've seen lumber camps bigger than this."

Kubuto Falls, like most other towns and cities, rested atop a small hill to protect it from the spring floods. The pagoda stabbed high above the other buildings, its white walls reflecting the sun's light. Green Shihbeian tile covered the roof of each level, and a finial carved to resemble Aaron's FTL

Vergo, a seven-pronged rod, pierced the sky. Near it, the pagoda's granaries also thrust above the village's buildings.

A crowd had formed by the time we arrived at the town's gates. Lean men and women, leathery skin darkened from years under the sun, bodies bent by hard labour, clasped their hands overhead in thanks.

"When's the last time you saw so many people as skinny as these?" I asked Talia under my breath as we approached.

"Cull of '29."

"That's what I was thinking."

Young children darted about, watching with wide eyes as we passed through the town's gate. I must have been about the same age when I saw my first falchilo. I had been in town picking up tools for my father. Five falchilo, their pace accelerated by their black kiraso, had sped their way to the pagoda like dark angels. I forgot to pick up the tools dad needed as I ran home to tell him what I had seen. I earned a scolding for the forgetting, though later that night, over dinner, he proudly told the rest of my family what I had witnessed. I had thought they might have come for my sister Tondra. She was sick with green fever, and I hoped the falchilo were there to investigate whether Malamiko caused her illness. Of course, they weren't—they were on their way to the borderlands to cleanse fields under Malamikan attack. Tondra survived the green fever, but it left her weakened, unable to fend off the strep throat she caught later that year, ravaging her body with fever for a month before killing her.

The people of Kubuto Falls began clapping. I forced a smile and waved. There were cheers, and someone, a woman, began singing "Donna of the Harvest." Before she had finished the first line, the entire crowd took up the hymn, and we were accompanied by song as we made our way to the pagoda grounds.

"Smile and wave," I said to Talia as I nodded at the crowd.

Her thin face was frozen in a rictus smile. "Why does it always gotta be 'Donna of the Harvest'?" she asked through her teeth while waving.

The road led past weathered walls of slapdash buildings to the pagoda gardens, where it passed under an arch enveloped by vines. The gardens were lush with green bushes lining a small pond and trees reaching high above the rest of the town's buildings. "Whatever blight's destroyed their crops has spared the pagoda gardens," Jak said with an accusatory tone.

A woman with grey hair, face as sun-dried as the rest of the villagers, stood in front of the archway. Beside her stood a man, younger than she, his hair still dark, though the face under his beard had weathered many summers under the sun. He wore a knee-length tunic, wine-red in colour with gold fringe, denoting his status as a kavaliroj noble.

"They only send out a low ranking paisajista to greet us," Jak said, noting the simple brown tunic worn by the old woman. "Shouldn't at least the gepatro paisajista be here to greet us?"

"The head of a pagoda has many duties. They may be out in the fields," I said.

"Or," Talia said, "this hick town's too small to warrant a gepatro."

The woman held up her hands, and the sounds of the crowd faded. She gave a paisajista's blessing: "May you be filled with loving-kindness. May you be well."

"*Mia korpo estas via shildo,*" I replied.

Greetings over, it was time to start the show for the crowd. "Welcome, Majstro Falchilo," she said with the passion of one speaking from a well-worn script. "I am Luksa, paisajista of Kubuto Falls."

"And I am Alechjo," the man beside her said, making sure the people saw he was part of this conversation, "the town's reeve."

"I'm Kredo. When will the pagoda's gepatro be back?"

A glimmer of annoyance appeared on her face, but she hid it quickly. "Kubuto Falls has no gepatro. I am the sole caretaker of these lands," Luksa said, her chin striking forward ever so slightly.

Talia was right. The pagoda was small but well maintained, and the gardens were beautiful. But with the surrounding fields failing, the Tero Kreinto would need to think about sending someone of higher rank. And Luksa was *old*. How could she be the sole caretaker here so long and never rise past the rank of paisajista?

Here, in front of the entire town, wasn't the place to start that conversation. The people of Kubuto Falls greeted us as saviours. They needed to see unity of purpose, and they needed to see we were taking control of the situation. "I want to meet with you right away, Luksa, to learn everything you've discovered about what's afflicting your crops. Then I'll want to tour the affected areas and speak with the farmers."

"Whatever you need, Majstro," Luksa said.

"All of Kubuto Falls is at your disposal," the reeve added.

"Do you have stations to charge our kiraso?"

"Of course. This way," Luksa said.

Talia caught up to me. "'I'm Kredo'?" she said, mimicking my voice. "That's your intro? They sing and clap, and you reply with 'I'm Kredo' and a bunch of orders?"

"Did you think I'd sing back to them?"

She grunted in derision. "You got no flair, Kredo."

"These people need a hero right now, not a song and dance."

"Well, not the way you dance."

"Talia."

"Yes, Majstro," she simpered.

"Shut it, or I'll have you working night soil into the pagoda gardens."

Dawn found us giving offerings at a shrine of Jinjing, Founder spirit of air, sunshine, and flowing water. The shrine had once been one of three ancient power stations built of Founder's stone. That stone, beaten by a millennium of weather, diverted the paths of flowing water to turn ancient coils of copper inside giant magnets within each of the buildings.

"One of them still works," Luksa told me, a little prideful, pointing to the uppermost shrine. "It gives enough power to light the pagoda and run the mill."

Much like the town, the falls after which Kubuto Falls was named did not impress. Over the span of about half a kilometre, the land angled down. The river cut through stone, and jagged rocks pierced the water. White rapids skipped down these stone steps and filled the air with their rushing hiss.

After a quick prayer asking for the Founders' guidance, I touched Jinjing's symbol, *I*V*, carved into the shrine's wall. I scanned the faces of the crowd gathered in the stunted fields —they looked hopeful, as though I had already found the cause of their crop's failure and fixed it.

Turning to Reeve Alechjo, I said, loud enough for the crowd to hear, "I want you to take Falchilos Talia and Jak to speak with the farmers. Start with the farms most affected by the blight. Paisajista Luksa, you'll take Falchilo Esper and me to the fields. I want to see the crops first hand."

Upon hearing I was sending him off with Talia instead of going with me, Jak frowned—it was almost a pout! "Cheer up, young pup," Talia said, reading Jak's disappointment. "The Majstro's doing you a favour because the only thing worse than interrogating dozens of farmers is peering at fields of dirt all day. You might even get to use your axe!"

"What's the axe for?" Alechjo asked.

"It's for making things *exciting*," Talia said, draping an arm over his shoulder. "Lead on, noble reeve. Let's start with the young farmers first. Someone handsome."

We marched our separate ways across fields of stunted, dying grain as the crowd dispersed. Luksa had to use a walking stick. Keeping pace with her was an adjustment after several days of kiraso-powered marching. "The town's been looking forward to meeting you, Kredo," Luksa said as she led us along a dirt road following the river. "Your stories reach us, even here. The people are praying for another miracle of Eta Monteto."

"Let's hope their prayers are answered," I said. "How long have you been paisajista here?"

Her smile didn't touch her eyes. "It's not polite to inquire about a woman's age." She continued walking. "Forty-two years this spring," she finally answered. "When I was first sent here to guard the lands, I was barely older than her," she said, nodding at Esper. Luksa studied her. "Xinhua's eyes, I can't believe I was ever as young as that." Esper blushed.

"Forty-two years as paisajista, and you never took the tests to rise up the ranks to a gepatro?" I asked.

"What difference would it make? It doesn't matter what they call me; I'm the only member of the Tero Kreinto minding this region." Her tone was defensive, and she looked sternly ahead, not making eye contact. Why the antagonism? "You've never had crop failures like this before?" I asked.

"No, never," Luksa said. "Even in good years, our yields aren't what they used to be, and we've had droughts before, back in '28 and '29. But the floods were good to us this year; the sun shines. I've studied the fields for Terran pestilence and sent samples to the Tero Kreinto in Firstsite and Lan Hu for study, but we've found nothing. Nothing the paisajista can see would cause this. That's why the Tero Kreinto sent for you." She didn't sound like she agreed with the Tero Kreinto's decision.

Esper asked, "Aside from this crop failure, you say your yields aren't what they used to be. Why is that?"

"The ebb and flow of nature's cycles," Luksa replied. Her response sounded rehearsed, like something she'd say to farmers worrying about their crops.

"That's no answer," I said.

She shrugged. "That is all the answer we have."

"Your soil's not eroding?" Esper asked.

"Of course, it's not eroding! Your parents were still filling their diapers when I became paisajista," she said. "The crops are rotated; we have good compost and regeneration procedures. The soil's as good as it ever was. If it was something with the plants or the land, the paisajista could deal with it without your help."

"I studied our records on Kubuto Falls before I came," I said. "You've had contamination in your fields before."

"Yes. The fields I'm taking you to now. We had falchilo inspect them four years ago and cleanse them." Accusation laced Luksa's voice.

"Your fields are prone to contamination," I said, a statement, not a question.

"Those fields are close to Malamiko. Every few years, falchilo come and burn our fields. They tell me they're cleansed, but a few years later, the falchilo are back laying flame to my fields."

My thoughts drifted to a strange comment from a recent conversation. *Our allotment chips don't buy as much food here as they should.* "How are your food stores?" I asked.

"Fine, why?"

"You have enough to last until the harvest?"

A frown's deep crevasse split her forehead underneath her mane of grey hair. "Ration's for the likes of you are at twenty chips a day. We're not at Cull levels yet—we're fine."

"I met some travellers on the way here," I said. "They were saying their chips didn't buy as much food as they should. Has the peg of allotment chips to calories slipped?"

"They are mistaken," she said, iron in her voice. "The linking of allotment chips to calories is a sacred duty. We paisajista do not let the peg slip." We walked in silence, the only sound that of our boots crunching the dirt. "The ration is razor-thin; people are hungry, yes," she added. "But Rendezvous is soon. Perhaps this will be the Rendezvous of Reunion."

"Praise Donna, let it be so," I said. I didn't trust her—the tone of her voice, her unwillingness to look me in the eye, set me on edge.

"Praise Donna, let it be so," she echoed. Then: "We're here."

We stood by a field of winter wheat, the green stalks sparse and stunted as they were everywhere. I crouched and examined the ground. I called Esper over. "Tell me what you see here."

She gently brushed stalks of wheat aside as she examined the soil. "Contamination. Looks like blue-leaf weeds. They're always the first Malamiko to contaminate our fields."

"And what does that tell you about our crop failures?"

She considered the question a moment. "Do you think this is causing them?"

"I'm asking you."

"The manlibroj tell us the blue-leaf weed itself is harmless. It's an early invader, conditioning the soil for ringweed and creeping micelio. It's those two which choke out our crops."

"The manlibroj are right," I said. "This blue-leaf's not our culprit."

"This is the only field that's contaminated," Luksa said from the road. "The rest of the fields for hectares around have no signs of contamination that I can see, no Terran disease either, and yet they, too, fail."

"Is your soil always like this?" Esper asked.

I scooped up a handful of soil. A light brown crust covered its surface. It wasn't like the soil around the farm where I grew up, but I don't know if I would have thought anything unusual about it.

Luksa gave Esper a grudging look of respect. "What an interesting question," she said. "It's always been prone to forming a light crust, but I don't remember it being so pronounced when I first came here. But maybe that's my memory playing tricks as I try to find a reason for our crop failures."

"What's causing the crusting?" Esper asked.

Luksa shrugged. "Some terran biological agents might, but we tested for that with the samples I sent to the Tero Kreinto and found nothing. Dry soil would do it—but we've had plenty of water. Over-cultivation, or removing organic residue and leaving the soil bare, but we've ruled that out. The manlibroj tells us high salt concentrations could do it. We've no way to measure that anymore, but nothing's changed with how we amend or irrigate the soil for thousands of years. Could be the nature of the soil in this area."

I took the GC from my pack. "Let's start testing to ID the boundaries of the contamination."

"Is that a GC?" Luksa's voice was little more than a whisper. Her eyes were wide with shock and reverence.

"It is." I stood, holding it in two hands before me. "This GC was made on Earth—it touched the same air the Founders breathed—and it arrived on the *Artemis* in 316. The greatest falchilo to ever use it was Jocho Venka, who eventually rose to become Kapo Falchilo in the 1700s."

"May I touch it?"

"No." I enjoyed denying her more than perhaps I should, but something about her rubbed me the wrong way. "This is the only GC that remains. The only other person who will touch it is whoever the Tero Kreinto finds worthy after I join my ancestors." A bit of a white lie, as I have had Talia fetch the GC from my pack on many occasions, but I didn't want anyone I didn't trust mucking about with one of our most sacred artifacts. Luksa's lips tightened, but she bowed her head in acquiescence.

"We'll have to mark the boundaries of contamination and cleanse the field, but this blue-leaf isn't what's causing these crop failures." I turned to Luksa. "You said these fields were close to Malamiko, but the river's got to be a kilometre wide here, with Malamiko on the other side."

"Follow me," she said, walking further down the road to the river's edge. "There," she pointed. A little more than twenty metres across the shallow water was a spit of land. Its surface was covered with chest-high orange tubules ending in broad, blue, plate-shaped leaves. "We call it Malamiko Island."

"By the love of Donna, that's close," I said. "The river looks shallow enough you could wade over to it. Has that island never been terraformed?"

"Once," Luksa said, "but any Terran soil was washed away generations ago. It's always been Malamiko Island as long as anyone living today's known it."

I pointed back to the hill atop which Kubuto Falls sat. "It's no more than a five or ten-minute walk to town. You live so close to it?"

"The town was here first," she said with a shrug. "We've never had anything worse than the blue-leaf."

"We'll have to cleanse the island, too."

"The falchilo always do," she said. "But it always comes back the year after."

My anger got the better of me. "Becoming a gepatro is more than a title. It's training. Your crop yields decline; you live with Malamiko right here," I stabbed my finger at the island. "This is too much for a paisajista to deal with. You should have become a gepatro, if not for the title, then for your duty to this land."

"Malamiko is not the duty of the paisajista. That's the falchilo's sacred responsibility. Malamiko fields from the ruins of Port Donna advance on us from the south, but the only falchilo fort in these parts is thirty kilometres away in Vojo Fino, and it's been abandoned since the Cull of '29. I can't even count the number of times I've watched your order cleanse these fields since then. And now my crops fail across this entire region, and you blame me!"

We are an island in a sea of Malamiko. We cannot hope to cleanse the world, yet it is the world that closes in on us, threatening our existence. I stared at Malamiko Island, watching the water rush around it. Here was one more front where Malamiko pierced our borders, trying to strike at our heart. My stomach twisted in gnawing hunger.

We scoured the nearby fields the rest of the day and found nothing other than the small plot of blue-leaf. As to what was attacking the rest of the crops, we had no idea.

"We should cleanse this whole region," Jak said as we cleaned the joints of our kiraso in Kubuto Falls' central plaza.

"Wow," Talia said, wolfing down dry bread. "That's one . . . extreme option, I guess."

"Nothing from your interviews has been of use?" I asked —again—putting aside my own kiraso.

"Bah!" Talia said. "If they're not blaming their failed crops on their bloody neighbours for some imagined slight, they're accusing the Founder city of Aaronsburg of bringing a curse down on us for its 'arrogant dreams of expansion' or some rot. If we listened to them, we'd cleanse half the bloody town then charge the palace in Aaronsburg."

The sun was setting, splashing a red fan of light across the sky while people lounged in clusters for their evening meal, though most of the plates were spare. A woman was beating out a gentle rhythm on a drum.

Talia muttered under her breath as she fished out something stuck between her teeth. "I think they're grinding up bloody grain stalks in their bread."

"Ersatz bread," I said. Jak stared at me blank-faced. "They're adding filler. Same thing happened back in '28 and '29."

Esper was sitting on a wooden stool at the far side of the plaza, surrounded by a large group of children ranging from little more than toddlers to young teenagers. She was teaching them something—I couldn't hear what from this distance. The children were starving, and she did her best to distract them from the pains in their stomachs—a born teacher. Perhaps she was telling them the miracle of seeds.

"We should cleanse this place. Everything." Jak said again,

wiping the smile from my face. "It's the safest choice. You found contamination by Malamiko Island. You've said yourself Malamiko's changing. Somehow it's killing these fields, and we can't detect it. Cleanse it. Cleanse it all."

"That's hundreds of hectares," Talia said.

Luksa was speaking with the city's reeve and several other men and women. People seemed content. "The allotment is already at pre-Cull levels," I said.

"If we have to Cull, then we Cull," Jak said. "It's better that than losing all of Duatero."

What was it about young men that compelled them to believe every problem could be solved if only you punched it hard enough? I had to admit, though, I was losing patience with this investigation. "You don't need to remind me of the necessity of the Cull. But triggering one when we have no idea what's going on is daft."

Jak stared at the ground, jaw clenched. Talia rolled her eyes. "Aaron's breath, don't pout about it," she said to him.

"I'm not pouting," he said, raw anger in his voice. Talia's eye's narrowed at his tone, her features taking on a dangerous aspect, a wolf appraising her prey. "Damn it, I'm starving," he said, wisely changing the subject. "Don't they have anything besides bread with sticks and twigs in it to eat?"

"Bear your burden with grace, Jak," I said, my voice heavy with warning. "We suffer so Duatero might survive. The hunger you feel is a noble sacrifice. It's how we'll earn our seat at the Founder's table."

"I'm sorry, Majstro. I won't show weakness like that again."

"Good. Now, we've let Malamiko Island stand long enough," I said. "We'll burn the island tomorrow and the land contaminated by blue-leaf." Both nodded.

"And what about the rest of the fields?" Jak asked.

I honestly had no idea. "There's been no other Malamiko we can detect. We'll keep looking, and then we'll widen our search along the borderlands."

The next morning we strode out to the fields by Malamiko Island, escorted by Luksa and Alechjo. The paisajista looked at the markers we had staked. "Must you really cleanse so much?" she asked.

Oh, Luksa, I thought. *We'd cleanse so much more if Jak had his way.* "Yes," I said. "There may be more once we've discovered what's causing your crops to fail."

"Do you have any ideas of the cause?" she asked.

"We're working on it."

"How long do these types of investigations usually take?" Alechjo asked. Something in my expression caused the reeve to hurriedly add, "The town's on edge, Majstro Falchilo. Their worry increases with each passing day."

Normally, his question would not have irritated me, but our lack of progress set my teeth grinding. "Tell them with this cleanse, the first stage of decontamination is complete." That should content them for a while. I removed the flam-jetilo from the harness at my back and turned to my falchilo. "The wind's coming from that direction, so we'll start our cleanse—" The bell from the town's pagoda interrupted me as it began ringing madly. The reeve and paisajista looked at each other, alarmed.

"What's going on?" I asked.

"That's the town's alarm," Alechjo said. "Kubuto Falls is under attack."

We stared at each other in surprise while the pagoda bells rang. "Talia," I said.

"Yes, Majstro."

"Power up the gun."

SIX

"THAT BASTARD PETRO," Alechjo said, running toward town as the pagoda's warning bell clanged.

I stopped Luksa, who was about to take after him. "Who's Petro?" I asked.

"The reeve of Fisheto—a town a few kilometres downriver."

"You expected him to attack, and you didn't tell us?"

Luksa pulled away, starting to head after Alechjo. "We didn't think he'd actually do it. You have to help me stop them."

Which presented a problem: Stelara's Kodo. This is the code that describes the proper behaviours of the falchilo, and we are all sworn to abide by its laws. It forbids falchilo from fighting in secular battles. If someone attacks us or any member of the Tero Kreinto or its property, they're treated as a contaminant, and all bets are off. But otherwise … "Esper, you know where the school is. Take the children and see they make it to the pagoda," I said.

Luksa stopped and turned back, her grey hair blowing in her face. "Not the pagoda. They'll attack the pagoda grounds."

"They wouldn't dare," I said.

"They're after the granary."

"They'll burn if they touch the pagoda grounds," I said. "Esper, stay out of the fight. Get the kids to the pagoda and keep them safe. Defend the pagoda if you have to. Jak, Talia, you're with me."

The kiraso powered our sprint, winging us to Kubuto Falls with the speed of a sling bullet, leaving Luksa and Alechjo far behind. In the village, men and women ran in every direction. The crashes and yells of fighting rose up over the buildings from the far side of the village. Screams sounded from everywhere; the pagoda bell rang.

Esper peeled off, heading toward the school, while Jak, Talia, and I ran toward the sounds of fighting. My kiraso, one with my body and my intentions, went into full combat mode, its helmet enveloping my head and shield spiralling open. I grabbed my rod and snapped it to full length as we ran.

We arrived at the heart of the attack at the main gate. The village's wall barely deserved the name. It was waist high at best and had already been overrun. Dozens of men armed with spears and daggers were entangled in battle, stabbing, pushing, and punching each other. On the rooftops, men and women with slings fired stones into the invaders.

"Kredo," Talia said beside me, gun in her hand, "we're falchilo. People—actual people—are not our enemy."

"I know. Hang back. We'll help the wounded and—" Beside me, a man drove a spear into another man's belly, dropping him to his knees with a grunt. The violence of it shocked me, and I tapped the spearman with the tip of my rod. It was a pure reaction, my body acting before my thoughts could catch up. The jolt of energy from my rod knocked him off his feet and onto his back, where he lay motionless. He could be dead. The touch of a rod didn't guarantee death, but it was possible. I didn't even know which side he was on, invader or defender.

Beside me, the man on his knees looked at the spear protruding from his belly, the far end resting on the ground. His hands, stained with dirt and blood, held the wooden shaft. He looked up to me, brown eyes wide with fear, and then back down to the spear in his gut. He cried out, a wailing moan, reminding me of the terrified bleating of sheep brought to slaughter, again and again, setting the hairs on the back of my neck on end.

The press of bodies enveloped me, and Stelara's Kodo or not, I was in the fight, pushing the throng of fighters back with my shield. I had my rod out, ready to use if someone attacked me, but no one came at me directly. Slings whistled overhead. The invaders were armoured, wearing vests of wooden stakes banded tightly together worn over a shirt. The defenders of Kubuto Falls were just men and women going about their business in town, and most wore simple tunics or jupo.

Voices called out around me. "Falchilo! Falchilo!"

The battle lulled, and I had a moment to look around. Talia moved through the combat like a dancer. She was trying not to use her rod, knocking attackers back with her shield instead. A little way away, Jak was cracking the handle of his axe into people's heads and bashing them with his shield.

Other voices rose. "Falchilo!" The cry came from the attackers, and they pushed away, leaving us as they gave chase after the village's defenders.

"Haa!" Jak called out, arms outstretched to either side.

"They're scared of us!" Rivulets of blood trailed down the front of his shield.

"They respect us," Talia said. "There's a difference."

"Though if Luksa's right and they've come to invade pagoda grounds, we might not be able to count on their respect for long," I said.

I searched for the man with the spear in his gut. He was a short distance away, slumped on his side, hands still clasping the shaft of the weapon protruding from him. He moaned softly. He needed a kuracisto to tend his wounds—or, more likely, peacefully end his suffering—but in a town as remote as Kubuto Falls, the nearest healer was probably days away. I placed my hand on his shoulder, and he roused somewhat. "Founder's grace protect you. We'll be back as soon as we can to help."

I led Talia and Jak into town after the invaders. Screams, yells, and the clatter of wood and steel crashing into each other sounded from everywhere. Down a narrow lane to our left, a flurry of movement caught my eye. I heard a woman screaming and a child crying.

"This way." I ran down the lane in time to hear fabric ripping as I saw an invader tear at the gown the woman wore, exposing her breasts. He stained her pale skin, groping at her with hands filthy with blood and dirt, while two other men held her thrashing body down. A fourth man watched on, his foot pinning a young boy to the ground who was calling out to his struggling mother. All of them, except the man madly grabbing at the woman's breast, faced us and saw our approach.

Things happened fast. Talia sped past me, blasting one of the men off his feet with the gun, and then sent another blast into the back of the man on the woman. The wonton, defiling violence of the scene drove Stelara's Kodo from my mind. I stabbed my rod into the man standing on the boy. The shock knocked him into the wall of a building with a hollow thud before he collapsed to the ground like an armful of dropped logs. I turned to face the last man. Time slowed. Sailing between Talia and me, Jak's axe tumbled end over end. I saw grimy stains of blood on its head and handle as it spun on by, embedding itself in the crook of the last man's neck and shoulder with a resounding crack like you might hear when breaking a drumstick off a chicken or when you crack a stick over a knee. The force of the blow sent him staggering. He lost his footing and fell on his back.

Talia crouched down to help the woman cover herself as her son scrambled to her. I walked over to the last man, axe jutting out of him. His breath rasped, and his eyes lolled, coming eventually to focus on me. I had never killed a human before. That's not what we falchilo are. Malamiko is our enemy, our only enemy. But sweet Donna, what kind of beast rapes a woman in front of her child?

I placed a foot on his chest and took a firm grip of the axe's handle, hefting the weapon free, ripping a scream out of him as I did. Blood pulsed out the wound; the man moaned, a sad, pitiful whimper, eyes wide in panic. Feebly, he brought his hands to the gaping wound, trying to staunch the flow of blood. The woman's screams and the sound of ripping fabric echoed in my ears, and I couldn't bring myself to help him. I thought about hitting him with the rod, ending his suffering. I chose not to. This wasn't me picking a side in a secular fight, I told myself. I hadn't violated Stelara's Kodo; I'd stopped a vile crime. He died before my eyes, and while the light in his eyes faded all I could think was, *Is it a sin to take satisfaction in evil's suffering?*

Screams from elsewhere in the city pulled my attention away from him. I tossed the axe back to Jak. "Bring them," I said pointing to the woman. Talia had managed to help her cover herself. The boy cried as he and his mother clung to each other. "We're making a run for the pagoda."

"Luksa says they're attacking the pagoda," Talia said. "You want to take her into the fight? Maybe I should take her out of town."

"The paisajista said they're here for the granary," I said.

"Which is on the pagoda grounds," Talia replied.

"I have a plan, and I'll need you and Jak. To the pagoda." I went back out into the main roadway. The fighting had moved on ahead, leaving a trail of bodies in its wake, blood leaving dark stains on the dirt road. Though a falchilo's enemy is Malamiko, we ultimately see ourselves as defenders of humanity. *Mia korpo estas via shildo*, the falchilo blessing— my body is your shield. That promise sat like a heavy stone in my gut as I passed the bodies of the dead and wounded.

We ran toward the pagoda, catching up with knots of fighting men. Along the rooftops, women and some men ran with slings whistling in wide arcs over their heads, firing into invaders below, but a few of the attackers had managed to clamber up the sides of the buildings and were starting to engage them in close quarters.

I scanned the chaotic pack for Reeve Alechjo, or Luksa, for anyone who seemed to be in command but saw no one in charge. "Fall back to the pagoda!" I yelled. "Kubuto Falls, to the pagoda!" We made our way quickly through the fighting throngs. Some invaders moved to intercept us, but once they saw our kiraso, they backed off.

I grabbed Jak's arm. "Go that way," I said, pointing down a narrow laneway that led to another street. "Tell everyone to fall back to the pagoda. You're falchilo; they'll listen to you. Go, be quick," I said, pushing him on his way. "Take them to the pagoda," I said to Talia, pointing at the woman and her son. "I'll meet you there." Talia ran on ahead with the woman and boy.

I ran to other streets, calling out, signalling a fall back to the pagoda before making my way there. Jak had arrived already, and he and Talia ran to meet me. In ones and twos, the defenders ran past us to the pagoda grounds. I tossed my flamjetilo to Jak.

"No weapon for you?" he asked, catching it.

"Nope."

"What's the plan?" Talia asked, her gun resting on her shoulder.

"We're going to stop these people from slaughtering Kubuto Falls," I said. "Follow behind me, one to either side."

"That's it?" Jak asked. "What do you want us to do?"

Talia caught where my plan was going. "Act like you're cock of the walk," she said, "and like you ain't scared of shit."

"Watch your language," I said.

"Damn it, Kredo, I am certain the Founders swore."

"Enough," I said. The attackers were exiting the streets like hungry coyotes from earthen lore, loping into the plaza leading to the pagoda ground. "Helmets on," I said to my falchilo. "I want you to be faceless." Their helmets enveloped their heads, but I kept my own face exposed. I stepped out, facing the onrushing attackers. "If they touch pagoda grounds, they're contaminants, and we cleanse them, everyone." They did not slow their charge. "Jak. Warning blast."

He stepped forward with the flamjetilo, and with a click, waves of energy belched forth, distorting the air, and the ground in front of us erupted in a line of fire. A stillness settled over the plaza as the attackers stopped, the coyotes unsure whether they should or could tackle the prey before them.

"The pagoda grounds are sacred," I called out loud enough everyone could hear over the crackle of dying flames. "Who sanctioned this attack on the Founder's sanctuary?" They replied with silence. "Who!"

A man stepped forward. He was kavaliro, a nobleman, judging by the steel helm and breastplate he wore, now dulled by dirt and blood. He walked up as the fire died and took off his helmet, revealing short grey hair, a long beard, and a tan, weathered face. "I am Petro Georgido, reeve of Fisheto. We're here for the food stores, Falchilo. Let us pass."

"It's *Majstro* Falchilo," I said.

"Apologies, Majstro," he said, his tone notable in its absence of contrition.

Buried among the stern faces of his soldiers, I noticed others whose brows furrowed with uncertainty. Not enough to turn the tide yet, but the start of an undercurrent. "It is the sacred duty of the paisajista to distribute food, not yours. Who are you to undermine the Founder's grace?"

"This is a battle between our towns. It doesn't concern you, Falchilo," the kavaliro said, again neglecting my rank. "Kubuto Falls is cursed. Step aside and let us finish what we've started."

I stepped over the smouldering embers of Jak's fire until I, completely unarmed, stood before the kavaliro, his fighters behind him, and I said so everyone could hear, "I am Majstro Falchilo Kredo." Whispers of recognition wafted to my ear, and the kavaliro's eye's narrowed as he digested this. Fame has some benefits. I spoke over the man's shoulders to his troops, trying to turn the undercurrent into a torrent leading away from the pagoda. "Your reeve has put you all at great risk. I am here investigating possible Malamiko contamination." A cold stillness washed across the plaza. I turned to the kavaliro, stared, and said, in a voice only he could hear, "Pray I do not find *you* contaminated."

His jaw clenched at my threat, and his eyes darted to Jak and the flamjetilo he held. Finally, he leaned in speaking in a voice only I could hear. "We need food."

"The allotment is sacred," I said. "It has kept Duatero strong enough to survive Malamiko for thousands of years. We're all hungry. Our hunger is the price we pay to stay strong through the lean years. The Founders smile on such sacrifice."

"My people don't hunger. They starve," the kavaliro said, anger in his eyes. "Paisajista Luksa did not give us enough food to last through to harvest with the allotment chips we have."

"That cannot be true," I said, looking once more at the troops behind him and seeing for the first time the gauntness of their faces, and the desperation in their eyes.

"It is," he said. "Luksa has forsaken her sacred duty. She favours Kubuto Falls, hoarding food here while we starve. The Founders punish this transgression with crops that fail for no reason." Strains of desperations entered his voice. "I mean no disrespect to you or the Founders, Majstro Falchilo, but what's going on here isn't the work of the Founders; it's not the way of the Tero Kreinto. Kubuto Falls is bringing us to ruin."

The paisajista are fools, I found myself thinking. They should have Culled last year before winter but didn't, cutting the allotment short instead as they pinned their hopes on lies to draw us out to Rendezvous. Through the Cull, we could reduce our population to the land's carrying capacity in a controlled, calculated manner. Without it . . . my eyes wandered to the bodies littering the streets behind the attackers, a haze of dust and smoke hanging in the air.

"It is not my place to distribute food on behalf of the paisajista," I said. "But if you take your soldiers and leave Kubuto Falls now, this is what I will do. I'll send a message to my superior, Kapo Falchilo Mihaelo. He speaks directly with the Unua Paisajista. I will have him speak to her on your behalf."

The kavaliro's eyes widened at this. "The *Unua*? You can send word to her?"

"I promise she will hear what you have told me. And I'm here now investigating what's causing the crop failures. The Tero Kreinto is fixing this. Leave Kubuto Falls. These people are not your enemy—our enemy is the blue fields that lurk outside Duatero."

He thought this through. "How long until the Unua hears of this?"

"Days."

"My people starve. How can I tell them to wait?"

"We're all starving. When Duatero prospers, we all prosper. When it suffers, we suffer together. It is not the people of Kubuto Falls who strike at you. It's Malamiko. And I swear on my kiraso, we will stop it. *Mia korpo estas via shildo*."

The kavaliro considered a moment. His eyes flicked to Jak, lingering on the flamjetilo. Was he honestly still thinking of attacking pagoda grounds? He'd have to know if he did, I'd be free to set my falchilo against him without reservation. Were his people so far gone they'd follow him against the Tero Kreinto? He looked down as he came to his decision. "Please, send your message quickly."

"I will."

"Today."

"I promise."

He looked at me, lines of shame and frustration etching his face. "We will go."

I turned and addressed his soldiers. "Your reeve has earned the Founder's favour today. The Unua Paisajista will hear of how you suffered and make things right!"

His followers mumbled softly to each other as the kavaliro turned, ordering them out of the village.

To Talia and Jak, I said, "Find Luksa. I'm getting some answers out of her."

As the soldiers were leaving, a cheer rose from the people of Kubuto Falls, many of them racing out to tend to the wounded, others calling out for lost loved ones.

We worked our way through this bustle of people looking for Luksa, through the pagoda, and through the surrounding gardens. Finally, we found her. She was lying flat on her back, her head in the lap of Reeve Alechjo, her dead eyes glassed over, staring lifelessly into the sky. A crimson circle stained her brown tunic around a dark hole.

The reeve looked at me, eyes wet with tears, face twisted in grief. "We are cursed. Cursed!" He turned to look at her lifeless face while rocking her gently. "Who kills a paisajista?"

So much for answers. I considered chasing down the attackers from Fisheto to bring them to justice for this murder of a member of the Tero Kreinto. I didn't, but my guilt for killing those beasts in the alley vanished. Luksa's failures— the failure of the whole paisajista order to call a Cull last year —brought this on. I turned to Talia and Jak. "Help with the wounded." Around us, people ran as they searched, or tended to the wounded. Men and women cried as they hugged one another.

There were no children.

"Wait," I said. Talia and Jak turned to look at me. "Where's Esper?"

A moment passed as we stared at each other. "You don't think they'd kill a school full of kids, do you?" Talia asked.

"You saw what they were doing to that woman and her son," I said. "When you're hungry enough to kill, you're . . . animal. This is what Malamiko does to us."

As one, we took off at a full sprint down dirt streets to the school. There had been fighting here. Scattered bodies littered the streets, both wounded and dead. Two children lay prone, one face down, a stab wound in her back, another resting on his side, the dirt in front of him stained by his blood. The invaders had attacked the school. This would make it in my report to the Unua, too. I rushed to the school, entered, called out Esper's name. It was a small building, two rooms, both empty.

"They got out," Talia said.

That didn't mean they lived. If Fisheto's soldiers killed Esper, damn my promise to report to the Unua, and damn their starving stomachs, by the Founders I'd chase down that kavaliro and those following him and cleanse them all. "There's only one entrance, so they would have exited to the street," I said, stepping out of the building.

Jak was there, investigating. He squatted down by the body of an attacker, turned him over, and then removed the corpse's protective vest with some struggling. A black patch of burnt flesh surrounded by red, nearly purple skin dominated the body's torso. "Rod," Jak said. "Esper got one of 'em." He stood up, surveying the street. "I wouldn't have thought she had it in her."

"The attackers would've come from that direction," Talia said, pointing down the street.

"Right, so Esper would probably take the kids this way," I

said, pointing the opposite direction. We followed the dirt road. It quickly came to the town's edge, leading to the ring road lining the wall. Beyond it lay a field of stunted wheat, and beyond that, the waters of the Jinhuang River glittering in the late morning sun.

I set Talia and Jak to searching for Esper while I returned to the pagoda to find Alechjo. Nearby, a man climbed a ladder to the top of a building and looked out over the streets and rooftops. He cupped his hands to either side of his mouth. "Amika!" he yelled. His bare chest swelled as he inhaled a deep breath. "Amika!"

Behind me, a woman's voice, shrill, tinged with panic, called out the same name. Other men and women began calling out other names. It had not taken long for Kubuto Falls to discover most of their children were gone.

I found Alechjo in the pagoda gardens. The wounded that could move or be moved came to the garden, and Alechjo had recovered enough from the paisajista's death to try and impose some semblance of order. He was speaking with a young man, giving him orders to head to the city of Kolo and bring back a kuracisto.

I pulled Alechjo aside. "The town's children are missing."

"Missing?"

I nodded.

"Did those bastards take them?"

"You stand on pagoda grounds—watch your tongue. I don't think so. Starving people don't steal more mouths to feed. Esper was with the kids, and it looked like she beat off at least some of the attackers."

"I . . . Well, where did they go?" he asked.

"You tell me. If they were going to go anywhere to hide, where would it be? Is there some cave, some hill, or woods nearby the children would know about?"

"I don't . . ." I caught the trace of a thought quickly entering his mind, quickly discarded. "No, there's no place nearby."

"Are you certain?" I asked. "These are your town's children. Anything. Any hint, any idea, no matter how unlikely, tell me."

"No," Alechjo said, more confidence in his voice. "Outside of the town, there's nothing nearby. In town, they could be in any of the houses. Anywhere, really."

Jak approached, and I left Alechjo to speak with him. "Anything?" I asked.

"No sign of 'em, dead or alive."

Jak and I began gathering the frantic parents into ordered teams and sent them searching building to building. When Talia returned, I had her organize a group to begin searching outside the town's walls.

The sun scaled the sky, a burning, unrelenting eye glaring down at us. I began to wonder if the attackers might have taken Esper and the kids hostage to make sure I held my end of the bargain. Petro would have to know that would only bring the full wrath of the falchilo down on him.

A runner came into town, screaming, "They found them! By the bend in the river, they found them!" He ran past too quickly for me to ask if they were alive or dead. I ran, my kiraso powering me past the throngs of people.

A large group had gathered halfway between the town and the river. I pushed my way through the crowd and out the other side. I had not realized how tied up in knots my guts had been, but when I saw Esper standing there in front of the town's children, the tension washed off me.

A hand on my chest stopped my advance. It was Talia, her helmet activated. "Helmet up," she said. Esper's brown hair was wild and unkempt, face smeared with dirt and sweat. She held a toddler in her arm. Around her, children clustered, clothes soaking wet. Older ones held younger ones, some holding back the little ones who might otherwise run to their parents. And beside me, a good twenty paces away, those very parents were on their knees, crying and praying.

"Don't come any closer!" Esper shouted.

"What have you done?" I asked.

"We . . ." She looked back over her shoulder, then to me, desperate worry in her eyes. "They were attacking. They killed some of the children, but I got them. More were coming, so we ran out of the village. They were chasing us, Kredo. We ran to the only place they wouldn't follow."

There, directly behind her, sat Malamiko Island, its blue fronds waving, taunting, threatening me. We were supposed to cleanse it today. *Not you, Esper*. The helmet of my kiraso engulfed my face.

"Should we prep the flamjetilo?" It was Jak, his own helmet activated.

"What is wrong with you?" Talia asked him. "We have the GC. She would have known that before taking them there. No need to get fire-happy."

This was true. Still, Esper had taken an extreme, borderline irresponsible risk. If the GC confirmed she or any of the children had been infected, I would have to cleanse them. Any other falchilo squad, lacking a GC of their own, would probably cleanse them out of hand to be safe, or, if they were close to a Founder city with a Tero Kreinto, maybe send them for quarantine and testing where they would probably die anyway, mad from the isolation.

"Talia, charge your gun. If anyone makes a break for it, take them down," I said.

She grunted in frustration as she cranked the power shaft

on her weapon. "I like you, Esper," she said. "Don't make me shoot you."

A weight squeezed my chest as I took the GC out of its case. I studied its golden casing and grasped its black handle. It was so old—older than the mountain kingdom of Shihbei. It had outlived the kingdoms of the Classic Kronoj and the empire of Lan Hu. And I knew it would not work forever. Was today the day it failed?

I crossed the distance to the cluster of children, stood right before Esper. She stared at me with sad eyes. "You chose not to activate your helmet," I said. "It would have saved you."

She shook her head and brushed some loose hair out of her face. "If any of them are contaminated, I don't think I could live with myself if I didn't face the same threat."

"You are a foolish girl." I kept myself from saying more, struggling to hold my anger in check.

She lowered her head, stared at the ground between her feet. "I am sorry, Majstro Falchilo. I didn't know what else to do. One of the children said they had explored the island before, and nothing happened."

The children had explored the island before. How could Luksa not know her own charges were wandering lands contaminated with Malamiko? Maybe she did know. She had much to answer for, but now the only ones she answered to were the Founders.

I raised my GC to Esper. "No," she said, raising her head to look me in the eyes. "Do them first," she said, nodding to the children surrounding her.

I hesitated a moment and then motioned a young boy toward me. He stepped forward, face nervous, as though he'd been caught red-handed in some boyhood escapade and was now facing the harsh retribution of an angry father. If only those were the stakes he faced. If he were contaminated, I'd have to cleanse him and watch him burn to ashes while his parents looked on in tears. That would leave a scar. How many of these kids would I have to cleanse, I wondered, looking at their faces. I'd have rather found the lot of them with spears in their guts.

I raised the GC to the boy's arm and pressed the activation trigger. He winced at its prick. A moment passed as the machine hissed and churned. Green light. The boy was clean. Esper almost dropped to her knees in relief.

"Don't celebrate yet," I said. I nodded to the boy, sending him running across the field into the arms of his crying parents. I motioned another kid forward. Green light. Same with the next. Over the next quarter-hour, I tested all the children; green lights for everyone.

Esper and I were the only ones left, and we faced each other as a breeze began to take the edge off the day's heat. My shock and anger had passed. I spoke quieter now. "You took a big risk."

"I saw them kill children," she said, tears rimming her eyes, her voice wavering. She looked so young. Having just finished her training as a falchilo, she'd be twenty at most. She'd spent the last four years cloistered in the sanctuary of the Tero Kreinto, and before that, living on a farm. She was trained to expect violence from Malamiko, but the violence we visit upon one another? Perhaps it overwhelmed what her childhood experiences had prepared her for.

"I killed two of them," she said, her voice a whisper. "They weren't contaminated. They were men, people."

Had I expected too much of her? She was intelligent, brilliant even. She was courageous against Malamiko. But still young, still scrambling up the cliff whose peak marked the separation between girl and woman. "None of us were there," I said. "You had to act. Sometimes life does that. The children are alive."

She didn't smile, didn't seem comforted. She'd learned a hard lesson today. Time to see if she lived to benefit from it. I brought the GC to her neck. "Ready?" I asked.

She nodded. I tested her.

Green light.

SEVEN

WE CLEANSED Malamiko Island the next day. I let Esper do it. Then, we continued our study of the fields around Kubuto Falls while the town recovered from its attack, searching for some clue to the crop failures. After two days of rooting through dirt and stunted stalks of grain, I knew no more about what was causing these failures than I did on the day I arrived. This was a waste of time.

Exhausted, I made my way to the town's pagoda. Excited chatter about a caravan arriving rippled through the small clusters of people I passed. It sounded like several kuracisto had accompanied it. Good. Many in the town were wounded, and they needed healers.

The wooden floors of the pagoda creaked as I walked to the office I had claimed. It was cramped, cluttered with potted plants and notebooks Luksa had left in it, but it had a desk and writing equipment where I could prepare my reports and record my observations for the day.

I was stunned to see Mihaelo sitting at the desk. He looked up from a notebook he was reading. "Afternoon,

Kredo," he said, as though his presence in Kubuto Falls was the epitome of normalcy.

"Kapo, I …I wasn't expecting you here, Kapo." I stood straighter, then bowed my head in respect. "It's good to see you."

He gave me a look of disbelief and said in his quiet voice, "Good to see me? No one likes it when their boss shows up unannounced." He nodded toward a chair buried under a stack of ledgers, inviting me to sit. "I read your report and decided to come here to see what's going on. Brought some kuracisto with me, too."

"The reeve will be grateful for your help," I said, placing the ledgers on the floor and taking my seat.

"Have you read through any of Luksa's notes?" he asked, holding up the book he was reading.

"No, I've been in the field."

"Of course. That's where any good falchilo should be. But ever since my leg vaulted me into the lofty heights of administration, my life has become one of reports and letters." I could see the sneer breaking through his cool reserve. "Every once in a while, though, they tell you something useful." He nodded to a page. "I've never been the strongest in math—that's another skill you get to pick up when they give you a desk—but looking over Luksa's records for the last harvest, Fisheto's reeve was telling the truth."

"You told the Unua of Fisheto's situation?"

"I did."

"Will she help in light of what you've found here?"

"I doubt it." Mihaelo folded his hands on the desk while he looked at me. "There's no food. I don't think Luksa was alone in shorting the allotment."

Our allotment chips don't buy as much as they should. I told Mihaelo of my conversation with traders on my way to

Kubuto Falls. Mihaelo nodded his head and said, "The paisajista blundered—" The sound of Talia entering the pagoda with Esper and Jak came from outside the office. "Oh good, your falchilo have returned. Have them join us for a walk in the pagoda's gardens." He must be missing the camaraderie of working in the field with fellow falchilo. He had been a man of action before a sentinel's pincer cracked his femur.

I gathered the other falchilo, and we went back outside. Like the town itself, Kubuto Fall's pagoda was small, and its grounds humble, though immaculately maintained. We found a short path leading to a modest pond.

"You must discover what's causing these failures quickly," Mihaelo said, carrying on our conversation as he took a seat on a stone bench overlooking the pond. The shade of overhanging trees gave relief from the sun.

"Obviously," I said. Talia immediately took a seat beside him, to which I raised a disapproving eyebrow that she ignored.

"Well, yes, obviously," Mihaelo said, massaging his leg. "But there's more beyond our starving people at play."

I cocked my head. "Oh?"

"Omaro Adamido is causing trouble," he said, voice barely louder than the breeze through the leaves. Omaro Adamido VI was the krono of the Founder city of Lan Hu and constantly angled for ways to strengthen the once-great empire. "The paisajista aren't saying so openly," Mihaelo continued, "but they've miscalculated. They should have Culled last year. Because they didn't, people starve. They were hoping to stretch things out to Rendezvous, but … Anyhow, Omaro's been openly offering to help the Tero Kreinto manage the allotment. As winter wore on and rations thinned, it became less of an offer and more of a suggestion.

Left unchecked, he may soon escalate his suggestion to a demand."

Jak shook his head. "Lan Hu, always scheming. It's a dead empire, but Omaro's too stupid to see it."

My thoughts flashed to Fisheto's attack on Kubuto Falls. "When a ruler's people starve, they feed them, find a scapegoat, or find their head on a pike."

"Gentlemen, the Kapo is talking," Talia said, patting Mihaelo on the leg.

Mihaelo gave her a quelling glance. "The crop failures you investigate play into his hands."

The town surrounding the pagoda was grubby at the best of times. I couldn't imagine it playing any kind of role in power politics. "How does what's happening in Kubuto Falls help him?"

"Kubuto Falls is not alone," he said. "There are several unexplained crop failures across Duatero."

"Where?" I asked.

"The western plains of Aaronsburg. Xuanhe also has widespread failures. Not all are as bad as Kubuto Falls, but this year's harvest is going to be a disaster."

My stomach knotted as I stared into the pond's surface. "We're being attacked."

"Attacked?" Mihaelo asked.

"We have dark wanderers that can talk. Our crops fail for no reason." My thoughts turned to Malamiko Island, close enough to Kubuto Falls that Esper and the town's children could wade to it, a beachhead for Malamiko to creep into our lands like worms chewing through the dirt. "There is something here. Something new." I would have liked to study Malamiko Island, but we'd turned it to ash.

"Your reports say the GC shows nothing," Mihaelo said.

"I know."

The silence hung. Mihaelo caught my unspoken fear. "You doubt the GC?"

"I don't know." Shrugging, I turned to him. "The GC is ancient. We should expect it to fail." Mihaelo said nothing, leaving me to speak into the silence. "I took it apart last night and inspected all of its components."

"And what did you learn?" he asked.

"The GC's fine. All its parts are old but still operating within specification."

Talia spoke up. "Aw, Kredo, you didn't have to ruin your night to figure that out. It still detects all the background markers of Malamiko. You can see that every time you calibrate it."

"We don't know what caused Kubuto Fall's crops to fail. Founder cities bicker and vie for dominance. Meanwhile, *something is attacking us*. In a way, I was hoping to find something wrong with the GC."

"Xinhua's eyes, why would you hope for that?" she asked

"Because the fact it's working means Malamiko has evolved some way to avoid detection. If the GC had finally failed, at least we might still be dealing with something we know. But with the GC working, this must be something new, and I don't know how to fight it."

Mihaelo leaned back, stretching his leg out. "If you, with the GC, can't find out what is happening, then . . ." He turned to look at me. "Then we have a very serious problem. Several of them. The entire legitimacy of the Tero Kreinto rests on our ability to avoid famines and to protect us from Malamiko. The starvation caused by the paisajista's unwillingness to Cull undermines the first. That something attacks our crops, and we are defenceless against it undermines the second."

Jak scowled. "What will the Tero Kreinto do?"

Mihaelo shrugged. "Lan Hu tax collectors encroach into

trade routes claimed by Aaronsburg. We'll fan that tension into war to keep Omaro occupied and take Lan Hu down a peg."

"Wait, what?" It was Esper. "War?"

"I'm afraid so."

"Can the Tero Kreinto bring Founder cities to war?" Esper asked.

"The kronoj war easily enough," Mihaelo replied. "It is only the hand of the Tero Kreinto on their reins that keep them from each other's throats. We but need to loosen our grip, and their old hatreds do the rest."

"How . . . How can the Tero Kreinto have such control over them?" Esper asked.

Mihaelo gave her a patient smile, one a father might give a child when explaining why summer must end. "We control the food and allotment. That gives us control over all else. And it's a good thing, too. It's only through our management we survive. Can you imagine if the kronoj, with all their petty bickering, managed food distribution?"

Esper's eyes were wide with shock. "But war? We'd actually bring them to war?"

"Why not?" Jak asked. "If they kill themselves, it lessens how deeply we need to Cull. And by directing the people's anger at each other, the Tero Kreinto is free to continue its battle with Malamiko."

Mihaelo stared at Jak with narrow eyes. "Very astute." Jak's chest puffed up. Mihaelo turned to Esper. "The sooner you find what is attacking our crops and destroy it, the faster our granaries will fill, and the sooner our need to distract the people through war ends."

"I don't think we're going to find it in Kubuto Falls," I said.

"No? Where then?"

"Vojo Fino."

Mihaelo stared at me, an eyebrow raised inquisitively.

"Luksa told me of it," I explained. "It's a town near here. It sits on the border of our lands where Malamiko from the ruins of Port Donna pushes up against us. There's an abandoned falchilo outpost there. Perhaps with easier access between the town and Malamiko, our enemy will strike more openly."

Mihaelo contemplated my words. "Good. Go there. I'll find another falchilo squad to finish investigating whatever fields you haven't got to yet here. Now, come," he said, struggling to his feet, with Talia quick to help him. "It cools quickly at night, and my leg would rather be inside as the temperature drops."

"Majstro, a word," Esper said as we neared the pagoda steps. I waved the others on ahead and held back to speak with her. "Kredo, you can't really support what the Tero Kreinto is doing?" she said once the others were gone.

"How can you ask such a thing?"

"The people starve. Isn't that suffering enough? To bring them to war now . . ."

A child's idealism still clung to her. "We're not *bringing* them to war. They fight all on their own."

"But Stelara's Kodo—we don't fight secular battles."

"We're not warring with them. They're warring with each other. Look, you saw what they did here in Kubuto Falls. We have a sacred duty—nothing less than our survival in this world. The Tero Kreinto directs the attention of the kronoj away from us so we can focus on our sacred task."

"It seems dirty."

Her words brought back the unsettling memory of a man, spear in his gut, wailing in fear and pain, as well as the sound of a gown ripping and an axe spinning end over end through the air. "It is dirty. That is why we must draw away from such matters, so our minds remain uncluttered while we battle our true enemy."

Be good, Kredo. My mother had said that to me when I left to join the Tero Kreinto. I'd been a boy, then, and every day since, I have tried to honour her charge. Esper's idealism grated under my skin as we entered the pagoda to get ready for the evening. *You can't really support what the Tero Kreinto is doing.* Was what the Tero Kreinto doing good?

It was necessary. The Tero Kreinto sustains us. Malamiko's greatest evil is it makes us kill our own. This whole dirty business—towns attacking each other, city-states going to war—this was Malamiko *forcing* us against each other. Focus on the hunt.

EIGHT

"WE'RE STAYING *HERE*?" Talia asked, voice dripping with disappointment. We stood before the western door of an abandoned falchilo outpost on the outskirts of Vojo Fino.

"It's not so bad," Esper said. "There's a charm to it."

"When did creepy become charming?" Talia asked.

"This is where we stay," I said.

Vojo Fino. The name meant Road's End in the tongue of the Classic Kronoj. It reeked of pessimism.

Talia stood, hands on hips, her face reminding me of a mythical wolf disappointed to find its prey was all skin and bones, no meat. "This town's got three pagodas we could stay at," she said. "I even saw an inn on our way here. Why stay someplace that's old, and abandoned?"

The main building was circular, two stories high, and the adjoining tower had an additional two levels above that. It was built of stone rather than mud brick—made to last. Moss covered the walls like a layer of paint, and the surrounding gardens were wild and overgrown with weeds. "Vojo Fino is the last town before the borderlands. It should have a permanent falchilo presence here," I said. "This outpost shouldn't be abandoned."

"Why is it, then?" Esper asked.

"After the Cull of '29, there weren't enough falchilo to guard the length of our border." I walked to the door, examining it. Thick, sturdy wood from the forests of Lu Guang, stained a dark brown, chained shut with solid-looking links. Three columns stood to either side, their capitals carved with images of birds, falchilo battling sentinels, human busts, and bees. A triangular lintel rested on the columns, and on the inset surface of the triangle, an engraving of a deer, white paint peeling from it. I smiled at my falchilo. "We're back."

From my pack, I withdrew the key Mihaelo had given me, unlocked the chains barring the door, and entered.

All the furniture had been removed, and the large circular chamber we entered stood empty. "Well," Talia said, coming in behind me, "it's roomy."

In the chamber's centre stood a two-floored shrine. A double set of stairs lined its outer walls to its second floor. "I don't recognize who it's to," Jak said, looking at the shrine.

"There," Talia said, pointing at the multiple engravings of deer painted white covering its walls. "Shen Ling Zhao, Founder of Xuanhe."

"How do you know that?" Esper asked.

Talia shrugged. "Grew up in Xuanhe. Paid enough attention to my aunt's preaching to figure out who founded the damn city."

"Talia, language," I said.

"Sorry, Majstro. *Illustrious* city."

"Look," Jak said, pointing through a door in the lower level of the shrine. "An aŭtomato!"

I hurried over. Time had blessed this aŭtomato, ancient servant of the Founders, preserving its metallic body and eight legs in excellent condition. On its back rested a sturdy platform where goods may have once been placed as it transported them from one area to another. The builders of this outpost, no doubt, built it around this aŭtomato to honour and protect it. "It's beautiful," I said. Jak placed a wood engraving of Founder Neil he had carved at the aŭtomato's base as an offering, and we took a knee and prayed.

We walked around the main chamber, inspecting the outpost. There were three apses on the eastern wall with a sanctuary built off the northernmost one. They were empty now, but the outlines of where altars and paintings once hung still marked the walls.

"That's the entrance to the tower," I said, pointing to a passage in the southeast section of the chamber. "The living quarters will be there. Talia, I want you and Jak to inspect this place. Make an inventory of what we'll need to make it livable, then go into town to get the supplies. If the town has any power, then this place should be hooked up to it. We'll need it to charge our kiraso. Check to see if we have power. If not, bang on the door of the Reeve's Hall and get it hooked up. Esper, you're with me."

I left with Esper close behind. "Where are we off to?" she asked.

"We're starting our investigation."

Vojo Fino exuded a combination of moods. On first look, it exuded melancholy. Once fine villas lined the road we walked, their plaster, coloured with faded paint, had flaked off, revealing sections of the mud brick underneath. Large estates once home to wealthy merchants had been converted to apartment complexes, filled now with dozens of families, or had been taken over by businesses and merchants. It seemed a town stuck in a dream remembering days of glory past. Interspersed between them sat abandoned buildings, their collapsing roofs and hollow doors gaping like missing teeth in a rictus smile.

At odds with this melancholy, people with quick and bright energy filled the road, paved with stone smoothed by the tread of a million feet over centuries. From a window above, a man's voice lifted in a happy song while he worked and spilled out on the street below. People bowed in deference to us as we passed, and I could hear the murmur of "falchilo" ripple through the crowds.

We arrived at the Reeve's Hall, a building similar in size to the falchilo outpost. Its paint, much like other buildings, was faded, though I could see where they had made repairs to the plaster. A four-tiered pagoda stood across from the hall. It was well maintained: its paint was bright, and several paisajista were out working in an immaculate garden. We went to the pagoda.

A man wearing the robes of a gepatro—ankle-length brown robe, cinched at his waist by a dark green belt with tasseled ends—introduced himself as Denizo Matido and took us in. He offered us tea in clay mugs but no food, even though I was starved from the day's travels. "I hope you understand," Denizo said by way of apology, "we've no food to spare in these times."

"You keep a tight rein on the allotment, even in your own pagoda," I said.

"When Duatero suffers, we suffer together," he said. I drank my tea, hoping the flavoured fluid would distract my stomach from its hunger. Denizo spoke into the silence. "It is good Firstsite sent falchilo. I've written some requests to Kapo Mihaelo."

"Your crops have failed, too? You suspect Malamiko contamination, then?"

He shrugged. "Our crops failed despite plenty of water

and sun. What else could it be? We live along the border-lands. Malamiko encroachment is a common threat."

I grew up in the borderlands south of Lan Hu and so knew well the dangers of living so close to the advancing tides of a world trying to reclaim its own from alien invaders.

I placed my mug down. My stomach grumbled—the tea only reminded me of my starvation. "Do you think you'll be able to draw the allotment out to Rendezvous without a Cull?" I cursed myself for asking as the words fled my lips—I was tired, irritable, and letting my hunger lead the conversation.

He smiled a thin, humourless smile. "We will know soon whether we have enough for the rest of the season. With Founder's grace, we'll make it without having to Cull." He spoke the lines with a fluidity suggesting the reply was well-rehearsed. I was probably one of hundreds of people who'd asked him that same question since harvest's end.

"Can you give me a list of farmers most affected by the failures? I'll want to speak with them."

"Of course—I have a list already prepared. If you want to get a start, Karena's crops were a complete loss last year. Her husband passed two years back, and she's been running the farm with her sons. She hasn't taken the failure well—you'll find her at a tavern near the edge of town."

We finished our tea, and I thanked him for his time. The tavern Denizo directed us to was in a building of ancient brick, bleached by thousands of sunny days and pitted by winds that had blown generations before my father walked the lands. The roof sagged, tired of this life, waiting for the owner to hire a team of roofers to put it out of its misery. Standing before it, I wondered how many things the building had been before the tavern took up residence in it—impos-sible to say. Inside, the wood floor creaked with each step, and dusty tapestries coloured the walls. Though it was mid-afternoon, a small collection of men and women reclined on benches. The pungent, sickly sweet stench hanging in the torpid air suggested mead filled the mugs they nursed. Though we lacked food, alcohol seemed plentiful. When I asked the barkeep for Karena, he led me out a door in the back to a narrow alley and pointed at a woman passed out in a pool of piss and vomit.

"Poor woman," Esper said, covering her mouth and nose from the stench.

"Get me a bucket of water," I said to the barkeep. "No, two buckets." It took a dousing from four buckets and some scrubbing before we'd cleaned her enough that I was comfortable having her touching my kiraso. We slung Karena's arms around each of our shoulders and dragged her semi-comatose back to the outpost, where we were surprised to find a group of people kneeling in prayer before the western doors. On the stairs sat bundles of offerings: wreaths of flowers, some clothes—and plates of cheeses, honeycombs, apples, and bread.

"We can't accept food," Esper said quietly as we approached. "These people are starving."

She was right, but, "These people gave their food as offering to the spirits, thanking them for our arrival. How would they take it if the spirits refused such a gift? How would the spirits take it if we denied them their gifts? No, we'll take the food to the pagoda tomorrow for redistribution."

One of those praying spotted us and called out, pointing. As one, they all turned, hailing our arrival, begging for blessings. "Take her inside," I nodded toward Karena, her head lolling like a ball on a rope between us. "I'll deal with them."

As Esper took the full weight of the woman and began

moving to the door, one of those offering prayer pointed his finger at Karena, and asked in a voice rising above the others, "Is she contaminated?"

This could get ugly. Esper was quicker than I to answer. "No," she said. "Her crops were severely attacked by Malamiko. We're helping her."

"My crops were also attacked," someone called out.

"And we'll help you, too," I said, a firm edge in my voice. "*Mia korpo estas via shildo.*"

They bowed their heads, and as one replied, "*Tiel estu.*" I motioned Esper into the outpost and spent the rest of the afternoon blessing the crowd and speaking with a stream of the faithful and desperate come to pay us their respects.

"Is it true?" a young man, maybe eighteen or so, asked when I came to give him my blessing. "I heard Tatjiana IX, krono of all Aaronsburg, has given herself to Malamiko and sent a pox down the Jinhuang that destroyed our crops."

I wondered whether this was a rumour spread by the paisajista to fan the flames of war or if this was something these people came up with on their own. "If anyone is contaminated, doesn't matter if they're a krono, a farmer, or even a member of the Tero Kreinto, the falchilo will cleanse them. If Krono Tatjiana were contaminated, she'd be ash."

The young man persisted. "I also heard Lan Hu defies the Tero Kreinto and hoards food while we starve."

"The Tero Kreinto controls food, not the krono. Ask the paisajista—they'll tell you." I blessed him and moved on before he could ask more questions. Usually, giving blessings was the boring part of the job, but I got the sense I was tiptoeing my way through a nest of sleeping sentinels.

The next morning, once Karena had sobered up enough, we began questioning her. I let Jak lead the questioning. Turns out he enjoyed it.

"I'm telling you, it's Radulfo," Karena said, sitting in a chair in the middle of a room in the tower of our outpost. She flinched back from Jak, a look of wretched sickness on her face. Her head must be pounding.

"Oh, Radulfo is it?" Jak said. He was leaning into Karena so close their faces almost touched. She tried to avoid eye contact with him. "You hear that, Talia?" Jak said, straightening up. "It's Radulfo. I guess we've solved the case and can go home." Talia rolled her eyes.

"Radulfo doesn't pay proper respect to the Founder spirits of Sabine and Dorian," Karena said. "That's what's allowed Tatjiana's pox into our lands." My ears pricked at this comment.

"There's no evidence of a pox," Esper said. She'd missed the important part of Karena's comment.

"Ah, Sabine and Dorian," Jak said. "They your guardian spirits around here?"

"Yes," Karena answered.

"So, I'm confused," Jak said, his forehead furrowed in an exaggerated mockery of confusion. "If it's Radulfo not paying his proper respects, why'd your crops fail as much as his?"

"Leave her alone," Esper said. "She's scared."

"She should be. Everyone's crops failed," Jak said, turning on Esper. "And someone knows why. If you don't have the strength to dig for the truth, what use are you?"

"Lay off Esper, will you," Talia said.

My falchilo were losing their focus. I cleared my throat. It was enough to snuff out the growing argument. "This Radulfo," I said to Karena. "How has he not been showing proper respect to your guardian spirits?"

"He's made no offerings to the shrine. He's too busy building his fence, he tells me. What good's a fence if the spirits aren't made to feel welcome?"

"A fence?" I asked, my heart rate rising.

"Around his yard. Says he's gotta get his fence built. Got his whole family at it, digging ditches and pounding posts in. All he's got is chickens! Keep 'em in their pen, I say. Why fence your whole yard? Damn fool."

"Mind your language," I said, though I hardly noticed her curse with how excited her answer made me. Talia, too, sat up, suddenly taking an interest in the questioning.

"Sorry, Majstro. My head beats something awful." Karena said, head bowed in contriteness. Esper's eyes widened in understanding. She'd also noticed it.

Jak laid into Karena again. "Let's talk about you and your crops." Talia was about to say something, but I waved her to silence. I wanted to see if Jak saw what the rest of us did. "Tell me of the Malamiko you've found on your lands," he said.

"There's nothing," Karena said. "No Malamiko I've seen."

"If not you, maybe your sons, then."

"My sons are good boys. They'd tell me if they saw Malamiko."

He didn't see it. I nodded to Talia.

"Xinhua's eyes, Jak," Talia said. "You get so into intimidating people you don't even notice when you've found what you're looking for. Missing spiritual activities? Building a bloody fence around his whole bloody yard? Digging ditches?"

"It's nesting," Esper said.

Realization dawned on his face. "Yeah, I get it," he said. His cheeks flushed as he glowered at Esper.

"Enough," I said. A sense of strength and confidence washed over me. We'd been farting around for days in Kubuto Falls and found nothing but weeds. But today, we will finally face our enemy—stage two contamination. My falchilo had hunger in their eyes. They could feel it too. "Today, we hunt."

"Is this everyone?" I asked.

Radulfo bowed, a nervous smile on its face. "It is, Majstro Falchilo."

The sun shone, but the wind was crisp. Chickens clucked a mindless tattoo somewhere in the yard, out of sight behind a barn. My dad had chickens. They'd peck at my hand as I collected eggs. I hated that, but who could blame them for protecting their family. All things want to live. It's no one's fault everything can only live at the expense of another.

Alongside Radulfo stood its wife and two sons, one nearly an adult, the other in the throes of adolescence. Their eyes darted from falchilo to falchilo, worried frowns on their foreheads. Stage one and early stage two contaminants look like people, but if you don't have a GC, you can identify them through dark splotching along the nervous tissue. The only way to view that without killing the suspect was to remove an eye and examine the optic nerve extending from it or dissecting it to study retinal tissue. Sometimes, if you're lucky, late-stage two contaminants had dark speckling along their mucous membranes, visible around their mouth, nose, and eyes. I noticed Radulfo's oldest son had this pattern under his nose—from a distance, you'd mistake it for an adolescent's moustache.

Fear, nervousness—I marvelled at how well Radulfo's body mimicked these emotions. It wasn't until stage three they started to lose their ability to mimic our humanity, except for the shells. At stage two, all contaminants still aped our emotions perfectly. If you weren't looking for the signs of nesting, you could have a conversation with them and never know you were no longer speaking to a human.

"The pagoda's register says they have a daughter. She's missing," Talia said. Her face—all our faces—were covered by our helmets, and we stood before the nest, dark angels, scythes of the Founders, ready to cut.

I turned to Radulfo's body, stared at it, letting the silence hang.

Radulfo was about to answer, but its wife spoke before it did. "She went to town."

"Is that true?" I asked Radulfo. It nodded.

"Huh," Talia said. "We came from town. Don't remember passing a girl on the way there. You remember that, Jak?"

"Nope," Jak said. His rod was out, fully extended, resting on his shoulder.

"She often cuts across the fields. You'd probably not see her on the road," Radulfo's body said.

A few buildings sat scattered across the yard: a house, a couple of barns, a well. Beyond the yard, fields of stunted and spindly pear trees sat like a plain of skeletal hands grasping toward the sky. The family hadn't been building a fence so much as an earthen wall around the perimeter of their yard— a line of defence to protect the nest. In the yard, they'd begun digging a series of drainage ditches to channel water, all classic signs of nesting. The daughter's absence suggested it'd be the host. We needed to watch out for it—that's the one that couldn't be allowed to get away. Which building would it be in? Someplace safe, easy to defend, easy access to water and food. Would this nest have decoys, too, like the one we cleansed earlier this spring?

"Why don't you make life easier on you and your family," Jak said. "Tell us where it is."

I studied the response of the creatures before us, looking

for a telltale hint, eyes flicking toward a building, a nervous glance over a shoulder. Nothing.

The body of Radulfo cocked its head, mimicking an expression of confusion and fear. "Where '*it*' is?"

"Don't bother," Talia said to Jak. "It won't tell you."

"Founder's grace, enough of this. Let's get on with it," I said. I took off my pack and withdrew my GC. The black speckling under the older son's nose clinched them for a stage two nest, but I wanted to see if the GC was still working properly.

Radulfo dropped to its knees, hands out before it as I walked to it with my GC. "No, please," it said, voice almost breaking into tears. "We've done nothing wrong! We're good people, this is a mistake!" The mother's body wrapped a protective arm around the adolescent's body, the older son's body stared at me, wide-eyed, frozen, as though paralyzed by fear. I didn't need to use the GC—the diagnosis was obvious. Still, I wanted to see . . .

Stepping toward the body of Radulfo, I pressed the nozzle of the GC into the man's hand and activated it. He winced. The machine hummed. Blue light. Malamiko. Good—it still worked.

A dark figure surrounded by a hazy black nimbus stepped out of a barn about ten metres back. It turned its head toward us with effort, as though its muscles were dried meat. Shields spiralled open, and Jak took a step back. "A dark wanderer!" Talia called out as she drew her gun. "The nest's stage four!" Two mounds of soil in the yard shifted as two sentinels crawled out of their burrows, shaking the dirt off as they stood.

Stage four? Couldn't be. Radulfo stared at me with a look of fear unchanged from a moment before, its last expression frozen on its face. It could be a shell, but shells don't carry on conversations—they're … well, they're shells. They're in late-stage nests for appearance. But, it had conversed with me seemingly with a mind all its own, like a stage two contaminant. A stage two contaminant in a stage four nest? Or was this something different?

Radulfo threw itself into me, its fist banging off my helmet while the elder son dived for Jak, tackling him. The mother and adolescent screamed as they dived at Esper. The mother produced a small hatchet and swung. Esper's shield blocked the blow, but the adolescent dived into her, driving her back. We were all stunned. Shells weren't supposed to attack, either.

Talia fired her gun, shattering the tranquility with a sizzling crack. Her shot knocked the dark wanderer back a pace, and then it charged as the two sentinels sought to outflank us.

Radulfo was trying to pull my shield down, but its strength was no match for my kiraso. I flung him away like a handful of pebbles and got my shield up as the dark wanderer fired its thorns. They ricocheted off my shield, and then the full brunt of its charge slammed into me, hurling me off my feet. I hung in the air a moment, weightless, before crashing to the ground, the GC hitting the dirt some distance away.

My vision reeled. I couldn't breathe. Talia yelled at Jak and Esper, "Keep the sentinels off my back!" and then the sizzling crack of her gun fired, then again and again.

Struggling to my knees, thorns from the dark wander drilled into my shield like a drum roll. Jak was struggling under a sentinel's attack. Radulfo and its wife were attacking Esper while the second sentinel angled to attack her with its pincers. Talia was dodging the attack of Radulfo's two sons while firing her gun at the dark wanderer. The dark wanderer was badly injured but still coming at me on hands and knees. I took the flamjetilo from its harness on my back, powered it on, shouting, "To the human whose body this once was, your torment is over. Tonight, you dine with the Founders!" I unleashed a wave of energy, and the dark wander belched into flame. "To Malamiko who has stolen this body—*burn!*"

The shells' bodies were still human and easy to dispatch while wearing the kiraso. I smashed my shield down on the mother, crushing it to the ground in a bloody pulp, and then kicked out and caved Radulfo's head in—its previous expression of fear and worry still etched unmoving on its face like a holiday mask.

The sentinels, though, were much tougher beasts. One of them turned, its vestigial human face flapping on a bony protuberance as it moved. It kicked Jak with its hind legs, sending him flying before he skidded into the ground. I ran and took Jak's place before it could strike at Talia, who was turning the crankshaft to charge her gun. My shield bashed into the sentinel with all the strength of my kiraso. The creature stumbled back a step and then renewed its attack, trying to angle its pincers around my shield to snap at me, all the while that horrible, human face jostled up and down.

Radulfo's older sons tackled me around the waist, dragging me to the ground. The sentinel was about to trample me when Talia shot it, knocking it back. Radulfo's younger son leaped on her back, clawing at her head. "You bloody brat!" Talia screamed as she grabbed the boy and flung him across the yard to crash into the side of a barn. The sentinel charged her, and she barely dodged it. She shot it two more times in the flank, dropping it, as I bashed the head in of the son attacking me.

Esper screamed. She was on her back underneath the second sentinel that was beating on her shield with its pincers. Talia had one shot left in her gun before she had to recharge, and she fired it directly into the sentinel's torso. It stumbled, wavering. Then Jak was there, blasting it with his rod, and I joined him.

We stood, each of us breathing heavily. My suit's indicator told me I was down to sixty-two percent power. Silence settled over the farmyard. Talia marched over to Radulfo's body. "Shells don't talk!" She punctuated each word by stomping on the tattered, bloody mass that was Radulfo's head. I grabbed the GC, checking to make sure it was all right, and then we gathered and inspected each other to ensure the dark wanderer had not hit any of us with its thorns. I gave the rites and cleansed the bodies. "Find the host," I ordered as the corpses crackled and popped under the purifying flames.

We found it in the cellar underneath the house. There were no decoys as we had found in the other nest earlier this spring. A stage four host is a black mat, a fungus-like fuzz covering the dank surfaces of its den. Like so much else we'd experienced these past weeks, this host was different. The black mat covered the walls and ceiling in its seething mass, that was normal. But opposite the door, embedded in a shifting blanket of black hyphae, was a small girl, about eight or nine years old. It began a plaintive, wailing cry the moment the light from the open cellar door pierced the room's gloom.

"Xinhua's bloody eyes," Talia whispered. We entered the room behind our polycrysteel shields.

"Jak," I said, "was the host you cleansed with me a couple of weeks ago like this?"

He had his axe out as he crouched behind his shield. "No, Majstro. It was a carpet of black, just as the manlibroj teach."

The child's body began to writhe, and with great effort, it

heaved and pulled its arm free of the dark mat. Then a leg came free with a slurping, sucking sound. Soon, the entire body pulled away from the seething tendrils, took a step, and then collapsed to the floor, its chest heaving as it emitted the piercing wail of a child's cry.

We surrounded it, standing behind our shields, weapons out, ready to strike should it try to escape or attack. It looked from one of us to the other, staring at us with wide eyes mimicking fear. It brought its knees to its chest and cried inconsolably. I allowed myself to believe that on some level, its tears were genuine. It's comforting to believe Malamiko can feel as much fear as it makes us feel.

I knew Talia had the strength to do what was required, and I suspected Jak wouldn't think twice about destroying a host in a child's body. Esper, though, her fondness for children had clouded her judgment in Kubuto Falls—enough to expose her and the children under her care to incalculable risk. Time for her to prove herself. I passed the flamjetilo to her. "You know what you need to do." She stared at me, her face covered by the black void of the helmet's mask, and then turned to the host. Its child-like cries cut the air like a bell.

"Help me." The host's voice fought its way through its sobs, its face a mask of fear and misery. Esper stood, flamjetilo pointed at the ground, unmoving. With her helmet engaged, I couldn't see the expression on her face belying the emotions causing her to hesitate. My jaw clenched. The Tero Kreinto trained her for this, trained her to act without hesitation, even when Malamiko contaminates the body of one you cared for. She knew this was a nest, and still, she hesitated.

"Should we GC her?" Esper asked.

"We're not exposing ourselves to it. You know what the result will be," I said. She had to act. If she was to have a life in the falchilo, she had to act. I began to doubt, my thoughts flying back to Esper on Malamiko Island with her helmet retracted. Suspicion flooded my mind—could she be contaminated? I began to question the wisdom of handing her the flamjetilo. Would my shield afford me any protection from its rays if she attacked?

She powered the flamjetilo on, and it came to life with a resonant twang. The host wailed. My body tensed. If Esper swung the nozzle toward me, could I hit her with the rod before she fired? It'd be a close thing.

She gave the rites, her voice loud and harsh. She aimed the flamjetilo at the host, and the air in front of her distorted in rippling waves moving toward the host's body. It erupted in flames, along with the black mass surrounding it, sending an unearthly screech that seemed to make my bones ache along with tendrils of thick, black smoke. Tension poured off my body, and I chastised myself for doubting Esper, though I took the flamjetilo from her a little more eagerly than intended. "Good," I said to Esper. "The child's spirit rests easy now because of what you've done. Be proud." Her featureless helmet looked at me and nodded.

BY THE TIME we finished cleansing the area and made it back to town, the sun was setting, ember-red fans cutting through the clouds. As unsettling as the nest was, today was a good day. After accomplishing nothing in Kubuto Falls, the thrill of having done something buzzed through me. "Next, we need to find how Malamiko contaminated Radulfo's family and root out the source," I said. "Each step gets us closer to discovering what is happening to Malamiko and our crops."

"The borderlands are only a few kilometres away," Talia said. "And beyond lie the plains of Malamiko reaching all the way to the Nanhai Ocean. Plenty of spots for another nest to hide."

"Perhaps the girl—the host, I mean," Esper said. "Before she was contaminated, the girl would have had friends. We could find out where they played together. It might narrow down where we search." Esper had been quiet most of the day since cleansing the host, carrying out her duties with silent stoicism. Hearing her thinking aloud again, planning how best to attack Malamiko raised my mood further.

"Good idea," I said. Action. Forward momentum.

"What's this?" Talia asked, pointing ahead to our outpost as we approached. A wagon sat on the road in front of the outpost with attendants tending to oxen still harnessed to it.

"There're some nice estates around here," Jak said. "Maybe it's some kavaliro seeking our favour with a worthy offering."

"Bah! As if we have time for useless butt-kissers," I said. We increased our pace. One of the attendants—he wore the black shirt and pants of falchilo—saw us approaching and went into the outpost. As we arrived, Mihaelo, leaning heavily on his cane, stepped out to greet us. "Founder's grace," I said, "What are you doing here?"

"We cleansed a stage four nest, unlike any nest you've ever seen before," Jak said before Mihaelo could reply, like a proud son boasting of accomplishments to his father.

I knew Mihaelo well and could tell something troubled him by the crease in his forehead. Still, he turned to Jak with a smile. "This is excellent news. Well done, all of you. I look forward to learning of this nest, but I didn't come to check up on you. Perhaps you could all find something to do while I speak with Kredo."

Talia looked at me, and I was surprised to note a rare

frown of worry on her brow. "Come on, children," she said, waving Jak and Esper along. "Grown-ups want to talk."

Once they left, Mihaelo faced me. "I wanted you to hear this from me," he said.

I could not imagine what new horror would inspire him to journey so far to speak to me in person. "What is it, Kapo?"

"Maraja Ravida III, Unua of the Tero Kreinto has made an announcement. She's finally admitted we haven't enough food to last to Rendezvous. There's going to be a Cull."

The news was a punch in the gut, though I wasn't surprised to hear it. "How deep will the cut be?"

"Kredo, I've seen the lists. Your mother's being Culled."

I . . . well, honestly, I didn't know what to feel. These were words. That's all the news was. Words. "My mother?" I thought of the last time I saw her. Dad's funeral. That was . . . Founder's grace, was that fifteen years ago already? No, sixteen. How had time slipped away?

"I'm giving you leave to be with her at the Cull," Mihaelo said.

"I . . . No, but the crop failures . . ." My mother? I was falchilo. *My* mother was being Culled? *My* family?

"Go to her, Kredo," Mihaelo said in his quiet voice.

I was *fixing* this. "We've cleansed a nest here—a new kind of nest. There'll be others. We have to find them and clear the area."

"Your team can search while you're gone."

"But . . ." I realized I'd failed utterly, and events had moved past my ability to make it right. All that was left to me was to wonder what I should have done and hate myself for not knowing, adding a list of *what-ifs* to the cart of regrets I pulled along behind me. I was stunned at the cruelty of the world and shaken at the realization that this cruelty was an echo of my own weakness and inability.

Mihaelo placed a hand on my shoulder. "I've sat around enough campfires listening to you tell stories of your family to know the nature of their character," he said. "I think I also know you well enough to understand why you keep them at a distance. Kredo, your mother is going to die a hero of Duatero. A *hero*. She's earned the right to have her child by her side."

NINE

TRANSIRI, a tarnished crown on a hilltop, had once been my home. The contours of the land fit into my memory like a puzzle piece. I approached a gentle swell in the road, one last bump before ascending the hill that would take me to town. I had forgotten this bump, a marker I had used as a child to gauge how much longer until I hit town limits.

The Founder roads between Lan Hu, Xuanhe, and Port Donna once met in Transiri. It was a hub, a junction between realms. That was centuries ago. Now the road leading south to the ruins of Port Donna was abandoned. With the great city's destruction, Malamiko advanced, pushing into Transiri's borders. It was a hard land to work. I remember Dad struggling to hew a life from it. I remembered bitter summers of toil and labour and disappointment.

Tomorrow was the Cull. I could have made it earlier, didn't intend to arrive so late, but my feet were slow. This was the first time I'd walked this road since Dad's funeral. I had avoided coming here. Not overtly, mind you, but it never felt right coming home; it felt like I hadn't finished the business I'd abandoned my family to complete. And so, I found it easy to distract myself with work. Malamiko always threatened, my mission still unfinished, still too soon for my triumphant return.

There is a strange feeling when returning home after an absence. The brown mudstone buildings lining the road, many too poor to even have a coat of plaster, looked as I remembered them, and yet they were alien. My memories were ghosts of an existence that had died on the day I left; these buildings had lived a life since then, aging under sun and rain and wind. Those who stayed behind built new structures and repaired old ones. The faces of the people were different, as though the cast of players populating my childhood had been replaced by different actors. As a boy, people in town would say hello, greeting me by name. Now, strangers gawked at the falchilo striding by.

How would my family react to seeing me? Gaja was heartbroken when I first left to join the Tero Kreinto. I remember her tears late one spring night under dark clouds as she begged me to stay. We'd been so close in age, we'd shared the entirety of our lives to that point together, and I broke her heart. Little Fondo, my only surviving brother, was proud of me. His idol was going to join the Tero Kreinto. He was too young to understand what that really meant. My mother . . . well, my mother had buried six of her children. She was used to letting go. She'd held me in an embrace for long moments, then released me. "Be good, Kredo," she'd said.

I'd seen them all at Dad's funeral. Gaja had grown into a handsome woman, married, her first child sitting on her hip. "Mother misses you terribly," she'd told me after Dad's service while she and I walked in the gardens surrounding the pagoda. "She'll never say anything to you—doesn't want to distract a falchilo from his important duties. She would be so happy if you visited. I'd be so happy." A year later, Eta Monteto happened, and I learned how fragile our existence on Duatero is, how close we are to the brink. I had abandoned my father and joined the falchilo to keep my family safe. How could I face them while their crops still failed and Malamiko invaded their fields? Unfinished business. Time passed.

I wandered through town and found myself on a street I never frequented as a child. We grew up outside of town on a farm. There were no stores on this street to visit. I'd had no friends along this road, had no reason to walk along it. Gaja and her family lived here now. I remembered it from Dad's funeral. The boy she bounced on her hip then would almost be a man now, with a brother close behind. She'd lived a life on this street, a street that meant nothing to me. A river branches, and the new stream carves a course for itself out of dirt and stone with only memories of the shared path behind it.

A woman came to the door of a building I stood in front of, stepping out onto the road. For a moment, I thought it was my mother, but no, it was Gaja. Had so much time really passed? The girl I knew was gone. Deep lines of worry and care creased her face now; hunger pulled at her skin. She was gaunt but had a stout frame, a woman who'd worked hard all her days, who'd hewn a life out of the borderlands between Duatero and Malamiko.

"Kredo, is that you?" she said.

"It is."

She came and hugged me. "You look so old," she said, crushing me in her arms.

For moments we stood like that, holding each other. "How's Mom?" I asked.

Gaja pulled away, a smile on her lips and tears in her eye.

"She will be so happy to see you. Fondo's coming over later. We'll all be together again."

She led me inside to a small, cramped room, a faded carpet on the dirt floor, bright tapestries hung on the wall illuminated by a fire in a nearby hearth. Her husband greeted me. I shook hands with my nephews, one a little taller than me, the other just about even.

"Kredo?" a voice said from the far end of the room. In my memory, my mom is a giant. Strong and kind, she was my world as a child. I recognized my mother's face on the woman coming forward, but little else. Where once my mother was tall, she was now bent, her back hunched at right angles. Where once my mother was strong, age had wasted her muscles away, her step fumbling and uncertain. Her eyes still held kindness, though, and so much joy. "Oh, Kredo," she said. "My brave falchilo is home."

My heart sank to see how frail she had become. She was a mountain, eroded by years of blowing wind and driving rain until only a shallow hill remained. I was afraid if I held her too tight, she'd crumble into sand, slipping away through my fingers. She showed no such fear as she hugged me with all the tremulous might her thin arms retained.

"Tomorrow night, I'm going to dine with Father," she said, her voice a whisper in my chest. "And Tondra, Paulo, and all my missing children. Tomorrow night I'm going to meet the Founders."

I needed to be strong, to keep a brave face so she would keep her courage as she made the sacrifice Duatero had called on her to make. I wasn't sure if I had that kind of strength, if anyone did. "I know, Mom."

She pulled back, looked at me anew, wonder in her eyes. "Is that your kiraso?"

I hadn't worn it for Dad's funeral. Was this really the first time she'd seen my kiraso? "It is." I pointed to the image of a bird with a twig in its mouth etched on my breastplate. "It arrived on the *Jingwei*, worn by Founder Tod C. Levitt, Trooper First Class."

She lightly touched the image on my chest, whispering, "Founder Tod C. Levitt." She looked at me with so much pride, tears rimming her eyes. "It's beautiful. This was touched by a Founder, and it protected him from harm." She looked at the image on my chest again, eyes wide with wonder. "I have never touched a Founder artifact before. Father would be so proud of you."

A commotion at the front door pulled our attention. Little Fondo and his family arrived. He saw me, smiled, crossed the room, and embraced me in a hug. I had to stop thinking of him as *Little* Fondo. He'd grown into a man, working the land my father had worked. He was so much younger than me, just a boy when I left. Now, his face had taken a beating from the elements, all creases and folds of skin. He was thin, and his back stooped like my father's. He was being beaten down by the land that had beaten down Dad, and a stranger looking at us side by side would have a hard time telling whether he or I was the elder.

We dined together as a family. We laughed at old stories. Gaja's younger son had a good voice, and he honoured us with a song, my mother and sister singing along. They asked me to tell them of my time as falchilo, and I told them of Eta Monteto, telling them of our harrowing attacks on two nests and the riots that happened as the floodwaters forced us to wait in town before attacking the third. I told them of the sentinel cracking Mihaelo's leg and the assault Aprila and I made on the final host.

I did not tell them of Aprila's contamination and of how I had to cleanse her in the thick mud of spring rain. The night was dark enough with the Cull tomorrow. We'd been good friends, she and I. The rains remind me of her.

"Another story!" Fondo's youngest child, a girl just entering adolescence, demanded.

"I think it's time for bed," Fondo said, eliciting groans from the children. I could understand why Fondo wanted to stop the storytelling. He didn't want me filling his children's heads with tales that might inspire them to leave, following in my footsteps. And so, the final night with my mother came to a close, leaving me alone with nothing but the dark, sleepless hours before dawn.

WE GATHERED on the dirt road in front of Gaja's house in the morning. My mother's blue robes snapped as a late spring wind pulled on them. It didn't seem right that the wind should blow so hard today, whipping my mother's hair, chilling her as she prepared to make this great sacrifice for her people. She didn't seem to mind. She watched brown leaves from last fall pile up along the leeward side of the building, hunched, frail, with a smile on her face and love in her eyes. My sister readjusted Mom's robes and pinned her hair, making her look beautiful in defiance of the whistling wind.

Down the street, another family clustered outside their door grouped around a thin grey man and an old woman beside him, both in the blue robes of the Culled, both holding tightly to each other. The grey man was speaking to a young boy, extolling final words of love or perhaps advice, conveying something for the boy to take with him past this day.

My young brother Fondo stepped out of the house onto

the street, dressed in a tunic hanging just above his knees. The clothing was simple, roughly worn, but I could see he'd spent time cleaning it as best he could. He'd grown into a good man.

My mother grasped my arm for support. "I remember how you used to play in the leaves in our yard," she said to me. "Do you remember? You were such a happy child. You'd run from pile to pile, jumping and crunching them under your feet." She looked at me with a smile. "I have such good memories."

How could that be true? She'd buried so many of her children before they'd reached the age of five. Every year was a fight for survival filled with constant fear Malamiko would advance further, tainting farmlands and contaminating neighbours.

"I remember you'd wrestle me down," Fondo said, smiling. "I'd fight so hard, and I could never beat you. You'd grind leaves into my hair."

"Oh," Mom said with a guilty laugh, "Father never liked when you did that."

"He'd set me to cleaning the yard," I said, remembering.

Nearby, the pagoda bell rang. An unnatural stillness settled over the town. It was time. I exchanged a look with Gaja, her lips tight. She closed her eyes, turned away. Fondo came up beside her, placed an arm around her shoulder.

"Such good memories," Mom said, patting my arm.

Silence hung in the air. Even the wind calmed. I remember one of my math tutors at the Tero Kreinto explaining you could divide the interval between any two numbers in half and then divide those halves again, and then again, all the way to forever. Imagine that! An infinity between moments, an eternity between the fall of each grain of sand in the hourglass. I couldn't make my legs move, didn't want to say a word, didn't want to breathe or do anything that might set the gears of time turning, sending the next grain of sand crashing down like a wave dashing a child's castle built on the sandy banks of a river.

"Your father is waiting for me," my mother said, her voice quiet. "I had a dream last night. He came to me. He told me not to be afraid. He'll be there, waiting for me, where he can hold me, and he'll never have to let me go. Come," she said, waving Gaja and Fondo closer. She grabbed Fondo's hand, placed it on her shoulder, held on to Gaja with one hand, me with the other. "I want all my children to hold me as I walk."

She began to shuffle down the street, short steps, unstable. Gaja and I had to support her as she led us toward the pagoda. Along the way, we joined others wearing the blue robes of those marked for the Cull. Old men, old women, a young boy with a lame leg shuffling on wooden crutches, others, so many of them joining our ranks, family and friends surrounding each of them with damp faces, dams too weak to hold back tears. Behind us, townsfolk, those lucky enough to not have someone in the Cull, slowly followed. No one spoke a word. Only the whisper of wind and tramp of feet hung in the air as we approached the pagoda grounds.

As we entered the courtyard, Fondo's and Gaja's children began setting down cushions and blankets for us to rest on. As we waited, Mom spoke quiet words to Fondo, hugging him with all the strength her frail arms possessed. She moved to Gaja with her weak, faltering steps. A whispered exchange, a hug given, a hug received. She came to me. I did not know if I had the strength to face this.

She looked up at me—she was once so tall—placed a cold hand on my cheek, her eyes wet with tears. "I have prayed for you every day of your life," she said, controlling her voice through tears that wanted to come. Who would pray for me now? "I have prayed for your safety as you face Malamiko. I've prayed for your happiness, Kredo. Since you've gone, I've prayed you find what it is you search for. Find what you search for, Kredo. Find it and be happy." She hugged me with all her strength; I held her as I would a delicate, dried flower that you might shield from the wind, lest it blows to pieces.

She pulled away, held me at arm's length, looking up at me. "Be good, Kredo."

"I will." My voice was the raspy whisper of dried sand crunching underfoot.

"Be good."

She struggled to settle onto her cushions, her three children rushing to aid her. I sat on mine, looked around the courtyard, seeing for the first time the number of those called to the Cull. This seemed like a deeper cut than that of '29 to my eyes. Not all those Culled seemed so old. Beyond the families of the Culled, the entire town gathered, young children clinging to the legs of mothers, staring at us with curious eyes.

A middle-aged man in the yellow robes of the kuracisto came to us and kneeled before my mother. "Founders thank you," he said, head bowed. He stayed like that a moment in reverent silence. Then, he placed a wooden cup in front of her filled with a liquid. "When the bell rings, drink it all, quickly. You'll fall asleep, and then you'll dance amongst the Founders." He covered the cup with a wooden plate and moved on to the next family. None of us looked at the cup, ignoring it with iron determination.

The pagoda's gepatro—a woman I didn't recognize—stood before the gathered town, gave a sermon I didn't hear, read verses from the manlibroj that slipped by me unnoticed, and prayed prayers that my mind did not register. She fell silent. I closed my eyes, trying to grasp that eternity between the falling grains of sand. The pagoda's bell rang: a sharp peal cracking the morning.

A moment hung, then my mother shifted. "I'm going to Father now." She leaned forward, took the plate off the cup none of us looked at. "Will it hurt?"

"No, Mom," I said. From my training at the Tero Kreinto, I knew well what would happen. "You'll fall asleep. You'll dream, and then you'll be with Dad." The finality of these words struck me with surprising strength, a sling bullet hitting me in the chest, and I had to look away. I had to be strong for her, giving her the strength she needed.

She raised the cup. "Founders, guide my children," she said, her voice soft as she spoke her last prayer of this life. Eyes squeezed shut, she gulped the drink down. "What happens now?" she asked.

I took the cup from her, set it aside. "You lie down now," I said. Her children helped her lay back, her head nestled on Gaja's lap. Fondo held one of her hands, I the other.

"How long will it take, Kredo?" she asked, looking up at me with eyes I would never see again.

"Not long. You'll feel tired soon. When you do, close your eyes. Dream."

"I think I feel it already. Would it happen so soon? Is this how it's supposed to happen?"

"Close your eyes, Mom." She did. "Dream." My voice tore at my throat. Fondo's head was bowed, tears dripping from his eyes. Gaja ran her hand along Mom's head, humming a gentle tune, a lullaby I remembered from my childhood. Mom's chest rose and fell rhythmically as she breathed. Several paisajista were going throughout the courtyard, distributing plates of food—platters filled with round loaves of bread, piles of fruit, stacks of cheese, bowls of honeycombs, and carafes of beer with cups for all.

Mom's chest rose and fell as the wind whistled through the trees in the pagoda garden. Her breathing came shallow. Her body seized. I clutched her hand tightly; I heard a sob. It was my own. Her body relaxed. Her chest rose no more.

She was gone.

I held her hand in mine, held it tight, as I had a moment ago when she was alive, but the only mother I had now was one of memories. Such a small, subtle difference between life and death. Is that all it takes to end the life of the woman who brought me into this world?

As the eldest, I still had duties to perform. I took the carafe of beer, poured out a drink for each of us, even Fondo's young children. We waited as, around the courtyard, similar scenes played out. Once the last of the Culled had passed, the gepatro who'd given the earlier sermon grabbed her cup, stood, and addressed us.

"Founders, greet our heroes," she called out, her voice loud, trembling with emotion. She turned her cup upside down, spilling its contents onto the dirt. Around the courtyard, throughout the streets beyond, we overturned our cups, every one of us, our drinks splashing on the ground, a libation, our first offering to our newest ancestors to enter the spirit world.

"The Culled love us," the gepatro said. She moved to a platter of food she had at hand, exchanged her cup for a loaf of bread. "They died so we'd have food. They died so we'd know hunger no more. Now, we honour their sacrifice by breaking bread. Treasure the gift they have given us. Remember this gift with each meal you eat from now until the Founders call you home." She led us in prayer.

BEFORE THE BREAD, *the baker*.

Before the baker, the miller.
Before the miller, the farmer.
Before the farmer, the land.
Before the land, the Tero Kreinto.
Before the Tero Kreinto, Donna.
Tiel estu.

I REACHED FOR OUR BREAD, broke it, passed pieces to Gaja, Fondo, all their children, and then, though none of us had an appetite, we ate, the food dry in our mouth, tasting like ash.

GAJA AND FONDO had invited me to stay, to journey with them to our family's mausoleum out by the farm where we'd put mom to rest, but the morning after the Cull, I hugged them both and made my way back to Vojo Fino and my fellow falchilo, pushing my kiraso to its limits. The look on Gaja's face when I told her I was leaving . . . how many times would I break her heart?

But I am falchilo—a *majstro* falchilo—scythe of the Founders. I hunt Malamiko to keep Duatero safe. The battle with the land broke my dad and sent a half dozen of my siblings to the grave. And now, after decades away, I come back only to hold my Mom's hand as she was Culled.

Mom died—Dad died—because I *failed*. Gaja and Fondo could never understand that. To them, Malamiko is a capricious force of nature, a hardship to bear as one bears the spring floods. But I'm supposed to protect Duatero from it. I left to save them, and each funeral I returned for was a beacon of my failure. Mom died proud of her son, the falchilo, never realizing the Cull happened because Malamiko beat me. Our crops withered while I scratched my head and impotently rooted through the dirt. No more. *No more!* I'll die before I let Malamiko force another Cull on us.

I marched like a person possessed, my kiraso propelling me to great speed, catching only brief hours of sleep. It was late at night when I stormed into our outpost at Vojo Fino. I hammered on the doors where my falchilo slept. Where were they?

"Kredo?" someone behind me asked.

I spun on the voice. It was Esper, her brow etched with worry, a candle in her hand casting dancing shadows on the wall. "Where are the others?" I demanded.

She stepped back from my anger. "I don't—"

"Where!"

"I—Talia, I think, is at the inn," Esper said.

"Get her. Get Jak. Get them both here. Go!"

She ran off. I lit lamps and then paced in circles around the shrine in the outpost's main chamber. Jak arrived first, running. He was wise enough to say nothing, sensing my mood. I continued pacing. Esper and Talia finally ran into the room.

"Kredo, are you okay?" Talia asked, breathing heavily.

"Someone in this town knows why the crops are dying," I said. "The nest we cleansed, someone knows how they got infected. Friends of their kids, neighbours, someone knows how they brought contamination into our lands. Find them! Bring them in! I want answers!" I caught an eager look in Jak's eyes. Good. We needed to get aggressive.

"Mihaelo told us about your mom," Talia said. "Do you think maybe you should take some time—"

"Time?" I said. "Time? By the time I was six years old, my mother had buried six of her children. Six! If our family 'took time' for every fucking funeral, we'd never have accomplished anything!" All three of them stood dumbfounded, eyes wide. I'd just sullied our language. I needed to get control. "Friends of their kids, friends of Radulfo, his wife, neighbours—get them. Bring them in."

Talia looked at me, uncertain. "Now? It's the middle of the night."

"Yes, now! You can dance when we've stopped Malamiko. I want answers!"

TEN

ELEKTI WAS NINE YEARS OLD, dark hair, dark, almond-shaped eyes, and she'd been crying so long it was giving me a headache. Jak was the reason she was crying. Elekti was a friend of Radulfo's daughter. The daughter was the host, so it made sense to start with her friends, see if we could piece together where it got contaminated.

"Tell me where in the borderlands you played!" Jak snapped at her, slapping the table between them with an open palm. She wailed, and, sweet Donna, her tears seemed to provoke him. He grabbed the table and flung it aside, sending it cartwheeling into the wall. Elekti screamed as she cowered under her arms, squealing at a pitch that drove daggers into my ears.

"Jak, enough," I said. "We'll give her a minute." I led Jak out of the room in the outpost's tower. Once outside in the dim hall, part of me wanted to chastise him, but I remembered the kids back in Kubuto Falls playing on Malamiko Island, remembered my brother Paulo playing with a wiggler, remembered the feel of my mom's hand in mine. The children of the borderlands had to lose their comfort with Malamiko.

"Let me try again," Jak said. "She knows something, I can feel it. Listen to her, she's about to crack."

I waved him off. "She cracked a long time ago. Give her a minute." We waited in the hall, Jak pacing like a caged animal, Elekti screaming for her mother.

Esper came into the hallway. She cast a worried frown at the door behind which the small girl shrieked. "I found her," she said, pointing at Talia, who stumbled in behind her, face pale, hair a mess.

"Bah," Jak said, throwing his hands up in the air and stalking to the other side of the hall, where he leaned against a wall, arms crossed.

"Are you quite hungover?" I asked Talia.

"No—only got, like, ten minutes sleep last night," she said. She put a hand to her head, swayed. "What's that noise."

"Her name's Elekti," I said. "She was a friend of Radulfo's daughter."

"Xinhua's eyes, she's bloody loud," Talia said.

"Jak's softened her up," I said. I caught Esper giving him a disapproving scowl. My eyes narrowed. Who's she to cast judging glances at Jak's ways? She led the children to Malamiko Island—she had to lose her comfort with Malamiko, too.

"My head's in a vice," Talia said, bleary-eyed. "I gotta make that kid shut up."

I waved my hand to the door. "She's all yours. Esper, work with Talia, see what you can learn about where Radulfo's daughter got contaminated."

They went in, closing the door behind them. Jak stewed in silence. In moments, the wailing quieted to sobs, which then faded away completely. "Sometimes you need a hammer," I said to Jak, "sometimes you need honey. You're my hammer; they're honey." I expected him to scoff or deride Talia and Esper. Instead, he processed my words, a thoughtful expression on his face.

Beyond the window at the end of the passage that lit the hall lay rolling fields of fruit trees, their branches bare in the crisp late-spring sun.

After some time, the door opened, and Talia and Esper exited. Esper cast Jak a dark glare he seemed oblivious to. Talia leaned back against the stone wall and slid down to plop on the ground. "There's an old abandoned town not far from here," Talia said. "They stumbled on it one day, explored it. Malamiko had claimed it."

Jak stepped forward. "That little— Why didn't the little brat tell me that?"

"Probably 'cause you're an ass," Talia said.

"Language!" I snapped.

"Oh, swearing's off-limits again?"

I shouldn't have lost control last night. "You are falchilo. You are in a falchilo outpost. Speak with respect."

Talia looked at me, an appraising look in her eyes and a smile on her lips. She seemed relieved. "Apologies, Majstro," she said.

I rubbed my forehead, frustrated. "What's with these border town people wandering off into the blue?" Maybe when you lived on the edge of civilization so close to Malamiko, you became complacent to its dangers. "You two," I pointed at Jak and Esper. "Prep our gear. We're going to check it out." The two left, leaving Talia and me alone.

"You look wretched," I said.

Talia looked at me. "Way to make a girl feel special."

"We're going into the borderlands. I still need you to babysit Jak and Esper."

She smiled. "I'll be okay. Find me some grub, and I'm good to go."

"Find your own grub and get ready quick. I want to check out the abandoned town and be back before dark."

She struggled to her feet. "Jak's a brute," she said.

"Sometimes—"

"Don't give me your hammer and honey story," she said. "I've seen Jak in taverns, back when we were in Firstsite and you and Esper were buried in the library. He's not a nice man."

"He's got strength. It just needs . . . tempering."

"Being mean's not strength, it's weakness. And stop counting Esper out. She's young, but she's got wisdom. She's the one who got that kid to talk about the town."

Talia and I had worked together for so long, I shouldn't be surprised she'd know my worries over Esper. "Are you done lecturing me?" I asked.

"Yeah, I think so."

"Good. Get some food, stuff your face, and get ready to hunt." I locked Elekti's cell and went downstairs.

Someone was banging on the western doors. Curious, I opened them, and a man, about the same age as my brother Fondo, stood, gaping at me. "Aaron's breath, why are you banging on the door, man?"

"Elekti, is she okay? I heard her crying."

His skin was darker, but I could see the resemblance in his eyes. "Are you her father?"

His head bowed. "Yes, Majstro."

"Your daughter's been playing in the borderlands!" I said, stabbing my finger in his chest.

An anguished cry escaped him, and he pulled on his hair.

"I tell her to stay away. I tell her to stay away from the borderlands!"

"Yeah, well, you got to do more than tell. You've got to put the fear of Malamiko in her."

"Is she . . ." he couldn't bring himself to say it.

"Contaminated?"

He bowed his head. "Is she?"

"I don't know." The GC had cleared her, but I figured he needed to sweat a little bit. Maybe sitting with the uncertainty would get him to keep his kids on a shorter leash. "We're going to an abandoned town overrun by Malamiko that your daughter found. We'll see what we find there. It may shed light on whether she's contaminated or not. Now, go home. We've got work to get to." I closed the door in his face.

THE ABANDONED TOWN WAS a ghost on a small rise, unaware it had died long ago. From this distance, I could see a low wall surrounding the perimeter and the outline of buildings rising behind it, like any one of hundreds of towns dotting the land. A stillness undermined its casual normalcy, though. Brown Duaterano scrub brush had grown over the dirt road, along with robust, vibrant blue Malamikan plants. Along either side of the unused path lay fields of dead fruit trees, once-living tombstones extending to the horizon.

We trudged to the old town walls, our kiraso in full combat readiness: helmets enveloping our head, sealing us off from the world, keeping us safe from contamination, rods out, shields opened and ready. The town's wall was mud brick, chest high, and collapsing like an old ox with a sagging back. The wooden gates had rotted, and they lay on the ground in a decomposing mound. Tiny blue fronds poked out from the mound and reached out to embrace the sun.

"Does this town have a name?" Esper asked.

"Not anymore," Talia said.

We passed through the gates into the sepulchre of a town. Hollow windows and doorways leered at us as we walked. "An abandoned town would be quite the thrill for kids to explore," Talia said.

"Kids ought to know better," I said. "Parents aren't putting the fear of Malamiko in them."

"Or when their kids are in danger, they lead them into Malamiko to hide," Jak said, obviously baiting Esper, a taunt she chose to ignore.

"On the bright side," Talia said, "after cleansing Radulfo's farm, parents—"

"What was that?" Esper cut her off.

We looked to where Esper was pointing. The road led ahead. Mud-brick buildings lined either side, dark hollows of windows staring out. "What'd you see? Where?" I asked.

"Five buildings in, on the left. I thought I saw something move on the roof."

Nothing moved. Just a gentle wind. "Jumping at shadows, now?" Jak asked.

"Save your meanness for Malamiko," Talia said.

"I got plenty of meanness for everybody," he said.

"Enough. Prep the gun," I told Talia. She withdrew it from her holster and turned the crankshaft to charge it up. We followed the main hard-packed road, the carcasses of buildings flanking us. I stepped up to a window, its gaping maw opening into a room bathed in shadows. The roof was caving in. It was empty, save for an old table standing off to the side.

We continued. I could see the top of the pagoda above the roofline, and we made our way toward it. Rounding a corner, we saw the pagoda gardens. My fist tightened. No bushes grew here anymore. Trees stood, brown, leafless, dead, blue vines wrapping around their trunks. And there was more.

"The stream's been dammed," Esper said, pointing to a narrow creek bed running around the periphery of the garden. "And an irrigation channel's been dug, leading to the granary."

"Another nest?" Jak asked.

"Looks like it," I said. Something seemed . . . off. Were there decoy dens like we saw early this year? Didn't seem so. "Stay sharp." What was it? I couldn't tell what was causing the hair on the back of my neck to stand. Walking side by side, we overlapped our shields to create a protective wall as we advanced.

It attacked. The dirt on the road in front of us erupted, a geyser of turf and sod. A shape leaped at us. It battered into Talia's shield, driving her back, leaving a gap in our wall. I drove my rod into the thing and gave it a full blast. It thrashed on the ground. A sizzling crack sent my ears to ringing as Talia shot the beast, the force of the blast bouncing it off the ground to flop dead onto the road some distance away.

We reformed our shield wall and approached the creature's corpse. "It's a sentinel," I said.

"Ain't like no sentinel I've ever seen," Talia said. It had the shoulder pincers and powerful legs of sentinels but was short, built low to the ground, and long, about half the length of a human, the last third of which was a tail.

"Its face . . ." Jak said, pointing at the vestigial face hanging off the front of the sentinel. It had a hole for a mouth but scaled skin and no eyes, no nose. "It doesn't look like it was ever human."

"It infected an indigenous life form," Esper said. "Of

course! If the contamination evolved on this planet, it would have native hosts."

"Don't let yourself get carried away," I said. "Why would Malamiko contaminate itself? Makes no sense. No, this isn't contamination; it's where contamination comes from. It's the source. These are Malamiko's soldiers. They live out here in the blue where they attack the unwary travelling the borderlands, contaminating them, and returning them to rot us from within."

Esper's brow furrowed. She didn't seem convinced.

"You've seen these before?" Talia asked.

"Once."

"Eta Monteto," Esper said.

"Good guess," I replied.

"Not a guess. I read the paper you and Mihaelo wrote."

"Glad someone remembers their studies," I said.

Jak kicked the sentinel's body. "We never saw them before Eta Monteto, and now you've seen them twice. Why is that?" he asked.

Esper answered before me. "Both in Eta Monteto and here, we encounter these nests outside of Duatero's borders. With Malamiko advancing on lands once ours, we're starting to encounter them more frequently."

I could see why Jak scowled at her sometimes. She was always jumping in with answers. She was thoughtful but naïve. I've fought Malamiko longer than she'd been alive; I knew it at a visceral level. "No," I said, "it's because Malamiko is changing. If there are records of these types of nests in the manlibroj, I haven't read them." As massive as the manlibroj are, the sections covering contamination were closely studied. If they mentioned nests like this, I would have read about it. "This is something new," I said, stepping over the body of the sentinel. "Come on. The irrigation ditches lead to the granary. That's where the host will be." We advanced. We'd made it three steps when the grounds throughout the pagoda gardens erupted, spewing forth dozens of sentinels—the strange, pure sentinels, like the one we just put down.

Talia began a falchilo battle prayer: "May the grace of the Founders be with us." She brought her gun to her shoulder.

"And may Donna, Star of the Fields, lead us to safe roads," I finished. *"Tiel estu!"*

WOOD SPLINTERED and cracked as Jak's axe thunked into the granary's door, echoing across the strange garden.

"Xinhua's eyes, Jak, hurry!" Talia said as she spun the crank to charge her gun. With a grunt, he reefed at his axe, ripping it from the door. He swung it high overhead, hacking it again into the wood.

We had fought our way to the granary, but the door was jammed shut. Esper and I were shielding Jak and Talia as they worked—Jak on the door, Talia on her gun. The strange sentinels skittered across the ground, closing fast. "Brace yourself," I said to Esper. "These aren't like human sentinels —they can leap overhead, landing behind your shield."

"Any other tricks?" Esper asked. The lead sentinel dived into my shield before I could answer, driving me back. My feet slid on the ground, pushing me into Jak, crushing us both into the splintering door. Esper stabbed her rod into its flanks, sending it writhing. Talia fired the gun, and then again, dropping two sentinels in mid-leap, tearing chunks of flesh and clear, thick fluid off with each shot.

Jak flung himself shoulder-first into the door. It was a wreck, gaping holes where he had struck it, barely hanging on its hinges, like a wet rag hanging off a hook. "Shield first!" I said, but too late. He threw his shoulder into the door, popping it off its hinges. I grabbed him, flung him back, took his place, shield first. The sentinel inside the granary leaped into me, hammering me into the ground with a force that caused my bones to ache.

The sizzling crack of Talia's gun rang out. The shot flung the beast away. With a fluid, graceful movement, Talia was in the granary's now hollow doorway, firing into the darkness beyond.

"Shield first, Jak," I said, getting up. "The host is always guarded by sentinels."

More sentinels were arriving. "Hold the door," I said to Jak. "You two," I said, indicating Talia and Esper, "with me." We entered the cavernous hall of the granary, wide grain pits, empty now, lining either side.

"Xinhua's eyes, I've never seen a host this big," Talia said. It was everywhere. From light shining through the door and high windows, I could see its mat of black hyphae covering the floor and climbing up walls into darkness, a seething blackness, source of Malamiko's greatest evil. I unholstered the flamjetilo, powered it on. It came to life with a hum.

"Aren't you going to give it the rights?" Esper asked.

"No," I said. "The rights are for contaminated humans. This is pure Malamiko. It just burns." I remembered holding my mother's hand as she convulsed. "You hear that!" I called out to the host's blackness surrounding us. "You *burn!*" And it did. I torched it, the flamjetilo calling waves of flame forth from the host's surface for minutes on end. I drained the flamjetilo's battery as I sent wave after wave of fiery destruction on my enemy.

Talia was pulling on my arm. "Enough, Kredo. The building's going to come down on top of us."

We stood in a cavern of flame, the host withering and smoking. "Everybody out," I said. We left, joining Jak by the shattered door. Beyond him in the gardens, the strange sentinels stood, watching us as they paced.

"Why aren't they going down?" Jak asked, calling out over the crackle of flames behind us. One of the sentinels shuffled to the side, seeing if it could outflank us. The sentinels were supposed to fall dormant once the host burned, but these ones cautiously moved, trying to find an angle of attack.

"Kredo?" Talia asked, positioning to cover our flank. "The host's burning. The nest's supposed to die when the host burns. Is this what I think it is?"

"Yep," I said, as warm waves of heat lapped my back through the door—no retreat that way. "Stage five."

Stage five—multiple fully formed nests scattered over kilometres, forming a network with one another. Multiple hosts; multiple minds controlling the nest. Mihaelo and I were the only living souls to encounter a stage five nest and survive. Until now.

Of course, we hadn't survived this one yet.

As one, the sentinels turned and scuttled off in different directions, scurrying away into the underbrush and the dark alleys between buildings beyond the garden.

"Unexpected," Talia said.

"This host is completely destroyed," I said. "There's nothing worth fighting for here. The other nests are calling them."

"How nearby are the other hosts?" Esper asked.

"I have no idea," I said. "In Eta Monteto, three hosts were spread out over fifteen kilometres. How typical that is, who knows? The other hosts could be anywhere. We don't even know how many hosts there are; we won't know until we burn the last one and the sentinels drop."

"That kid," Jak said. "Elekti. She'd know."

"Haven't had your fill of terrorizing small girls?" Talia asked.

"Think about it," Jak said. "She and Radulfo's daughter came here. How'd two girls not even ten years old survive a stage five nest? Radulfo's daughter only made it 'cause she was contaminated—the nest let it return as a host to contaminate us. And Elekti?" He let the question hang a moment. "What are the odds Radulfo's daughter got contaminated and not Elekti?"

"He's right," I said. "Listen, in Eta Monteto I was only able to partially cleanse the second host, wounding it rather than killing it, before sentinels overwhelmed us. As we retreated, sentinels carried slabs of what was left of the wounded host away. We followed them straight to the third host. Any contaminant in the area will know where the other hosts are. And if we can find another host and wound it, sentinels will come to take it to another host for reabsorption, with us following."

"C'mon," Esper said, "she's just a kid. We tested her with the GC, and she was green-lighted."

"I think I've been too reliant on the GC. If Elekti's a host, it may be our best hope of finding other hosts," I said. "We head back to town."

ELEVEN

JAK SWUNG OPEN the door to Elekti's room, slamming it against the stone wall. The young girl screamed, scurrying into a corner as we entered. Jak kneeled in front of her, grabbed her wrists, and forced her to face him. "You're going to tell us where your hosts are," he said.

"If she's not infected, she won't know," Esper said, coming in behind and pulling Jak back.

"Everyone, out of my way," I said, pushing through the room, readying the GC.

"We tested her already," Talia said from the door. "She was green-lighted."

"I'm testing her again." I grabbed Elekti's arm, placed the GC's nozzle on her skin, and stopped. The GC's indicator light shone red. Not the yellow of calibration, not the blue of Malamiko infection, not the green signalling no contamination. Red. I stood up, looked over the GC in my hands. On the display screen, written in the script of the Founders, was the code "F.201."

"What's the matter?" Talia asked.

Ignoring her, I powered down the GC, counted slowly to twenty, and turned it back on. The red light shone, a tiny, evil little eye returning my stare, "F.201" on the screen.

"Kredo?" Esper asked. Talia silenced her with a quick gesture.

Elekti had curled into a sobbing ball on the floor. I motioned the other falchilo to follow me into the hall. Talia closed the door behind us. "What's wrong with the GC?"

I was grinding my teeth, and I tried to force my jaw to relax. "It's giving me an error code. I *knew* it was acting strangely. And dropping it on the ground when I took that hit from the dark wanderer back at Radulfo's farm probably didn't help."

"Which code?" Esper asked. I showed her. "Do you know what it means?"

Of course, I knew. I was granted the honour of carrying the final GC. I knew every aspect of its functioning. "Pneumatics shutdown. The pneumatics control board needs replacing."

All three looked at me, worried frowns creasing their brows. "Are there any left?" Talia asked.

"No," I said.

"How can you be so sure?" Esper asked.

"Because I carry all the spare parts that are left with me in its case. There are four injection ports, two sputter ion pumps, five pressure regulators, one separation column, and one focusing lens. That's it. There are no pneumatics control boards." Even in the time of the Founders, we lacked the industry to build such technologies. Everything came from Earth. All we have are the parts the Founders left us, and as each of these components succumbs to time, the blessings of the Founders draw further away.

The three of them stared dumbly at me a moment. Elekti's

cries came muted through the door. "There's a bloody stage five nest outside of town and no GC," Talia said. "What are we going to do?"

"It's okay," I said, though my gut ached. "We're not the first falchilo to work without a GC."

Jak seemed to stand taller; Talia grimaced. Esper's eyes widened, and she took a step back. "We should check with the other Tero Kreinto first," Esper said. "They can check their archives. Maybe they have old pneumatics boards they lost track of. A visual inspection of their inventory—"

"No," I cut her off. "Sending word to all the Tero Kreinto and waiting for a reply will take months, maybe longer, and for what? I already have all the working spare parts with me that are left. There's a stage five, pure Malamikan nest hours away. We must act."

Esper pointed at Elekti's door. "So, you're going to do a visual inspection?"

I powered the GC down. "Yes. We have to act." I stared at the GC, one more Founder artifact lost to us.

"But you already tested her with the GC when it was still working and cleared her. Why would we need to test her again like this?"

"Radulfo's daughter was a host!" I shouted. I was losing control, and I breathed calm into myself. "What are the odds she'd be contaminated and Elekti'd be fine? They played in the borderlands together. The GC took a hit when I dropped it at Radulfo's farm."

Esper covered her mouth with her hands and turned away. Jak stood, arms crossed, ready for action. I turned to Talia. She had her hands on her hips, resigned to what we had to do. I said, "We're going to need a small knife and boiling water."

ELEKTI'S EYE stared at me. The rest of the girl sobbed softly, curled up on a table at the back of the room, blood matting her hair to her head like a honey-soaked rag, drenching her clothes and bandages wrapped around her face. It was late. Our outpost had power, so a bulb made in the city of Xuanhe —the last place on Duatero where artisans still have the skills to manufacture such wonders—dimly lit our room.

The contamination targets nervous tissue initially, leaving a faint black speckling—a way to identify the contaminated before outward signs manifest themselves. There are a few areas of the human body where you can expose a significant amount of nervous tissue without killing the person. I held up her eye, level to my face. The eye was an excellent candidate for examination, what with the optic nerve dangling from its rear and retinal tissue housed inside the orb. And if they were free of contamination, the person could live a full, healthy life, less one eye. Barring infection, that is, but a town as big as Vojo Fino would have a kuracisto to help prevent that.

Removed from her head, the pupil had dilated to unusual size, almost obscuring its brown iris. Beyond the iris, a dense web of red capillaries like strands of torn cotton covered the otherwise white sphere, ruptured, no doubt, from the trauma of its removal. The stench of blood, a metallic, warm smell, filled my nose. Elekti began to wail again.

Jak had a set of knives for carving wood, and one was the perfect size and sharpness for cutting out the eye. I picked up that knife again and began my efforts to scrape and cut off fat and muscle clinging to the back half of the eye, enshrouding the optic nerve. It was a painstaking, patient task, reminding me of dinners spent cutting gristle clinging to meat, only here

I required a kuracisto's precision so as not to mangle the nerve beneath. The electrical light was as wondrous as it was feeble, and it only cast a dull amber glow that danced and flickered. I paused, breathed in calm, and offered a silent prayer to Jinjing, Founder spirit of air, sunshine, and flowing water, whose power charged our light, asking for him to keep our bulb burning brightly. Periodically, I dunked the eye in a clay bowl of water, washing away blood and loose tissue.

"Pass me that white cloth," I said after maybe a dozen minutes of work. It was Esper who unfolded it, laying it before me on the table. I placed the eye on it and began inspecting the nerve dangling from its back that I'd uncovered. The others crowded around me. We each wore our kiraso, first, to supplement our strength to hold Elekti down when we cut her eye out, and second, so the helmet's visor could augment our sight as we made our inspection. Even so, Founders' grace, it was so hard to tell what we were looking at. Having suffered its removal from Elekti's body, compounded with my cutting at it with crude tools, the tissue was bloody and torn. I held it up, trying to get decent light on it.

"I don't see any signs of contamination," Esper said.

I couldn't tell a bloody thing from what I was looking at. Bringing calm authority to my voice, I said, "Can't say anything conclusive. The tissue's too mangled. We'll try the retina."

I began my attempts at dissecting the eye with the knife. The tissue was hard to cut, and the orb slipped easily from under the blade. I tried to pierce it with picks and awls in Jak's collection, and after several tries, I managed to puncture it, spilling clear, viscous fluid onto the white cloth. From my initial puncture, I worked the knife in and then began cutting through the hard tissue, eventually bisecting the eye. I took the back half, fingered out the remaining fluid, and then forced it inside out to view the retina on the eye's back wall. Shiny oatmeal-brown coloured nervous tissue stood out against the black backdrop of the rest of the eye's interior.

It was the border, where the pale brown of the nervous tissue bled into the black background of the inner eye, that my heart sank. The tissue was so irregular, and the border more a blending into one another than a clear delineation. I was looking for the telltale black specks on brown tissue the manlibroj tell us indicates contamination, but was what I was seeing contamination, or the dark tissue of the inner eye showing through? I'd always had the GC as a majstro—I never actually had to diagnose contamination this way before.

"I think I see some speckling there," Jak said.

"Where?" Esper asked.

"There," he said, pointing, his kiraso-clad finger hopelessly too thick for the task of pointing out what would be no bigger than pinpricks.

"That's normal tissue," Esper said.

"Naw, it's speckling," Jak said.

I stared at it, wondering, frustrated, hating Malamiko for leading us to a place in our lives where we found ourselves peering at the insides of a girl's eye. I zoomed in with my kiraso's visor, but still, nothing was clear. "What do you think, Talia," I asked.

She leaned over my shoulder, took a close look in the light we had. I noticed Elekti's blood on the breastplate of her kiraso, a dark smear on black armour. "I don't know, Kredo. Maybe we should quarantine her; wait and see if contamination develops."

"It'll take weeks, maybe months, for the contamination to develop into something visible," I said. "There's a stage five nest hours from town. If we wait, we could lose this whole area." My stomach burned. This seemed so wrong, but what else was there to do? We are dying. We had to find something to defend ourselves from. *I* had to find something to defend ourselves from. I am falchilo, and I will not allow another Cull to happen.

"Her retina's fine," Esper said. "Look, you can see it's the dark under-tissue of the eye blending in with the nervous tissue."

"No way," Jak said. "That's speckling."

"How would you know what speckling looks like?" Esper asked. "All we ever dissected were sheep's eyes. We've only seen pictures of speckling in the manlibroj."

"Yeah, and in those pictures, that's what speckling looks like," Jak said.

"No, it's not!" Esper screamed in wild anger.

"Enough," I said, silencing them. I was Majstro Falchilo. The decision was mine. An image of my brother Paulo, playing with a wiggler in the yard, came to mind. I remembered the cold touch of my mother's hand. The sound of Aprila's arms and legs flapping in the mud as the death throes took her echoed in my ears. So many holes in my heart, and still Malamiko keeps taking.

Focusing all my will, all my energy, all my powers of observation, forcing my old eyes to focus, to read the signs lain before me, I stared at the remnants of the eye in my hand. There it was—that was it! "It's contaminated."

"Kredo, no," Esper said.

Talia sighed.

"Agreed," Jak said.

I showed the eye to Esper, pointing with Jak's awl. "There. Don't you see it? Speckling."

Her voice broke. "You're wrong."

I wasn't. Ignoring her, Jak said, "Assuming the closest nest is near the one we cleansed, if we get Elekti's body out there early morning and wound it, sentinels should be there before noon. With luck, they'll lead us to the second host before nightfall."

"Good thinking," I said. "Tie it to the table. We'll post a guard overnight to make sure it doesn't escape."

"No!" Esper drove her body into Jak, her strength augmented by the kiraso, and sent him crashing into a wall with the force of an ox. He collapsed on the floor. Talia lashed out, clocking Esper on the side of the head with her fist, sending her sprawling over a stool with a clatter.

"Enough!" I yelled. Talia stepped back to break off the fight, but Esper, fumbling to regain her feet, struck out with her rod, driving the tip into Talia's leg, sending a bolt of energy into it. Talia's body convulsed, then flopped to the ground. I ran to her body, screaming. Her helmet covered her head, and I fumbled with the external manual override at the back of her neck to withdraw it so I could see if she was alive. Esper grabbed Elekti and ran.

The rod could kill. If Esper killed Talia . . .

Jak slowly rolled onto his belly and rose to his hands and knees. "Jak, get up. Get Esper!" He lumbered to his feet and stumbled out the door. I calmed myself, forced my hands to obey as I worked the manual override of Talia's kiraso. The helmet retracted. Her head lolled in my hands, her face motionless. *Founders, favour me*, I prayed; *favour Talia*. My body tensed as I checked to see if she was still breathing.

Faint, shallow, her chest rose and fell with weak breaths that fogged the outside of my visor as I leaned over her face. Praise the Founders! Still, the rod strike would have burned her. She'd need a kuracisto to tend to the wound it would leave. But first, Esper.

I ran out the door, down the stairs, and out onto a street whose only illumination was the stars. Where were Jak or Esper? Commotion sounded far to my right, heading into town. I was off, running toward it, charging down stone streets, the buildings a blur flashing past me.

Screams sounded a block away. I quickly closed the distance. I found them on the main road, the one that leads out of town, lit by the light shining through nearby windows and doors. Elekti was on the ground, curled fetal in a ball. It didn't cry or moan. It just lay there, spent, blood weeping from its torn eye socket. Esper stood in front of it, shield out, rod forward, facing Jak, standing with his own shield and rod. Their commotion had brought a crowd.

"This isn't right, Kredo!" Esper said, tears in her voice.

"It's contaminated," I said, pointing at Elekti. A collective gasp escaped from the crowd like the ripples of a pebble dropped in a pond. More than one window and door closed, while those who remained stepped back.

"There's no speckling. You're guessing," Esper said.

"What's gotten into you?" I asked her. "This is not how we do things. You could have killed Talia."

"It's Malamiko Island," Jak said.

"What?" she asked.

"Esper's contaminated," Jak said. "From Malamiko Island."

"That's low, even for you," Esper said.

"What else could explain it?" Jak asked. "It attacks a falchilo with lethal force to protect a host. Stelara's Kodo is clear about what that means."

My chest tightened. I scanned the faces of people watching this unfold. "Jak, not here." It was too late. Everyone watching would have heard one falchilo judge another one contaminated. And didn't they hear us pronounce Elekti contaminated, too? A dark falchilo trying to free a contaminant—this story would spread like wildfire through town.

"Elekti's not a host! She's not contaminated!" Esper said.

"*It,*" I said, "is contaminated. Put your rod down."

"Promise me you won't hurt her," Esper said.

"This isn't a negotiation. Put your rod away."

"Promise you won't hurt her," she said again, raising her rod to me.

Jak charged, ramming her with his shield, slamming her into a wall with a hollow thud. Chunks of plaster clattered on the ground at her feet. Esper tried to manoeuvre her rod to strike back. Before she could, I grabbed the edge of her shield, pulled it down, and punched her with a blow that sent her head, helmet and all, careening into the wall, breaking off more plaster. She slumped to the ground in an unconscious heap.

"We should take its eye, confirm that it's contaminated," Jak said, nodding toward Esper.

Around us, dozens of people stared from doorways and windows. What would they think if I let this pass? What would Jak think? What he said had a logic to it. She exposed herself on Malamiko Island. Malamiko was changing. Could Esper be contaminated? Could I cut out her eye? "No. We'll quarantine her." *A good compromise,* I thought.

Jak almost spoke, seemed to think better of it. After some thought, he finally asked, "Really?" with a voice drenched in disapproval.

"Yes, really." My gut tied itself in knots. "Something new is happening to Malamiko. We need to understand it. We'll send Esper's body to Firstsite for quarantine. The falchilo there can study it, maybe help us figure out what's going on." That was a good idea. This was a good plan, a wise plan.

"Take Esper," I said to Jak. "Don't . . ." Don't what? Don't hurt her? Don't kill her? She'd attacked Talia to defend a contaminant. She should be cleansed. *It* should be cleansed, that's what Stelara's Kodo says. "Go easy on . . . just . . . don't wreck our specimen."

TALIA HAD NOT REGAINED consciousness by dawn, despite the ministrations of Vojo Fino's finest kuracisto. Perhaps that was for the best.

Jak and I dragged Elekti's body out of town, far into the fields on a cold and rainy morning, near to the abandoned town where we burned the host the day before. It had continued bleeding from its eye socket through the night, but it clung to life. Mortally wounding a host worked before in Eta Monteto, calling forth sentinels to bring the wounded host to another nest for reabsorption. In this way, we had tracked down host after host, ending the threat of contamination.

It didn't work today. We moved some distance away and hid, waiting for sentinels to come. The rain intensified, then passed, leaving only dull grey clouds. It moaned. It fell silent. It cried, and it tried crawling back to town, collapsing into the mud after only a couple of metres. It cried more and fell silent again. More rain fell. It called for help, it begged for help, it prayed to the spirits for rescue before falling silent one last time.

As the clouds overhead thickened, we stood over the corpse of Elekti's body, a tiny figure splayed in the muddy field. Just like Aprila that day outside Eta Monteto where joy was stolen from our victory.

"Why didn't the sentinels come to save it?" Jak asked.

Why indeed? "She must have been a secondary."

"A secondary?" Jak asked.

It had to be true. "Yes," I said, gaining confidence as my mind worked through it. "It's a secondary." I began to laugh as it all came clear, relief flowing through me like a cleansing stream. "It's a secondary infection—sentinels only come for wounded hosts, and Radulfo's daughter was probably the only host in town."

"And Elekti's family?" Jak asked. "Always test the family, that's what the manlibroj say."

"Yes, of course," I said, remembering Elekti's father who'd banged on the outpost door, the man who reminded me of Little Fondo. A dirty business, this. "We'll get the records on the family from the pagoda when we get back."

I pulled the flamjetilo from its harness on my back, powered it on, and stared down at the unmoving body of Elekti as the rain fell, thin arms and legs like broken branches akimbo in the mud. I closed my eyes, saw Aprila's body in the rain, her long black hair splayed in pools of muck, lifeless eyes staring at me before I cleansed her. She had been the first person I'd cleansed. A fellow falchilo. A friend.

My eyes opened and stared at Elekti. "To the human whose body this once was . . ."

TWELVE

THE NEXT MORNING found me in the garden of the falchilo outpost cutting back a tenacious patch of morning glory to bring order to the unruly yard. I was angry the falchilo had let it come to ruin. "Nature will serve us," my father told me one summer afternoon decades ago as I was breaking my back working compost into our fields, "but you have to *work* it, every day, or it will let you starve." The coiling thin vines of the morning glory snaked everywhere, and I lost hours pulling them from the ground and from around the branches of other overgrown bushes.

A din of shouts in the distance tugged me away from my work. I stashed a handful of leaf-covered vines in the compost bin, made my way to the main road, and looked toward town to see what was going on. A group of falchilo walking alongside an ox-drawn wagon approached. A mob of people shouted at them from either side. I strained my ears to hear and caught some fragments. "Cleanse the beasts!" "My neighbour is a…" "… crops die!"

The Cull had given us food, but it took our family and did

nothing to save our crops from ruin. The people of Vojo Fino were scared and angry.

The squad of falchilo pulled past the crowd, and the people lingered, staring at their backs before going back to their lives. The falchilo approached and came to a stop before the outpost. The leader wore the blue armband of a second. He stepped forward. "Majstro Kredo."

"Yes, I'm Kredo." I recognized him. "Falchilo Zahario, isn't it?"

He smiled and stood a little straighter. "Yes, Majstro. Good memory."

"We worked together before. Where was it?"

"I was part of a squad assigned to help you investigate a nest outside Orasteppo. That was six years ago now. How's Talia."

My mood darkened, but I tried not to let it show on my face. "She was wounded recently, but she's healing quickly." Physically, at least. Before he could ask more, I added, "I suppose I know why you're here."

"Yes," he said, producing papers and passing them to me. "We're here for the contaminant, Esperanta Sagido. I've orders to take it to quarantine in Firstsite."

I knew this moment would come, but a dark pit still opened in my gut at the words. "Of course." I gave his squad directions to the cell where we held Esper. While his men were gathering the contaminant, Zahario looked back to town. "People are still raw from the Cull," he said.

The icy shadow of my mother's stone-cold fingers still haunted my hand. "The Cull leaves a hole in us."

He nodded in agreement. "I don't get why we still farm so close to Malamiko's borders."

Shrugging, I said, "Our yield per hectare is going down as

it is. We need to use all the arable land we can to keep Culls at a minimum."

"I guess," he said. "You sure you want to send the contaminant to quarantine? Cleansing it in town would be cathartic for the people, don't you think?"

"No!" He looked at me, as shocked as I was at the intensity in my voice. I breathed calm into myself and thought quickly of something to explain my outburst. "The contamination is changing. We need to understand these changes if we're to fight it. Esper must make it to quarantine where we can study it."

The other falchilo returned, Esper in chains between them. I hadn't spoken to it since the night of its capture. As the falchilo led it from the outpost, it looked at me with Esper's eyes. "Is Talia okay?" it asked on its way past me.

The other falchilo looked at me, waiting to see how the Hero of Eta Monteto responded to contaminants. I replied with something like, "You can strike at us, wound us even, but you'll never destroy us," or some such bravado.

They left, and I returned to my garden, where I sat in the dirt surrounded by wild bushes flowering in the sun. Esper had so much potential. Such wisdom, such keen intellect. That was over now. Did I make the right choice? Yes, I think so—with the changing nature of Malamiko I couldn't ignore her behaviour.

I went inside, grabbed Esper's gear, and took it to my office. I began going through it, deciding what to return to the Tero Kreinto, and how to dispense with the rest. I found her almond seed in a faded leather pouch. The sun shone through the window of my office as I held it up and felt its rough shell between my finger and thumb. I remembered Esper's story. Through this, life enters the universe—not a seed but a miracle.

Should I keep it to plant in Donna's Garden when I returned to Firstsite? Whatever goodness Esper might have done was gone. I fancied the idea of a tree, her tree, living on, growing, maturing, producing nuts of its own that would one day feed her people.

I went to the kitchen and tossed it in a cooking fire. Malamiko infects living things, and it was changing, becoming something we didn't know how to fight anymore. Imagine if Esper had contaminated this seed, and then I were to plant it in our first Tero Kreinto where paisajista, falchilo, and kuracisto would feed off it.

After it burned, I thought to write to Gaja. I even went to my office and pulled out pages of reed paper and lampblack ink from my desk but could think of nothing worth saying. It didn't feel right writing to her; I don't know why. Pages, pregnant with intent, left blank.

Salvation from this darkness came the next day. Mihaelo sent twenty falchilo for me to command. As farmers tended their orchards, we swept out into the borderlands, searching for the stage five hosts. It did not take long to find one and then another soon after. Momentum! I pushed my falchilo deeper into the borderlands—I wanted to eradicate this contamination before Rendezvous. The people of Duatero needed a victory. I needed a victory.

Throughout that week, we rooted out the contamination. The tactic of wounding a host to lure sentinels to retrieve worked once more, as it had in Eta Monteto. These were real hosts, fully developed masses of black hyphae clinging to wood or stone.

By the end of the week, we had nearly destroyed the stage five nest at our borders, though it cost the lives of eight falchilo. My reputation grew immensely. I was already the hero of Eta Monteto, the first attack on Duatero from a stage five nest. Now, the hero of Vojo Fino was added to my epithet. And yet, on mornings such as this, a sense of utter failure overwhelmed me.

My anger caused me to hammer on the door a bit too harshly. A man about my age opened it, hurriedly tying his jupo around his waist. Seeing a majstro clad in full kiraso at his door, he quickly bowed his head and asked how he might serve.

"Is she here?" I asked. I didn't have to say who. He knew.

"Yes, Majstro," he said, almost stumbling over his words in his eagerness to answer my questions. "Upstairs, with our son." Behind him, his wife stood in the common area, head bowed.

"Get me a bucket of water," I said to her. "You," I said to the man, "show me his room." He led me up an old, well-worn ladder through a hole in the ceiling to a dark hallway with creaking wooden floors, and to a door. The house had the musty smell of people packed too close together.

"This it?" I asked.

"Yes," he said, bowing once more. "My son, Majstro, he's of an age where his choices—"

I held up a finger, silencing him. "Your son has nothing to fear from me." I flung the door open, and it slammed hard against the wall with a resounding crack. On a straw bed in the room, a young man bolted to his feet, naked, shock tearing him from slumber. Beside him, Talia lay face down, equally naked, unconscious.

The youth froze, seeing who I was. I ordered him out of the room by stabbing my thumb over my shoulder, and he tripped his way past me. Talia's back rose and fell as she breathed. Her naked body was lean and muscled. I could see the pink wound on her leg where Esper's rod had burned her. The kuracisto had given her ointments and salves that healed the wound quickly and prevented infection. Physically, she had already fully recovered from Esper's attack and was in as good health as she'd ever been in.

"Where's that water?" I asked over my shoulder.

The mother appeared, handing me a clay pot with a reed handle, bowing as soon as I took it. I sent the family away. The room stank of piss-soaked straw and mead. I dumped the water on Talia.

"Shit!" She sprung to hands and knees, shocked to consciousness.

"Language."

"Oh, it's you," she said, flopping to her side. With tremendous effort, she heaved herself into a sitting position. "Bloody . . . Where're my knickers?"

"I assure you, I do not know."

"I . . ." Her head hung low, like an autumn leaf barely clinging to its branch. "I wish you didn't see me like this."

"Me too."

"No, I mean naked." She moaned and reached out an unsteady hand in my direction. "Pass me that bucket," she said, and I gave her the one I had used to douse her. She thunked it on the floor between her feet, leaned her head over it, her dark wet hair hanging limply around her face with bits of straw in it.

"You going to be alright?" I asked, crossing my arms. She answered by holding up a hand to me, gesturing for me to give her a minute. I shook my head, muttering a prayer to Donna, moved to her, and held her hair out of her face. Her body heaved as she began vomiting. Moments passed as she retched, and I looked away, trying, failing, to evade the smell.

Her body stilled and then began to shiver. Searching

about, I found a dry blanket and wrapped it around her. "This room stinks," I said. "Clean it up; clean yourself up," I said. "Jak's squad found another sub-nest, a big one, a day's march into the borderlands. We're leading the rest of the falchilo out to meet him. I want to leave this morning."

I left her, then paused at the top of the ladder leading to the lower level. Talia had always been one to live life to its fullest, but lately, she seemed prone to excess. Wanton drunkenness, once a rare event for her, was becoming commonplace. I wanted to talk to her about it, but she wasn't one for heart-to-heart conversations, and her performance in the field was as solid as ever. She was proud; a tough woman. It was through dance she expressed herself, not words. She hadn't been dancing so much, lately, not since her wound. I had talked to a kuracisto about it, but he said her leg was fine, and she could dance if she wanted.

A sound came to me, rippling down the hall, a tiny stream of noise. Talia was weeping. I quietly made my way down the ladder, giving her privacy to deal with whatever it was she was dealing with, and left the house without a word to anyone.

THE NEXT DAY, I marvelled as Talia, clad in kiraso, came alive in battle. She seemed at peace as she rolled out of the path of an oncoming sentinel, at one with the ebb and flow of nature as she fired her gun and then leaped behind the shield wall formed by the remaining falchilo. We were a day's march into the borderlands, further than any human had been in modern times. Scant were the hints that humans once dominated this land: a few skeletal fruit trees that blue Malamikan vines had not yet pulled under, the occasional mound of mud brick on hilltops where farms and estates once stood, but not much else.

Talia saw me coming out of the entrance of an ancient, abandoned dolmen that housed this sub-nest's host, holstering the flamjetilo as I stepped into the dazzling sun. I nodded my head, letting her know I finished wounding the host. Time to watch the sentinels. If other hosts remained, they would gather what was left of this host and take it to another, with us close behind. Talia ordered the falchilo to withdraw from the entrance to the host's den. In lockstep, my falchilo moved away while maintaining their shield wall, Talia and I taking cover behind them. Nothing to do now but take up a position some distance away and wait.

"Look at the sentinels!" Jak called out. I strained to look over the shoulders of the falchilo in front of me, saw several sentinels stumbling.

"Looks like they're dancing a jig," Jak said. "What's it mean?"

Smiling, I turned at Talia. "It means this is the last host of the stage five nest. With no other host to establish control over them, the sentinels are losing connection to the nest."

"You hear that!" Jak called out. "We did it! We destroyed a stage five nest! We're the Heroes of Vojo Fino!"

My falchilo gave a cheer while the sentinels tripped and stumbled in the field of blue before us. They called out my name, again and again, pumping their rods in the air. Talia slapped me on the back. "I suppose this is going straight to your head, ain't it," she said. I smiled, tossed the flamjetilo to her, and told her to go finish off the host to strike the killing blow.

We arrived back at Vojo Fino near the end of the next day, and news of our victory swept like a stiff breeze through town. The reeve called for a celebration that night. In a matter of hours, it seemed to my eyes the entire population of Vojo Fino and surrounding lands crammed themselves into the central square between the town's reeve's hall and central pagoda.

Gepatro Denizo stepped up onto a bench while carafes of mead and beer passed through the crowd. A young paisajista, younger even than Jak, filled my clay mug with beer. Denizo led us in a prayer of thanksgiving and remembrance. Then he turned to me, hand outstretched. "It was not just the people of Vojo Fino who fell to this contamination. Many falchilo died at the hands of Malamiko. Majstro Kredo, would you lead us in a prayer remembering those brave men and women who died so we might live?"

Talia turned to look at me, eyes wide. "Oooh. Did no one tell him how bad you are at speeches?"

I gave her a sidelong glance and then stepped forward. The crowd fell silent. The sun was setting behind buildings, painting the sky glowing-ember red as it did. All I could think of was Esper standing over the body of a little girl, standing up to Jak, standing up to me, to the whole bloody Tero Kreinto. Was there some other way? Did she see something that I missed? She almost killed Talia. Cleansing nests— that's what I was made to do, and I was good at it. Nests were easy. Yes, Elekti was dead and Esper in quarantine, but we destroyed a stage five nest. This was a mighty blow against Malamiko. But this thing with Esper . . .

People stared at me. Talia was right. I'm horrible at speeches. I raised my mug, and the assembly raised theirs. "Malamiko's greatest evil is it replaces the person behind the eyes of our loved ones with monsters. It forces us to take our own." *How do I finish this? How do I make this make sense to these people, how do I make them understand why I did what I did to their neighbours, to their daughters, to Elekti, to Esper?*

"Mia korpo estas via shildo."

"Tiel Estu," they mumbled quietly back. I upended my cup, pouring its contents on the ground, and everyone in the square did the same, a libation, honouring the spirits of the falchilo who'd fallen in our battle with the stage five nest, as well as the families who'd succumbed to contamination.

Denizo let the silence hang a moment, then he said, "The Founders favour us. A stage five nest is cleansed. Our lands are safe. Tonight, we celebrate the life the fallen have given us."

The crowd cheered, and all the tension and pain the people of Vojo Fino held, first from the Cull, then from our merciless hunt for the stage five nest that had, sadly, cut into their own people, was released in one of the happiest celebrations I have ever seen.

The paisajista lit a bonfire that roared in the town square, casting giant shadows of dancers on the walls of the pagoda as night fell while dozens of ouds, drums, and reed pipes sang their songs to the sea of stars rippling in the dark heavens above.

"Storytellers will sing your song for ages to come," Jak said, taking a seat beside me and toasting me with a mug of mead. "Before you, no falchilo had ever even known about stage five nests. Now, you've destroyed not one but two. Greatness follows you." He hoisted his mug aloft, spilling some of his drink over the rim. "Kredo!" he shouted, and other falchilo took up his call, chanting my name. Before I could reply, he was up, joining the press of bodies dancing around the bonfire. Talia danced and danced and danced. Seeing joy grab hold of my best friend's body once more filled me with happy satisfaction.

I wish I hadn't burned Esper's almond seed.

THIRTEEN

"THIS IS BLOODY *AMAZING*!" Talia said, skipping through the Rendezvous crowd. Neither Jak nor I shared her exuberance for throngs of people. The population of Firstsite had easily doubled, if not more, since we were here last, and an entirely new city of tents and stalls had sprung up on the surrounding plains. It was Rendezvous, and mad, frenetic energy filled the air. Sounds of a city gone mad in celebration rose into the sky. The beat of the drums pulsing underneath the undulating scales of reed pipes, and singer's voices wrapping around the dancing rhythms of lyres and ouds, sounded from dozens of different directions, intermingled with each other in the space above the city's rooftops, and there joined with the clapping of audiences keeping time, and the cheers of revellers.

Talia bounded in front of me, taking both my hands in hers. "Sweet Donna, we have to go to the Market."

"Sweet Donna, no," I replied.

"Come on, you have to buy a sky lantern for Rendezvous night."

"That's six days away. Plenty of time."

She grunted and waved dismissively at me. "Suit yourself. The Market's always got magicians and acrobats. I'm off." She looked back at me over her shoulder as she pressed on. "Tonight's ritual is Purify. Will you celebrate it with me?"

"I will. Meet me at the falchilo barracks after sundown." I turned to Jak after she'd left. "What are your plans for tonight?"

"I'm meeting up with some friends from my days as an initiate."

I pushed my way through a group of people stopped in front of me. Why do people in crowded streets think it's okay to stop walking? "Make sure you leave plenty of time to get to where you're going." The next few hours of our lives were spent pushing our way through the masses to the Tero Kreinto. Even there, on sacred grounds, the pathways were filled with people, though the atmosphere was much calmer than the city outside.

I only had time to set my gear in a cell and wash before Talia found me to begin the ritual of Purify. Together we walked the gardens surrounding Aaron's tomb. She was buzzing with energy, skipping and chattering without pause. "I don't know how you do it," I said. "You've spent the day pushing through the crowds, and you're more charged up than I've ever seen you. I spend an hour in the crowd, and all I want to do is nap."

"You're old, Kredo."

"You ain't as young as you used to be, either."

She elbowed me in the ribs. "You shut up."

The paisajista had done wonders preparing the Tero Kreinto for Rendezvous. The paths throughout the gardens were lined with lanterns, casting an eldritch glow on the leaves of trees overhead that twinkled off rippling streams of water. It was a warm night in early summer, and small groups of people walked together throughout the gardens. Talia and I gave silent prayers at the menhir over Aaron's tomb, its front surface dominated by Aaron's symbol, the seven-pronged FTL Vergo, engraved in the cold block of Founder stone.

From there, we walked until we found an empty bench overlooking a stream to begin the ritual of Purify, the first of five rituals before Rendezvous night. Our objective was to cleanse our spirits by speaking aloud our greatest sins. I had a hard time choosing what to share. It seemed guilt haunted me about a great many things. "I don't know what to confess."

"That's what you get for being boring."

I smiled in reply and remained silent.

"Tell me about your family," she said.

I shouldn't be surprised Talia knew what weighed on my heart before I did. "It is only in the last few years I realize how much hardship I caused them," I said. I could feel my mother's spirit nearby as I continued, like a warm blanket surrounding me on a cold morning. "Our farm was south of Transiri, near the borderlands where Malamiko from the ruins of Port Donna creeps into Duatero. It was . . . It was a hard land. My mom lost six kids. Six! How do you keep going after that?

"My sister was fifteen when I left for the Tero Kreinto, my brother only eleven. I left my father to work that brutal land alone. Eight years later, he was dead. It would be more than a decade after that before the self-centredness of youth passed enough for me to consider how my choices may have impacted his life. Still, even today, my absence wounds them. My mother lost a husband and six children, and I might as well be the seventh for all the times I visited her. And now . . ." I could still feel her cold hand in mine as she passed to the spirits. "Now, she'll never have the child she deserved, at least not in me. I didn't even stay to see her interred in our family's mausoleum, Talia. What's wrong with me?"

Be good, Kredo. I remember the reverence in her eyes as she touched my kiraso, the joy in her smile as she listened to her grandchildren sing. I sat a moment. You are supposed to feel cleansed from the confession, or so the paisajista teach us, but the weight of guilt chained to my neck still pulled me down. What more was there for me to say? What else should I confess? That doubt plagued me in my battle with Malamiko, or that I don't know if judging Esper a contaminant was the right thing to do? Is doubt a sin? Was I good? Malamiko's greatest weapon is its ability to make us kill our own. The sin is Malamiko's, not mine. "*Absolvi min,*" I said, bringing my confession to a close.

Talia cupped my head in her hands, stared at me with a lopsided smile that seemed to hold a world of compassion in it. "Purify," she exhorted the spirits.

"Your turn," I said.

She faced the stream, and her forehead scrunched up as she wrestled with her thoughts. I waited. Perhaps now I would learn more about what was driving her to drink lately. "I've killed people, Kredo," she finally said—not what I was expecting. "At Kubuto Falls, those bastards raping that woman, I killed two of 'em. They had it coming, but I—*me*—I took their lives. I know being a falchilo means making hard choices, and you've known me long enough to know I make those choices. We're at war with Malamiko, and blood's spilled in war. But I broke Stelara's Kodo. The falchilo are not at war with the people of Duatero. I think that's why their deaths have been weighing on me. And that kid, Elekti. Xinhua's eyes, that kid just kept crying, screaming. I try to sleep, but I keep hearing her scream in my ears. I tell myself it was a contaminant, that Malamiko made it cry to twist the knife. But I don't know. And Esper . . ." She looked on the verge of saying more, then stopped. An abyss of time opened. Finally, she said, "All this twists in me. *Absolvi min.*"

Malamiko made all this happen. I wanted to tell her that, just as I tell myself, to let her know she was blameless. I wanted to say it was right for her to come to the aid of those who need help, that the raiders in Kubuto Falls intended to attack the pagoda and steal grain, and her choices, as hard as they were, were righteous. But it was the ritual of Purify. There is no counselling, no judgment, only forgiveness. I cupped her head in my hands and stared her in the eye so she knew I understood her, so she could feel she was forgiven. "Purify."

We spent the rest of the evening holding hands as we walked the paths in silence, following the babbling brooks winding through the old city. We hugged, then went our separate ways. The next day, I requested the records of the Tero Kreinto's study of Esper. I was curious, obviously, but I worried about Talia, also, and thought confirmation of Esper's contamination would allay some of the guilt she felt.

I scanned over the report's pages. It had been questioned, observed, and then tested for contamination. Reports such as these had only three possible conclusions: contaminant, likely contaminant, or free of contamination. Contaminants are cleansed. Non-contaminants are released. Likely contaminants are observed in quarantine.

Written in hastily scrawled script at the bottom of the report: "Likely contaminate. Recommend observation until fall, then cleanse." The conclusion wasn't surprising. If they marked it contaminated, Stelara's Kodo mandated immediate cleansing. Denoting it a likely contaminate gave us time to study it further. To my surprise, a surge of relief flooded me. My doubts had weighed on me, but confirmation of my suspicions freed me from a weight I'd been carrying around in my heart.

I wanted to share this finding, but over the next couple of days, I saw neither Jak nor Talia. Jak was reconnecting with falchilo he trained with, and Talia disappeared in the ongoing festivities. I dared to venture out of the Tero Kreinto and into the mad city to visit Donna's pagoda for the ritual of Thanksgiving. And for Charity the day after, I worked with the kuracisto tending the sick in the hospital on Tero Kreinto grounds. The next day was the Festival of Fertility, and I spent it alone—I am at a stage in life where such festivities are behind me, or, perhaps more truthfully, I have no one who I'd wish to celebrate with, and I had no desire for the company of a stranger.

The next morning, Talia found me working in the garden deadheading a patch of nasturtium. We needed to keep the blooms fresh for the bees—if the bees die, we die. "Always, I find you in the muck," she said, kneeling beside me.

"It's the farm boy in me." I stopped what I was doing to look at her. "Last night was the Festival of Fertility."

"It was," she said, a conspiratorial gleam in her eye.

"It's still morning. What are you doing up?"

She shrugged. "Maybe I'm still up from last night. I suppose you spent your Festival of Fertility locked alone in your room self-flagellating or something."

"Cleaning the joint actuators of my kiraso, actually."

She looked at me, a crooked smile on her face. "And no one's fallen in love with you, yet. Strange. It's a good thing you're so boring. You could really be abusing your power now if you wanted to."

"My power?"

"Kredo, the streets are on fire with the story of how you destroyed the stage five nest in Vojo Fino. I don't think there's a soul in the city—man or woman—who'd deny you a request." I grunted dismissively. "Anyhow," Talia continued, "I'm pulling on my connections to score a date with the Hero of Vojo Fino tonight. Tomorrow's Rendezvous, and tonight is the Celebration of Fellowship. Tonight, we walk the streets, arms draped around our friends and family. The spirits don't want us to be alone tonight."

"You're right, I guess." I imagined walking the streets with Talia. No hunting. No Malamiko. Just two friends. "I'd like that."

"You'll like this next bit less."

I frowned. "What is it?"

"I'm gonna guess you haven't got your sky lantern yet."

Blast it. "No. Not yet."

"That means you're coming with me to the Market to shop." She slapped me on the back before I could reply. "You'll want to change into something less muddy. Meet me in front of Donna's Hall in twenty minutes?"

"Before you drag me kicking and screaming into the market, we need to talk about Esper."

Talia's mood crashed in her features. "What is it?"

"I've read the report on its investigation."

"And?"

"It concluded likely contaminant. Cleansing's slated for the fall."

Talia stared at the dirt a moment. "Likely. That's as conclusive as they could get?"

"'Likely contaminant' gives time to study it. Given the unique nature of this contamination, that's to be expected."

"The report said that?"

No. "That's how the Tero Kreinto works." But that's not the type of thing you'd document in a formal report.

"Hey, forget it," Talia said, and I couldn't read the tone in her voice. "It's Rendezvous, and I'm not letting you get out of shopping with me."

———

THE MARKET WAS a packed mob shuffling from stall to stall, all to the background noise of braying animals, a half-dozen musicians playing different melodies, and the hubbub of a thousand voices. On upturned barrels or makeshift stages, performers in bright, colourful tunics swallowed swords, juggled bewildering arrays of fruit and vegetables, or blasted balls of flame from their mouths.

My exploits in Vojo Fino may be famous, but no one outside of my few companions knew what I looked like, allowing me to pass through crowds unnoticed. Intricately coloured tapestries hung from the sides of buildings, and the stench of sweat, animals, food, and spices attacked my nose like a pack of drunk teenage boys on a rampage. The Cull was behind us. Tomorrow was Rendezvous. It was a time for hope.

The pressing masses gave me a fierce headache but watching Talia skip as she slid through the crowd, leading me to a sky lantern vendor I *have* to see to believe," filled me with a quiet peace. I bought my sky lantern and brought it back to my quarters in the Tero Kreinto. Rendezvous was a sacred time, so I ground my own ink from a sumi ink stick and inkstone and used a goat-hair brush to write my prayer on its side.

That night, Talia knocked on my door. "It's still a little early," I said, seeing her.

She grabbed my hand, pulled me out of my room. "The party's starting."

"The party hasn't stopped for a week."

She winked at me and pulled me down the hall, out of the barracks, and into the Tero Kreinto complex. There, we made our way along the roads and pathways into the city. We wandered the streets of Firstsite, arm in arm, amid crowds mad with celebration. We hugged strangers and sang together.

Sometime late in the evening, we found our way to an aŭtomato, lit by hundreds of lanterns, in a large open area in the elbow of the Southfork Aqueduct where it turned south out of the city. The aŭtomato was the size of a house, resting on treads that hadn't moved for a thousand years, and was made of metal losing the battle with time, eroding and flaking away. Someday it would be a pile of dust, and still, we'll gather and worship it. A large crowd had come together, and somewhere sounded the beat of drums with oud and pipes twirling around its rhythms. Somehow, Talia got me dancing.

After many songs, I had to take a break. I leaned against a tree, watching Talia twirl amongst the swaying mass of people. She had a lightness about her, as though gravity, too, leaned beside me, forgetting to hold her to the ground while it watched her dance.

So enrapt was I watching her move that I nearly missed the man with a knife coming to kill me. I saw a blur in my peripheral vision, a shape coming at me, lamplight glinting off a metallic surface. I dodged, more by instinct than design, but the blade slashed through my black shirt and sliced into the flesh of my chest with a scarlet flare of pain.

How many were attacking me? I called out to Talia, heard the screams of other revellers as my assailant and I stumbled into the crowd, dagger slashing. There only seemed to be one attacker. I didn't even see who it was—all I saw was the blade flashing. Without my kiraso, I am only human—human speed, human strength—and I stumbled, tripping over the feet of someone. My attacker dropped on me. I held the knife at bay, its point a hand's width from my chest, but he leveraged his entire weight over the blade, and slowly, my arms started giving way. I called out for Talia again.

A blow struck him, whipping his head to the side like a ball whipping around a tetherball pole, and he collapsed. Above him, Talia stood, a big rock in hand, the giant aŭtomato looming large behind her. "Aaron's dank breath, Kredo, what's all this?"

"I don't know. He came at me."

"Who is he?"

I turned the body over and looked at the face. I stepped back, shocked. How did it find me here? How in all the Founders' grace did it find me here? Had it been following me?

"Kredo?" Talia pressed.

"It's Elekti's father," I said, looking at its eyes reflecting the blackness of the night sky.

The answer struck Talia, knocked her back a step. Her eyes closed, the rock dropping from her hand. "Elekti? Didn't her dad escape into the borderlands?"

"Yeah."

"How do you know it's her—*its*—dad?"

I remembered it banging on the door of the falchilo barracks. Saw those same features in the body staring lifelessly at the stars above. "I met it before, in Vojo Fino, before we knew Elekti was a contaminant."

I placed my hand on her arm. "Thank you, Talia. You saved me. I was two heartbeats from dining with the Founders." I noticed the celebrations were still ongoing. No one gave us even the slightest attention amid the chaos of the night.

"Is he . . .?"

"You killed it," I said. *It.* Was Elekti's father an "it"? Stelara's Kodo was clear on what attacking a falchilo meant. "Only contaminants attack falchilo." Or heartbroken fathers. Contaminants nest. They send dark wanderers into the fields to infect anything in their path. They don't send out human-looking secondaries for targeted attacks against falchilo. They don't track their prey across the land and attack one specific individual in a crowd. At least they never used to. Still, if Elekti were infected, its whole household would be infected. That's how it worked. If.

"Only contaminants attack falchilo," Talia echoed. She stood, stunned, as though she'd woken from a dream.

"You okay?" I asked.

"Yeah, great." She kneeled beside the body. "Help me lift it. Let's get it back to the Tero Kreinto and cleanse it." She still seemed like she was walking in a haze.

"You sure you're okay?"

"Bloody yes, Kredo. It's . . ."

"What?"

"I don't know, I guess . . . shit, Kredo, you're bleeding," she said, pointing at my chest.

My shirt was torn and soaked with my blood. Looking under my shirt at the wound, I said, "It's okay," though I couldn't really see anything given the darkness of night. I was still standing and so figured it must not be that bad.

"Get your shirt off, and let me look at it." Without waiting, she yanked my shirt up. "Aw, blast, that's nasty. You're gonna need stitches, at least. You got to sit down."

I waved her off. "It's fine. I'll have the kuracisto stitch it up."

"Kredo, you've been cut."

"No, look, it's okay. It didn't cut anything important. I can get back to the Tero Kreinto. It'll be easier than you going there and bringing kuracisto back again."

She did not look convinced. "If you say so."

We carried the contaminant back to the Tero Kreinto for cleansing, one of its arms slung around each of our shoulders. My wound erupted in blazing pain. No one gave us a second glance, assuming, no doubt, we were taking a drunken companion home. At the hospital on Tero Kreinto grounds, Talia hovered nearby while a kuracisto stitched my gash under the illumination of a fluttering light bulb, and then she made sure he gave me a salve to prevent infection.

"Rub the ointment on the wound twice a day for a week, whether you think it needs it or not," Talia said, walking me back to my cell in the falchilo barracks.

"I heard the instructions," I said.

"Yeah, well, I know you ain't one for letting others tell you what to do."

She walked me to my quarters, hugged me hard enough to hurt my wound, and then she left without a word. I wanted to tell her to lay off the drink tonight, but she rushed down the hall almost at a run and was around a corner before the words made their way from my heart to my mouth.

My wound ached, and I tentatively touched it, wincing in pain as I did. Tonight would be an uncomfortable night's sleep. I eased myself onto my bed and stared at the ceiling, gingerly running my fingers along the bandages on my chest.

Only contaminants—and heartbroken fathers—attack falchilo.

FOURTEEN

THE CROWD FILLED the courtyard and spilled into the streets beyond the Tero Kreinto complex like a pot boiling over or a river surging over its banks and spilling out onto the plains beyond, the type of crowd only Rendezvous can attract. It seemed all the city, and a good bit of Duatero besides, was trying to crowd around Firstsite's Tero Kreinto. It was a beautiful summer morning: crisp air, bright sun peering over buildings. People thronged the surrounding gardens, keeping to the paths, careful not to trample bushes and plants, yet shoulder to shoulder, front to back.

The ointment the kuracisto gave me to daub on my wound dulled the pain to a slight tingling underneath my formal clothes. In addition to the discomfort, I was tired. Dreams of little Elekti crying kept waking me. Bad dreams are the lot of most falchilo. Despite these bothers, I stood with the grin of a child witnessing a carnival for the first time.

"You seem in good spirits," Mihaelo said, standing beside me.

"Few are the sights that can rival this." I cast my hand out across the ocean of my people standing before us. Jak, Talia, and I stood as honoured luminaries among the platform party on the patio at the top of the stairs leading into the Hall of Donna. From our vantage point, we could see the crowd extending far back to Dorian's Gate and into the city beyond. Only the highest-ranking members of the Tero Kreinto stood on the patio beside us.

Jak echoed my thoughts, nodding toward the pavilion at the base of the stairs where the royal rulers of the five Founder cities sat, three men, two women, all dressed in gaudy gowns and finery. "The kronoj do not join us on the platform?"

Mihaelo adjusted his weight on his cane as he leaned in and smiled faintly. "Celebrations such as this are a good reminder to them of their place."

"So, how'd we score a spot up here?" Talia asked. Dark shadows lay under her eyes, her hair was a bit unkempt, and I swear I smelled stale beer on her breath.

Before anyone could reply, the air was sundered as the bell tower to the north began ringing. A cheer rose from the people in the courtyard and along the cramped roads and alleys throughout Firstsite. As one, from the foot of the Tero Kreinto to the trampled grounds of the pilgrim's tent-village in the fields beyond and in cities, towns, and villages across Duatero, our cheers rose to the sky, loud enough that any emissaries approaching from Earth, should they be on their way, could hear our joy.

Drummers, hundreds of them lining the levels of the Tero Kreinto and positioned in the crowd throughout the city, began a slow, rhythmic beat, a pulse pumping energy through a lost colony of humanity. Reed pipes began playing, wrapping their melody around the drums' rhythm, people began to clap and stomp their feet in time. Today was a good day, an auspicious day. It was Rendezvous.

Behind us, the Hall of Donna's wide doors opened, and the crowd went into a frenzied madness, my voice and stomping feet adding to the pandemonium. Through these doors, Maraja Ravida III, Unua Paisajista, head of all Tero Kreinto, our leader, the Voice of the Founders, stepped forward. Whereas the kronoj at the foot of the stairs dressed in elaborate costumes, the Unua wore a simple white robe, cinched at the waist with a golden belt with a golden sash draped off her shoulder. This close, I could see the lines time had etched onto her face: the crease of a brow furrowed too often, lines of laughter crinkling her eyes. Hair, as white as her robes, was bound in a knot, secured with a golden net. In her right hand, she held Aaron's FTL Vergo. This was a staff on the head of which was affixed the Vergo—the real Vergo, not a replica—a cylinder about the length of a forearm with seven finger-sized prongs on its end.

The Unua wasted no time and began clapping, keeping the rhythm of the drums, her body gently swaying, the length of her robes swishing around her ankles. She began to sing, and the voices of all those surrounding the Tero Kreinto, all those throughout Firstsite—throughout Duatero, no doubt—joined her. Talia slung her arm around mine and Jak's shoulders. Beside me, Mihaelo sang, and my voice joined in too.

It was an old song, one of the oldest: *Fino Kunveno*—Final Reunion. It told of the power held by the people of Earth, the ability to cross the gulfs between stars. From this cradle, the Founders sprang and came to Duatero. For thirty-five Rendezvous, each one nine years after the previous, Founder ships came to Duatero with supplies, new colonists, and word from the homeworld. Cities grew, and the Tero Kreinto churned native soil into something more divine to grow our food.

During the thirty-sixth Rendezvous, the Founder ships did not appear. They have never appeared since. No one knows why.

The song ended, but in the courtyard, throughout the city, and across our land, drums went on, feet stamped the ground, hands clapped in time. Duatero's heart beat still. We remained. Hear us, Malamiko, and rage at your failure; hear us, Founders, and take pride in your children's strength.

We are lost. Abandoned. But every nine years, we have hope. Perhaps tonight would be the Rendezvous of Reunion, and new supplies would arrive, new technologies, materials, and skills long lost. Perhaps with new parts, we could repair the Tero Kreinto, and they would return to life, creating fresh soil so that we might push Malamiko back. Perhaps. I didn't think anyone really believed it would happen. But, perhaps, just perhaps, tonight was the night. Doubt was for tomorrow; today was for hope.

The Unua raised her hands, and a wave of silence washed over the crowd. She turned, and she looked at me—the Unua, looking at me! She called out in a voice that carried over the heads of the people gathered in the courtyard. "Majstro Falchilo Kredo, step forward."

This promised to be awkward. I stepped forward. The Unua turned to the crowd. "Malamiko attacked our southern border with one of the largest nests we have ever seen. It contaminated mothers and fathers! It contaminated our children! It destroyed our crops, and it forced us to Cull!" She hung her head a moment, and an icy stillness hung in the air. "We sent our greatest falchilo, Majstro Kredo, the hero of Eta Monteto, to do battle with the Enemy. The battle was long and hard, and many fine falchilo died." I thought of Esper standing up to Jak, defying me, almost killing Talia. "But the Founders smile on us. This is a special Rendezvous—more special than most—for not more than a few days ago, Majstro Kredo, with his falchilo, cleansed the last nest, bringing peace and safety to our southern border!" I rubbed the wound on my chest, wondering if that was true.

The mass of people erupted in wild cheers, stamping their feet and clapping their hands. Not knowing what else to do, I raised my hand, waved at them, then swung my hand to include Talia and Jak. Jak was basking in the roar of the crowd, fists overhead. Talia seemed as awkward as I felt, forcing a smile and waving.

The Unua stepped down the stairs, and the sea of people parted before her. The platform party, including myself, followed. Behind us, the kronoj stepped in line, followed by the rest of the crowd. Over the next hour, the Unua led her people down the well-worn stone road of Spero's Way and out onto the fields east of the city where the path leading to the Landing began. There she waited for Firstsite to empty, its people crowding the plains. Music played. People laughed, held hands, hugged. Bells from every pagoda rang. Tonight could be the night. A breeze blew, bringing change. You could feel it. The world knew tonight would be the night the Founders return. Reunion.

Attendants brought collapsible chairs for Kapo Mihaelo and me. Jak stretched out on the ground, basking in the warm sun, while Talia sat beside him, hugging knees to chest. The kapo massaged his thigh and nodded toward a nearby pavilion where the kronoj rested. "Their body language speaks volumes, doesn't it?"

"I don't get your meaning," I said.

"The fellow there on the left," he said, indicating a balding man in his thirties with jet black beard immaculately maintained. "That's Omaro Adamido VI, krono of Lan Hu. The woman with him is Ina Helenida, krono of Xuanhe." The woman was young, late twenties, with dark skin, hair, and eyes.

"Lan Hu and Xuanhe, always scheming," Jak said.

"What's Xuanhe gonna do?" Talia said, staring at the ground. "Lan Hu's got Xuanhe completely blocked in. If Xuanhe wants to trade anything, it's gotta go through Lan Hu before it gets anywhere else." Jak grunted dismissively.

Mihaelo pointed. "On the far side of the pavilion, far away as possible while remaining in the pavilion's shade, is Tatjiana of Aaronsburg with Cezaro of Shihbei—Tatjiana seeks Shihbei's assistance against Lan Hu. And between both groups, studiously alone with his retainers, is Dimitro of Lu Guang, ready to profit selling iron and lumber to either side. The lines of war take shape."

"You figure there'll still be war?" I asked. "Even after our success in Vojo Fino?"

"Absolutely," Mihaelo answered. "Our crops are still failing. Thanks to the Cull, we'll be able to support the people we have through to next year. But after that . . ." His words struck me in the gut.

Jak sat upright. "Even after cleansing a stage five nest?" he asked.

"Yes," Mihaelo said. "The Unua maintains the opinion war will distract the kronoj, allowing us to continue our work."

Still. Even now, I had failed. What killed my mother still attacked, hidden, walking among us.

"I understand a contaminant from Vojo Fino attacked you here last night," Mihaelo said, fixing me with a hard stare. I nodded. How did he know? I hadn't time to submit a report yet. "And you were wounded?"

Ah, the kuracisto must have told him. "It cut me with a knife. Nothing significant. All I needed were some stitches and ointment that smells like rotting leaves."

He nodded his head thoughtfully, and I caught his eyes darting to my chest. "That is unusual behaviour for a contaminant," he said. "Unprecedented. Something is happening to Duatero, something we've never faced before. The Unua has ordered that we focus all the resources of the Tero Kreinto on solving this. Nothing has a higher priority. Whatever you need, anything, it's at your disposal. Do what you have to do to fix this. Whatever action you need to take, you have my blessing."

All the resources of the Tero Kreinto, what good were they, what good were ten times those resources when I hadn't a clue what I needed, when I didn't even understand what I was fighting anymore?

Nodding my head again, I said, "*Mia korpo estas via shildo.*"

He smiled a thin smile. "*Tiel estu.* Ah, good, look. The festivities are about to continue." The Unua climbed upon a wooden platform and began a sermon, after which she led us to the Landing. There, a cyclopean stone pathway laid in the manner of a labyrinth took up nearly fifty-two hectares of what was otherwise prime farmland. In the centre of the labyrinth, the Landing itself rose to the sky, giant tapestries filled with imagery of the Founders hanging from its walls. Following the Unua's lead, the populace of Firstsite entered and made its way along the labyrinth, drawing ever closer to the Landing.

Mihaelo's leg caused him to lag, and Talia slowed her pace to keep him company while I walked ahead. The march through the labyrinth took most of the day, and the sun was setting behind the silhouette of Firstsite by the time we made it to the Landing.

I remembered a winter's night from years ago. I was still living at home, a child, and it was Dongzhi Festival—the winter solstice. We sat by a fire, huddled together for warmth, and my father told us the story of the Landing, of how Founder ships would set down there. He sat on a stool, Gaja, Fondo, and me sitting on thick blankets on the ground as he told us how back in the time of the Classic Kronoj, Venka the Ironheart had built the walls encircling it, walls that had stood for thousands of years, carefully maintained, occasionally added to by other kronoj seeking glory, or seeking favour from the Tero Kreinto. My father told me that all kronoj who had paid for its upkeep and built new additions had their name inscribed on the inside of the wall, right where the Founders could read them when they returned. I had never set foot on the fields within the walls to see if this was true—those fields were holy, and only paisajista attaining the rank of altaj, or the Unua herself, may lay foot on that holy ground.

As the sun set, lanterns came out to shoo the darkness back. It was a clear night, and a river of stars shone overhead. I scanned the sky for the constellation of Aaron's Cross, spotted Terosuno—Earth's sun. I remembered another night under the stars, Esper sitting by my side telling me of the miracle of the seed, the gate through which life entered the universe, and my heart ached. I had liked her. Smart, able to quickly read a situation, willing to act—she had had such potential.

Scattered throughout the masses of people, drummers and reed pipers played slow, reverent tones. The Unua led us up a set of stairs wrapped around the Landing's wall, leading up past banners inscribed with the symbols of Founders—the Eye of Xinhua, Donna's spiral, and Aaron's Vergo dominated. A soft, warm breeze set them to fluttering. The platform party and other senior members of the Tero Kreinto followed the

Unua, then the kronoj and their retainers, and then as many people as the ramparts could hold. The rest would watch the ceremony from the ground.

Lights—actual lights!—illuminated the interior of the Landing. These lights, built by artisans from Xuanhe and powered by a nearby dam, lit the five aŭtomato scattered across the field of stone, and I gave a silent prayer of thanks to Founder Jinjing for their illumination so I could witness the wonders within this sacred space. On the eastern side of the Landing, a series of lights lit the Spero Temple. On the fields outside the Landing, a sea of lanterns held by masses of people slowly drifting through the labyrinth dominated the plain. Time ceased its forward march as we grasped for a moment, grasped for that infinity between falling grains of sand. The night deepened; stars brightened. Tonight would be the night. The Founders couldn't abandon us forever.

The Unua led us along the worn stone of the ramparts, taking us to the Tower—a structure rising high above the plains on the northeast portion of the wall. The Tower and Spero Temple were some of the first structures built on Duatero, predating the wall by nearly a thousand years. The second set of stairs led from the ramparts up to the top of the Tower, and at the base of the stairs sat a giant bronze gong. This is where the Unua stopped, and we filed in behind her. We waited as the ramparts filled and music played. At some signal known only to the Unua, she picked up the hammer and crashed it into the gong, sending a reverberating peal splashing across the field.

Silence. The music stopped. Conversation stopped. Only a gentle breeze whispered. The Founders were almost here. Mihaelo, along with the sanministro, head of the kuracisto order, escorted the Unua up the stairs to the Tower. I winced, watching Mihaelo struggle with his leg. His thigh must be raging in pain after such a long walk. But this was Rendezvous. If ever there was a time to drive through pain to do what your duty demanded, this was it.

At the top of the tower, the three leaders of the Tero Kreinto lit the signal fire, and in moments its raging tendrils of flame and smoke danced into the sky, visible, no doubt, from Firstsite's walls and from the heavens above to guide any incoming ships to us. I couldn't see from my angle but knew the Unua would now be entering the very Tower itself, alone, while the kapo and sanministro stood sentinel by the signal fire. The crackle and pop of burning wood carried on the breeze.

We waited. I could feel the pressure of the spirit world, so close to us now, pressing around us. My mother was here, my father, lost brothers and sisters: they stood by my side, embracing me. An entire people, living and passed, waited in silence, breath held. Tonight would be the night; you could already feel the Founders among us. The signal fire burned, its flames beginning to slacken.

Was this taking longer than usual? It seemed that it was. Perhaps, even now, the Unua was speaking with the Founders. The crowd's eyes turned upwards, looking for the telltale ripples of light in the night sky the legends said signified the Founders' return. Had something happened? Gentle murmurs began to rise. Was that a ripple in the heavens or smoke obscuring the stars?

Movement on the tower, shadows moving in front of the dying signal fire, drew a gasp from the crowd. I strained to see what was happening, looked to the sky for the lights. From the tower's top, another gong sounded, its peal racing across the plains. As one, every voice, my own added to the ritual chorus, asked, screaming, "Have the Founders returned?"

A giant lid slammed shut on the signal fire with a resounding clang that shattered the night, snuffing the flames, plunging the top of the tower in darkness. I lowered my head and closed my eyes. Not tonight. Our problems were still ours to solve. Throughout the plains, every man, woman, and child responded in a whisper, giving voice to the gentle breeze. *"Tiel estu."*

I pulled the sky lantern out of the pack I bought with Talia yesterday. Beside me, Talia and Jak did the same, as did thousands of others across the Landing. I lit a long wick from the flame of a nearby lamp and used it to ignite the fuel cell of my sky lantern. It smouldered, a slow burn, its light dim and orange, and I held the body of my sky lantern over it. The fuel cell's heat rose, causing the structure to inflate, its light filling the expanding orb, a firefly awakening. In the crowds below, lanterns began to float skyward, glowing, flickering balls rising slowly, lazily, as though they knew there was no rush, as though they knew the sky would always be there for them as we released our hopes and dreams, our worries and our fears, up, up into night's blanket.

Even the kronoj of our great Founder cities had their own lanterns, gently rising away from their outstretched hands. I wondered for a moment what prayers they painted on their sky lanterns, but my own lantern interrupted my thoughts as it began to rise. It turned as it floated away, and the prayer I wrote on its side, the same prayer I wrote nine years ago during last Rendezvous, came into view. Last Rendezvous, I sent this prayer to my father. This one was for my mother. Two words: "forgive me."

It joined thousands of rising lanterns, a slow-moving river of lights flowing away from the Landing, lifting high to where the clouds looked down on us, to be picked up by the wind where they would travel far across the land. Perhaps some would travel far enough to make their way to the Founders, and some of our prayers would be answered.

THE NEXT MORNING, a violent hammering on the door of my cell woke me, the mid-morning sun cutting through the shutters of my window. "What? Yes?" I said, bleary-eyed and groggy, throwing back the blankets. The door swung open before I could get up, and Mihaelo entered, hobbling on his cane. He still wore his sleeping gown, and black and white whiskers clung to his cheeks and chin. I shot to my feet. "What is it, Kapo?"

"There was a quarantine breach last night. Esper—it's escaped."

FIFTEEN

"HOW?" was the only word I could force out my mouth. People don't escape quarantine.

"She had help," Mihaelo said. "Get suited up. We're going to check its cell." He looked down, realizing for the first time he was still in his sleeping gown. "Meet me at the quarantine entrance in ten minutes," and he was gone. I got Jak up the same way Mihaelo had awoken me and sent him after Talia.

Minutes later, we gathered in a grey, windowless room in the basement of the falchilo barracks, each of us, including Mihaelo, clad in our kiraso. I couldn't remember the last time I saw Mihaelo in the kapo's kiraso. It was spectacular. Named after Patrol Trooper Liang Qiu, it had arrived on the Founder Ship *Pixiu*, and the ship's emblem of a winged lion with two horns was engraved on its breastplate. It was the oldest functioning kiraso on Duatero and completely unique: the shoulders were more pronounced, the helmet had sharper angles framing the face, and the colour was dark grey rather than the black of more common kiraso.

Before us stood a heavy door of steel. Flickering lights cast the room in dancing shadows, and I touched a bulb, giving a quick prayer to Founder Jinjing.

"Aaron's dank breath, what's this I hear about Esper escaping?" Talia asked.

Mihaelo cleared his throat. "Come with me." He turned away and led us through the steel door. We followed him down stairs of grey stone lit by sputtering lights and then along a hallway to the quarantine cells.

"There are not many who know of its escape," Mihaelo said. "You'll keep it that way. Only myself, the Unua, and the Majstro Falchilo of the guard who found the facility abandoned. And now, you three."

We approached a polycrysteel passthrough window, revealing a grey room beyond. Mihaelo led us into the cell, and our helmets enveloped our heads as we entered. It contained nothing but grey walls, a mattress, a blanket, and a narrow hole in the floor for prisoners to piss and crap into. Where will you run to, Esper? Where should I start looking? "You told me it had help escaping. Who?" I asked.

Mihaelo sighed. "Its guards last night. They were falchilo, every one. While we were celebrating Rendezvous, members of our own order helped it escape. This the Unua doesn't know yet. I'll tell her once we learn more about what happened."

Talia whistled, and I stood mute like a fool. "Were the guards contaminated?" I finally managed to ask.

"We must assume so," Mihaelo said. We stared at him, stunned. Had contamination pierced the heart of the Tero Kreinto? "Without the GC, who to trust is a bit of a guessing game," he said. "But I trust you, Kredo. You suspected Esper's contamination and brought it in. Find it. Cleanse it. We must remove this cancer before it spreads. Now more than ever, the falchilo must be merciless against

Malamiko—we must show we have control over this threat."

"Yes, of course."

Jak crossed his arms, and Talia, hands on hips, looked at the floor. "We'll need access to its cell. Full records of its activities while under quarantine and profiles of the missing guards. We'll start at once."

Mihaelo assured us we'd have full access to all the Tero Kreinto's records and left us to plan our investigation.

"Come on, Kredo, you don't think Esper's contaminated, along with all the bloody guards," Talia said once Mihaelo had left.

"What falchilo would free a contaminant?" I asked.

"A *likely* contaminant," she retorted.

"It attacked you. It could have killed you."

"She was protecting that girl. You know she's got a soft spot for kids."

"That '*girl*' was a contaminant."

"I don't think Esper agreed."

"Stelara's Kodo is clear. Attack a falchilo, assist a contaminant, and you're—"

"I know, I know. A 'likely contaminant.'"

"Esper went to Malamiko Island with her helmet down. I had my doubts about her contamination, too. But now this? What falchilo—what *human*—would attack a falchilo to free a contaminant? What human would break that 'likely' contaminant out of quarantine?"

"I don't know! But do you think contaminants have sleeper agents sitting in our Tero Kreinto waiting to pull a prison break? That's not how the contamination acts."

"We don't know how the contamination acts anymore."

She paced back and forth, then stopped, head down. Beyond her, the hallway stretched, lights fluttering and gasping for life, battling the darkness. Esper escaped down that hall, fading into those jerking shadows that buzzed and crackled with each flicker. "This has got us jumping at the wind. How many people are we gonna cleanse?" she asked.

"We're not going to cleanse any *people*. What's gotten into you?"

She looked at me, frowning, dark rings under her eyes. "I'm tired," she said. "It's been a hard couple of weeks."

Jak decided to stoke the fire. "You can always sit this one out."

Talia tensed, a spring ready to pop. "You ain't near man enough to start messing with me." Her words were a wolf's warning growl.

"Just trying to help," Jak said.

"Enough," I said. "Esper had the makings of a great falchilo. Not a good one—a great one. We're going to find it and figure out what's happening. We're not going to let Malamiko make a mockery of what she was." *I'm not going to let Malamiko drive us to another Cull.* "You're either going to help me, Talia, or you *are* going to sit this one out. Which is it?"

She did not answer right away, turned her back, and stared down the hall a moment. Was she going to leave me? Did she really carry so much doubt and guilt? Her shoulders slumped, then shrugged. "I'm with you. Where else would I be?"

<hr>

SOMEONE HAD GIVEN Esper a reader connected to the manlibroj. A reader! I sent Jak to find out which guards were so charitable with our Founder artifacts, believing Jak would adequately express my displeasure on my behalf.

He met me in an office Mihaelo had given us to conduct our investigation. "The reader was signed out by Falchilo Herina," Jak said.

"Where is she?" I asked.

"Gone. She was one of two guards missing the night Esper escaped."

"What do you know of Herina?"

"She transferred to Firstsite this past winter, along with the other missing guard, Serchanto."

I rubbed the heel of my palm in my eye, asked, "Where'd they transfer from?"

"No one knows," Jak said. "There's no record of them before they arrived. The names are probably fake."

"A majstro falchilo would have signed their transfer."

"Their transfer papers are missing."

I sat back, my chair creaking, wondering if they had help from someone still here or if they were working alone and had managed to steal their transfer papers from records before they left. "Speak with the other falchilo. If they were here since winter, others would know them."

Jak left to carry out his instructions. I suited up in my kiraso and made my way to the quarantine level and into Esper's cell. The reader was still on the mattress. Sitting down, I powered it on and scrolled through its history. What does a contaminant waiting for cleansing—or planning escape—read?

Improved biomass productivity of X^{kd} transgenic COE wheat.

Influence of the time emergence of blue-leaf weeds on yield loss of barley and rye.

Methods to determine nitrate and nitrite levels in water and soil extracts.

· · ·

FOUNDER'S GRACE, who reads this stuff? I imagined the body of Esper sitting on the mattress, reader propped on its knees, hungrily devouring the manlibroj's library.

Leaning back against the wall, I made myself comfortable and began to read.

"PORT DONNA?" Talia asked with a look of startled confusion.

"Port Donna," I said, leaning back in my chair in our office—it was padded, comfortable, but that creak annoyed me. "That's where Esper's going."

"Burn that. I thought Port Donna was at the bottom of the Nanhai Ocean," Jak said.

"Port Donna didn't sink," I said. "A tidal wave struck, destroying it. The next year was the year without summer, and then the Black Cull the two years following. It was years before anyone got around to mounting a return to Port Donna, and by then, Malamiko had reclaimed its lands, repelling would-be explorers. It's been lost ever since."

"What makes you think it's heading there?" Talia asked.

I motioned her and Jak around the reader and began scrolling through Esper's reading list.

Talia scanned through some of the papers Esper had read. "Was the woman studying for a bloody exam?"

"I think it was looking for ways to destroy our crops. Look at these reports marked in red," I said, running my hand down the list of reports. Easily two-thirds of them were red. "These are references it couldn't access."

"Why not?" Talia asked.

"Because they're on disc at Port Donna," I said. "The

paisajista of Port Donna were producing a huge amount of research and weren't able to upload it all to the manlibroj before the city fell. All that work was lost when the sea rose to claim the city, leaving us with only dead links."

Talia leaned back, arms crossed, and said, "Growing up in Xuanhe you'd hear stories of barges getting caught in the river's tides and getting pulled too far down the Okcidento, right to the mouth where it spills into the Nanhai. They'd come back with tales of ruins seen through the blue brush of Malamiko, still echoing with the cries of the city's spirits."

"So, you can get there by boat from Xuanhe?" I asked.

"If you believe the tales of barge sailors," Talia said. "Most of 'em would say anything if they thought it'd get them laid."

"If Port Donna's Tero Kreinto survived, those discs would still be there," Jak said.

"Exactly," I said, laying the reader down on my desk. "And the Tero Kreinto were built by the Founders, and if anything could survive the destruction of the city, it would be Founder buildings." Hadn't Esper once made the same argument to me? Even when human, Port Donna called to her.

Talia frowned. "Do you think Esper would risk travelling so far into the blue?"

"It's a contaminant. What's it got to fear from the blue?" Jak said.

Talia scowled but kept quiet.

"Regardless," I said, "Port Donna's our only lead. That's where we're heading."

SIXTEEN

I TURNED BACK to the river barge captain we were speaking to. "So, you've never seen the ruins of Port Donna. You're sure."

"No, Majstro, only a fuckin' fool would let their boat slip that far into the blue."

My head ached. The noise, the abuse of the language the Founders gave us, the dead ends, they were tying the muscles in my neck and back into knots. The healing wound on my chest itched. We stood on the Founders' Quay in the southern city of Xuanhe. The sweltering heat smothered us like a warm, wet blanket you couldn't escape, and the stench of the docks—fresh fish and kelp harvested from the farms mixed with the body odour of a hundred dock hands—seemed almost a tangible thing, suspended in the thick air like a foul molasses you couldn't clear out of your nostrils. Around us, a cacophony of sounds roared in a continual eruption: the clatter of wood slamming on wooden decks, the lap of water slapping into the wall of the quay, the hollow thud of heavy objects dropping onto decks of river barges, and above it all, droning like the buzz of a hundred beehives, a ceaseless stream of curses escaping the lips of the men and women earning their living along the docks.

Jak stepped forward. "Watch your tongue. You're speaking to a majstro."

The sailor bowed his head, "Pardon my language, Majstro."

The thermoregulators of our kiraso protected us from the heat—sort of—but with the helmet down, sweat still slicked my hair. Several docks over, soldiers dressed in the colours of Xuanhe marched aboard ferries for transport across the Okcidento River. Almost as soon as Rendezvous ended, Aaronsburg declared war on Lan Hu, as did Shihbei far to the north a day after. Xuanhe, ever the faithful ally to once-great Lan Hu, declared war right back. And all the merchants in eastern Lu Guang rubbed their hands together and prepared to sell lumber and iron to whichever side (or sides) had the allotment chips to afford their prices. With the summer half over, it'd be a short fighting season before the Tero Kreinto called the people back to tend harvest, all but guaranteeing the war would drag out to next year.

The barge captain must have found my silence unsettling, and a need to fill it overcame him. "You ain't the first falchilo to be asking about this," he said. "Three others came the other day."

Several other dockhands I'd spoken to had told me much the same. I repeated the description I'd been given from others: "A man—a majstro with dark skin and hair, almond-shaped eyes with two women?"

"Yeah, that's about right. You know 'em?"

From the descriptions I'd been given so far, one of those women was Esper, but the other two were a mystery. "I have a message for them. Do you know where I can find them?"

"No idea. The Tero Kreinto, probably."

They were not at Xuanhe's Tero Kreinto. I'd already checked. "Do you know if they managed to book passage to the mouth of the river?"

"I don't know, Majstro. I wish I could be of more help."

Thanking the barge captain for his time, I let him get back to his duties.

"You're letting him go?" Jak asked. "The last dockhand was certain this captain had been to the ruins."

"Yes, I'm letting him go." I wiped the sweat from my brow with the back of my hand, but it was clad in the kiraso's glove and was not absorbent. "You think we'd have any better luck than we've had with the half-dozen other captains we've talked to? They're afraid we'll label them a contaminant for venturing so far into the blue."

"Or," Talia interrupted, "maybe they're afraid they'd earn the reputation of a lousy captain, unable to control their barge among the current and swells of the Okcidento. Bad for business if that rep gets about." I turned to look at her. She'd been silent through most of our investigation. Her short dark hair was matted to her face, and she had a sly smile that I knew meant she was about to give me grief. "You frustrated enough you're open to some advice?" she asked.

"You got something to say?" I asked in reply.

"You're going about this all wrong," she said. "If you were a people person, you'd know this already."

"I suppose you know the right way?"

"Yeah, I do." She took Jak and me by the shoulder, leading us off the quays toward the walls of Xuanhe. "Why don't you guys find a temple to pray at or something. Maybe snoop around, see if you can figure out where Esper or those other dark falchilo have been hiding. Give me some time, and I'll find someone to take us to Port Donna."

"You got family around here, don't you?" I asked.

"An uncle and aunt, and a handful of cousins."

"Think maybe you'll get a chance to see them?"

"Since when did you become so concerned about family?" she asked. "Go be bland somewhere. I'll let you know when I've found passage."

Jak and I left to search the city. Xuanhe had five inns, and Jak and I visited all of them before nightfall, trying to find Esper and her dark falchilo. The Lamb's Head Inn, a block northeast from the Night Market and its flickering lights, had guests matching their description, but they'd left the day before.

As for Talia, apparently, the "right" way to find passage to Port Donna's ruins involved hitting the taverns and getting hammered. She woke me the next morning before dawn by beating on my door. Groggy and disoriented, I lit a candle and opened it. She leaned drunkenly on the door frame with a smug smile plastered on her flushed and sweaty face. "You up?" she asked, carefully enunciating each word, though it still came out a slurred mess.

"What is it?"

"Heard you're looking to book passage to Port Donna." She swayed and slipped off the door frame, stumbling to catch her balance. She began to giggle.

"You found someone to take us?"

She nodded, eyes wide. "I did. Her name's Dezi. Says to meet her at dock twenty-three tomorrow. It's important you remember that," she said, stabbing her finger into my shoulder, "because I might not."

"Good hunting, Talia," I said. "Catch some sleep. We'll go to see her first thing this morning."

Talia's body jolted with a deep, resonant hiccup. "Oh, I don't think Dezi'll be up and about first thing."

As night turned to day, the sweltering heat and humidity blossomed into a deluge of wind and rain. A little after noon, Talia led us down dock twenty-three to meet the barge captain who had agreed to take us to the mouth of the Okcidento River where the ruins of Port Donna lay. I found myself having to watch my footing on the slick wood of the docks as the rain pelted me. "Is that her?" I asked, pointing to a woman making repairs on a barge.

"Yep," Talia said. Her hair hung in damp strands around her face. She was pale as a skeleton, except for the rings under her eyes, which were black as coal.

The wooden boat was banged up and patched in several areas. The captain, her hair long and grey, hanging limply and wet around her face, looked in about as good condition as her boat. "Where'd you dig her up?" I asked.

"We got kicked out of the same bar," Talia said with a wink. Dezi saw us approach and stood to greet us.

"Falchilo Talia tells me you've seen the ruins of Port Donna," I said.

Dezi nodded. "And she told me you'd pay me to take you there."

"The Tero Kreinto will reimburse you for your time and effort," I said.

"Good, good. Storms like this blow in off the Nanhai all the time. Safer to wait 'til it blows over."

"How long do you think that will take?"

"Maybe a week."

"We're not waiting."

"Sure, sure. So, the Tero Kreinto'll reimburse hazard pay, too, then?"

Jak stepped up right into her face. "Serving the Tero Kreinto is all the payment you need. You're speaking to Majstro Falchilo Kredo, the hero of Eta Monteto and Vojo

Fino, and we're the only reason your city's not being overrun by sentinels and dark wanderers."

"Easy, Jak," I said with enough of an edge to shut him down. To Dezi, I said, "Your service to Duatero will be properly compensated. I want to leave as soon as possible."

"Sure, sure," she said. "The sooner this is over, the happier we'll all be. We'll leave when I finish fixing my boat."

We left the next morning. The rain stopped, replaced with suffocating heat and unsettled skies. "Too rough, too rough," she told me. "The winds are still too rough to risk heading down the Okcidento. And those clouds got more rain in 'em," Dezi said, but I forced her to begin our journey. Esper had a head start on us. Risk or no, it was time to hunt.

The barge pulled away from the Founder's Quay early morning and began floating down the waters of the Okcidento carried by the tide, our progress slowed by stiff headwinds. Dezi had told us to plan for a one- to two-day trip to Port Donna's ruins, and as many days back, depending on tides, winds, and shoals, plus however long we explored the ruins. We had supplies for a week, and I found myself worrying we may be short as the wind blew into us, pushing us back while the tide pulled us forward.

I stood on deck and watched Xuanhe slowly pass by. The quay went on for kilometres, filled with a seemingly unending supply of boats and sailors. The giant red-tiled dome of Xuanhe's Tero Kreinto peaked above the city's spalling walls, catching the morning sun. Ferries went back and forth across the river, and many boats, sails unfurled, moved upstream to trade with northern ports of call. Dezi and her crew navigated us through the thick river traffic, not with great skill, mind you, as we thumped into more than one barge while making our way. With each collision, Dezi's crew would line the railing, and the other barge's crew would line theirs, and they'd hurl curses at each other.

By late morning, the quays transitioned to undeveloped waterfront as we passed the boundaries of the city into the lands beyond. Thick boat traffic made its way up and down the river, and I could see the fences of kelp and fish farms poking out of the water. The fields beyond contained orchards of apples, pears, and figs. Mihaelo had told me our crops still suffered, and I could see the truth of his words. Sparse clusters of leaves lined the branches, many of the leaves already brown, though autumn was months away. As those sick orchards drifted by at the pace of the river's current, I wondered how many years we had before we had to Cull again.

Talia leaned on the railing, watching the men and women mucking around the kelp farms, waist-deep in water, while Jak sat on the deck, back against the railing, arms folded over his stomach. The sun set with us still in the lands of Duatero. Dezi dropped anchor, and we slept on deck, under skies buried by thick layers of clouds that did nothing to cool the thick, humid heat. As dawn brightened the sky from black to grey, we continued our journey. The river curved south, and we left the lands of humanity behind. River traffic faded until we were alone. Brambles of blue vines choked dead and dying fruit trees, and I could see orange and blue reeds clinging to the river's bottom along the banks. Dezi spent her day on the prow of the barge with a long pole she used to test the river's depth and to help navigate the barge around deadheads and sand spits hiding beneath the river's surface.

Jak, Talia, and I engaged the helmets of our kiraso. We were in Malamiko lands. Dezi and her crew had no such protection, but I figured if we stayed away from the shores, they should be safe. Still, it was a risk. The sooner this was over, the better.

By mid-morning of the second day, the skies opened, releasing a waterfall of rain, as though a giant grey bladder holding an ocean of warm water above us had been cut. The river turned south, and a fierce wind struck us, slowing our advance to a crawl. Dezi was at the front of the barge with a pole, trying to navigate the barge around a sand spit as the wind tossed the boat. She yelled at her crew, and they set to with oars and poles to keep the barge from running aground.

"We need to go back," she said to me once she got the barge into the flow of the river again, her hair and clothes plastered to her thin body like damp rags hung over a broom- stick. "I can't steer the boat in this wind, and the water's muddy, so I can't see shit."

"You're speaking to a falchilo. Mind your tongue," I said.

"Don't matter who I'm speaking to, I can't see what's under the water's surface, and I can't control the boat. We need to wait for the weather to settle."

"We wait for nothing! We're almost there; we're not turning back."

Dezi mumbled words I couldn't make out and returned to the chore of navigating her barge. I couldn't fault her for her nervousness—the world around us was wholly alien, enough to set anyone on edge. Thick walls of blue foliage lined either bank, dipped into the current, and it seemed to me this dense jungle breathed, swelling to and fro with the wind. Strange branches of foliage—not trees, but rather long orange stalks with blue fronds—bent over the water as though reaching out to pluck us off the boat with grotesque hands. The wind made a strange sound here, as though some creature roared behind the gale.

The river turned east again, the current picked up, and

our boat began racing. We made great time, though our speed bothered Dezi. "I can't test the river depth at this speed," she complained. "We could crack our hull against a sand spit or deadhead, and I'd never see it coming." I ignored her. We had to press on. I was done with waiting.

We came around a bend. "Will you look at that," Talia said, pointing ahead. Not even a kilometre in front of us, the river widened into a vast expanse of water, tips of white dotting the waves. This was the source of the roar: endless waves crashing on the surf. The Nanhai Ocean. I had never seen such a thing. I doubt any of us had. There sat no obstructions to mar our sight, no hill, no copse of trees, no island of rock, just a plain of waves reaching to the ends of the world. That gulf was the world, I a pebble.

I found the thought of this tiny barge alone in that vast expanse, merely a mote in the sea, terrifying. This ocean wounded us—it destroyed Port Donna. What hope would our tiny boat stand if not even a Founder city could survive the ocean's wrath? Surely the waves would dash us to pieces. How deep was the water beneath that surface? Could the mind even comprehend such depths?

Dezi seemed to share my fear. "Drop anchor!" she yelled to her crew as the current pulled us toward that tremendous expanse like a magnet pulling iron. She cursed and yelled as her crew dropped the anchor. We waited, my gut in knots, for our boat to slow and stop. The river's mouth where the Okcidento spewed into the Nanhai drew nearer. The anchor finally caught on something on the river's bottom, and the rope snapped taut, tugging the boat to a stop.

"Xinhua's eyes, Kredo, have you ever seen such a thing?" Talia asked, giddy as a child.

"Never." To the residents of Port Donna, the site of the ocean would have been commonplace. There were tales of traders sailing across these waters, traversing the Nanhai from the mouth of the Okcidento to the mouth of the Jinhuang River. Years ago, I saw a painting in Lan Hu's Tero Kreinto of Port Donna in its heyday: proud buildings rising above the ocean of blue while people swam in its tides. But the ocean was lost to us centuries ago. A thick band of Malamiko rests between us and it.

"There," Jak said, pointing. I strained my eyes through the driving rain, magnifying my vision through my helmet. I thought he might be mistaken, and then there it was. A faint outline of concrete quays, nearly sunken below the level of the water, overwhelmed by dense blue vines of Malamiko.

"You want us to dock the barge?" Dezi asked beside me.

"No," I said. "You'll risk contamination. Remain anchored here. We'll take ourselves in with the rowboat."

We clambered into the boat once it had been lowered into the water. The waves tossed the small craft about like a leaf on the wind. "Aaron's dank breath," Jak said, hands gripping the railing. "You sure this is a good idea?"

"You guys never been in a bloody boat before?" Talia asked, plopping down on a seat. "You're way too stiff. Loosen up. Roll with the waves."

"Burn that," Jak said, refusing to release his grip on the railings. A wave crashed into our boat, sending it slamming into the side of the barge, nearly knocking me overboard.

"Anybody here beside me know how to swim?" Talia asked.

"Talia," I said, "row us to shore."

"Aw, you guys are bloody babies," she said, crawling over Jak and taking up the oars.

The waves tossed us, water sloshing over the rails, filling the floor of our boat, and the current pulled at us, drawing us further down river toward the ocean while Talia heaved on the oars. Founder's grace, I thought for certain that if the waves didn't capsize us, we'd be drawn out into the endless Nanhai. But Donna watched over us, and somehow Talia pulled us alongside the ancient quay, though we were much further down the river than where the barge had anchored.

Jak scrambled out of the boat, clinging to roots and branches choking the quay. His movement caused the boat to roll, and Talia and I desperately grasped for something to grab hold of as we fell into the river. What happened next was a blur. The boat flipped, and I found myself underwater, my kiraso drenched and weighing me down, and the current —I couldn't believe how strong the current was. I got a hold of something and struggled to pull myself up. Hands grabbed hold of me—it was Talia—and, combined with my kiraso's strength, pulled me onto the surface of the quay. Jak was beside me, on hands and knees, soaked and gasping for air.

After hauling me up, Talia watched our boat, upside down now, spin as the river's current flung it out to sea like a farmer might pitch a shovel of compost onto his fields. "Well," she said, taking a seat on the quay, her feet hanging over the edge in the water, "fuck."

SEVENTEEN

BOTH JAK and Talia sat on the quay, shoulders slumped. Sometimes you need a hammer, sometimes honey. My falchilo looked dejected, so I opted for the latter. Getting to my feet, I said, "It's not the end of the world. The barge is still there. We'll figure out a way to get out once the weather clears." I helped Jak to his feet and patted Talia on the shoulder. "Besides, if Esper's still here, she'd have her own boat we can take. Let's go find the ruins of the Tero Kreinto."

Talia got to her feet. I was expecting her to take a shot at Jak for panicking and tipping the boat, but she kept quiet, filling me with both relief and worry.

I waved at Dezi, signalling we were all right, and then we turned and entered the overgrown ruins of Port Donna. Along either side of the path, thick, fungal-like branches and rope-like roots of Malamiko choked structures of Founder stone. These buildings protected us from the wind, but we could still hear it howling overhead, moaning through abandoned hallways and whistling through hollow windows. The rain came down in a heavy mist, filtered by the vegetation overhanging the broken roofs of buildings, revealing brief windows of grey skies amid dense, blue foliage. Over it all, the ocean waves crashing into the surf roared.

How can I describe the feeling of walking past buildings so familiar, so like the architecture of other Founder cities, yet empty, lifeless, unrecognizable in their desolation? Through breaks in the choking vegetation, I spotted familiar symbols etched into stone panels: Donna's spiral dominated, but I also saw the seven-pronged pictogram of Aaron's FTL Vergo and the Eye of Xinhua, amongst others. Generations of feet walked the street I now walked, lives were lived here, and then emptiness. Ghosts. The last echoes of talk, laughter, and shouts had reverberated off these walls so long ago.

We walked down those streets, and it seemed the city, broken, tired, asleep for centuries, now roused itself to watch us pass, its gaze haunted by what it had seen and lost. The wind sighed down the streets, seemed to whisper, "Remember," into my ear. Is this the destiny of all we create?

We made slow progress. Thick roots and vines buried the roads as if some tentacled beast sat digesting the city's remains, making the footing slippery and uncertain. Many streets progressed for only a few blocks before ending in swamps, forcing us to backtrack and probe for new paths forward. We were not alone. Along gables and high branches, strange creatures, long, low to the ground with four legs and lengthy tails, skittered through the foliage, darting out of sight whenever I turned to look at them. They had no eyes, no discernible head, really. Just long stalks protruding along a line down their back.

Talia saw what I saw. "Hope they're not hungry," she said.

"Keep the gun handy." A mass of wigglers, hundreds of them, scuttled across a wall and around a corner, making chittering, glottal clicking sounds as they moved.

"How will we find the Tero Kreinto in this jungle?" Jak asked, his first words since capsizing our boat. His tone did not convey fear or frustration but rather awe at how completely Malamiko had consumed Port Donna.

"If it's still above water, we'll find it," I said, though, Founders save me, I wasn't sure that was true. No post-Founder buildings survived—their material of construction was not nearly strong enough to withstand centuries of neglect. Even the Founder buildings were little more than rubble or stood on the verge of collapse.

That was when I first heard the creatures that had been following us, and I say 'heard' only because I have no other word for the experience. It was a deep rumble, felt in my bones and in the hollow pit of my stomach rather than registered in my ears, and it sent shivers down my spine, like the feeling you get when someone passes behind you.

They called to each other in this way from the rooftops and branches along either side of the street. We grouped close together, shields open and rods out, save for Talia, who aimed the gun at the rustling branches above us. It had been a dream of our people to reclaim Port Donna. As the strange calls of these alien creatures passed through me, I knew it would remain a dream. How could we? Our Tero Kreinto, once the creator of fertile soil, silent now for generations, our last GC malfunctioning, our guns few and dwindling, how could we beat back the tide of a world reclaiming its own lost lands?

My booted feet sunk into the muck, and I couldn't pull myself out. "Here," Jak said, reaching a hand to me. I grabbed it, and together we struggled to free me from the land that seemed intent on subsuming me. With a slurping sound, I pulled one foot free, set it on firmer ground, and then got the other one out. Ahead of us, dense Malamikan foliage choked the road. I had destroyed two stage five nests—but would cleansing two nests, ten, or even twenty, leave a mark against the immensity of the world that birthed them? Duatero was an island in a sea of Malamiko, and my life's work was a bucket, digging into waves that stretched past the horizon, sloshing against the rising tide.

I focused my mind on finding a roadway leading to the ruins of the Tero Kreinto. The rain stopped, at least. With our stores of food on Dezi's boat, a hunger reminding me of the Cull twisted my stomach as we marched on. Branches, curled claws of blue, appeared out of the mists, and from every direction came the sound of dripping water—plip, plip, plip, a thousand metronomes, each keeping their own time.

"What are we going to do about food and water?" Jak asked. Apparently, our stomachs were in sync.

"What's important is we stop Esper and the dark falchilo helping it," I said.

Jak said nothing but took out his axe and swung petulantly at a nearby branch.

"If you're looking for a more self-interested answer," Talia said, "Esper's group will have supplies. You'll eat when we find them." She couldn't resist adding, "Assuming they haven't overturned their boat, too."

Jak took the bait. "I didn't knock over our boat!" He jabbed his axe in Talia's direction to punctuate his point.

"I didn't say you did," Talia said, hands raised in mock surrender.

"For the love of Donna," I said, stepping between them. "I am not going to listen to you two bicker, so stow it."

We marched in silence for what must have been hours. The cloud cover began to break, and water on blue leaves and branches began to steam in the summer sun. The thermoregulators of our kiraso protected us from the heat; it'd be sweltering without them.

An hour later, we found an avenue wider than the others. We followed it deep into the heart of the city. A short time later, we spotted what could only be the central spire of the Tero Kreinto rising above the top of the blue jungle. I could see that its surface was covered in tiles of white porcelain, and though these tiles had fallen off in great sheets, exposing the grey Founder stone beneath, enough remained to catch the afternoon sun and reflect it in dazzling brilliance. *Sweet Donna, this must have been beautiful in its day.*

The spire reached eighty, maybe a hundred metres in the air, and a replica of the Vergo still capped it. Webs of blue vines wrapped around the spire, veins pumping poison into the old city's heart, weighing the mighty structure down. I was watching a generations-old battle, fought so slowly it appeared frozen in time, caught in that endless moment between falling grains of sand. The Tero Kreinto stood, cracked, its outer layer of skin peeling away, walls covered in an indigo fungus beginning to crumble but still standing against the onslaught. *Fight!* I wanted to yell at it. *Fight against the tide of Malamiko! Show me something created by humanity can resist the Enemy's advance!*

We pushed our way through the Malamiko jungle toward the spire, Jak leading the way, hacking a path through the undergrowth with his axe. We came to a river, a small arm of the Okcidento delta bisecting Port Donna. Large bricks of Founder's stone broke the surface of the waterway at haphazard intervals. Across it sat the Tero Kreinto compound, ruined walls lining its perimeter. This close, I counted four lesser spires surrounding the central tower. I could see niches along the face of these spires in which stood statues of men and women, covered in multi-coloured porcelain tiles that were flaking away. Silent they stood, for centuries, scarred spirits glowing in the day's light, maintaining a sad vigil over their dead city.

Maybe seventy metres to our left, remnants of a bridge that once led into the Tero Kreinto compound sat in ruins. To our right, a bit closer, another one sat, this one still in one piece. Crossing it, we entered the Tero Kreinto compound. Pavilions of green Founder stone lined the road, their terra-cotta roofs collapsed in heaps on the ground, the blue fungus unable to conceal the spiral symbol of Donna repeated along the columns. As we left the bridge and stepped onto holy ground, I allowed myself to believe the growth of Malamiko was not as dense here as the rest of the city. Perhaps the spirit of the Founders still paid some heed to this lost land.

Statues cast in green stone of animals foreign to us— elephants, horses, lions, and other creatures I recognized from legends of old Earth—lined the path we followed to the main entrance of the central buildings. The doors had been forced open—recently, as evidenced by branches and roots hacked and cleared away. Esper had been here, perhaps still was. Beyond the door, a dark hall loomed. What I would have given to have the time to soak it all in, to study the mosaic tiles cracked underfoot or the images carved into the walls, covered by a thin veneer of blue fungus. But we were on the hunt for an enemy. And so, we entered, cautiously, staying close to the wall, clinging to shadows, peering over our shields, rods at the ready. Talia led, gun first. We cast our senses ahead, eyes trying to penetrate the gloom, ears straining to catch the sound of a stray foot on a loose stone.

We entered a large, central atrium. When the Tero Kreinto still functioned in the age of the Founders, this area would have rumbled with life as the machinery created soil for our expansion. Now, it was a vast, wide-open space, lit by shafts of light cutting through holes in the roof, stories above us, and pouring in through shattered windows. On the far wall, the entryway to the borehole led down to the potash mine deep underneath the building. Giant pipes that once pumped water into the mine pierced the building's floor, and exit pipes that transported the solubilized potash led outside. At the far end of the building stood the compost bins, each one the size of a small building. Beyond those would lie the fermentation plant. To our left sat the giant alkali vats.

The main area of the floor was a massive trench, a hectare in size, with ancient turbines that once churned the soil. Tunnels, where aŭtomato brought in Duaterano soil, pierced one side of the building, and exit tunnels pierced the other where the aŭtomato would transport the pre-terano soil back out to be mixed with the natural soil of nearby farms to create fertile land for our crops.

This place was like every other Tero Kreinto I'd visited where paisajista, falchilo, and kuracisto mingled and worked, except wrapped in stillness, a dying echo. Unbidden, the image of Firstsite's Tero Kreinto sprang to mind. Was it destined to one day lie abandoned, too, while Malamiko reclaimed its mouldering remains? The thought revulsed me and sent white-hot rage up my spine. I will not let that happen.

By the faint light, I could see the dust on the ground we walked had been disturbed by other human feet clad in boots. I hardly needed such clues to guess where Esper would head first. "We'll check out the manlibroj library," I said. "It'll be in one of the smaller towers." We crossed the vast space, over a bridge spanning the trench in the floor, and took a dark stairwell, lit only by faint bands of light peering in through small windows on each level, and began searching the towers. The library was in the second tower we investigated. There we paused, letting the silence wash in, straining our ears for hints of others. Nothing.

Signs of our enemy's presence abounded. Tables and chairs had been cleared. A pile of garbage, food scraps mostly, sat in a corner. They'd spent days here, camped out in this room.

"Looks like we missed 'em," Talia said. "Where are the discs stored?"

"There," I said, pointing to an array of metal cabinets spanning the length of the wall. I opened the nearest one. It contained rows of discs interspersed with large, empty patches. I opened another cabinet. More of the same. "Looks like it scoured the library," I said, taking one of the remaining discs out to view.

"I wonder how she decided what to take and what to leave behind," Talia said.

"It had plenty of time to make its selection while sitting in quarantine," I replied. "And plenty of time to sit here searching for them while we wasted time in Xuanhe."

"Power's getting low in my kiraso," she said. "Whaddya think the odds are this place still has a power supply and a functioning charging station?"

I closed the cabinet I was looking at. "Poor. My joint actuators are stiff, too. My suit needs maintenance, especially after getting dumped in the river."

"Majstro!" Jak shouted. He was standing by a window, pointing. I ran over, Talia close behind.

The side of the Tero Kreinto complex we entered was bordered by the arm of the Okcidento river. A moat bordered the remaining three sides. Perhaps once, it created an idyllic scene, marking the boundary of holy ground from the rest of the city. Now, the water in the moat lay stagnant, and some Malamikan algae turned it a sharp cobalt blue. Along this moat, making its way to the tributary, a boat sailed. The eyes of my kiraso zoomed in, bringing to clarity those aboard. All of them wore the kiraso—Esper and its dark falchilo.

Without a word, we raced downstairs in a mad scramble, jumping floors at a time. Our kiraso propelled us at speed through the Tero Kreinto's door and into the tangled growth choking the compound beyond, smashing through branches and leaping over thick roots. By the moat, the growth of Malamiko was thick, blocking our view of the boat. We made our way as best we could, but the closer to the moat we got, the slower our pace as large, fungoid trunks obstructed our path.

I pushed through the jungle to its edge abutting the moat, had to cling to a branch to keep from stumbling into the putrefying waters. The boat was maybe two hundred metres ahead. "Talia," I said, "gun!"

She looped an arm around a thin trunk, leaned over the water to get a view of the boat. "Gun's only effective up to fifty metres when powered by the hand crank."

"They're getting away! This is our only chance! Shoot! Aim for the sails."

Talia took aim. She pulled the trigger. The gun's sizzling crack echoed, skipping across the water like a stone. Nothing. She fired again, then stopped to crank up the gun's energy.

Though her shots didn't reach the boat, the sound of their report did. Three figures stood on the boat's stern, watching us as they pulled away. The central one stepped forward, head encased in its helmet. Esper. It looked like her kiraso, even from here. I zoomed in with my helmet's eyes, got a good look at it. It stared back at me through its faceless mask as its boat pulled further away.

The figure behind Esper wore a red armband, the markings of a majstro falchilo. The remaining dark falchilo, an armband of blue denoting it as the majstro's second, raised a gun and fired. Jak and Talia ducked back into the undergrowth, but I stood, unflinching. Didn't Talia just prove our guns were ineffective at this range?

"Xinhua's eyes, they have a gun!" Talia said.

"They are dark falchilo, and they have all our tools," I said, watching Esper reach out and push the barrel of the gun down.

"We've got to get closer," Jak said. "Come on!" He broke away, pushed inland, away from the thick vegetation where he could bring the speed of his kiraso to bear, Talia close behind him. I stayed for a moment, my gaze locked once more with Esper's. *Where are you going now? Where does a dark falchilo hide?*

I raced after Jak and Talia. We did not catch up to the boat. It turned from the moat up the arm of the Okcidento, making its way upstream to the main body of the river, propelled by the wind in its sail and a tide that seemed to be rushing inland. In silent anger, we watched it sail up the tributary to where it entered the main river. There, I expected it to turn north toward Xuanhe, and indeed, it started doing just that. Then, it turned south.

"Where's it going?" Jak asked. "It's heading toward the Nanhai."

A realization hit me, and a cold sweat broke out on my back. "They spotted Dezi's barge and are heading for it. They're going to sink it and abandon us here."

We raced back to the bridge, crossed the tributary, and hurled ourselves headlong through the Malamiko jungle toward where we thought the quays resided.

The power on Jak's kiraso gave out first, dropping him down to human speed. "Regroup back at the Tero Kreinto!" I shouted as we sped away from him. In the heart of the jungle, with few visual markers, we could do little but guess our way as we worked around dead ends and swamps. Talia's suit lost power later, leaving me alone to continue bashing my way toward where I thought the quays were.

I came out of the jungle along a crumbling seawall facing the Nanhai. Somehow I had ended up heading south to the sea rather than west to the quays. Though the sun shone on where I stood, a grey fog buried the horizon and sat on the ocean as though waiting for its moment to advance. The mouth of the Okcidento and Dezi's barge would lie to my right. I ran that way, making good time along the ruins of the seawall. My path soon met up with the Okcidento and turned north. I followed it a short distance to the quays where I thought we had arrived.

Dezi's barge was gone. If I needed further evidence of Esper's contamination, the fact she'd sunk and killed a barge of innocent sailors was it. We were stranded in these ruins.

The power on my kiraso gave out on the way back, and I found making my way through the growth terribly difficult with unaugmented strength. It was dusk by the time I made it to the Tero Kreinto. Jak and Talia rushed to greet me.

"What's the news?" Talia asked.

"We've got problems."

THE SUN HAD SET, smothering the interior of the abandoned Tero Kreinto in darkness. Our movements created enough of a charge to power the low light visors of our kiraso, which allowed us to see, though the world was cast in unearthly green hues. If you stood still for too long, though, it would power down until you walked a few more steps. Talia sat on the ground, leaning on a wall, knees to chest. Jak paced, hands on hips.

Talia broke the silence that had settled on us. "How do you know Esper killed Dezi and her crew?"

"Her boat was gone," I said.

"But Dezi might have left with them."

"She wouldn't abandon falchilo here."

"She would if other falchilo told her to," Talia said. "She wouldn't know they were contaminants."

Talia had a point. One of them wore the red band of a majstro. With the helmet up, Dezi might have even thought it was me.

"Why are you trying to defend it?" Jak asked. "It killed Dezi, it didn't kill Dezi—who cares? Either way, it abandoned us here to die."

"It abandoned us here to die," Talia echoed, hanging her head. "We all know that's not true. We're not going to die here."

"You've some ideas on getting us out?" I asked, glad to get Talia off the topic of Esper.

"This is a port city. We're going to find a boat. And if there are none left intact, then Jak's gonna take his bloody axe and chop down some big trunks of trees, or whatever these things are growing here. Then we're gonna take some of these vines wrapped around everything, lash those trunks together into a raft, and then we're gonna pole our way upriver when the tide comes in until we're close enough to Xuanhe that a passing boat picks us up."

"With the power in our suits drained, our moisture recirculators won't work," Jak said. "Are we going to have enough water to make it back?"

"We're surrounded by water," Talia said. "We can always boil some, push comes to shove."

"No," I said. "We're not withdrawing our helmets in Malamiko lands. Not to eat, not for water, not for any reason. That's how Esper got contaminated, and I'm not losing another falchilo to the same mistake. Anyways, our physical movement will charge our energy packs enough to maintain some basic systems," I said. "If we can make it back to civilized lands in a couple of days, we should be okay. We'll be starving, but we'll be okay."

"And then what?" Talia asked.

"What do you mean?" I asked.

"We get back to civilized lands, and then we do what?"

"We continue the hunt for Esper."

She said nothing in reply. I told Jak, "Give us a moment," and he left with a shrug. I sat on the ground alongside Talia. "Esper's gone," I said.

"Is she?"

"Yes." I let that hang in the air.

"I wanted to catch up with her," Talia said, "to see with my own eyes . . . I don't know. I figured if we could see her and talk to her, we could see what's really going on."

"Esper had the makings of a great falchilo. She was a good woman. She was young; she went into Malamiko without her helmet, and she got contaminated and died. Now that thing is using her body to attack us. It's using her body to hurt you. You know this. You've been a falchilo a long time now."

"Right. 'A likely contaminant.'"

"This goes beyond Esper. There are the dark falchilo, who infiltrated the Tero Kreinto at Firstsite. There is something rotten in Duatero, and Esper is wrapped up in it."

"Yeah, I suppose. I guess the sooner we get out of here, the sooner we can end this."

I put my arm around her shoulder, squeezed her in close. "Exactly."

The next morning, we searched for boats along the waterfront, but all we found were their decaying remains. It took the better part of a day to lash together enough logs to make a suitable raft for the three of us and another two to pole our way upriver. We emerged from Malamiko lands emaciated and delirious from dehydration. Kelp farmers rescued us a day out from Xuanhe.

In the months that followed, we found no sign of Esper.

EIGHTEEN

"FOUNDER'S GRACE, Jak, I thought I told you to keep her out of trouble." On the other side of the door leading to the tavern, a woman screamed, a man cursed, and furniture crashed.

"Talia wears the blue armband of your second," Jak said, with a tone suggesting I'd made a grave error in judgment. "If she gets it in her head to not listen to me, what do you expect me to do?"

I *had* been enjoying the day. We arrived in the city of Kolo late morning after spending the last couple of months patrolling the lands of western Aaronsburg, looking for a sign of Esper or the dark falchilo. The Founder cities warred through the summer. I'd heard stories of several skirmishes, some towns changing hands, but no major upsets or victories. The harvest had been miserable, and the paisajista scaled back the allotment for winter to where it had been before the Cull. Every time my stomach knotted in hunger, I remembered my mother's hand in mine as she died. I remembered my father breaking himself in the fields, and imagined farmers today, still breaking themselves, but for little more than a garnish for the plate.

Winter was deepening, and we were on our way to Firstsite. I had set Jak and Talia to securing our lodging at the falchilo barracks nestled between the pagodas of Liam the Swift Companion and Donna of the Golden Hills in the heart of the city. Meanwhile, I strolled the aŭtomato gardens in the west end, wandering amid pavilions of carved stone housing aŭtomato of every shape and size, from waist-high six-legged carriers to house-sized contraptions on rollers with long, articulated arms ending in large buckets or claws. Scattered throughout the park were shrines to Founder Dorian, Sabine, and half a dozen others.

It was, therefore, with a calm and peaceful state of mind that I made my way to the barracks, whereupon Jak hit me with his news: Talia had been drinking again. It had been a couple of weeks since she'd drunk to excess, which I had hoped signalled a corner turned for her.

Another crash and volley of yells came from inside. I opened the door and entered into a tableau frozen in time for a single moment. Talia had a young woman, late teens, maybe early twenties, on her back on a table and was clenching the neckline of her robes. Talia's other hand was raised high in a fist. Behind her, a young man was getting up off the floor, benches and tables scattered around him. Everywhere else, a sea of shocked faces either stared or leaped to get out of the way.

Talia brought her fist down, smashing it in the young woman's face with a resonant crack. Her fist was up and down in the woman's face again before the young man had regained his feet and tackled Talia.

"For the love of Donna, enough!" I yelled. Talia ignored me, slipped out of the man's grip, and was on her feet. She tried to kick him while he was still on the ground, but she missed, lost her balance, stumbled into a bench, and fell on a table, sending her, the table, dishes of food, and cups clattering onto the floor.

"Jak, get her," I said, pointing to Talia, who was already trying to get to her feet but slipping on spilled food and drink. The young man was diving for Talia, but I managed to grab him by the collar and pull him back. "Enough!"

Jak smacked Talia in the face, the sound like the impact meat makes when a butcher slaps it on a counter. She collapsed to the ground like a heap of rags. "Jak! What are you doing?" He looked at me with an innocent expression that seemed to say he'd only done what he thought I'd told him to do.

"You," I said, finger in the face of the young man. "What's going on here?"

"It's her!" he said, pointing at Talia, his face flushed and hair dishevelled. "She's been putting the moves on me. I see from her uniform she's a falchilo, and so I tell her I'm engaged, all polite like, and she hauls off and attacks my fiancée." The young woman on the table had begun to cry and moan, her nose and mouth smeared with blood.

"Go. Look after her," I said, pushing the young man to his fiancée.

"Fuck, Jak," Talia said behind me, her words swimming in inebriation. "You sucker punch me again—"

"Silence!" I yelled at her. "What's gotten into you?"

"He hit me," she said, angry, using an overturned bench for support as she tried to sit up. Her mouth was bloody. She lost her balance, collapsed to the floor. She rolled onto her back, pointing unsteadily at Jak. "Stelara's Kodo tells us what to do. Let's quarantine 'im."

"You stupid—" I caught myself before I said anything I'd regret. Talia lost consciousness, her head lolling on the floor.

I apologized to the young couple, promised them I'd send for a kuracisto to tend to the woman, and then speak to the gepatro paisajista of one of the nearby pagodas to ensure they would have a feast for their wedding day. I made reparations to the innkeeper. Then, with Talia slung between Jak and me, we left, heading for the falchilo barracks.

A squad of soldiers tramping down the street eyed us with curiosity as we went our way. Soldiers were common in the streets as Lan Hu was preparing to defend Kolo against Aaronsburg's army next summer. Jak waited until we were some distance away. "What do you want to do about her?" he said, nodding his head toward Talia.

"I'll talk to her when she's sobered up tomorrow."

He let that sit a moment. The air was chilly, brisk on the cheeks. "I think we should leave her at the barracks."

"She'll be fine," I said, a tone of warning in my voice.

Jak pushed on, either brave or oblivious. "Come on, Kredo, we can't trust her when she's like this."

"*I* trust her," I said, staring him in the eye until he looked away. She'd been in a downward spiral since Port Donna. I still hoped she'd swing back to her usual self. We walked on in silence, the barracks only a block away. "And what about you? You hit her—a fellow falchilo. In public! We are holy warriors. We are what keeps Malamiko at bay. How do you think this affects the people when they see us fight amongst ourselves?"

I could tell Jak was wrestling with fear at my anger, and a small part of me was impressed he found the courage to carry on, to defy me and my rage. "How do you think it affects the people to see a falchilo act like a drunken boor? Is she acting with the honour demanded by Stelara's Kodo?" he asked. "I think the people would expect us to be outraged, and I think the people would take comfort in seeing us take decisive action to stamp it out. I think Stelara's Kodo demands no less from us."

"I've had enough of your thinking for one day." We arrived at the barracks and dragged Talia to her cell. Several young falchilo saw us on our way, casting a curious eye at Talia, but saying nothing. I ground my teeth. First the soldiers, now falchilo—a campaign of whispers would follow in our wake, and it wouldn't be long before Kapo Mihaelo summoned me to inquire about my second's conduct. A muscle knotted on my shoulder as I thought about how that conversation would go.

We lowered her onto her bed and left her to recover. A falchilo, a young woman in her twenties, approached as we closed Talia's door. "Majstro Kredo?" she asked.

"What is it?"

"I have a message for you." She handed me a folded paper. From its texture, I'd say it was made of wood pulp, the kind typically used in the region of Lu Guang or Shihbei. I dismissed her and read it.

Jak caught my look. "What is it? Is everything okay?"

"Yes. Fine." I held up the paper between us. "Change of plans. We're not going to winter in Firstsite."

"No? Where are we going?"

"Your old stomping grounds—Lu Guang. According to this note, last spring, a ferryman was taking a group across the Jinhuang River to Lu Guang. He caught sight of their cargo. He had no idea what it was; told a local paisajista about it."

"What was it?"

"Discs. His passengers were carrying discs. It must have been Esper and her crew." We had been looking for Esper, but now that we had our first sign of it, I was worried. How would Talia take it, finally coming face to face with whatever contaminated Esper? "Sleep well tonight. Tomorrow we head east."

Talia greeted the next morning with a round of body-quaking vomiting. The side of her face was discoloured, dark purple, the colour of the sky the moment before dawn, and swollen to the point her eye was almost forced shut. "What happened last night?" she asked, sitting on her knees on the wooden floor, bucket in front of her filled with her retch, tentatively opening and closing her jaw.

I sat on a short stool facing her, trying to ignore the stench rising from the bucket. "You don't remember?"

"No," she said, plugging the nostril on the unbruised side of her face with her thumb and then blowing a long, bulbous string of clotted blood out the other into the bucket. "Ugh—did I get in a scrape?"

"You did."

"Did I give as good as I got?" she asked, a weak smile flashing across her pale face.

"You beat a defenceless woman—a girl more like—for the crime of being engaged to a boy you took a fancy to."

She rested her head in her hand, a look of sickness and misery on her face. "How bad?"

"Bad enough." It was a blessing she'd forgotten it was Jak who hit her.

"I'm sorry, Kredo," she said. "I . . . Maybe I need a minute to myself, okay?"

"Our hunt for Esper continues," I said.

"Did it ever stop?" She kept her eyes on the ground, head cupped in her hands.

"She was spotted crossing into Lu Guang. We're heading there today."

"Yeah, well, we falchilo do what we gotta do to keep Duatero safe, don't we?"

She looked so weak and sick, and seeing her like this hurt deep in my chest. "How long have we worked together?"

"Aw, come on, Kredo, don't give me this."

"How long?"

She grunted and spat, missing the bucket this time. "I think it's, like, fifteen years now."

"Fifteen years you've been by my side. Together, we've travelled the length and breadth of Duatero. We've saved each other's lives; we've saved towns and cities. You've always been wild, Talia, but lately . . . I don't know if I can trust you."

There. I said it. I was surprised how much it hurt. She looked at me, a broken heart painted on her bruised and swollen face, the pain in her eyes was a spear stabbing me in the gut. She looked down again. "You can trust me," she said, her voice a meek, sad shadow of itself. "It's just . . ."

"It's just what?"

"It doesn't . . . I don't know. Things don't *feel* right."

"It doesn't *feel* right?" I repeated.

"This whole thing with Esper stinks. It feels off. Everything's felt off since Vojo Fino."

"You think I'm not torn up by doubt? I haven't known what's going on since dark wanderers started talking and nests built decoys. You know what we fight. Malamiko's greatest evil isn't that it kills us. It's that it makes us kill our own. That's what's happened with Esper. The only way we'll survive is if we have the strength to strike Malamiko, even when it wears the face of a loved one. Once we find Esper, we can figure out what's going on."

"Yeah," she said, rubbing her eyes with the heels of her hands. "I'm being stupid."

"Look," I said, resting a hand on her shoulder. "If you need some time, I can have you assigned to the Tero Kreinto in Firstsite for a spell. Let you catch your breath. It's only a day away from here. You can try wearing down Mihaelo's will."

"Don't you dare," she said, stabbing me with eyes wide with fear. "Don't you *dare*. I'll rot behind a desk. I'm with you, Kredo. I'm with you to the end."

NINETEEN

FEW THINGS FILL me with such a mix of awe and sadness as The Gates of Lu Guang. Why we call them "The Gates," I've no idea, but that's what they have always been called. They were, in fact, the ruins of a bridge that once spanned the vast distance to the far shore of the Jinhuang River where the lands of Lu Guang begin.

But "bridge" seemed too pale a word to capture the wonder of what The Gates truly were, even in ruin. You could see it kilometres away, its pilings like the stone legs of a titan, breaking through the water, reaching skyward, piercing the grey ceiling of clouds where they arched over, and connecting one piling to its opposite. From the tops of these cyclopean pillars, steel cables, thicker than a strong man's body, sloped toward the shore where they remained anchored to blocks of stone and iron buried in the ground. Midway up these giant pillars hung the road, so wide it seemed as though the Founders had risen plains of stone into the air in blithe defiance of gravity. My eyes traced the line of this road to a point a quarter way across the river where it ended in a jagged length of twisted steel like the frayed end of a broom, giant chunks of Founder stone still trapped in their tangled web. My heart ached as I scanned the long expanse of empty air.

I have travelled to Lu Guang many times, yet every time I have seen The Gates they fill me with the wonder of a child seeing the sky lanterns at Rendezvous for the first time. And they fill me with a sadness that sits in my gut like a stone. I have contemplated why these ruins affect me so. I have seen the wonders of the Founders. I have seen the Tero Kreinto, once a force of change and salvation, now quiet. Why doesn't that wondrous equipment fill me with the same awe and melancholy?

I suppose it's that I can't even begin to imagine how the Tero Kreinto once functioned. Tales of how they changed this planet, changing the soil through what might as well have been magic, were little more than myths. But a bridge—I *know* what a bridge is. And to see these ancient pilings, even in ruin still piercing the sky and catching the clouds, and to know in my heart such marvels are so far beyond what we could ever now create shows me the true face of how far we have fallen with such brutal honesty. What power the Founders must have possessed that they could turn something as mundane as a bridge into a wonder.

A modest city simply called The Gates sat on this side of the Jinhuang, a port of call for traders and travellers, where they might rest before riding a ferry from the western shore to the eastern, where the walls of Lu Guang begin. Aaronsburg had wrested control of it from Lan Hu this past summer, and the ruins of battlements and burned-out defensive fortresses attested to the struggle from earlier this year. To either side of the road rose large earthen mounds, newly dug: mass graves of fallen soldiers, I suspected. Even now, soldiers clad in the livery of Aaronsburg and its ally Shihbei scurried over these ruins, like bees repairing a damaged hive, in anticipation of Lan Hu trying to reclaim the city next year.

We arrived at The Gates late afternoon on the day of Dongzhi Festival, which marked the winter solstice. The air was chill, freezing my face and coating the grass lining our path with a dusting of frost. We approached the city walls. The guards let us pass with only a cursory check—not even the armies of the Founder cities dared to stop those on business for the Tero Kreinto.

We prayed and made offerings at the shrines of Dorian and Sabine, and then we walked to the docks, busy as traders moved goods to and from Lu Guang in preparation for tonight's Dongzhi feasts. We looked for the dockmaster, found him yelling at a barge crew for unloading their goods in an area that the dockmaster managed to communicate amid a string of profanity was reserved for some other purpose. The docks were slick, the thin layer of water covering them freezing in the cold air, and we had to walk carefully so as not to slip.

He bowed his head as he saw us approach. "Merry Dongzhi, Majstro. Lookin' for passage across?" he guessed. "Plenty o' traffic. Oughta be able to set you up right quick."

"Perhaps in a bit," I said, pulling out my message from the Tero Kreinto. "I'm looking for," I scanned the document for the name of the barge captain who'd reported seeing the discs smuggled across, "Vik Panido."

"Are ya?" the dockmaster said.

"You know him?"

"Aye, he's worked a barge here for years."

"Where is he? I'd like to speak with him."

The dockmaster looked worried. "I'm afraid he's gone to be with his family for Dongzhi."

"Where's that?"

"Aye, just a minute, then." The dockmaster walked away, yelling for one of his assistants. They spoke for minutes together, then called others, adding them to their conversations.

Finally, he came back to us, his lips and forehead bunched up as though he was readying himself to deliver bad news. "Near as we can figure, he's gone to Pordegeto, a couple of days upriver if ya barge it and the weather's good."

It wasn't Vik who interested me, and I didn't want to run all over Duatero finding him. I wanted Esper.

Jak was staring at some customs officials inspecting offloaded cargo on a nearby dock. "Do you guys keep records of what goes and comes on these barges?"

The dockmaster looked at him cautiously. "Yeah. Doesn't matter who's in charge of The Gates; they want to make sure they're getting the tax they feel they're due. Why?"

I picked up Jak's cue. If we could find out more about who was with Esper and what they were transporting with them, it might give us a lead. "We'll need to see those records. We're interested in a shipment Vik made earlier this year."

He looked like he wanted to swear but thought better of it. "Can it wait until tomorrow, Majstro? Today's a busy day. Once Dongzhi's over, it'll quiet down."

"We can take the records with us and study them at a nearby inn," I said.

His face screwed up, clearly uncomfortable with the suggestion. "I ain't supposed to let the records leave the dock."

Talia slapped him on the shoulder in an exaggerated display of camaraderie. "We're falchilo. You can trust us," she said.

Emotions churned on his face as he looked at his docks. With a shrug, he said, "Fine, since you're falchilo and all."

"Fantastic," Talia said with a smile. She looked at me and said, "And I was worried Dongzhi night would be boring."

"WELL, THIS IS STRANGE," I said, looking up from the records. We lounged on cushions as we ate a Dongzhi feast prepared by the family running the tavern near the pagoda where our kiraso were getting charged up. The common room was nearly empty—the winter rains discourage all except the toughest of travellers, and Dongzhi is a time to celebrate with family, anyways, rather than carouse local drinking holes. Right now, aside from us, the only other person in the room was the barkeep's daughter, who strummed an oud by the hearth, gently humming a Dongzhi carol as she played.

"What is it?" Jak asked. He left off spooning yule dumpling soup into his mouth to lean over and look at the ledger.

"I found the entry for the date Esper crossed. Vik transported an unspecified number of people. Their cargo included personal items, including the discs, as well as a box of glass ornaments from Xuanhe, a couple of canisters of salt and other baking goods, and, get this, a nugget of silver ore. Have you ever seen silver outside of a palace? They paid a steep tax on it, too."

Jak looked at the list and shrugged. "Plenty of metalworkers in Lu Guang. Most of 'em work with iron or steel, though."

"But just a nugget?"

Talia, who had been swaying to the tune of the oud with closed eyes, sighed loudly, letting us know our conversation was drowning out the music, and began to dance to the young girl's song. She hadn't danced for a long time, and I was happy to see her at it again.

The innkeeper came over, placing a large carafe of beer on the table. "Fresh stock," he said. "Released by the paisajista this afternoon for Dongzhi."

Jak began to pour a cup for the two of us. "We'd better drink off some of this before Talia notices." I agreed, though it felt a betrayal. Talia, though, seemed content to dance by herself. So, Jak and I drained our first cup on the floor as a libation to the ancestors and then poured ourselves another and sat back into our cushions, enjoying the music and warm fire. I suspected we might see a dusting of snow by morning. Jak stretched out, crossed his ankles, and rested his cup on his belly.

"You grew up in Lu Guang," I said to him.

"Not in the city itself."

"If the metalworkers don't work with silver that often, do you know how hard it would be to find the one who worked on this kilogram of ore?"

"Oh, it wouldn't be too hard, I'd think," Jak said. "Working on silver would be strange enough. Plus, Esper would've had to pay them well enough to stick in their memory, given demand for weapons and armour these days. Life's never better in Lu Guang than when Aaronsburg and Lan Hu start going at slitting each other's throats."

"Seems a dark way to make a living," I said.

"Bah," he waved a hand dismissively. "The way I figure it, each soldier that kills another is one less mouth to feed, holds off the next Cull a bit longer."

"Is that what you figure."

"It is. Culls make us look bad, make us look like we failed. Let 'em do that nasty bit for us."

I remembered walking my mother to the pagoda courtyard during the Cull, me, Gaja, and Fondo. "People are more than mouths to feed." I was going to say more, but a sound from outside stopped me. I couldn't make it out clearly over the sound of music. Shushing the daughter and then Talia as she began to complain, I strained my ear. We all heard it—it was getting louder. Screaming.

I moved to the window to see what was happening but saw nothing. I was terribly exposed, naked without my kiraso. The barkeep came out into the main room, worry painted on his face. Screams were rising in pitch, and the sound of wood and windows crashing could be heard now. His daughter looked at him as she set the oud down and asked, "Are we under attack again?"

Founder cities didn't fight their wars through the winter, but if the paisajista were still fooling with the allotment like they did this spring, who knows what desperate acts armies could do.

"Get in the kitchen with your mother," he said, pulling a club out from behind a counter.

"Should we make a run to the pagoda to get suited up?" Jak asked.

"The screams are coming from the direction of the pago-da," Talia said.

"Best to get to the pagoda. If this is a repeat of Kubuto Falls, it could be brigands heading for the granary. Kiraso or no, we'll make our way there and protect pagoda grounds as need be."

The barkeep nodded to us as he went into the kitchen after his daughter to protect his family. We slipped out the door onto the street. The night was frigid, and a freezing mist filled the air.

It wasn't the army of a Founder city attacking. It wasn't starving brigands, either.

We heard screams from a nearby house. A door shattered, its shards cartwheeling in the air. Light from a warming fire spilled onto the street, and a form bathed in shadow stood silhouetted by the dancing light. I stared a moment, my eyes adjusting to the darkness as I tried to make sense of what I saw.

It wasn't shadow that bathed the figure. It was a dark haze hovering around a humanoid figure covered in black, rag-like scales. "Aw, you're bloody kidding me," Talia said.

A dark wanderer was rampaging in The Gates. It turned its head to look at us, and as it did, its scales ground against each other with the sound of dry leaves underfoot. "Get back inside," I ordered as I turned to run. "Go!" We sprinted back into the tavern and slammed the door behind us as thorns thudded into it. All three of us leaned into the door to brace it. A moment passed. Another. A force like an ox charging slammed into the door, jarring us, but we held fast.

"Talia, get out through the kitchen and make your way to the pagoda," I said. *Whump!* The door shuddered. "Get suited up and take this thing out." She was the fastest. If we had a chance, she was it.

Whump! The door took another vicious hit. "And you're going to do what, stay here and bore it with a sermon? You won't last two minutes."

Whump! "Then you better fucking hurry!" Jak shouted.

"Jak!" *Whump!* "Language! Talia, go!" She grunted in frustration and then left.

Whump! The braces holding the wood of the door together were falling apart, and the beams were snapping. "On my word, run for a table and use it as a shield. I'll draw it away; you attack with your axe." *Whump!* The door was almost in tatters. "Go!"

I ran. The dark wanderer crashed through the door. I

knocked a table on its side and hid behind it. Thorns splintering into wood shuddered the surface of the table. The beast raged through the room, smashing benches and tables. I peered around the edge. The beast was chasing after Jak, who was struggling to carry a table in front of him as a shield. I grabbed the top two legs of my table, picked it up, and charged. Yelling, I drove my full weight into it, table first. I felt like a small child trying to tackle a grown man. This was my first time fighting a dark wanderer without my kiraso. The thing reeked of fetid swamp water.

From my position behind the table, I couldn't see its punch coming. The force of the blow sent me crashing over benches and shattered the table I'd been using as a shield. I banged my head and shoulder, and something jabbed into my back, sending spears of pain down one side of my body. The thing loomed in my line of sight like a black wraith, its dark halo hanging over it. I still held a table leg in my hand. I threw it at the dark wanderer and rolled for cover.

From behind his own table, Jak yelled and swung his axe into the beast's head with a wet crack. The creature stumbled but kept its feet. With a grunt, Jak hefted the axe out of its head and ducked. It punched Jak's makeshift shield and sent him and the table slamming into a wall.

I grabbed another table and held it in front of me, and took another charge at the creature. I couldn't see where I was going and only glanced off the dark wanderer. It grabbed the edges of my table and tried to pull it away. I hung on with all my strength, and it dragged me as though I were a rag doll. The thwack of Jak's axe sounded again, and the dark wanderer tossed me aside like a toy it was bored of. I landed hard. There was nowhere nearby to get cover from the beast's thorns.

The sizzling crack of a gun shattered the air, and then

three more times. My ears rang. Nothing moved. I rolled over and saw a kiraso-clad Talia stepping into the room, turning the crankshaft to power her gun. My body ached, and I accepted Talia's hand to my feet. "You're okay?" she asked. It came across as half question, half surprised exclamation.

Jak pulled himself out from behind a table. "Nice hit, Talia."

"It's what I do."

I motioned Jak over. The body of the dark wanderer was beginning to dissolve into a viscous black putrescence. It gave off a thick stench of rotten meat, and we had to move closer to the fresh air of the door. "You've got to inspect us," I said to Talia.

"Aw, bloody … I don't think I could cleanse you," she said as she withdrew her helmet.

"Just inspect us. We'll figure out what happens after."

She looked Jak and me over for a sign we'd been hit by a thorn. A crowd was beginning to gather by the door. "You're fine," she concluded.

My two falchilo were still flushed from the battle. "This is going to be a bad night. The dark wanderer would have hit a lot of people before it got here." Behind them, more and more people gathered outside. Was Talia still up for this? I steeled myself for what came next. "We've got a lot of cleansing to do."

TWENTY

THERE WERE TWENTY-THREE IN ALL. Some came quietly, knowing what they had become and wanting to be cleansed before they hurt their families. Others cried. Some screamed and needed to be dragged as they thrashed and kicked until someone jabbed them with a rod to silence them. Their families followed similar patterns, some giving up their cherished spouse or children with tears of heartbreak, while others fought us with such violence we included them in the cleanse. As the dawn rose on a snowy gray morning, the people of The Gates quickly turned on themselves, angry gangs bringing us anyone with a scratch or mark for inspection.

We corralled the contaminants in the tavern where the remains of the dark wanderer moldered and had the city's soldiers help us keep guard as we continued searching. We sent word to the Tero Kreinto in Lu Guang, just a ferry ride across the Jinhuang. By mid-morning, a score more falchilo joined us. A crowd of townsfolk formed outside the tavern, some yelling curses at the contaminants within, others calling for us to release their loved ones because there must have been a mistake. By early afternoon, I was satisfied we'd caught all of them.

Twenty-three contaminants. Some were sullen and quiet; others shouted they felt fine and should be freed. I walked into the tavern with Jak and Talia to figure out how we were going to cleanse so many. Jak wanted to burn the tavern down with them in it. But I believed the human was still alive in them somewhere and wanted a mercy kill before the cleansing flame.

The contaminants fell quiet and backed away as we entered. All except for one male dressed in a traveling cloak, which held its ground as it stared at me. I returned its stare, curious. "Are you Majstro Kredo?" it asked.

"Who are you?"

A female stepped forward, tears staining its face. "He's not from here," it said, its voice rising in hysterics.

"I'm talking to it," I said, pointing to the male.

"He brought the contamination with him!" The female's voice was a banshee's wail. I snapped my rod to full length, and it stepped back, trying to silence the sobs that shook its body.

"I was sent to find you and give you a message," the male said.

"Who sent you?"

"Majstro Bao."

"Who?"

"He's a falchilo, like you. He says you met earlier this past summer." Was it talking about the dark majstro we saw in Port Donna? "He wants to speak with you about Esperanta. He'll wait for you in Pordegeto until a week after Dongzhi. After that, he's moving on."

Talia shook her head. "This is messed up."

Bao? That sounded like a Founder name. Strange. What parents would have the hubris to name their children after the Founders? "What do you know about Majstro Bao? Was Esperanta with it?" I asked.

"I never met him before," it said. "I was doing a lumber run up by Pordegeto this fall. He found out I was planning on heading south and paid me to look for you and give you that message. He was alone when we spoke. I don't know no Esperanta. I gave you the message like he asked. I helped out with falchilo business, right? Do you think that might be worth cutting me a break here?"

"A break? You've been contaminated by a dark wanderer's thorns."

"I have a good constitution. It just nicked me, anyways. Barely even a scratch."

"Wait here," I said and led Jak and Talia out.

"Lot of things pointing us to Pordegeto," Talia said once we were outside. "First the barge captain Vik, now this. Are we going to head there?"

"Yes. But, I still want to know what Esper was up to in Lu Guang with its silver. I don't want the trail to get too cold there. For all we know, the dark majstro could be trying to lure us away from Lu Guang."

"That guy said Majstro Bao would only stick around a week after Dongzhi. Do we have time to muck about in Lu Guang and make it to Pordegeto in time?" Talia asked.

I turned to Jak. "You used to live around here."

He shrugged. "It'd be tight. Depends how much time we spent in Lu Guang. Depends on the weather, too. Winter winds blow off the Shandong Mountains, and a trip that'd take a day in the summer could take a week."

I gave it some thought while staring at the tavern. "The

dark wanderer also means there's a nest at least stage four somewhere near here we need to deal with," I said.

The crowd growing outside began chanting: "Cleanse! Cleanse! Cleanse!"

"Let's finish here, then work out our next steps," I said.

I gathered the falchilo from Lu Guang. We rushed the tavern. A dozen falchilo lined the perimeter of the room, making sure nothing escaped while the rest, including Talia, Jak, and me, began administering mercy kills by gun or rod. Contaminants screamed. Some charged us. Others bolted for doors or windows, only to be tossed back by the falchilo standing guard. Some contaminants wrestled other contaminants down, enough of the human still in them to know what needed to be done for the safety of Duatero. Bodies shuddered in their death throes, and blood from gun wounds pooled on the floor and stained the kiraso of many falchilo.

I strode up to the messenger. "Aw, come on. Please?" it said, a smile on its face, equal parts pleading and obsequious. I hit it with my rod, the shock jolting it off its feet and onto its back. I shocked it again to make sure it stayed down. Once done, the falchilo laid a cleansing fire on the tavern, setting it aflame. The crowd cheered and shouted prayers into the sky.

Esper spotted going into Lu Guang; the dark majstro in Pordegeto; a stage four nest . . . somewhere. I could set the falchilo of Lu Guang to hunt down the nest. They knew this land best, so that made sense. Jak, Talia, and I could split up to search both Lu Guang and Pordegeto. This presented me with a problem. Typically, Talia, as my second, would be the obvious choice to send on her own, and then Jak would come with me. But with her recent behavior and drinking, I couldn't trust her alone.

My eye sought out Talia in the crowd as the fire roared. She stood nearby, eying the tavern morosely. She had a large clay mug in hand that she was drinking from. She stood with Jak, who looked at her with disapproval out of the corner of his eye.

I stalked up to her and grabbed the mug out of her hand. "Hey," she called out, startled.

"What is this?" I held it to my nose and smelled it. Beer. "Where'd you get this?"

"I got it from the back of the tavern as we were pulling out." I crushed the mug, my kiraso augmenting my strength to grind it into powder. "Xinhua's eyes, Kredo!" she said, stunned, as beer slopped to the ground.

"No more drinking," I said, finger in her face. "We were attacked last night, and we've got several leads to follow. I need you sharp."

"Okay, okay," she said, hands up in surrender, taking a step away.

"I'm sending Jak into Lu Guang to find out what Esper did while it was there. I think it went to a metalsmith to do something with that silver. You're coming with me to Pordegeto to hunt down the dark majstro." Jak stood a little straighter.

"I can handle the search in Lu Guang," Talia said.

"No, I'm sending Jak. He grew up around here, so he knows the area. It's time to try him out on his own."

"Is this about the drinking, Kredo? Because if it is, I've got it under con—"

"Just—" I silenced her with a raised hand. "I want you with me, and that's the way it's going to be."

She looked at me, and she looked mad, like an ox lowering its head, flaring its nostrils before it charged. I don't know if I've ever actually seen her that angry. I wondered for a moment if she was going to push it, turning this into something ugly. But, she ground her teeth and left without a word.

"Just you and her," Jak said as she pushed her way through the crowd. "You sure? Is she the one you want to walk into a trap with?"

I took a sidelong glance at him. "Yeah, we'll be okay."

He shrugged. "Maybe it's a good thing. Maybe one-on-one, you can steer her away from the drink long enough for her to break the addiction."

"It's not an addiction," I said. "She's always been wild. She needs to get it under control, again, is all."

"Sure. Fine," he said. "I saw a man in my lumber camp poison himself on the drink when I was—"

"She'll be fine. Drop it."

TWENTY-ONE

"MISERABLE DAY TO be on the water," Talia muttered.

We stood on the deck of a barge heading north up the Jinhuang. The rain was turning to snow, coating the deck with a slick layer of slush, and a fog rested on top of the water, reminding me of steam coming off a hot mug of tea. The wind was calm, so most of the crew were working the oars on the lower deck, rowing against the lazy current. Our only companion was a pilot on the prow of the boat, pole in hand measuring the depth of the river, and the helmsman at the rear, implementing the occasional order the pilot shouted. The winter was grey, leeching colours out of the world, replacing them with mud and dampness. It seemed the only sound on all Duatero was the lapping of paddles dipping into the river's surface, little bloops, like small stones dropped into water.

I was starving. "We'll arrive in Pordegeto early evening," I said. I was also exhausted, but Malamiko wasn't giving us time to rest. "I want to find the barge captain, Vik, as soon as we arrive. We'll question him about Esper, and then we'll track down this dark majstro."

"What if Vik's dead, or if Majstro Bao has moved on?" Talia asked.

I studied the brush lining the eastern shore. The wet snow was starting to stick to their branches, turning them into white ghosts. "Jak's going to meet up with us at Pordegeto, so he may have news. Either way, Esper and its secondaries crossed the Jinhuang into the eastern border of Duatero. If the trail goes cold in Pordegeto, and Jak turns up nothing in Lu Guang, we'll focus our search to the far east, where Lu Guang and Shihbei meet Malamiko."

I turned to face her. Her skin was so pale, made even starker when contrasted against the blackness of the kiraso she wore, and dark shadows smeared the hollows under her eyes. Her face was puffy, as though she'd been crying. She was my friend. She was my family, really, and I was losing her somehow, and I didn't know how to keep her from slipping away. I wanted to say so much to her but only managed, "We didn't get any sleep last night. Might not get any tonight, either, if things get lively in Pordegeto. Why don't you get below deck and catch some shut-eye?"

"Why don't *you* catch some shut-eye?" she countered and then smiled as she added, "You look wretched."

I smiled. I hadn't lost her yet. "Maybe in a minute. I grew up on a land-locked farm and still enjoy watching the river pass by."

She shook her head as she turned to go. "You are so boring." She went down the hatch to the lower deck to sleep.

The morning stretched on, mirrored by the endless, torpid river we made our way up. I leaned on the barge's rail, the slow dip of the paddles like a clock ticking through molasses, and my mind raced, keeping sleep from me. The unending sameness—mist hanging over the river, drizzling snow—made it hard to measure the passage of time. It must have been close to noon when another barge appeared ahead through the thinning fog.

I activated my helmet and strained to bring whoever was on deck into focus, my visor zooming in. Fifteen people armed with spears and slings. I called out to the pilot and pointed at the troops.

"The Aaronsburg army patrolling their side of the river?" he said, hopefully.

"I don't see Aaronsburg's standard anywhere." The crew of the other ship drew anchor, and oars began to pull. They were moving with the current.

The pilot pulled his pole out of the water, watching the other barge we were drawing nearer to with every slap of our boat's oars. "Bandits!" he called loud enough for his crew to hear. He ordered us to reverse course, but our momentum pulled us forward. The other barge was moving to approach us from the centre of the river to force us ashore. Our pilot shouted at the helmsman to pull us deeper into the river, but as our forward momentum vied with the new direction our oars were pulling, the helmsman was unable to manoeuvre us.

Moving to the hatch leading below deck, I shouted, "Talia! Talia! Get up here!"

They were close enough by the time she fumbled her way up that we could clearly see the men and women on their deck without the kiraso's augmentation. "Got a plan?" she asked.

Assuming these were simple bandits and not contamination, we had to be careful not to overstep our bounds. "We're going to talk our way out of this."

She shrugged. "I think you've had better plans, but I got nothing to top it."

I gave her a sidelong glance. "Charge up your gun, just in case."

"Sounds like you got two plans," she said, drawing her gun as she began churning the crank to bring it to full charge.

I strode to the prow of our boat, careful not to slip on the slush as the deck shifted with the gentle waves of the river. "This boat is on falchilo business. Let us pass," I called loud enough for them to hear on the other barge. They did not change course.

"Drop oars," the pilot ordered his crew. "We surrender!" Still, the barge came at us.

"You're not going to fight for your boat?" I asked.

"We've nothing to steal. Nothing worth getting killed for."

Talia stood beside me. "Stelara's Kodo. If these aren't contaminants—"

"I know—" I couldn't say more as their barge broadsided us, sending us tumbling and sliding along the slick deck. Grappling hooks lashed the two boats together, and the bandits poured over the railings onto our deck as the two boats began to spin from the force of the impact.

Quickly, the invaders got our crew on deck and began manoeuvring both boats into shore. They moved with discipline and efficiency and seemed comfortable handling their weapons. These were not starving farmers. They'd done this before. I found their captain and got right in his face. "This boat is on falchilo business. You are disrupting the work of the Tero Kreinto."

Their captain was a sickly, gaunt man, wet mousy hair plastered to the side of his head and greying beard that was a tangle of mats. "This won't take long, Majstro," he said.

"Let us on our way, immediately."

"Sorry, Majstro, but I've mouths to feed. Since the Tero Kreinto ain't taking care of it, nothing left but to take matters on ourselves. If your crew plays nice, we'll be done, and you'll be on your way inside twenty minutes."

I balled my fists. With my kiraso, I could pick him up and fling him into the middle of the river as I might toss a stone. "Allotment of food is the sacred duty of the paisajista. You break holy law by stealing it from others."

"Holy law?" The captain was angry as he spoke. "The paisajista short-changed us this spring, Culled us this summer, and starve us this winter. It's them who's broken faith with us, not the other way around."

"This isn't a debate. I'm not going to allow you to defy the will of the Tero Kreinto." I snapped my rod to full length.

He sneered and looked at his fellow bandits. Those who weren't working the oars or rudder were guarding our crew, who sat on the wet deck, hands clasped on top of their heads. "If these falchilo move to stop us," he called out so everyone on deck could hear, "start killing prisoners."

"Please, Majstro," the pilot of our boat pleaded with me. "We've nothing for them to steal. Let them search and be on their way."

I stared hard at our pilot a moment. He was serious. "Fine," I relented.

The bandit captain noticeably relaxed. "Wise move, Majstro. Now, if you'll kindly surrender your weapons." I braced my feet, crossed my arms, and gave him a stare that dared him to try and disarm me. He considered this and then said, "Fine, keep them. But if you make any moves that make me nervous, blood starts flowing."

They brought the barges to a clearing along the shore and unloaded us onto the beach. They had our crew on their knees in the wet snow while several of their thugs searched the ship. Talia and I stood aside, watching these marauders rifling through the gear of our crew. My mood worsened as we waited. I was cold, exhausted, and hungry, and now these thieves were wasting my time. We might not make it to Pordegeto before night fell, thanks to this.

"Seventy-three allotment chips—that's it?" the thief captain exclaimed once his band finished their search. Some of his fellow bandits swore angrily. The captain shoved our pilot to the ground and loomed over him. "Where's your cargo? Where's your food?" First the raiders at Kubuto Falls, now this. Our crops failed. We were all starving. Who were these filth to demand more from good, honest men and women?

"That's it," our pilot pleaded. "I told you we had nothing."

"We were their only cargo," I said, stepping forward. "You've wasted enough of the Tero Kreinto's time. You've taken all these people had to give. We're leaving now."

"Oh, no, you don't, falchilo," the thief captain said, walking up to me, dagger in hand. Was this fool going to threaten me?

"What are you doing?" one of the bandits asked behind his captain.

"Look at their armbands. This here's a majstro and his second," the captain said. "I'll bet the Tero Kreinto will pay dearly for their release. They'll have to release their secret stores of food for us. Picture it, enough flour to gorge yourself on."

"Don't be an idiot," I said, motioning to our pilot and crew to follow me as I turned to go to our barge.

"I ain't done with you, falchilo," the captain said. He grabbed my arm and spun me toward him, knife poised threateningly. I punched him. In the face. With the full strength of my kiraso. With one blow, I caved his head in and sent his body tumbling a good ten metres.

I expected his followers to surrender—lop the head off, and the beast dies, right? But these men did not balk at the show of force. One of them raised his spear to stab a prisoner, which set Talia into action. In a blink, her shield was opened and swatting one bandit out of the way to clear her shot at the spearman with her gun. She fired, ripping the would-be murderer off his feet.

After watching me send their leader flying with a single blow, and Talia shooting another, I was hoping the rest would run. No luck. They attacked.

A man was shouting orders, organizing their attack, and it hit me—these weren't wild marauders. They were soldiers, some dregs left over after the summer's fighting ended who figured they'd use their strength to prey on the weak, under-mining the sacred allotment in the process.

Stelara's Kodo allowed me to class these thieves as conta-minants now they'd chosen to attack, so I drew my flamjetilo, powering it on. "Protect the prisoners," I said. "I'll use my flamjetilo to scatter their troops."

"May Donna, Star of the Fields, lead us to safe roads!" Talia yelled. *Tiel estu*. Her gun cracked beside me, and waves of energy belched forth from my flamjetilo, setting the grass and brush lining the river's bank alight, forcing the bandits back.

I was hoping the flames would drive the troops to flight, but the damp snow snuffed the fires out almost as soon as they lit in a fit of hissing, like meat sizzling on a frying pan, releasing a wall of steam and smoke. I could hear someone ordering them to charge through. The river was at our back, giving no means of escape for our crew.

Turning to our pilot, I said, "Get your crew on the boat.

Talia, with me." My shield spiralled open. I leaped over the thick pall of smoke and steam, Talia right behind me. My feet squelched in the semi-frozen mud as I landed, and spears and sling bullets clattered off my shield. They advanced. Two groups tried to outflank us, a third coming at us head-on, a wall of steam and smoke behind us.

"To the humans whose bodies these once were, your torment is over! Tonight, you dine with the Founders!" I yelled, letting loose with the flamjetilo into the group charging directly at us. "To Malamiko who has stolen these bodies—burn!"

There is nothing quite as terrifying as the screams of burning contaminants. They erupted in flame as the waves of the flamjetilo hit them. Fire tore screams from their lungs. They ran in a wild panic, arms windmilling while dark smoke trailed into the sky. I blanched at the horror, then reminded myself these were not people as defined by our law. They were the Enemy. They undermined the allotment and struck at the Tero Kreinto's warriors. Their mad shrieks were the music of Malamiko dying. Certainly, there can be no sin listening to evil suffer. I tell myself that when I can't sleep.

The remaining two groups slammed into us, the mass of their bodies overwhelming both Talia and me. Talia, hiding behind her shield, jabbed her rod into the throng of attackers. They knew how to fight, and the two of us were pressed back to back. I unleashed another wave of the flamjetilo to more screams. Smoke from flailing bodies and steam from snow-covered grass rose above our heads.

What was wrong with Talia? Blows into her shield I knew she was quick enough to deflect and turn into a counterattack were knocking her back as she clumsily struck with her rod. Was she hit?

A contaminant thudded into my shield and grabbed the

barrel of my flamjetilo, forcing it to the sky. Another contaminant came at me with a spear. Clad in my kiraso, they were no match for my strength and speed. I dashed them away with my shield as I might toss a pile of papers in the wind. I watched them alight in flame through the smear of blood on my shield as I sent a wave of fire before me.

Contaminants were behind us. I found myself fending off blows from clubs. When I finally beat them down, I turned to see Talia, ahead of me by several metres. None of the would-be bandits remained, save their broken and burning bodies. The only sound was the rush of water along the river and the dying hiss of steam.

She was looking at the scene of our fight, shoulders slumped. "Xinhua's eyes, Kredo," she said.

I turned her to face me. "Are you okay?"

"Yeah, why?"

"You seemed sluggish."

She shrugged, looking to the river. "My kiraso—power's a bit spotty. And actually, after this fight, my suit's power is almost dry."

I glanced at my suit's indicator on the inside of my visor. "I'm pretty low, too." We did not have a chance to recharge them after cleansing the victims of the dark wanderer at The Gates. "Might not make it to tonight. Hopefully, Pordegeto has a pagoda with a power supply we can charge up at."

My sight drifted along the shoreline upriver. "Well, Founders' grace," I said. Two figures, clad in black kiraso, stood atop a low rise about a kilometre away. They were watching us. I pointed at them. "Guests."

Talia turned to look as I zoomed in with my kiraso. I could see the red armband of a majstro on one, the blue armband of his second on the other. "I don't see Esper," she said.

"Nor I." Their helmets were withdrawn. The majstro was

a male, short black hair, almond-shaped eyes, dark skin, thin goatee. The second was female, with similar hair, skin, and eyes. I didn't recognize either of them. "The dark falchilo?" What I thought was the goatee could be contamination spotting the majstro's mouth and nose, as sometimes happens.

"Beats me," Talia said

"Let's say hello. Keep your gun charged."

"Friendly, but not too friendly. Got it," she replied as she turned the crankshaft, charging her weapon.

They turned and ran. We gave chase. We closed the distance in moments, draining our kiraso further as they powered our sprint. Once we had crested the rise, I could see thick brush crept up to the shores of the Jinhuang. Travelling along the shore would be slow and painstaking. The two (dark?) falchilo were in a rowboat, pulling away from us at great speed as the one wearing the second's blue armband drew the oars.

"Aaron's dank breath," Talia said. "If they're the dark falchilo, I thought they wanted to meet with us." They pulled away, heading up the river—the same direction we were initially heading. Were the bandits with them? "Now what?" she asked.

I began walking toward our barge. "We push on to Pordegeto."

TWENTY-TWO

THE TOWN of Pordegeto came into view through the haze of wet snowflakes. I had never been here before. Pordegeto, its scattered mud-brick buildings clinging to the shore like mushrooms poking through the manure, its dock of decaying wood jutting onto the water like a fallen tree left to rot, did not impress. Perhaps the weather was affecting my mood. A winter storm was strengthening, and thick clouds cast a grey pall, creating a perpetual twilight. Despite my kiraso, I was cold and wet.

Talia horked and spat over the railings of our boat into the river. "Xinhua's eyes, what a stink hole." Her dark brown hair was soaking, strands clinging to her high cheekbones.

"Vik. The dark falchilo. All signs point here." I stilled my foot, tapping impatiently on the boat's deck.

Soldiers wearing the colours of Aaronsburg ran from a shack on a mound of mud at the end of the docks. They took cover behind barricades of wood and earth piled up along the river bank. "They've spotted us," our oarsman said from the cowl of a thick winter cloak.

The dark falchilo were active in this area. If they'd been here before, if they'd contaminated this town, this could get messy. "Talia. Prep your gun," I said as I powered on my flamjetilo. "At this distance, they can see our kiraso, so they know we're falchilo," I said, engaging my helmet. "If they try to stop us, we cleanse them. The whole lot."

It turned out they were happy to see us. A guard poked his head above the barricades. "Falchilo!" he yelled. "Falchilo!" others took up the call. The soldiers came out and ran down the docks to greet us, and men and women living in hovels within earshot opened doors to watch us approach, some of them donning thick cloaks and coming out to join the soldiers greeting us.

The soldiers helped us out of the boat, then kneeled in the wet slush, asking for our blessings. And so, Talia and I spent our first moments in Pordegeto standing in the falling snow repeating the litany, "*Mia korpo estas via shildo,*" to a growing body of men and women coming to greet us. At length, a group wearing the brown tunics of the paisajista underneath thick cloaks intervened and drew us away from the crowds.

"Founders favour you, falchilo," one of the women said, taking the lead. "I am Paisajista Ada."

"Kredo," I said, stabbing a thumb at my chest, "Talia," I said, stabbing my thumb over my shoulder at her. "Are you gepatro of this town?"

"Pordegeto is too small for a gepatro," she said. "But for all that, we feel truly blessed. It's been years since a falchilo has come through town. Now, you're our second group in as many months."

"Majstro Bao is one of them?" I guessed.

"Yes. And his second, Tai. You know them?"

"I've heard about them. Are there only the two of them? Another woman didn't travel with them?"

"No, Majstro, just the two."

So Esper remained elsewhere. Or was in hiding. "Where are they from, do you know?"

"I've no idea. I assumed they were from Aaronsburg, given that's the nearest Founder city."

"You've never talked to them; got to know them?"

"They keep to themselves. They've been staying in an old falchilo fort about an hour out of town on the road to Aaronsburg."

"Does your pagoda have any charging stations for kiraso?" I asked.

"We do, but they've never been used in the time I've been here. I have no idea if they work or not—our power supply is iffy."

"Talia, check it out," I said. "I'm going to find Vik. Once our kiraso are charged up, we'll pay Majstro Bao a visit."

"You sure you want to check out Vik now? You haven't slept since the dark wanderer in The Gates, and I don't know about you, but I'm starving."

"Shouldn't take long to talk to the barge captain. I'll meet you at the pagoda."

She shrugged and followed the paisajista up a slushy mud road leading up a rise. I asked for directions to Vik's family home from a villager. Pordegeto was small; everyone knew everyone. His family lived out of town, about a kilometre up the river. A quarter of an hour later, I was knocking on his door. Its reed construction and lack of mound raising it above the floodplain suggested the poverty of those within. A woman, perhaps my age, maybe a bit older, opened the door. She bowed her head as she saw my kiraso.

"I'm looking for Vik," I said. "Does he live here?"

"Vik's my son. Come in."

Something about her behaviour set my nerves on edge.

Was it her eyes, shifting quickly, avoiding my gaze? I stepped forward, looked closely at her eyes and the skin around her nose and mouth, looking for signs of contamination. She smiled nervously under my intense scrutiny, but she showed no outward signs of contamination. Behind her, a grey light coming through the windows lit a room. I could see a wooden counter behind her and a hearth with an open flame to the right. "Thank you," I said, stepping into the house.

A gun muzzle pressed into the side of my head. Hands out, I slowly turned my head, my gaze following the barrel of the gun back to a figure wearing a kiraso, its visor hiding its face. The dark falchilo. I finally got a good look at its kiraso, saw the etching of bow and arrow on its breastplate. A suit from the Founder ship *Artemis*, same as Talia's. Also like Talia, it wore the blue armband of a second.

The other dark falchilo, wearing the red armband of a majstro, stepped from the shadows behind the door. Its kiraso had the etchings of a bird, twig in its mouth—the Founder ship *Jingwei*, same as mine. I ground my teeth. That Malamiko had sullied a kiraso of the same vintage as mine filled me with a rage that burned in my gut.

The woman who answered the door bowed before the dark majstro. "Is everything okay, now?" it asked. "Are we safe?" Only contaminants need fear a true falchilo.

"You did well," the dark majstro said. "Go into the back room with your family, lock the door, and don't come out until we leave."

The woman fled through a door. I caught a glimpse of others, a young man and an adolescent girl, in the room beyond before the door closed, leaving me alone with the two dark falchilo. The dark majstro withdrew its helmet, revealing a lean, brown face with black stubble surrounding its mouth in a thin goatee. Probably to hide signs of contamination.

It stepped up to me. "Where's Talia?"

I planted my feet and crossed my arms.

It raised an eyebrow. "Fine. We'll do it the hard way. In the meantime," it reached out a hand, "your flamjetilo and rod, please."

I stared at it but did not move.

It shook its head. "Damn it, Kredo." Its second swung the butt of its gun into the back of my head, knocking me out cold.

FOUNDER'S GRACE, I hate headaches, and my head pounded as I came to. After the pain in my head, my first sensations were of cold and dampness. Someone was tying my feet together, and I bucked, trying to kick them. Someone cursed, but my feet didn't connect with anything.

"He's up," a female voice said.

I blinked the haze of unconsciousness from my eyes and found myself on the earthen floor of a dank room—the kitchen I had entered. Ahead of me, on the ground near the warmth of the hearth, I spied a clay bowl with a mound of dough rising in it. They had undressed me, and the ground was freezing and damp, moisture seeping up my undershirt and briefs. My feet were bound, my arms tied behind my back. My kiraso and weapons were in a pile on the floor.

Booted feet stepped into my vision. It was the dark second, its helmet still up so I couldn't see its face. It grabbed my shirt and yanked me up until I was sitting on the floor. My head throbbed.

"Easy," the voice of the dark majstro said. It sat on a nearby stool, back straight, hands on knees.

"He's dangerous," the dark second said, a female voice.

"*I'm* the dangerous one, am I?" I said, fighting off waves of nausea. I don't think I've ever been so exhausted and hungry. It was a debilitating combination when added to the vice-like pain in my head.

It looked at me, head cocked. "You quarantined Esperanta. Yesterday, I saw you defy Stelara's K—"

The door slammed open. The two dark falchilo whirled as three men stumbled in, one standing only with the support of the other, the third's face marred by a nose that was swollen and bent to the side, blood draining from it and caking its face and chest. They wore banded reed armour and carried spears but bore no livery of any Founder city.

"Report. Where's Talia?" the dark majstro said to one of the soldiers.

It fell to its knees. "She downed two of my men, Majstro."

"And where is she now?"

"She got away."

"She escaped? There were five of you! And you had the element of surprise, and her kiraso should have been drained."

I couldn't hide my smile. Good on you, Talia.

The mercenary captain sneered. "She slipped away and got the attention of an Aaronsburg patrol. We barely escaped."

The dark second—Tai—ran to the door, peered out of it. "Did the patrol follow you?"

"We got away clean."

"It's no matter," the dark majstro said. "Talia will bring them here. Time to go."

"What of Talia? Esper wanted her, too," the dark second said.

"If we're captured here, all is lost," the dark majstro replied. "Kredo's the important one. Get him to the boats."

I yelled. It was a small town and a quiet day. Talia might hear. I leaped off the ground as best I could with my arms and feet bound. I threw my body into the mercenaries, sent the injured one to the ground in a haze of curses.

Strong arms grabbed me in a bear hug. I struggled, thrashing my whole body. I tried to stamp on the feet of whoever held me. One of the mercenaries grabbed my legs, and I was manhandled out the door.

"Here they come," a mercenary said. A group of soldiers, spears in hand, were running toward us. Sprinting out in front of them, bearing down on us with terrible speed, came Talia. Her kiraso was drained of power, but sweet Donna, she was still fast.

"Get him on the boat," the dark majstro said.

Tai drew her gun as the guards dragged me to the river's edge. I yelled, "Talia! Gun!"

She didn't slow her pace, instead drew her own gun as the dark second swore and took aim. Talia dived for cover as she fired. I lost sight of the fight as the soldiers dumped me onto the floor of a boat. They pushed off, and one of them took up oars. It was snowing madly.

Yelling, I rocked the boat, hoping to capsize it. Cursing, one of them tried to hold me down. With a sharp crack, a blow struck me in the head, and I blacked out.

TWENTY-THREE

A BOWL CLATTERED on the floor by my head, waking me. Porridge, steam coming off, and a cup of water. No cutlery. How long had I been out? Where was I? No windows pierced these walls, the only light coming from candles flickering on a table where two guards sat playing a game that involved dice and several metal doodads. One of them nodded toward me. "Sleeping beauty's up."

The other guard grunted. "I'll let the majstro know." He got up and left the room through a heavy door reinforced with steel bands.

Famished and thirsty, I spooned the porridge into my mouth with my hand and washed it down with water. Once done, I was still famished and thirsty. I was behind iron bars, but the room was otherwise constructed of wood. A brazier glowed softly near the guards' table, giving off an anemic heat. I wore only my underwear, and I was cold. My head ached, and I could feel two tender goose eggs on my scalp.

"Where am I?" I asked the remaining guard. Speaking caused my head to throb.

"Lagofino."

Where was that? I called up my mental map of Duatero but could not place the name. The paisajista in Pordegeto said the dark falchilo were in an outpost about an hour out of town on the road to Aaronsburg. Could I be there? My last memory was of being hauled into a boat on the river, though, which would take me away from Aaronsburg.

My head, combined with the porridge I just scarfed down, made me feel ill, and I didn't feel much like questioning the guard further. Sitting in a corner, I tenderly probed at the bumps on my scalp. One was about two knuckles in size.

The dark majstro entered with the other guard and an officer, a woman. " . . . Tian Ti's snowed in," the woman said. "We may have to winter here."

Tian Ti—I recognized the name.

"We'll talk later, Fajra," the dark majstro said, closing the door, leaving the woman outside. It turned to me. "We haven't really been introduced, Kredo." It bowed its head, placing palms together over its forehead. "I'm Majstro Falchilo Bao Lido." It pulled up a stool and sat. Dark skin and hair, almond-shaped eyes, thin goatee—he was the majstro we saw on the river when the bandits attacked us.

"You're a contaminant, Malamiko, and you taint the kiraso by wearing it."

It smiled politely. "Is life always so black and white for you?"

"Yep." I stared at it, determined to find traces of contamination. I focused on the stubble around its mouth, trying to see if the short whiskers hid the dark speckling that sometimes became visible around the lips and nose in stage two contamination. Shadows cloaked its face cast by candles and the dull glow of the brazier.

"Was it so black and white at Kubuto Falls or along the

shores of the Jinhuang when bandits attacked? Or how about when Jak accused Esperanta of being contaminated?"

My eyes narrowed. "What do you want?"

"We wish to catch Talia alive." Good—Talia was still free. "Your second commandeered a squad of Aaronsburg soldiers to cross over into Lu Guang in pursuit," it said. "If Lu Guang finds Aaronsburg soldiers this side of the river, it could lead to a broadening of war. Fool woman risks much for you. With your help, we can capture her with minimal chance of injury —on both sides."

"We're in Lu Guang?" The falchilo outpost supposedly sat between Pordegeto and Aaronsburg to the west. That we were on the eastern banks of the Jinhuang in Lu Guang instead left me confused. "Where are you taking me?"

"Let's save that for later."

We sat, staring at each other through the bars. My head felt like it was going to explode. "You broke Esper out of Firstsite," I finally said.

"I did."

"Why?"

"Because Esperanta is not a contaminant."

"You don't know that."

"Oh, I'm pretty sure."

"But you don't *know*," I said. "It attacked a falchilo—could have killed her—to protect a contaminant. With no functioning GC, Stelara's Kodo is clear about how to proceed."

"Black and white, is it?"

"Black and white."

The faint clamour of pagoda bells rang through the walls. The guards and dark majstro looked at each other, and then the dark majstro turned back to me. "That's Talia and her followers attacking now. Help us capture her. Haven't enough died?"

I crossed my arms. It turned away, a look of disappointment on its face. It left the room, ordering the guards to keep watch over me as it did. I sat back down in the corner close to the brazier—it was cold in the room without my clothes—and waited for an opportunity to appear.

Tian Ti. I'd heard the name before. Where? I rubbed the side of my head. That goose egg was huge—no wonder my head ached. Then it struck me. The Tian Ti Pass. It was the road to Shihbei, last of the Founder cities, the jewel of the northern Shandong Mountains. They were taking me north up the Jinhuang River along the border of Lu Guang to the Tian Ti and from there to Shihbei. That's where Esper must be. So isolated, so hard to get to. So few had been there, the city seemed more fable than reality.

My thoughts turned to the dark majstro. Was it really contaminated, a new form of shell that looked human and did its nest's bidding? That would explain Elekti's father hunting me down and attacking. And Founder's grace, what was Esper up to in Shihbei?

The door to the guardroom opened. The candles had burned down low, casting thick shadows dancing slowly amid golden-red light splashed on the walls. Through the door, walking as though she hadn't a care in the world, a falchilo entered. The helmet was engaged, hiding the owner's face, but the blue armband denoted the kiraso was owned by a majstro's second, while the engraving on the breastplate identified the suit from the Founder ship *Artemis*. So like the dark majstro's second. But I knew this armour, knew the proportions of the woman who shaped it, and it was not the dark second.

The guards left their game of dice, stood up, and peered at her through the shadows. "Falchilo Tai?" one asked. I smiled.

It didn't know I was being rescued and that it was *my* second, Talia, standing before it.

"Why does everyone keep calling me that?" she asked. Her movement was a blur. Her rod snapped out and tapped the first guard in the torso. It jolted and collapsed to the ground. Before the second guard could move, Talia's rod swung around and jolted it off its feet, too.

The helmet on Talia's kiraso withdrew, revealing her sharp features. Hands on hips, she smiled at me, nodding toward my briefs. "That's cute underwear."

"It's great to see you," I said. "I heard you travel with Aaronsburg soldiers. Are they the ones attacking the town?"

She retrieved the key from the belt of a fallen guard and moved to open my cell. "They are. They're distracting everybody while I rescue you."

"Good work. Let's find my gear and get out of here."

As I left the cell, she thumped me in the chest with her fist. "Hey," she said. I couldn't read what was in her eyes. "Don't leave me like that again."

"It would seem even if I did, you'd just come after me."

She smiled. "We gotta find your kiraso. People will get the wrong idea of me if they see me wandering around with you in your underwear."

"Would the idea they get of you really be that wrong?"

She smiled and led the way out of the room.

"Your speed," I said, "it looks like you managed to charge up your kiraso."

"Yep," she said. "The pagoda in Pordegeto did have a charging rack. I figured I'd need to fight, so I sent Aaronsburg scouts to tail you guys while I charged up. With the kiraso at full power, I made pretty good time catching up."

I must have been unconscious for at least a day. "That's

good thinking. Maybe we'll make a majstro out of you yet."
She looked at me as though I were an idiot.

We looked for my kiraso in an office kitty corner to the vault they'd kept me in. Nothing. "Raise your helmet," I said. "The dark second's kiraso is from the *Artemis* like yours. The soldiers can't tell your suits apart. Anybody asks, you're taking the prisoner to a safer location."

"Check," she said, and her helmet engulfed her head. We could hear other people in the building, but we encountered no one. Most soldiers were out in the town fighting off Talia's allies. We followed a long hallway lined with doors. The walls, floor, ceiling were all made of wood. We looked in the rooms as we walked by, saw soldiers guarding windows with spears. Some of them turned to watch us walk past, but they paid us no mind. The hall turned a corner, leading to the back of the building and ending in a large room with a counter and benches. My gear rested on a table off to the left among a pile of supplies. We closed the door, and I began pulling my kiraso on.

"My suit's got no power, so I won't be much use to you for now," I said.

"At least this time, you've got an excuse."

I had one leg on when the door slammed open with such force the hinges tore partway out of the frame. Blocking the exit stood the dark second, shield open and rod in hand. "Talia," I said, "meet Tai."

"Oh, *you're* Tai," Talia said. "You're going to laugh when you hear this, but everybody here thinks I'm you." Her shield spiralled open, and her rod snapped to full length. She leaped at the dark second. It skipped out of the way of her rod but took the brunt of Talia's charge on its shield. In a blur, the two struck and parried each other's blows.

I had no time to put on my suit. Dropping my kiraso, I

dived for the dark second, trying to knock it off balance. With only a subtle movement, the dark second sent me sprawling onto the floor. Struggling to my feet, I got my shield band on. It spiralled open as I grabbed my rod. I tried to outflank the dark second while it and Talia exchanged blows.

In a flash of movement, the dark second kicked out. It hit my shield with the force of a charging sentinel. I was on my back, trying to suck air back into my lungs.

"Will you stop getting in my way," Talia said to me as she circled the dark second. She attacked. I stood and marvelled. She struck with such efficiency, such speed. The dark second was good, but Talia was better, a hail storm flattening fields, a bolt of lightning, flashing, then gone, leaving only a grumbling boom in its wake.

She feinted, struck, the dark second parried, she bashed it with her shield, drove her rod into its foot, blasting it with a good long charge. The dark second quivered as bolts of energy raged through its body. Talia withdrew the rod, and it collapsed, still shaking.

Talia looked at me. "I thought I told you to get your clothes on." I donned my kiraso. It was like coming home, like walking the streets of Transiri once more.

A sound from down the hall froze both Talia and me: a voice of command, calling soldiers to follow it. "It's the dark majstro," I said.

Talia pointed to the back of the room. A door led out to the rear of the building. With both Talia and me, we outnumbered the dark majstro, its second lying still on the ground by my feet. But my kiraso had no charge, and the dark majstro was collecting soldiers in its wake. Still, this may be our best chance to eliminate both dark falchilo.

"Take cover behind the counter," I said. This put the exit at our back, so we had a way out if the fight went sour. "You got your gun?"

"Of course, I got it—shit! It's gone!"

"What!"

Talia hopped the counter, me close behind. "Kidding, it's right here." She drew her gun. "'*Do you have your gun?*'," she said, mimicking me. "No, because I'm, like, five years old."

"Shut up and shoot whoever comes through the door."

She popped over the counter, fired twice, then dropped down again. Yells came from the direction of the door. I pulled my flamjetilo out from its harness on my back and powered it on. Indicator lights told me its battery packs had enough charge for a couple of good blasts, but that was it. Talia looked at it. "The dark majstro's got a flamjetilo too, doesn't it?"

The counter we hid behind was made of wood. So was the floor. And the walls. Ceiling, too. Maybe we should have run.

A scream filled with rage and pain startled me. Poking my head above the counter, I scanned the room. It was the dark majstro. It had entered, along with other soldiers who were now diving for cover behind benches. It sat on its knees, hunched over the body of its second. "Talia! Shoot it!"

Talia fired. The dark majstro leaped back. The shot missed, plowing into the wood of the wall behind it with a crack. The gun can fire four times before needing recharging. Talia had fired three shots. She fired the fourth into a soldier charging over our counter.

The dark majstro had been counting too. "Their weapon's finished. Charge them! *Kill them!*"

I stood and unleashed my flamjetilo. The wooden benches, floor, walls, soldiers, anything organic in the path of its beam, erupted in flame and, in the case of soldiers, screams. The dark majstro jumped out of the room before I could cleanse it. But its second still lay on the floor, and I made sure it burned. Its kiraso burned with it, and it broke my heart to destroy such a gift from the Founders. How could we trust the contaminant's taint hadn't transferred to it, though. No falchilo would wear such a suit again.

Over the crackle of flames, over the screams of those burning, I yelled the rites. "To the humans whose bodies these once were, *rejoice,* your torment is at an end!"

A wave of fire belched toward me. I ducked behind the counter, barely in time. The dark majstro was firing its own flamjetilo. The counter shielding us was in flames, the heat forcing us back. I moved to the side, found an angle to strike, and sent a wave of cleansing fire toward the dark majstro. It jumped back out of the room. A moment later, another wave of fire rushed toward us. Flaming embers rained from the ceiling.

Talia grabbed my shoulder. "I may not be a wise woman, but it seems like we should go."

I nodded. "Get us out of here."

She grabbed me and leaped toward the back door, her kiraso augmenting her lift-off. We slammed through the door and onto the snowy ground beyond. It was night—pitch black, snowing lightly—and I could hear the screams of soldiers fighting nearby and the whistle of slingshot whizzing through the air. Without power, I could only run as fast as a human. Before I could say a word otherwise, Talia slung me over her shoulder and bolted out of town and into the dark forest beyond. I've made more elegant withdrawals.

She circled back through the surrounding woods, trudging through calf-deep snow, back to the main road leading into town. By the time we got there, the battle for the town was over. Talia's soldiers had been outnumbered and had been overwhelmed by the contaminants defending the town. We caught up with two of them fleeing, one of them with a broken arm, but he could still run.

I expected the dark majstro to press its advantage and give chase, but nothing followed us as we retreated. The darkness was absolute, and so Talia led the way using the low-light vision of her kiraso. "So, what's next?" Talia asked after we'd marched for a while and were certain none of the contaminants were in pursuit.

"Back to Pordegeto to meet up with Jak," I said. "And to cleanse Vik's family."

Talia was silent for a moment. "Vik's family's contaminated?"

"They are in league with the dark majstro."

"Sure, but they wouldn't know it was a contaminant. All they'd know was a majstro was telling them to do something."

Black and white. We were dying while our enemy strengthened and evolved. Our destruction lay in the shades of grey. Better to cut too much than too little. "Stelara's Kodo is clear. If you harm or assist someone harming a falchilo, you're a contaminant." It was a hard choice, but I wasn't going to let my weakness allow Malamiko to lead us to another Cull. "Given the changes we've seen in Malamiko, we can't take a chance. We don't understand how the contamination works anymore, and until we do, we need to err on the side of caution."

"So we're going to burn them?"

"We're going to *cleanse* them." Such a dirty, nasty business, this. These choices we're forced to make—cleanse someone potentially innocent or free a potential contaminant —this was Malamiko's evil. "Once that's done, we're off to Shihbei."

"Shihbei?"

"Yes. I overheard the dark majstro talking. Esper is in Shihbei. It's almost over, Talia."

We made the rest of the journey in silence. It took us longer to return to Pordegeto than I expected. The snow kept falling, choking the road, and ice formed along the banks of the river, creating difficulty for us to get our boats out onto the water and across to the western shore where Pordegeto lay.

Jak was at the pagoda when we finally made it back. "The paisajista told me what happened," he said upon seeing me. "Are you alright?"

"Well, I owe my life and my freedom to Talia here," I said, arm around her shoulder. She gave a thumbs up.

"I wish I could have been here to help," he said.

"You were on your own mission. Speaking of which, did you find out what Esper was doing with the silver?"

"It had it turned into fine wire."

My face screwed up in surprise. "Like a necklace?"

"No. Just a small length of thin wire. That's what the metalsmith said."

"What for?"

"It didn't know."

I almost didn't catch that. "*It*?"

"Yep. The metalsmith was a contaminant."

Talia pulled away from me, arms crossed. "Really?" she said, voice tainted with accusation.

"Without a doubt," Jak said, crossing his own arms.

"You cleansed the metalworker," Talia said. It wasn't a question.

"I took it to the falchilo barracks where one of our sisters loaned me a flamjetilo, and I cleansed it myself."

"You're no majstro. What gives you the right to start accusing people of contamination and cleansing them?"

I stepped between them. "The same right you have, Talia, or any falchilo." I turned to Jak and asked, "You had a clear sign of contamination?"

"Speckling on its retina."

"You sent a report to Kapo Mihaelo in Firstsite?"

"I did."

"Good."

"You don't believe him, do you?" Talia asked, forehead furrowed in disbelief.

"Jak's a falchilo. He's received our training and has worked in the field with us for almost a year. If he says the metalsmith was a contaminant, then we need to believe him."

"No, we don't."

"Talia, enough! Why would he kill a metalsmith if it wasn't contaminated?"

"I don't know. Maybe he's got a taste for it."

Jak stepped forward. "Whatever Esper's working on is important to it," he said. "Do you think it would trust part of its plan to a human? Of course, the metalsmith was a contaminant. His spirit's free—*I* freed it. He's dining with the Founders, now."

"*Tiel estu*," I said.

Talia stared at me, shock on her face, and I stared her down. We had to be united, more than ever. We had to cut the rot out, and we had to cut deep. She raised her hands in mock surrender and pressed the point no more.

Good. Changing the subject, I told Jak, "I know where Esper is."

"Great! Where?"

"Shihbei."

"Of course," he said. "It makes sense. That's about as far away from civilization you can get and still be in Duatero. But the winters this far north are harder than what you're used to in the south. The Tian Ti Pass will be snowed in. Won't be passable until spring."

"We're not waiting," I said.

"The Shandong Mountains ain't a safe place in winter," Jak said.

"The dark majstro is out there still. If it reaches Esper before us, they'll move their nest, and we'll lose them. We'll charge up our kiraso, pick up supplies, and then head out. That is after we take care of one last bit of business."

Talia turned her back and walked away.

"What's that?" Jak asked.

THE HAZE of smoke drifted through the citizens of Pordegeto gathered, like wispy spirits walking amongst us. Jak was finishing the rites: " . . . and to Malamiko who stole these bodies, *burn!*"

"Burn!" the crowd screamed at the reed hut engulfed in flames, their faces twisted in hatred and anger. As loud as the roar of the flames and the jeers of the crowd were, the screeches of the contaminants—Vik, its mother, who had lured me into the dark falchilos' trap, and the rest of its family—burning inside rose above it all, shrill wails chilling the already cold wind blowing in off the Jinhuang. The people of Pordegeto screamed their rage at the contaminants burning in the house. It has always surprised me how quickly people turned on their neighbours. Perhaps it's fear my suspicious eye might fall on them. Or, maybe they want someone to blame for the hardships they've suffered. Faces contorted with righteous hate as a family died because we didn't know who the enemy was anymore—was this who I was fighting for? Did Malamiko make us this way, or have we always been like this?

Founder's grace, a contaminant's cries while burning are the stuff of nightmares, and these ones were going on and on.

Talia stood at the edge of the screaming throng. She was swaying, stumbling a bit to keep her balance. It looked like she'd been drinking. Watching her there, trying to stand, my heart broke. Should I scream at her, find her stash of alcohol, and pour it out? All I really wanted to do was find a quiet corner and sit with my head in my hands.

I walked up to her. She straightened as she saw me approach. "We done here?" she asked. "Off to Shihbei now?" She articulated her words carefully, trying to hide the slur that would give her drunkenness away. She wasn't strong enough for what we had to do. I saw that now, though I didn't understand it. She'd been by my side for years, never faltered once, never even blinked when there were contaminants to cleanse. I wondered—a thought that pierced my soul like a knife—what she would do when we finally faced Esper. Would she fight with the power and strength I knew she had? Would she have my back?

"Fuck, I hate the stench of burnings," she said, her face in a grimace that made me think she might vomit.

Leaving her behind would be best. Our quest was destroying her.

"I hate when they scream," she continued. "It haunts me. You hear it for days afterward. You hear it in your sleep."

But when I was captured by the dark majstro, she came after me. The old Talia came back when I needed her. I studied her face. Gaunt cheeks that usually reminded me of the mythical wolf of old Earth seemed skeletal now. Her eyes, moist with the drink, stared at me. They seemed to be crying for help, but I did not know how. She swayed, caught her balance. She was too young to be so broken.

I knew if I left her, she would drink herself into the grave. The road to Shihbei would be long, and we'd have to spend weeks in the wilderness. Away from towns and cities, she'd have no access to alcohol. Maybe time alone in the wilds of Duatero with us would clear the poison from her veins, let her get her thoughts straight.

Jak came up beside us. "Did you hear their screams?" He sounded like an excited schoolboy showing off a trophy to proud parents. "They went on, didn't they? Hearing evil suffer like that, you gotta love it." Talia's eyes narrowed, and the wolf was back in her features. Jak didn't notice. He was watching the crowd disperse into town and surrounding homesteads. "The people like it when they scream. They see we can hurt Malamiko. Lets 'em know we can win this fight."

"Is our gear ready?" I asked before Talia could say something she—or I—might regret.

"Yep," he said. "The mouth of the Tian Ti Pass is about a hundred-fifty, two-hundred kilometres upriver. Normally, that'd take the better part of a week by boat. This time of year, in this area of the world, it could take weeks, longer if we're snowed in, and there's not much in the way of towns if we run into trouble. You sure you don't want to wait until spring?"

Talia's face held no emotion, leaving me to guess what was going on inside her. "We leave now."

TWENTY-FOUR

THERE IS such beauty in winter's harshness. The silence of snowfall. Trees, frosted in white, standing guard along the river in a frozen menagerie. Ghosts exhaled with each breath. I was used to cold rain and thick grey skies. This northern winter was a wonderland of biting cold. Back home in the south, the temperature would drop from time to time, and we'd see skiffs of snow. That was rare, though—once, maybe twice a year or so. Here, though, along the northern reaches of the Jinhuang, the snow fell relentlessly in large wet flakes that piled up past the knees and soaked everything in freezing wetness.

As we travelled north, the river swung toward the Shandong Mountains, and fierce, freezing winds blew down off their slopes, so cold even our kiraso couldn't keep the chill from our bones. When it blew, it'd freeze the upper layers of snow, and we'd have to punch our feet through it to walk.

We travelled by small boat, using the sail when the wind was favourable, rowing when it wasn't. We went about our travels in near silence. We were alone for longer and longer stretches, and our daily routines were so repetitious there hardly seemed any reason for words. I pushed us to make as much distance as we could——I reasoned the dark majstro would be making its way to Shihbei to warn Esper and its nest—but it seemed either the wind blew so hard we had to stop lest we risk capsizing, or it didn't blow at all, leaving us little choice but to advance at the plodding pace of our oars against the current.

Little changed with Talia. She was quiet, withdrawn, but so were we all. Though never overtly drunk, I think she was still drinking. I never saw her in the act, but I was certain I could smell it on her breath some evenings and sometimes in the morning. I would watch her, try to catch her sneaking a drink, even look through her gear for a stash of alcohol when she was relieving herself in the woods, but never found direct evidence with which I could confront her. I started to doubt my suspicions. I shouldn't have. So many things I could have done, but choices close doors.

"I'll get more firewood," Jak said. We'd been camping on the shore for a couple of days, waiting out a storm. Our kiraso had been drained of power, and I had no idea when we'd next find a town with a functioning power supply to charge them. Our bodily movements kept enough of a charge to power our thermoregulators, but even so, the chill seeped through and chilled my fingers and toes.

With axe resting on his shoulder, Jak trudged away from the warmth of our fire. He had kept us alive. He knew these winters. He knew when storms were brewing. He knew to get the boat out of the Jinhuang before the banks froze over, knew how to find snow caves at the base of trees, hollows in the snow around the base of large evergreens where we could huddle together for warmth when the temperature plummeted, and he knew how to set tents in blowing wind and snow.

I set to checking our supplies, figuring out how to make them last long enough for us to get to the next town—a tough job since we didn't really know how long it'd take us to get there. Some time passed, then Talia shuffled close beside me and sat on her knees in the snow. She looked like she wanted to say something but sat there, hands fidgeting in her lap, lips tight together, like a schoolgirl working up the courage to ask an older boy to dance.

"What's up?" I asked.

"Not much," she said.

Should I give her space to speak when she was ready or push her to get whatever she wanted to say out? I was having a harder time knowing how to handle her.

"I remember when I first met you," she said. Her words were stiff, nervous, as though she were speaking from a script.

I smiled at the memory. "You'd have been just a kid out of the Tero Kreinto, probably younger than Jak is now."

"Don't let yourself lean on Jak," she said. This wasn't what she wanted to talk about. I could see from her relaxing features that she was off-script, relieved to speak of something else.

"I know you don't like him," I said.

"He's cruel."

"What we do requires hard choices."

"There's a difference between being hard and having no compassion. You're hard," she said.

"And what about you?"

She smiled weakly. She didn't seem to like where this diversion led and so switched back to her script. "I was an initiate in the Tero Kreinto when you cleansed Eta Monteto." An image flashed in my mind: Aprila on her back, blood draining into the muck beside her, shot by my hand, her hair, splayed in the mud moments before I cleansed her—cleansed *it*. "Your name was everywhere," Talia said. "The girls in my class had quite the thing for you, even though none of us had met you. It was your story that inspired me to take the falchilo's path. It seemed a grand adventure, better than pulling weeds as a paisajista. And when I graduated and found out I was assigned to Mihaelo's squad and would work beside you, that . . . well, there ain't been too many thrills that topped that."

"Did I live up to the hype?"

She smiled, staring at our fire. "I thought you were boring as mud bricks. Still do."

"And yet you remain." I'm not a fire, I'm a pillar. She needed that; she always has.

"Still, I figured I'd get you drunk, take you for a whirl, see if I could break the heart of the Hero of Eta Monteto." She *was* breaking my heart. I wanted to tell her that, but she continued. "It was one night. You were still a candidate for promotion to majstro, so you were still one of us, though more uptight than usual. The entire squad was camped out sitting around a fire, and you were talking about your dad. I don't remember the story—some crap about busting your hump for not digging a ditch deep enough or making you shovel out the chicken barn, or whatever. But I remember a smile in your eyes as you talked about him. I'd never seen anyone talk about their family with a smile in their eyes."

In all my years travelling with Talia, I'd never seen her open up like this. I didn't know whether to be hopeful, that maybe she was reaching out to me to drag her through this dark spell or if this was leading to a confrontation. Or to her quitting the falchilo. She kept her eyes on the fire, her features not giving me any hint of where she was taking this. "Anyhow," she said, "next day, you set me to cleaning your gun—the gun I carry now. Mihaelo sees me, gets his nose bent out of shape, 'cause he figures guns are for seconds, and I was just some snot-nosed rookie, and he starts taking a strip off me. You remember that? You remember what you did?"

"No," I said, genuinely curious.

"You came over, and you told him it was you who gave me the gun to clean. Well, Mihaelo turns and lays into you. *'The gun is a sacred weapon, entrusted to you, and you alone,'* or some yak-fodder like that. There you were, candidate for promotion, needing to impress the powers-that-be and all, and you told the majstro it was you who'd screwed up and given a sacred weapon to some kid to clean. You took the heat right off me. You weren't even there to start, could have held back and let me take it, and no one'd have even known you were there. I remember watching you get it from Mihaelo and thinking—knowing—you had my back. What you did that day made me think maybe with the falchilo, with you, I'd found a family that would put a smile in my eyes."

She looked at me, held my gaze for a second, then glanced down. "Kredo."

"Yes, Talia."

"I don't think we're on the right path anymore."

What was it about Esper that had Talia so mixed up? "We're the only thing that stands between Duatero and another Cull."

"Are we?" She didn't sound convinced.

"Yes."

"There's more than one way to dance. Rather than hunting Esper, maybe we should listen to what it has to say."

"Malamiko has nothing to teach us," I said. "It wants us dead, wiped off this planet."

"Do you really believe Esper is contaminated?"

"Yes. Firstsite's report concluded she was. Stelara's Kodo is clear—"

"Stelara's Kodo is just a rule book. The problem with rules is they never change. They don't let you exercise your judgment."

"These rules have kept us alive for thousands of years."

"But Malamiko's changed."

How do I make her see that this is why we cannot show weakness? "Would you have us allow contaminants to walk free among us? Allow them to continue destroying our crops, forcing us to Cull?" My mother *died*, and now Talia wants to go soft on contaminants. No. No more Culls, no more being Malamiko's victim.

"Then send Jak away," she said. "If you want to continue the hunt, at least send him away."

"Are you kidding? I need him."

"You have me."

"I don't trust you." The words were out before they even registered in my mind. She had a look on her face as though I'd stabbed her. It hurt to see it. "I'm sorry. I didn't mean it like that." What did I mean? That she was a drunk? That'd she'd lost faith in the Kodo? That she doubted me? "It's just—"

"It's okay, I get it." She looked past me. "Here come's Jak. Don't make it weird."

Jak came back, plowing through the snow, and dumped an armful of branches and logs by the fire. Did he overhear us? "Aaron's dank breath, the snow's coming down," he said. It didn't seem like he had heard us. He continued, "We're gonna need a lot of wood tonight for the fire. I think we all better get out there and collect as much as we can."

So far on this journey, I'd learned to trust Jak when it came to what we had to do to survive the weather. We spent the remaining hours of light collecting wood for the fire. That night, we had dinner of honey granola, a bit of porridge, smoked chicken meat, and tea while the wind howled in the blackness beyond our fire's light.

I didn't get a chance that night alone with Talia to respond to what she'd told me. My last words to her were too sharp, and I wanted to make things right. I laid awake, listening to the wind buffeting the fabric of my tent, wondering how to get her head back on straight.

THE STORM that hit was ferocious. Talia didn't speak to me the next day. Or the day after. I tried talking to her. She was cordial, but a wall had come down, and I was on the wrong side of it. With time, she might thaw, and I could reach her again. The storm broke the afternoon of the third day, and I resolved to continue our journey the next morning.

I woke that morning with a start. The wind still howled, and pre-dawn greyness smothered my tent. Something had jolted me out of my sleep. What was it?

There it was again. The sizzling crack of a gun in the distance. We slept in our kiraso to keep from freezing. After maintaining my temperature through the night, my suit had barely enough power to engage the helmet in fits and starts as I whipped open my tent flap and stepped out, facing the full fury of the icy wind. "Talia, to arms!" I shouted, moving to her tent. I dashed the flap aside and peered in. Empty. "Talia, report!"

Another crack of a gun sounded above the wind. "Jak?" No answer. Where was everyone?

The shots came from the woods, and I headed toward

them. There were footsteps in the snow, though new snow was quickly burying them, leading toward the forest. Jak emerged from the brush, helmet up, axe in hand. "That way!" he shouted when he saw me, pointing back at the woods.

"Where's Talia?" I asked as I approached him.

"I don't know. I was getting wood for the morning fire, and I heard the shots."

We both ran into the surrounding forest. Our kiraso, drained of power, did nothing to help us stamp our way through knee-deep snow. My movement gave enough of a charge to my batteries, but it wouldn't be enough to help in a fight.

We followed the outline of feet. I tried to hear more sounds giving a hint as to where Talia was but heard nothing but the wind, my feet punching through the snow, and my breath in my helmet.

I stopped, brought Jak to a halt, and strained my hearing, seeking any sound that might guide us. "You hear anything?" I asked.

"Just the wind."

"Keep moving." I couldn't help but think if we'd stumbled close to a nest, we'd be no match for sentinels without our kiraso's augmented strength and speed. We struggled forward, our feet plowing through the glazed surface of the deep snow. I wanted to call out, but we'd lose any chance of surprise if I did.

"Kredo, here," Jak said. I moved to him. He was in a clearing. The snow all around had been stamped down, and in the brightening dawn, I could see several dark red stains on the blanket of white. A form lay there, lightly dusted with snow. I thought it was a log at first—maybe my brain knew but couldn't accept it, and so didn't notice it right away. I almost tripped over it before realizing it was Talia's body lying face down.

"Talia?" I shook her gently. A massive red stain melted the snow around her. I turned her over, cradled her head in my hand. Dead eyes dominated her face, glazing over as I stared at them. I think I screamed for Jak. I don't know, don't remember much except I was yelling. I pressed my hand on a deep hole along her ribs, mindlessly trying to staunch blood that no longer flowed.

Jak was on his knees beside me. "Damn the dark, is she . . ."

"No!" I laid her down, started doing chest compressions. Every time I pushed down on her chest, a deep, sickening gurgle sounded from her wound, and dark blood burbled out onto the snow. "Damn it, Jak, cover her wound!" With a sound like cracking knuckles, I broke her sternum under the weight of my compressions.

"Kredo, I—"

"Do it! Apply pressure!" Jak obeyed. Frantic, mad, I pressed on her chest, tried breathing into her mouth, but my air hissed through the hole in her ribs, escaping between Jak's fingers as he tried to seal the wound with his hand. I kept at it. I don't know how long, but I kept at it. When I stopped, the day had brightened as the sun started to break through the clouds, and the falling snow had stopped, the morning banishing the pre-dawn grey.

Jak looked down at her. "She died in her kiraso, not a contaminant, but a falchilo." His voice was charged with emotion, wavering at the weight of his words. "She should be buried with her ancestors."

"Damn right."

Jak pointed. "Look, there." A little way away, partially buried by upturned snow, I saw a bladder, the kind used to carry liquids. I picked it up, smelled its nozzle. Beer. Talia had been drinking, was probably drunk, when her attacker struck. I tried not to picture her stumbling, reflexes slowed and mind numb from the drink as she fought, but the image came to me, a waking nightmare. I threw the bladder on the ground, stomped on it, again and again, grinding it into the blood and snow and dirt, cursing it, "Mother fucker!" fouling the language the Founders gave us to vent my rage.

"Kredo!" Jak had been yelling at me, I don't know for how long. "Kredo, tracks." He pointed. I could see in the light of day footprints moving away from the clearing. Pools of blood accompanied the trail. "She wounded it," he said. "Whatever attacked her, she wounded it."

"We're going to finish it," I said. "Where's her gun?" The gun I had given her to clean so many years ago, the gun that first bought Talia's loyalty as Mihaelo took a strip off me.

Jak found it and started turning the crankshaft. "Spread out," I said as we began to follow the trail. "Eyes sharp. If it's the dark majstro, it'll have weapons of its own."

We separated and marched for several minutes. I saw the aŭtomato first. The snow made it tough to spot, but the giant mechanical arm reaching out caught my eye, easily five metres long, lined with a ridge of snow starting to sparkle as the sun fought to banish the clouds, claw frozen open, clearly showing that here sat a Founder artifact. This forest was thousands of years old, planted by the Founders, and this aŭtomato had likely lain here, alone, lost, since that time. An undiscovered aŭtomato—a sign of the Founders' favour.

And at its base, sitting on the ground, back propped up against the aŭtomato's body, the dark majstro sat, its head lolling on its chest. Its shoulder was brutally mangled, torn flesh and bones exposed. Good girl, Talia. She must have shot it. I zoomed in with my kiraso's visor. It held a gun loosely in its good hand. It was struggling to draw breath.

It was unconscious. I took its gun without even rousing it and then knelt to pray at the aŭtomato. Doubt. Doubt had plagued me. I had doubted my ability to root out the enemy infiltrating our borders. But the Founders led me here, led me to this ancient artifact, this relic of their power. I could barely make out its form under the snow. I stood and began brushing it off. Trees and bushes had grown around and through it, plants from Earth subsuming its frame, its metal dulled and corroded by dozens of centuries. I could hardly tell what form the aŭtomato took in its halcyon days, but it was clearly a servant of the Founders and a giant one at that.

I shrugged off my pack, searched for some rations, and found a small package of dried fruit. Though starving, I laid it at the aŭtomato's base, an offering. I thought of a prayer my mother used to say.

*M*AY *all people everywhere plagued with sufferings of body and mind quickly be freed from their illnesses.*

May those frightened cease to be afraid, and may those bound be free.

May the spirits of our ancestors guard those who find themselves in trackless, fearful wildernesses.

May we find our way to dine with the Founders.

I'D HEARD her say it first at the funeral of my brother Paulo, who had played with a wiggler while I watched. *While I watched.* Everyone I love dies while I watch. There was nothing I wouldn't give to have Talia share this moment with me. Our very own aŭtomato. But she died here. Beneath my helmet, tears ran down my face.

But she died *here*. Her spirit would dance amongst these trees, would sit high up on that mechanical arm overhead, kicking her legs. Perhaps her spirit looked down on me even now. The thought gave me comfort, helped me smile through my tears.

The dark majstro moaned in pain as it awoke, wiping the smile from my face. It looked up at me, raised its good hand. "Kredo," it said, voice weak. It withdrew its visor, showed me its pale face, covered in a sheen of sweat. Bao was the name it called itself. A Founder name. "Mercy. Please—"

A shot rang out and I started. The dark majstro grunted as a force tore its chest open. It slumped over, blood drenching the snow.

Jak came into the clearing, gun at his shoulder. "Is it dead?"

"You fool, hot-headed … We could have questioned it before cleansing!"

"I'm sorry, Majstro," he said. "It killed Talia. I didn't want to take a chance with it so close to you."

A murderous rage shook my hands. I had wanted to be the one to cleanse it. It should have been me. All I had now was another empty hole that Malamiko had hacked out of my soul without even vengeance to fill it.

TWENTY-FIVE

"MY KIRASO'S still got a charge. I can leap at him, hit him with the rod before he sounds an alarm," Jak said. He laid on his belly beside me, peering over a cliff's edge, spying on a group of soldiers guarding a greenhouse in the mountains surrounding Shihbei. He wore the blue armband of my second.

After Talia had died, winter raged at us, slowing our progress to a crawl. We had pushed onward—recklessly, perhaps, as our boat nearly capsized several times in the bitter winds that stabbed daggers of cold into us. Through it all, a blackness had absorbed my soul and eaten the part of me that could feel. I had lost an important part of myself when Talia died.

The snow fell, the sun shone, the wind blew, and the waters of the Jinhuang flowed. The world did what it had always done. It was the same. Except it no longer had Talia walking its surface or dancing to the rhythms of the oud. It seemed wrong the waters should flow and the winds gust as though her death hadn't happened, as though her life hadn't happened.

When we finally arrived at the Tian Ti's trailhead, we recharged our kirasos, poured libations to honour Talia, and gave the pagoda's gepatro instructions to send her body to Xuanhe where her family could inter her in their mausoleum and her spirit could dine with her ancestors. The gepatro begged us to delay our crossing over the Tian Ti, told us the pass was closed, the risk of an avalanche too great, that it would only take a couple of weeks before warm winds would blow in off the Nanhai Ocean, melting the snowpack. But spring was coming, and with it a new planting season, and still we had no idea how Malamiko was attacking our crops. If we couldn't solve this soon, it was likely we'd have another crop failure this year.

Tian Ti Pass was a serpentine road of crumbling Founder stone lined with crenellated walls. It coiled around mountains and struck out across vertiginous valleys, slithered its way deeper into the Shandong mountains. We had made it to the outskirts of Shihbei yesterday noon. The dark falchilo had come from here, and I believed Esper was here now. I didn't know if contamination lurked here, and if it did, how far it had spread, so I didn't want to announce our presence.

Instead, Jak and I had searched the surrounding valleys and peaks. I had hoped the nest might be outside of Shihbei. Early that morning, we stumbled upon a Founder's greenhouse situated in a high pass, built into the wall of the mountain where the sun could blaze on it. Nothing strange about that, except workers had already cleared the snow off this one, and we could see activity underway inside. It seemed early for that. Even more curious, a group of soldiers camped at a crumbling nearby fort kept close guard. Why would soldiers guard a greenhouse in some isolated corner of one of the hardest-to-reach places on Duatero?

Jak wanted to attack. "No," I said. "We don't know if he's contaminated." I drew back behind the lip of the cliff we perched on. "The rod might kill him. We don't know who's an enemy here."

Jak shrugged and drew back from the ledge to join me. "Well, then, what's the plan?" he asked.

Were these guards contaminants, sentinels guarding their nest? Hosts usually like cold, dank places. The greenhouse would be too warm. "We'll wait 'til night. We'll have night vision, they won't. We ought to be able to get the drop on them, knock out the guards at the door without alerting the rest in the fort. Then, we'll see what's worth protecting in that greenhouse."

We drew back from the ledge and moved to a nearby slope free from snow where we could sit and pass the time. Jak took out a hand-sized wood-carved statuette of Talia he'd been working on and set to smoothing its surface with a tiny knife. Usually, Jak finished his wood carvings quickly, but he'd laboured over this one of Talia for days. This was the third one he'd attempted since her death, having discarded the previous two for imperfections only he could see. This surprised me. Jak hadn't had much respect for Talia when she was alive.

The sun shone. Snow melted. From our vantage point, it seemed we were on top of the world, staring down at white-tipped trees. Down one valley, huddled against a mountainside like a lamb snug in a bed of straw, sat Shihbei, its green tiled roofs and pale stone catching the sun, tendrils of smoke from hundreds of warming fires drifting upwards. High up along the mountainside sat the Tero Kreinto, the last one built by Founders. I knew it from legend. There in its heart sat the red stone structure of the Rugha Palace surrounded by the pale white stone of the Cangbai Palace with its elaborate battlements, calling to mind images of a roughly hewn ruby set in a frame of white marble.

The view, spectacular as it was, was ash to my eyes. All I could think about was what I might say to Talia were she here or how she might gripe about how bloody bored she was. A wave of rage washed over me with such intensity I shook.

"You okay?" Jak asked, looking up from his carving.

"It's good. Going to be a long day is all."

Jak shrugged and turned back to smoothing a feature on the statuette with his tiny knife. The day passed, the dripping of melting snow marking the passage of time. I dozed; had unsettling dreams. The sun set, and after darkness had fallen over the mountains for several hours, we returned to the Founder's greenhouse. I stared down from my ledge to two soldiers guarding the entrance, the visor of my kiraso allowing me to see in the green hue of night vision. I zoomed my visor in on the fort. "No sign of activity," I said. "Remember, no rods. We'll knock the guards out, drag them into the greenhouse, and then bind and gag them."

"Yeah, yeah," Jak said, exasperation in his voice.

"No axe, either."

Talia would have made some quip, asking if we were to tickle them into submission, or something off-handed. Not that, but something like it. I don't know what she'd say. She was quicker than I. Jak said nothing.

We leaped off the high ledge and dropped to the ground, dark angels descending from the nighttime sky, our kiraso absorbing the impact of landing. The guards didn't stand a chance and were unconscious in moments. We dragged them into the greenhouse and bound and gagged them with rope from our supplies.

I searched the building to see what they were working on —rows of soil, partitioned at regular intervals. "They're plants," Jak said, peering down into a soil box. A thin cotyledon of three tiny leaves barely poked out of the dirt. "What is it, do you think?"

"Grain," I said. I'd spent my childhood growing it. Even under the strange hue of night vision, I could tell by the shape of the plant what it was. Something gnawed at the back of my mind, though I couldn't place what. I took my rod out, snapped it to full length.

"What is it?" Jak asked, doing the same.

I stared at the tiny plant. It looked fine, but something about it made me uneasy.

Jak looked over at another planter. "Is it grain or what?"

"Yeah, I'm pretty sure." I looked at the tag on the front of the soil box. It read: *T. ara* pc^{xd}.

Jak read the label over my shoulder. "What in the dark is that?"

"'*T. ara*' is an abbreviation for the Founder symbol for wheat. I don't know the rest." I grabbed a pinch of soil from the container and rubbed it between my fingers. It had a thin crust like Esper first saw in the fields around Kubuto Falls.

We stared at it. "So, what do we do?" Jak asked.

"Keep looking, see if we can learn more about what's going on."

We searched, found row after row of planters, row after row of strange names. *S. cer* pc^{xd}, *L. sativa* pc^{xd}, *Z. mays* pc^{xd}— rye, lettuce, corn, and more, all modified in some way. Near the back sat a desk, and on it, I found books of log entries and notes. Sitting down on the wooden stool, I started flipping through pages to get a sense of what was happening, but I'd need to spend time reading them to really understand what they were undertaking here.

It became apparent we'd found all we were going to, and we'd learned nothing.

"I don't get it," Jak said. "Why the guards."

"These notebooks might have some clues," I said. Still, something wasn't sitting right. "Here, hold these." I passed the notebooks to Jak and went over to pick up a planter, the one we had looked at originally. I took it to the desk where I'd found the notebooks, lit the lamp sitting on its surface, and held it over the planter so we could see what we were looking at under normal light rather than the green-tinged view of night vision.

Jak gasped at what it illuminated and took a step back. I stared at it, a cold sweat breaking along my forehead and down my back. "What . . ." Jak struggled for words. "*What have they done?*" His voice came out as a harsh hiss, as though the spirits tore the words from his throat.

It was wheat. I'd spent enough years farming to know it when I saw it. It had the stalk and leaves of *our* plants, but in the lamp's light, its leaves were blue. Malamiko blue.

"It's found a way to contaminate our food," I said. "Mix these seeds with our own seeds, we won't know we're planting our own death until . . ." A cold bead of sweat dripped down my back. My skin felt cold and clammy, and I had to brace myself on the desk as I wavered. They may have already shipped seeds to mix with the seeds from the rest of Duatero. In a few short weeks, after the floods abated, farmers might start planting them. It could already be too late. Was this Malamiko's death blow?

Fondo. My thoughts jumped to my brother, of the last time I'd seen him at Gaja's house during the Cull, of his two kids, a boy and girl, asking me to tell them tales of my adventures. He would plant these seeds. His children would starve once the Malamiko took over his field. I stared at the contaminated cotyledon of grain, my heart fluttering like butterfly wings in the wind. I left my family to save them. Have I failed again?

A male voice called an alarm outside. I snuffed the lamp. "We've got to cleanse them," I said. "We've got to cleanse them all."

We erupted out the doors of the Founder greenhouse. A group of contaminants carrying torches was running to us, spears in hand. Jak had the dark majstro's gun—his gun now —and fired, again and again into the herd, dropping three of them with four shots and turning the rest back to their fort. I leaped into their midst, my rod striking and stabbing in a flurry, dropping contaminants around me as I advanced.

A blow struck my knee, driving me to the ground. A contaminant stood above me, spear high overhead in preparation for stabbing it through my chest. An axe thunked into its head, and it collapsed. Jak darted over my prone body, driving into another cluster of contaminants. I got up and fell to the ground after putting weight on my knee. Using my rod for support, I got up again and hobbled after Jak and the rest of the fleeing contaminants.

Jak had to stop before the fort, crouching behind his shield, taking shelter from sling bullets whizzing down from above like a hail storm. I limped up beside him, bullets hammering off my shield.

"You okay?" Jak asked, nodding toward my leg.

"Good enough." I took the flamjetilo from its holster, powered it on. "Smash open the door, then get out of the way," I ordered. "Then circle around behind and stop anything trying to escape."

We stood under cover of our shields. I limped forward, Jak pacing me. He kicked open the door, sending it flying off its hinges with the power of his kiraso, and I poured a river of flame into the building. The unholy screaming of contaminants filled the night like banshees screeching, echoed off the surrounding mountains, and reverberated down valleys and crags. In minutes it was over. We dragged the guards we'd left outside the fort into the Founder greenhouse and then cleansed that, too.

When we were done, when nothing of the guards or the contaminated seedlings was left but ash, my knee throbbed in pain, and I couldn't walk without the assistance of my rod for support. "If anyone was watching this ridge, they'd have seen the fire and come to check it out," I said. "We need to go. We can't be captured, not yet. Malamiko wants to contaminate our entire food supply, and we've got to stop it."

Founders' grace, my knee ached. With Jak supporting me, we travelled through the night, but my knee became worse, and I called a halt before dawn. We cleared an area of snow and sat, backs against a rock, watching the sun crack over the peaks of the Shandong Mountains, like it did yesterday, like it would tomorrow. But the world was different now. If Esper managed to send these seeds to the rest of Duatero, this would be our last spring.

While we distanced ourselves from the embers of the Founder greenhouse throughout the night, I'd been thinking about what we needed to do. "You need to go back over the Tian Ti Pass and get word to Firstsite," I said.

"Agreed," Jak said. "My suit's got power still. I can take you."

"No."

Jak stared at me. "I'm not leaving you here."

"Yes, you are."

"Their falchilo are contaminated, their army's contaminated—far as we know, all of bloody Shihbei is one big nest."

"Jak, as soon as the Tian Ti opens for traders, they'll be

able to take their seeds out along every trade route. Far as we know, they may have seeds sitting in our granaries from last year. Once the floods recede and seeding starts, it's too late. But Firstsite can track granaries with seeds from Shihbei and cleanse them before they're planted. Then you've got to get Firstsite to send help to root out the contamination in Shihbei.

"But we've got to act fast. Snows'll melt, opening the Tian Ti. Floods will come and go soon. You've got to get word to Firstsite."

"Burning granaries," Jak said. "So soon after our last Cull . . ."

"We'll need to Cull again," I finished for him.

"Your knee's just twisted. A couple of days, it'll be fine. In the meantime, I can carry you. We're going to do this. We're going to save Duatero together."

"Jak, Malamiko took Esper from me, and Talia, and . . . it's taken *everything* from me!" My shout echoed off the mountainside. I forced calm in my voice. "But the spirits of the Founders kept you alive. I've got to believe they did so for a reason. And this is it. Of all the falchilo I've known, only you have the strength to do what must be done. I know Esper didn't have the strength to do what you must do. Talia didn't either in the end. You do, Jak. If you do this, they'll make you a majstro. You'll be the Hero of Shihbei—that is your destiny. Malamiko has penetrated us deeper than it ever has, and we need to cut deeper than we've ever cut to cure ourselves. The spirits of the Founders kept you alive because you're the knife."

Pride straightened Jak's back, curved his lip into a slight smile. He turned to me. "What will you do?"

"As soon as I'm able, I'll find their food stores and start burning them; greenhouses, too."

"When do you want me to leave?"

"Now. I'll keep Talia's gun, my flamjetilo, and the food in my pack."

Jak rested the back of his head against the rock we were leaning on. "When I return, I will find you, Kredo."

"If I've been captured, assume I'm contaminated. Cleanse me. Don't allow Malamiko to make my body the instrument of Duatero's destruction."

He looked me in the eyes. "You can count on me."

I know Talia would not have had the strength to do what I asked Jak to do. The knowledge weighed heavily on me, but it was true. I remembered the pain of cleansing Aprila, so many years ago in the forests surrounding Eta Monteto. Pain that twisted me still. She—it—had cried, but it did not fight. Mihaelo was unconscious, the rest of our squad dead. "You could run." I had said that to Aprila. "No one would know." I had offered it life.

The look in its eyes stabbed me like a knife in my chest, burned me like the handle of a frying pan left too long on the fire. A look of absolute yearning, of desperately wanting to take my offer, to do anything other than face what must be done. Perhaps offering it that temptation was cruel. I hadn't intended it as such.

"You've seen what's become of contaminants," it had said to me. "Don't let me become that." It closed its eyes. "Do it." We'd fought together for months. She'd taken me under her wing when I first arrived in Mihaelo's squad. I lived, I succeeded, due to what she had taught me. "Do it now!" And I pulled the trigger—the trigger of the gun I now held, the same gun that had been Talia's—saw Aprila jolt off her feet, torso torn open by my shot, and I dropped to my knees, vomiting into the pools of mud.

Could Talia have survived doing that to me? In a way, I was glad death had ensured she'd never face such a choice.

Painful as it was, perhaps her death was a gift from the Founders. Even now, in this moment when Malamiko seemed ascendant and Duatero on the brink of destruction, I could still see the influence of the Founders' wisdom at work. They had, after all, led me to discover an aŭtomato hadn't they?

"Here, I want you to have this," Jak said, opening his pack and digging through it. He withdrew the wooden statuette of Talia he'd been working on. "I'd have spent more time smoothing it if I could."

I took the carving from him, felt its weight in my hands, ran my fingers over its surface. "It's perfect." The features of the face Jak had carved were so like the mythical wolf from Earthen legend. "I'm surprised. I didn't think you liked her."

His face held no expression. "I know she was important to you. I'm sorry she died." I said nothing, staring at the carving. Jak stood up. "May you dine with the Founders, Kredo."

"May Donna, Star of the Fields, lead you to safe roads, Jak."

He turned and marched through the snow.

TWENTY-SIX

STILL LIMPING, I managed to burn down one food store. It was in a valley about two kilometres from Shihbei—a stone building, cellar dug into the ground underneath it, guarded by two contaminants. I shot them with my gun and cleansed them and everything inside to ash. After that, my kiraso had no power, and I didn't trust any of the pagodas to approach for a recharge. My flamjetilo ran out of power, too. I spent an afternoon transferring the crankshaft from the gun to the flamjetilo, and then an evening cranking it up, giving it enough of a charge for one good blast. My knee burned and swelled to the point it barely fit in the leg of my kiraso.

I wanted to rest, knew my leg needed it, but the thought of my brother Fondo planting Esper's contaminated seeds this spring drove me on. Relying heavily on my rod as walking staff, I struggled through snowy mountainous terrain avoiding the roads while I hunted for more food stores or greenhouses. My knee limited my progress to one, maybe two kilometres.

The next day I found another greenhouse. It was an old

station along the Founder road. It was a metal frame structure with plates of transparent polycrysteel, the same material as my shield, forming walls and roof. Set beside the Founder road, it reminded me of a long jar turned on its side and half-buried, or a tunnel made of glass. The station was fully enclosed, and the Shihbeians had converted it over to a greenhouse. I observed it from a distance, hidden in a forest of thick trees and brush, the sound of dripping and running water everywhere as the snow melted under the sun. As with the other greenhouse Jak and I had cleansed, a small group of paisajista worked throughout the day while soldiers stood guard. I wanted to attack now, cleanse the paisajista working on these contaminated plants, but knew with my suit out of power and my knee the way it was, I needed to wait for night, when fewer people were around.

Unlike the greenhouse Jak and I first encountered, however, the guards here positioned themselves inside the building once everyone left and the sun set. They were adapting in light of my previous attacks. Using my night vision, my movements giving enough of a charge to power it, I counted four guards through the transparent walls working some mechanism to lock the door. This would be difficult. I'd need to use one shot of my gun to blast the lock to open the door. That'd leave me with three shots for four guards. I could shoot the lock, then come in and let loose with a blast from my flamjetilo. Not ideal, as that would not guarantee I'd cleanse the further back portions of the greenhouse, especially if the guards managed to flank me and force me to cover or retreat. Plus, being forced to hand charge the flamjetilo left it low on power, and I might only get one partial blast.

I decided I'd shoot the lock and then try to take out three guards with the remaining shots on my gun, and then hope I could crank up the charge on my gun before the fourth one rushed me. With the guards subdued, I'd have time to make sure I cleansed every contaminated seed and planter in there.

Things went well up to the point where I blasted off the lock. I entered the greenhouse, tracking with my gun for the first guard to shoot, but ran afoul of tripwire. It was a trap. With my knee as it was, I fell like a chopped tree and rolled on the ground. The tripwire was rigged to a giant plate of polycrysteel above the door, and when I triggered it, the plate dropped on me as I was scrambling to my feet, knocking me senseless.

When I came to, the guards were in the process of disarming me and removing my kiraso.

"Stand point," one of them said. "There are two others."

They thought I was here with Jak and Talia. The longer they believed that, the longer it would be before they sent troops to track down Jak. "It's a trap!" I yelled.

"Shut him up," a guard ordered. "He'll scare off the others."

Two guards gagged and bound me as I struggled and yelled. When done, they all stood tense, coiled springs, staring at the door. Hours passed. Of course, no one came. As the sun began to rise, cracking over the mountains, one of them asked, "So, which one do we got?"

"He's got the red armband," said another. "This'd be Majstro Kredo."

One of them squatted in front of me, bowed its head, and placed palms together over its forehead. "I apologize, Majstro. It ain't my desire to strike anyone of the Tero Kreinto. I pray you'll see what it is that we're doing, and one day you'll forgive me." It put a bag on my head.

I ENTERED Shihbei for the first time bound and gagged, tied in a sack, and strapped down in the back of a cart. My hands and feet were numb from the restraints. I tested my bindings, but I was tied up tight. The sounds of a crowded street came from all around me—people talking, yaks snorting, and wagons trundling over cobblestone.

I had to get out of here before they brought me to the nest. Talia died herself. Founders help me, I wasn't going to let myself become a dark majstro. I tried getting up, thrashed and squirmed, but I was tied down to the floor of the cart. I tried calling out over the gag, but my cries fit right in with the hectic background noise of the street. But really, what was I expecting? Without my kiraso, I looked like a man, a man in custody being transported by city guards. Most would assume I was a criminal.

My captors were taking me up a steep incline with zigzag-ging switchbacks. The sounds of the crowd lessened, replaced with soft murmuring voices, barely heard above the cart's creaking. After some time, we stopped. Hands, too many of them to count, grabbed me, freed me from my restraints, picked me up, and then dropped me to the ground before tearing off the sack I'd been stored in.

The sun clubbed my eyes, and I painfully got to my knees, my injured leg raging in pain as I tried to bend it, hands and feet still bound. I was in a small courtyard of dust-covered stones. The white walls of the Tero Kreinto rose before me like the pale cliffs of the Shandong Mountains, and at its base, a simple wooden door. Guards surrounded me.

Hidden in a sack. Taken to a side door. They didn't want my capture known.

The door opened, and an old woman exited. It wore the robes of an altaj paisajista—senior clergy, second only to the Unua—ankle-length brown robes, intricate geometric patterns embroidered in the fabric, with golden fringe, adorned with a red sash and belt. There were only five paisajista of that rank, one for each Tero Kreinto, and so I knew its name. "Altaj Karesinda Safirida." A contaminant? Was she aware of the contaminated seeds growing in Shihbei's greenhouses? It seemed safest to assume so.

It ignored me. "Is he the only one?" it asked the guards.

One of the soldiers placed my kiraso, gun, flamjetilo, all I had, at its feet. "Caught him trying to burn down one of our greenhouses. We haven't found the other two yet."

The dark altaj nodded to one of the guards who walked into the building and out of view. It inspected my kiraso, saw the red armband. "Welcome to Shihbei, Majstro Kredo," it said. "We were hoping you'd come, though we wished it was with less violence."

Movement at the door grabbed my attention. It was Esper, dressed in full kiraso. Her face was leaner, harder than I remembered it, with a patch over one eye. Her remaining green eye stared at me with intensity, an emerald catching the sun in the depths of its angles.

"Hello, Kredo," it said. I said nothing, studying it, trying to see if any sign of contamination marred the area around its lips and nose. If it were going to manifest signs of contamination, it would have done so by now unless it was a shell. "Where's Jak and Talia?" it asked.

An image of Talia, blood staining white snow, flashed in my mind. "Dead. They're both dead." They mustn't find out about Jak. He was our only hope.

The contaminant's face twisted, looked as though it might be sick. It mimicked our emotions so well. The trace beginnings of frown lines I didn't remember it having etched its brow. "Talia?" it asked.

"Dead!"

"I don't believe you."

"Look in my pack," I said. Esper's brow furrowed and head cocked. It moved to my pack and dumped its contents on the ground. It bent over to pick up the wood carving of Talia. "Jak made that before he died."

It ran its fingers down the carving's length. "Where is Bao?" it asked, refusing to look at me. Its voice was tight, as though it took great effort to speak the words, as if not wanting to ask a question it didn't want the answer to.

"Bao?"

"Majstro Falchilo Bao." Its voice wavered; its hands trembled. "We sent him to bring you here."

Esper's emotions seemed so genuine, the tightness of its lips, the slight shudder in its breath. Dread? Was the emotion Esper showed simply it playing human, or had Malamiko's time masquerading as a human given it some of our feelings? Maybe, somehow, the contamination stopped at stage one or two in Esper—maybe that was the change in Malamiko. Talia doubted Esper's contamination altogether. Perhaps I was wrong. Maybe Esper wasn't contaminated. Its emotions seemed so real. Doubt gnawed at me. But I'd seen stage one and two contaminants, perfectly normal-looking, confirmed by the GC when it still worked. I knew how well early-stage contaminants could pass amongst us. And in Vojo Fino, shells from a late-stage nest carried on normal conversations with me. How could I know if it was still Esper?

"Where is Bao?" it asked again. "Please tell me, Kredo."

The world froze, not even the breeze daring to move. An eternity between falling grains of sand. Esper's one eye was locked on the carving; the dark altaj stared at Esper, lips tight. Another blood-soaked clearing came to mind. "It killed Talia."

"No. That's not true."

"It killed Talia. And then we killed it."

Something broke in Esper. Its arms hung slack by its sides, its grip white-knuckle tight on the carving. It turned and staggered back to the door of the Tero Kreinto.

"Esper, I don't know what happened to you," I called to its back, "I don't know if your spirit can hear me but listen! Talia died free of contamination! She died trying to save Duatero!" But Esper had retreated through the door, vanishing into the bowels of the Tero Kreinto. "I will free you too! Founder's grace, I swear it!"

TWENTY-SEVEN

THEY IMPRISONED me in the Tero Kreinto's quarantine cells. Built with smooth walls seemingly carved from a single block of gray Founder stone, only the door of steel, polished smooth as ice and just as cold, a passthrough of transparent polycrysteel, and a hole bored into the floor no wider than my knee that served as my toilet marred the uniformity of my cell.

Esper did not visit me, nor did the dark altaj. They had abandoned me. The only sign they had not forgotten me completely was the food and water my guards placed inside the passthrough twice a day. I spent my time during those first days looking for ways to escape. I had nothing but time. But, the utensils my food and water came with were wooden, useless against Founder stone and polycrysteel, unable even to leave a mark that I might use to record the number of days I'd been here. I must have explored every square inch of my cell a dozen times looking for some crack, some weakness I could work on, but found nothing. I banged my cup along each wall, listening for a return tap from a neighboring prisoner, but only the silence of my thoughts replied.

This silence unnerved me the most. It was not the silence of the farm, where breezes blow, whispering through the leaves and stalks of grain, the grunt and snuffle of animals soft in the distance. Nor was it the silence of the city, where the air carries the murmur of voices on the street below, or the creak of the cart, or padding of footsteps. Here, in quarantine, the silence was utter and absolute, like my head was encased in stone deep beneath the surface where not even the strongest of vibrations might reach. I called out, and the silence absorbed my voice like a dry rag soaking up water.

During the first few days of my imprisonment, I thought through my predicament to distract me from the haunting silence suffocating my mind. They took me to the Tero Kreinto in secret, and even there, they still aped human emotions so as not to draw attention to themselves. The contamination had pierced Shihbei deep, but not completely. We hadn't lost yet.

Moreover, Duatero still had Jak. He was going to be the Hero of Shihbei, a new generation of falchilo to fight a new generation of Malamiko. How long had it been since he left? He must be over the Tian Ti Pass by now. If Malamiko ignored me long enough, if Jak could convince Firstsite to act, maybe I'd see daylight again.

Ah, who was I kidding? Even if I did manage to stay alive until the armies came, Jak knew what to do. He'd assume I was contaminated, and I'd spend the rest of my days in a quarantine cell like this, or he'd cleanse me. It's what I'd do—it's what I ordered him to do. He knows it and has the will to do it.

Days passed. It is a strange thing to feel your mind slip

away. The weight of my isolation crushed my thoughts, and I found myself talking out loud when I had believed I was thinking quietly. Restless energy burned through me; I paced constantly. Upon waking, I'd exercise—push-ups, sit-ups, squats, running and jumping on the spot, to the point of exhaustion, counting my reps aloud to thrash back the silence grasping at me.

A reader sat in the passthrough one morning when I woke. Was I hallucinating? I closed my eyes, letting darkness join forces with the silence for a moment. Part of me was afraid to open my eyes in case it was a hallucination. It was still there when I opened them.

Esper had been given a reader when it was in quarantine. Was it taunting me by mimicking its own experience? "I'm not going to play your game!" I shouted to the walls. They replied with a stoic quiet.

Days blended together. The plains of Duatero would be flooding now. Had Jak made it to a Tero Kreinto in a Founder City? Maybe. Depends on the weather. So much depends on the weather. Rain. RAIN! I would scream at the passthrough, banging my hands until they ached. The reader sat unmoved.

The spirit world began to visit me. Or maybe I was hallucinating. It started with lights at the edge of my vision, disappearing as I whipped my head to look. They quickly got more elaborate. I knew they were visions, knew they were the product of a mind suffering from isolation, but they seemed so real, so visceral. My sister Gaja appeared, not old, not like the last time I saw her, but young, from when I left her the first time. She pointed a damning finger at me. "Maybe *you're* Malamiko!"

Maybe I was. Maybe they had contaminated me, and this was my mind trapped in my head while my body did their work. Could that be? I walked through my memories. Was there a moment when I was contaminated, my skin pricked by an innocuous thorn? Maybe that knife wound when Elekti's father attacked me? And I'd fought that one dark wanderer without my kiraso. Talia inspected me after and gave me the all clear. But, if a dark wanderer's thorn had nicked me, would Talia have said anything knowing it would mean my death if she did? Was Esper trapped in a dungeon such as this while her body corrupted Duatero? Was my body by her body's side, even now bringing my people closer to ruin?

If I wasn't contaminated, what were they keeping me here for? Question me, torture me, gloat over me, execute me . . . contaminate me. Do something. But to keep me here, alone, to do nothing except keep me alive—why?

Of course, they had done something. I opened the passthrough and touched the reader's smooth cold surface. Founders had touched this device. Maybe even Yu Lifen had read reports from this very reader during the construction of Shihbei's Tero Kreinto. Picking it up, I powered it on. Someone—it wasn't hard to guess who—had already loaded a reading list.

Breeding of a transgenic phycocyanin-based T. Aestivum

A Novel Mechanism to Isolate genes encoding for ammonia monooxygenase and hydroxylamine oxidoreductase

Inhibition of N. europaea *by glucosinolate hydrolysis products*

Amongst many others. Hallucinations suddenly did not seem so bad. Then the location codes of the reports caught my attention. They had come from Port Donna's disc library.

I sat in a corner, reader propped on my knees, and began to read.

I was reading when someone knocked at the passthrough. It was Esper. It sat, arms crossed, leaning back in a chair on the other side as it stared angrily at me with its one eye. I had no chair, and the passthrough was too high for me to see through if I sat on the floor but too low for me to stand straight and see Esper. I bent over, hand on the wall for support.

How should I start this conversation? Esper did it for me. "You killed Bao." Its voice was thin, muted by the passthrough's polycrysteel.

"And its second, Tai."

A look of heartbreak broke its features, and it stood up to walk away. It stopped, took a breath, and resumed its seat. "Why?" It shot the word at me like a sling bullet. "Why didn't you listen to them? You never listened."

"We never really had a lot of time for conversation," I said.

"No, I suppose not. You were always one for action."

I remembered Bao's death, Jak shooting it before I could question it. "I've slowed down recently." I held up the reader. "Taken up reading."

"I'm not contaminated, Kredo."

Of course, it would say that. Every contaminant I've encountered that could speak has told me the same. I pointed at the patch over where its one eye had been. "You weren't cleared at Firstsite."

It lost control of its anger, knocking its chair over as it stood. "Staring at a mangled eye! What's next? Will we use tea leaves to root out contamination? Or sacrifice sheep to the Founders to coax them into giving us guidance?"

This wasn't going to be a productive line of discussion. "Tell me about this reading list," I said, changing the subject.

It placed a hand on either side of the passthrough and leaned in. "I know why our crops are failing."

I stepped back, arms crossed. "Do you?"

"Yes. Nitrifying bacteria."

I stared at her. "What?"

It picked up the chair and sat down again. "Good soil has a variety of bacteria that are essential for maintaining the conditions needed to grow crops. One class of these are the nitrifying bacteria. They're essential for converting nitrogen into a form our crops can take up. Without this process—without these bacteria—our plants can't get nitrogen. Without nitrogen, our plants die."

"So, what do you think is happening to these nitrifying bacteria?"

"A Malamikan bacteria has mutated, allowing it to survive in our soil. It's out-competing our nitrifying bacteria for nutrients. It's what's causing the crusting we saw on the soil by Kubuto Falls."

"How . . ." Did it expect me to believe this? "How could you know such a thing?"

"The manlibroj I got from the ruins of Port Donna."

"Port Donna's manlibroj are centuries old. How could they tell you the cause of our problems today?"

"I tested the soil myself, Kredo. I followed directions in Port Donna's manlibroj to make a nitrate probe and tested our soil."

"A nitrate probe?" Was that what it wanted with the silver wire and the glass ornaments?

"There's more," it said, lifting a small dish covered with a clear glass lid so I could see it through the passthrough. On the bottom of the dish sat a layer of some translucent solid the color of melted butter. Scattered across its surface were striated, flesh-colored lumps that reminded me of warts one of our neighbors on the farm had on his hands. "Following the instructions in the manlibroj, I've managed to isolate this Malamikan bacteria."

Reflexively, I took a step back. "That's Malamiko?"

"Yes," she said looking at it. "The scholars of Port Donna believed it was a symbiote of the contamination, conditioning the soil of the nest. On its own lands, other Malamikan bacteria compete with it, limiting its spread. But it has no natural competitors in our soil. This may have allowed the contamination to survive better on our lands, explaining why we see more stage five nests, and why its able to adapt better to human hosts than before."

I shook my head. It was trying to confuse me with technobabble. "Nitrate probes. Plucking invisible bacteria from the soil. These tools are lost to us. You say we do little more than stare at tea leaves, yet you'd have me believe you've tapped into some mystical power, that you've turned myth into reality." I wanted to say that we lose the technology of the Founders, not gain them, but I didn't want to speak that belief aloud.

"Use your eyes, Kredo," it said, holding its dish towards me so I could see the Malamikan bacteria. "The truth is here to see."

I began to wonder if, perhaps, I had been wrong about Esper. Doubt. Such a small, subtle thing. But isn't it always small, subtle things that cause the hero's fall. We hunt for monsters, ignoring the roots widening the cracks in our foundation. "Lies!" I must not let it warp my mind. All I had was its word on what that dish contained, and what it did to our soil. "Our crops die. We Cull, and we Cull again. And you tell me after one trip to Port Donna—one trip!—you've got it all figured out?"

"This is what the scholars at Port Donna were working on

when the sea rose to claim it. They knew this was happening! Look at the records at any Tero Kreinto. Yields have been dropping since before the city fell."

"We've lost the secrets of the Founders. Rendezvous comes and goes in silence. Our ability to fix the Tero Kreinto ended centuries ago. We're alone, it's no wonder our yields fall."

"We can fix this. The Altaj of Shihbei saw it too. She knew of my research when I was an initiate. That's why she sought me out and sent Majstro Bao to find me. And that's why he rescued me from quarantine. The Founders knew the secrets of moving genes from one organism to another. These records remained at Port Donna, and from my research as an initiate, I understand them! I can save us. I've been using this knowledge to try and develop strains of grain that can grow in native soil, that's what you found in the greenhouse. And more, Kredo! The scholars of Port Donna were working on ways to protect us from contamination, too. The Founders didn't abandon us. We have their knowledge, and we can use it to save ourselves."

"Enough of your lies," I said. "You're telling me you knew all this, had the manlibroj of Port Donna as proof, had the Altaj of Shihbei as an ally, and you said nothing to us? Esper would have told us what she learned. She would have made us see."

"Maybe before you quarantined me and took my eye!" It tore the patch from its face that covered its missing eye. An empty socket, a blackness deeper than the Nanhai Ocean filling it. The ragged skin surrounding the hole was puckered, like cracked lips. It jabbed its finger at me in a gesture pregnant with depths of accusation, and said, "You cast me away to die!" Its strength left it. Its arm dropped to its side, and it leaned against the passthrough. "We sent Bao to talk to you. We thought you might listen to another majstro, and then you could convince Mihaelo, and he the Unua. But you killed Bao. You burn what you don't understand."

We have such limits. Eyes that only see a drop in the ocean of light waves put out by the sun, ears that only hear a thin range of vibrations in the air, nerves that feel only what we can reach out and touch. We are so small, the universe so vast. We are blind, fumbling in the dark. How, then, are we to find our way?

Nitrifying bacteria. Could we truly know such a thing? Could we build the tools the Founders used to test for ourselves with any certainty, and then blithely move genes from one plant to another to keep us alive as Founder Donna once did? Were these thoughts Malamiko seeping into my mind, clouding my thoughts with doubt? Was this how cont-amination worked on its human host, twisting thoughts until you became Malamiko's puppet? My heart thudded in my ears. Could Esper prove these claims? Could I ever trust what it showed me as proof? Will there ever be enough knowledge to banish doubt?

No. Of course not. Only faith can banish doubt.

"I know Jak's alive," it said, its voice soft now.

My stomach knotted. Had they captured him? Was he in a cell down here in quarantine with me? Perhaps Esper was trying to trick me into revealing the truth. "Why do you believe that?" I asked. I tried to ignore the absence where its eye once was. The void there bored deep into my spirit.

"He convinced Firstsite to unite the armies of Duatero against Shihbei."

"Armies?" What had Jak told them?

"Yes, armies. Aaronsburg and Lu Guang are at the head of

the Tian Ti pass right now. Our army is holding them there. We believe Lan Hu and Xuanhe will arrive any day."

"Why do you think Jak had anything to do with that?"

"Because falchilo fight with them, and Jak is one of their leaders."

TWENTY-EIGHT

THAT NIGHT I dreamed of Malamiko. I dreamed I stood in a field of blue-leafed, plate-shaped fronds, the wind blowing in hushed gusts whispering through the growth, forming words as it did. *This world is not your home.*

The sun shone on my face in my dream, the Founder's warmth washing over me. "We have made our home here for two-thousand-six-hundred-forty-five years. We have passed the test of time. This is *our* home now."

You falter. You must repel an endless train of attacks, but I need only one victory.

The blue fronds shifted and grew, wrapped around my legs, my torso, my arms, and my neck, down my throat, choking me. I woke up gagging.

Reading helped to keep the mad boredom of isolation at bay. The papers Esper had selected for me were technical and challenging to read. I didn't understand much of it, but I understood enough to get a sense of how the scholars of Port Donna took genes from one organism and transposed them into others. I learned of the studies they performed on the soil and of the meticulous measurement of yields of genetically modified crops under a variety of conditions. I read the paper on how to build a nitrate probe and another on how to use it to measure nitrate levels in our soil.

We lost so much when Port Donna fell. The greatest intellects were drawn to that doomed city. Our best minds perished that day with most of their work on disc, waiting to be uploaded to the manlibroj. And then two back-to-back Culls after that—a third of our population gone. How much wisdom and experience did we lose as so many sacrificed themselves?

Naturally, I thought deeply about Esper, specifically, whether I still believed it was contaminated. Nothing in the reports I'd been reading contradicted what it had said to me. Of course, it had created my reading list, so it was likely biased. With the knowledge to transfer genes, it could have transmitted genes fatal to humans into grain seeds as easily as genes to help our plants thrive, as it had claimed. It would be safest to continue doubting it for now.

It came later that day, clad in its kiraso. It knocked on the passthrough to get my attention. "Is Talia really dead?" it asked.

I didn't say a word, but the expression I could not keep from my face seemed to tell Esper everything it needed to know. Its face looked so haggard.

It marshalled the strength to speak. "Are you ready to see more?" It worked some mechanism out of my line of sight, and then the door to my cell unlocked.

I placed the reader beside me and stood warily. "You're going to release me from quarantine?"

"For now. Come on."

I opened the door to my cell, and the cool refreshing air from the hallway kissed my cheeks. And there it stood, less than an arm's length away. I could have rushed it, slung my fist into its head. But it wore the kiraso. I'd be a lamb charging an ox.

"This way," it said. It led me through the quarantine block. "There is one more thing the scholars of Port Donna were working on you need to see," it said as we walked.

"Any hints?" I asked, peering through the passthroughs lining the walls to see if others were imprisoned. All the cells we passed were dark and empty.

"Have you read the paper on selenophile's sensitivity to racin-beta-five yet?"

I had no idea. "Why don't you refresh my memory?"

It looked at me, a hint of a proud smile creasing its eye. "Why don't I show you, instead."

We came to a hallway cast in darkness. Set out on a small side table made of wood was a tray with a bowl of food, a cup of water, and a pot of what looked like mushrooms. It picked up the mushroom pot and held it between us. They looked like the kind of growth I'd seen in gardens and homesteads throughout Duatero. "Smell anything?" it asked.

I strained my senses. The only smell I could detect was the earthy loam of the soil, and I told it as much.

"Good," it said. It picked up the tray and led down the darkened hallway. We went around a corner and then another. The darkness became nearly pitch, save for a light emanating from a passthrough window some distance away. It was to this passthrough it led me.

"With the hallway darkened, it won't be able to see us," Esper said.

It?

"Do you remember the stage four nest we encountered in Vojo Fino? The one we cleansed the day we learned of the Cull?" Esper asked as we walked down the hall. How could I forget? "You remember how it had shells that could carry on a conversation."

We arrived at the passthrough. Curious, I peered into the room on the other side. A young boy about eight years old stood in the cell, unmoving, a silent, life-like statue. An ingratiating smile was frozen on its face. Behind it where its bed should have lain rested a mound of black hyphae, its thin, hair-like tendrils moving gently, as though a gentle breeze blew in the cell.

"You captured a shell and its host," I said, impressed.

"Bao, Tai, and I encountered a stage four nest near the head of the Tian Ti pass. It had the same morphology as the nest in Vojo Fino. Shells that talked, dark wanderers. It even had decoy host sites. We cleansed it and captured these for study. Here, watch what happens when I turn the light in the hallway on."

Esper walked to a nearby control panel and flipped a switch. With a sputtering buzz, lights powered on down the length of the hall, and I gave a quick prayer to Jinjing. With the lights on, the shell saw me through the passthrough window, and its body came to life. The expression on its face turned to one of distress, and it spoke. "Please, sir, you have to get me out of here. Quickly, before they come back." Esper returned to my side, and the shell stepped back, fear now evident on its face. "Her," it pointed at Esper. "She looks nice, but she's mean and scary. She hurt me!"

Esper opened our side of the passthrough. "I've brought you something to eat." She placed the tray of food along with the pot of mushrooms on the passthrough's floor before closing our side.

The shell continued pointing at Esper, screaming. "She hurt me! She's a wicked old bat!" Esper stepped out of view of the passthrough. Once the shell lost sight of Esper, its aspect changed instantly back to one of pleading. "Please get me out of here before she gets back. I'm hungry and scared."

"Why don't you eat?" I said.

"Eat?"

"Yes, there's food right there." I pointed at the tray and then reached for the mechanism that opened the passthrough window on its side of the cell.

"I'm hungry," it said. It opened the passthrough door on its side, reached for the tray, and stopped. A strange, glottal gasp rose from its throat, and it backed away until it stood on the far side of the room. "I'm hungry." Its tone and pitch replicated exactly as before, followed by a strange gagging gasp. It made no move toward the passthrough.

"It's the fungus," Esper said, pointing at the mushroom pot. "Following instructions from the disc library, I've modified it to emit a chemical that the scholars at Port Donna discovered caused a severe reaction in the contaminated."

I closed my eyes, saw Talia on a bed of blood-soaked snow, and felt such depths of regret at the sharp words I spoke to her during our last conversation.

"Can you imagine it, Kredo?" Esper asked. "We can grow this fungus around farmsteads and villages to repel dark wanderers and contaminants."

In my heart, I knew Talia died believing Esper was not contaminated. Could I now allow myself to agree with her? That would mean I'd have to believe that rather than dying trying to save Duatero, Talia died in a drunken brawl with a fellow falchilo who stumbled upon her in the dark. Worse still, I started to think that maybe it wasn't Bao who killed her. Had Jak overheard her asking me to send him away? Wasn't it Jak who led me to the clearing and found the skin of beer? Hadn't Jak killed Bao before I could question him? Had I misjudged Jak that much?

"You saw the shell's reaction. We can use this fungus to help us identify early-stage contaminants, like the GC used to."

Could I allow myself to believe that—maybe—not everyone I had cleansed had been a contaminant? What would that make me if that were true?

"And the grains I've made—the secrets of Port Donna hold the key to our survival on this planet."

I leaned forward and rested my head on the passthrough window.

"Kredo?" I couldn't make myself reply. "How certain were you Elekti was contaminated?" she asked.

"How certain were you she wasn't?"

"I think my actions give the answer to that."

"And mine don't?"

The actions I took and the people I cleansed—what could I have done differently? Where was it that I lost the path?

Esper shifted her weight from one foot to the other. Her boot scraped the floor as she did. "Your mom had been Culled days earlier," she said. "We'd found a stage five nest out of town, and the GC had stopped working. I think you wanted to find Elekti contaminated so you'd have something you knew how to fight."

"I think you wanted to believe she was a little girl."

She sighed, crossing her arms. "I suppose we'll die never knowing which of us was right."

My memory jumped to Elekti's father. He hunted me down, tried to kill me. Contaminants don't do that. My doubt broke, like a wave on the Nanhai Ocean crashing on the rocks. It took an effort to speak, but I did, quietly. "No. You were right, I was wrong." I was a murderer, a torturer. *Be good, Kredo.* That was the last thing my mom ever asked of me, her last wish before sacrificing herself for Duatero.

"I need help, Kredo. I don't know how to make people see. I don't know how to make them believe me enough to plant the seeds I've created."

"They won't believe me, either."

"They have to."

I stood up straight and looked at her. She was so young. I couldn't imagine myself ever being that young. She had such an intellect and so many years ahead of her to exploit it. Such a gift. Though I might never match her intelligence, I'd been around a while. I knew how things worked. "The first falchilo that sees me will cleanse me as a contaminant." And I'd welcome it.

She seemed so small and fragile at that moment, like a child who'd lost a favourite toy and learned that not even her parents could bring it back. Her face hardened into anger. "I can save us. What are we going to do?"

A voice from behind me made me jump. "You'd better figure it out quickly." I turned to see the source of the voice. The dark altaj—well, just altaj, I supposed—stood at the end of the hall.

"What's happened?" Esper asked.

"The Tian Ti's fallen, and the army's of Duatero march on us. They'll be here any day."

IT CAME to me that my kiraso was really the only home I had now. It formed around my body, supporting me. This armour was worn by Founder Tod C. Levitt, Trooper First Class, who walked the very soils of Earth as a boy. Majstro Antono Spirita donned it the day the falchilo order was founded over a thousand years ago. It protected me as I charged the nests of Eta Monteto and kept me alive while sentinels pinned me against a catacomb wall on the day I first met Jak and Esper. And I wore it now as I prepared to defend Shihbei from forces I had unleashed.

"It's a beautiful day today, isn't it?" Esper said beside me.

I was pretty sure we were going to die. Still, the sun shone high in the sky. The temperature was perfect—not hot, not cold. The air carried the scent of pine.

Altaj Karesinda was on my other side. "A fine day."

Why do people insist on talking about the weather? "They're coming," I said. We stood behind barricades in the centre of the main road leading to the Tian Ti Pass, its crenellated ramparts winding into the mountains. Coming into view around a bend about two kilometres away marched the armies of Duatero, a large band of falchilo at the head. Though I had been told falchilo fought with the army, my heart dropped seeing them march in the vanguard. I took a rough count—there were easily a hundred falchilo. I had never seen such a large gathering of my brethren.

My shield spiralled open. This was my castle wall. My gun, rod, and flamjetilo were my armies that I sent charging into the Enemy. Energy thrummed through my body. Today was a day upon which Duatero turned. You could feel it. The Founders were silent, watching.

Our plan was first to parley, then failing that, fight to defend the last city the Founders had built and the wondrous gifts Esper had created. Shihbei was easy to defend. The only route leading to the city was the Tian Ti, and its rampart was only wide enough for about twenty soldiers. It was a punishing choke point, kilometres long.

Unfortunately, Shihbei's army had been destroyed at the Tian Ti's head. Survivors from the rout had trickled back over the past day, telling tales of falchilo shattering the army. The last line of defence now consisted mostly of young teenagers, women, the old, sick, and wounded. They manned towers lining the path of the Tian Ti as it approached the city, armed with slings, and stood behind barricades, spears jutting out. No one in Shihbei said a word. On the wind, you could hear the tramping feet of the invading army.

Shihbei's mayor stepped forward and walked toward the oncoming army as we had planned. He was going to vie for peace. Minutes passed. Falchilo marched at the army's head. It should have been me going out to negotiate with them; I'd have a better chance of convincing them to stop.

Or maybe not. The sizzling crack of a gun echoed off the mountains, and the mayor fell heavily onto his back. A collective gasp whispered through the streets of Shihbei. A falchilo ran ahead of the others, flamjetilo in hand, and cleansed the mayor. We watched in horror.

"Why would they do that?" Esper asked, aghast. "Why wouldn't they even hear us out?"

"This is a Cull," the altaj said as a thin tendril of smoke from the mayor's burning body twisted into the sky.

"Care to explain?" I asked.

The altaj sighed. "There was going to be another Cull this year. It would have been even worse after your boy Jak convinced them to destroy granaries that had seeds from Shihbei. Now, if they cleanse the entire city of Shihbei, they won't have to."

Already falchilo were leaping into the guard towers along the Tian Ti, and the screams of their defenders came to us on the wind. And still, the train of soldiers—hundreds upon hundreds of them—continued to appear around the bend. A few of the defenders manning the barricades around me were already turning to run. The faces of those who remained held terror. Though many had spears, more than a few had armed themselves with shovels and rakes. One boy had a broom.

Breathing deeply, I closed my eyes and prayed. *May Donna, star of the fields, lead us to safe roads*. Turning to Esper, I gave her my final command. "Run."

The screams from our defenders in the Tian Ti's towers now matched the volume of the thousands of feet marching toward us. "I'm not abandoning Shihbei," Esper told me. She hadn't forgiven me for what I'd done to her—probably never would—and she couldn't seem to speak to me without anger in her voice.

"Yes, you are," I said calmly. "You're going to gather your seeds, those mushrooms that repel contaminants, and all the manlibroj and discs you can carry that contain the secrets of Port Donna, and you're going to get them out of Shihbei to safety."

"Kredo—"

"You know that's what you must do. If Duatero is to have a future, you must do this. You," I pointed to Altaj Karesinda, "go with her. Help her. Esper must make it to safety with as much of her gear and materials as possible."

The invading army was nearly on us.

"And you, Kredo?" the altaj asked. "What will you do?"

I smiled as I drew my gun—Talia's gun. *"Mia korpo estas via shildo."*

A breeze blew a strand of the altaj's grey hair in her face. *"Tiel estu,"* she replied. So be it.

My helmet engulfed my head as I leaped over the barricades, my weak knee twinged as I landed, and I shot a falchilo who was charging.

TWENTY-NINE

SHIHBEI BURNED as the sun set. Flames snapped at the deepening twilight, the sharp smell of wood smoke choked the lungs of defender and invader alike, and glowing embers lazily rained down, buffeted by currents of wind. The defenders of Shihbei had been pushed back onto the very grounds of the Tero Kreinto. Even the paisajista took up arms to defend this holy site.

The armies of Duatero had spilled into Shihbei as relentless as the waters of the Jinhuang when they breach their banks during the spring flood. I fought with all my strength and guile, but I was the only falchilo to stand with Shihbei.

A collective yell rose from the attacking soldiers. They were once more charging the barricade I was manning with several dozen defenders. I stood up, shield open, flamjetilo in hand, and looked down on the narrow path below. Sling bullets ricocheted off my shield as attackers ran toward us. When they were almost at the barricade, I let loose a wave that immolated the front ranks. Burning soldiers ran in mad panic, shrieking. The world was chaos and smoke and the sickening crackle of burning meat. The charging soldiers retreated in terror.

I dropped back behind the barricade. That blast drained my flamjetilo. I had been fighting non-stop, draining my kiraso, and I was down to less than fifteen percent power. My knee ached, but it was holding up.

"Kredo!" a voice called out over the din. I recognized it. Jak.

Keeping my head down, I called back, "Sweet Donna, Jak, what are you doing?"

"Cleansing a nest."

"All of Shihbei is not contaminated."

"Firstsite says Shihbei is a nest and must be cleansed. So, Shihbei will be cleansed."

"This is holy ground. You know this isn't right."

"It's hard talking to you when I can't see you. Why don't you show yourself? Afraid I'll see the contamination on your face?"

"I'm afraid one of your falchilo will blow my head off."

"You'd rather we didn't give you a mercy shot?"

"Look, Jak, you've got to stop this. Esper has figured out how to stop our crop failures. And she's found a way to protect ourselves from contamination."

"Right. Sounds interesting. Why don't you come down, and we'll talk about it?"

"You and I both know you aren't much of a talker." I searched for a paisajista or anyone with authority.

"I suppose you're right," he said. The sizzling crack of a gun sounded, blasting a hole in the barricade no more than two metres away from where I stood.

I saw a paisajista nearby—a gepatro. "Kredo?" Jak called out. "Did that get you?" Saying nothing, I jogged over to the gepatro and told him to keep the defenders together and hold their ground.

"Where will you be?" he asked.

"I've got to make sure Esper makes it out." Without waiting for a reply, I turned and ran through the Tero Kreinto grounds, making my way to the Cangbai Palace.

A long path opened into a courtyard. There, three bodies lay lifeless, dark pools of blood staining the stone in the grey light of dusk. Nearby the sound of crashing wood and screams rampaged. A falchilo's gun fired somewhere.

A large building made from one mountainous block of white Founder stone rose from the far end of the courtyard. Wide stone stairs led to heavy doors made from redwood. White panels with painted blue spirals, the symbol of Donna, surrounded the doors. Above the door were six ornate balconies flanked by windows that rose like rungs of a ladder for giants. The Cangbai Palace. This was where Esper lived and worked while in Shihbei.

The front doors were barricaded and guarded by paisajista. I was about to approach when a squad of several dozen soldiers wearing the livery of one of Duatero's armies charged screaming from a side road. Slings whistled over the barricade, sending bullets whipping into the attackers. About five soldiers dropped, and the rest attacked, scrambling up the barricade where paisajista stabbed at them with spears, shovels, chairs, and any other item they had found.

My instinct was to help, but I knew Shihbei was lost. The only thing that mattered now was Esper had to escape with her discoveries—that's where my attention and efforts had to stay. I avoided the scrum and made my way to a side entrance, making my way along a covered walkway that flanked the length of the courtyard, leading to a passage clinging to the periphery of the Cangbai. Wooden doors spaced along the left-hand wall led into the palace.

Another dead body lay in the hall—friend or foe, I had no way of telling—and I stepped over it as I came to a door, indistinguishable from the others, and entered.

Flickering light bulbs lit the narrow hallway, casting strange, dancing shadows. The glowing orbs hummed softly with power, each flicker accompanied by a buzz reminding me of a bee defending its hive. I touched a bulb and gave thanks to Founder Jinjing for lighting my way through this darkness.

I was alone in the hall but heard voices yelling elsewhere in the building. "They've breached the entrance! Defend the altaj!" If Altaj Karesinda was here, maybe Esper was, too.

The whump of a flamjetilo sounded, followed by the sickening screams of men and women burning alive. I ran up a set of stairs, passing the altaj's personal guards running down. Grabbing one, I pulled him aside. "Where's the altaj?" figuring she'd still be with Esper.

"Third floor. Go, help her—defend the altaj!" The report of gunfire sounded from elsewhere within the palace. A bell rang madly.

Upward I ran and onto the third floor. I ran down a hall, then another. At its end, a small squad of invaders approached. They wore the livery of Aaronsburg and had no falchilo with them. They saw me, stopped, and saluted. They thought I was one of the falchilo with the attacking armies. I leaped down the hall, closing the distance to them in a heartbeat. With a flurry of blows, I sent their bodies scattering as a child might stomp through a pile of sticks and twigs.

More attackers appeared behind me. Before they had a chance to think whether I was ally or enemy, I darted toward them and scattered their crumpled bodies across the hall. For the moment, I was alone, standing in a hall, bodies littering the floor, a spray of blood on the white stone walls dripping down. A luxurious carpet lined the hall, a complex geometric pattern running its length. Paintings hung on the walls. Bells clanged through the palace, and it seemed from further distant, too, out in the Tero Kreinto compound.

Voices came from nearby. I ran through the unfamiliar corridors searching for them. When I found their source— more attackers—I sent them crashing into walls with the force of a dozen sentinels.

A woman's shrill voice begged for mercy. Then, Jak's voice. "To the human whose body this once was . . ." I ran, desperately trying to find them. The whoosh of the flamjetilo sounded, and then screams, screams like an ox sinking in the mud along the shores of the Okcidento River bleating in a panic the moment before it goes under, or a soldier losing a gangrenous limb to the kuracisto's saw, or a mad banshee screeching a dozen lifetimes of pain into the night.

I turned the corner and saw a nightmare come to life. Jak had his back to me. In front of him, a human body, unrecognizable in the flames, thrashed on the ground. "Was that Esper?"

He turned at the sound of my voice. "Majstro," he greeted me. The hall was hazy with smoke. "I promised I would cleanse you and not let the contamination make a mockery of what you've accomplished. I don't know if you're still in there to hear me, but I've come to fulfill that promise."

I screamed and charged, my shield spiralling open and my rod snapping to full length. He barely had time to open his shield before I drove into him. He fell backward into the flaming embers, sending a cloud of black smoke and sparks into the air. His kiraso protected him as flames on either side licked up a tapestry hanging on the walls tickling the ceiling.

I stabbed my rod at him. He rolled out of the way and was up, his own rod out now.

We deflected jabs from each other's rods and bashed each other with our shields. He was good, quick—his body was younger than mine. But I've been at this game a long time. Flames were spreading along the floor. The art and tapestries along the walls ignited. The wood of the ceiling above us was starting to catch. I let him force me back through the fire. When he stood in the epicentre of the blaze, I held my ground. His kiraso would give him some protection, but I wasn't forcing him into the fire to burn him. He was on the spot where the beam of his flamjetilo set the flame. The flamjetilo does not light kindling like a match lights straw. Rather, it causes the very substance of the target to erupt in flame from the inside out. The floor was char, and it gave way under his weight. He fell through and crashed on the floor below amid a rain of fiery detritus.

"Fuck," he moaned.

"Language," I admonished.

I did not leap down through the flaming hole to press my advantage. I desperately wanted to believe that it was not Esper he had cleansed, and so I ran, searching for her. Jak's footsteps thumped behind me. I took cover in a doorway, hiding as he sped past. I jumped him from behind, but some sense warned him, and he spun, shield open. Still, I hit him hard. The blow sent him crashing through a door. I attacked before he could get up.

I kept him rolling on the floor as I jabbed my rod at him. Whenever he tried to rise, I bashed him down with my shield. We were in a bedroom, the bed neatly made. Jak grabbed the legs of a nearby nightstand and hurled it at me. It crashed off my shield. He rolled under the bed, but I tossed it across the room, my strength augmented by the kiraso. He kicked out and drove the heel of his foot into my injured knee, and it buckled.

He dived at me. I used the momentum from his charge and flung him crashing through the wooden shutters of a window and into the night air beyond. It was a three-story drop. His kiraso would keep him alive, though the fall would hurt—a lot. That ought to slow him down.

My knee throbbed, and I struggled to stand. That nasty little thug probably remembered my knee was injured and kicked it again on purpose. I needed to use my rod as a support as I continued searching for Esper.

And then I heard her voice. "Kredo?" I don't think I've ever known such happiness. The Founders had not abandoned me. She was behind me in the smoke-filled hall, her helmet down, face covered with soot. She had a large pack and several boxes in her hand.

"What are you still doing here?" I asked.

"By the time I got all my supplies, the Tero Kreinto was under attack. Kredo, I think Jak murdered the altaj."

Yes. That's what he did. "You're still safe, and you have your supplies—that's what's important. We have to go. Now."

We ran. Esper had to support me as my knee could bear little weight. We ran downstairs and out into a courtyard. A building burned to our left, casting dancing shadows in the night, and in them, I thought I saw the spirits of the Founders, leaping, urging us on.

"There they are!" Jak shouted from some distance away. "Soldiers, after them! Don't let them get away!"

We bolted through a tangle of buildings in the Tero Kreinto complex. A dozen fires lit the night, soldiers yelled, and slings whistled. Fires illuminated a massive building of red Founder stone to my left, and we took cover in it. We ran past chapels and shrines, offices, and rooms. We crashed out a door into the night air, flames behind us, dancing.

Ahead of us, a Founder road clung to a ridge toward an outcropping of buildings less than half a kilometre away, and beyond that, the forests of the Shandong Mountains. Soldiers yelled behind us, their feet tramping the ground in pursuit. We ran.

We ran until I could run no more. My knee gave out, and I dropped. "Come on," Esper said, using her kiraso's strength to pull me to my feet.

"No," I said. "This is as far as I go." The road ahead wound into the darkness of the woods.

She punched me lightly in the chest. "Don't give up. Fight for Duatero."

"I will," I said. "But I fight a different fight than you. Take your seeds and plants and take them back to Duatero. Plant them. Plant the fungus where it will repel contamination. Plant the seeds where the grain will grow."

"But the armies of Duatero control the Tian Ti Pass."

"Then find another way through the mountains. I will buy you time to get away, but it is you who must save us."

She stared at me with her one eye. I wondered if she was going to argue more, or if she was going to tell me she needed me, that she couldn't do it on her own, and all the things people say when faced with too big an obligation. But, she breathed deeply, her shoulders relaxed, and she said, "I will find a way."

Would she? The Shandong Mountains were high and dangerous. She didn't have any food, and her kiraso's power wouldn't last the night trekking through the terrain. For whatever help they might be, I gave her my flamjetilo, drained as it was, and Talia's gun—Esper's gun, now. I was done with killing and cleansing.

"I burned your almond seed," I said, remembering another night under the stars where she taught me of miracles. Strange that I should feel compelled to confess that now. "I could have planted it in Firstsite's Tero Kreinto where it would grow and feed the future. Through it, life could have entered the universe. But I didn't because I was afraid, and so I burned it. Find another miracle to plant, and then plant it. Don't wait, don't show it to a fool like me."

I knew she had not forgiven me for all that I'd done, and I knew I could never deserve it, but still, she looked at me with a kind expression. "Founders smile on you," she said, and then she slipped away into the darkness.

I turned to face the Tero Kreinto. It was in flames, and it cast a baleful light on the mountainside. A group of soldiers was exiting it along the road that would take them to me. A falchilo led them. Jak. He saw me soon enough and screamed my name, his voice bouncing off the mountain walls like a stone skipping over water.

I snapped my rod open and engaged my shield. And then my kiraso ran out of power.

THIRTY

JAK APPROACHED, soldiers at his back and the fires of the Tero Kreinto casting him in silhouette. He was limping, and his kiraso seemed battered. His fall out the window must have hurt. Probably not enough to compensate for my kiraso's lack of power. "Where is Esper?" he demanded

"Dead," I said. "I cleansed her in one of the greenhouses outside of the city before they captured me."

He smiled a vicious, nasty smile. He had caught my mistake. "*Her*?" He scanned the dark woods past me. Turning to the soldiers behind him, he ordered, "Search the woods up ahead. There's a contaminated falchilo trying to escape."

"It's been cleansed," I said, still hoping to at least sow the seeds of doubt. "There's only me." I had to buy Esper time. Her kiraso still had power, so she could handle the soldiers if they found her. My eyes drifted to the flamjetilo harness Jak wore. He was the danger.

"Did you kill Talia?" I asked.

His expression told me the truth before his words. "She was your weakness, Kredo, and Duatero needed you strong."

I should have been enraged, should have burned for vengeance, but I felt only sadness. Talia knew the truth about him, but I did not listen. Her eyes had always been better than mine.

Esper. She was all that mattered now. Buy time. "We call native plants 'Malamiko'," I said. "The word means 'enemy' in the tongue of the Classic Kronoj. You broke Stelara's Kodo when you killed her, Jak. You are Malamiko."

"Can't resist giving one last lesson, can you?" he asked. "I don't know if you're alive in there and can hear me, Kredo, but I want to thank you. You were a good mentor. Through you, I've achieved great things. In honor of that," he snapped his rod to full length, "I will make sure you're dead before I cleanse you."

Before I could think, his shield spiraled open as his helmet engulfed his head, and he charged like a bolt of lightning.

I dropped to the ground in a ball rather than hit him head-on as I would if my suit had power. He slammed into me with the force of a charging ox and tripped over my prone body, his momentum sending him rolling along the ground for meters.

The impact of his legs sent pangs of pain through my ribs —he probably broke one or two of them. I struggled to my feet, keeping my weight off my injured knee as much as I could. Buy time. "Jak, there's no need for this." Pain stabbed in my chest as I spoke. "Listen to me." He probably did not yet realize my kiraso had no power. That might make him cautious and slow to attack.

That said, caution had never been one of Jak's traits. He charged me again. I tried to sidestep him, but he was too fast. He shield-bashed me with a force that took me off my feet and made every bone in my body throb. The breath was blasted from my chest when I hit the ground. "You've no power, do you?" Jak asked.

"Well, it's been a long day," I said, wheezing air back into my lungs. "Lot's of fighting, being the only falchilo defender of Shihbei and all. Your kiraso must be pretty low, too, after marching all the way here." I tried to get up, but my body wouldn't obey.

"My kiraso's fine. We didn't wear our armor for the march, so I can go on for a good long while, yet." He jabbed his rod at me. I managed to get my shield up, deflecting his blow off to my side. I stabbed my rod at him. He was over-confident, cocky, and that made him sloppy enough that I almost got him. So close—if only I were a little bit faster.

He stabbed at me, but I managed to roll out of the way. I tried to stand. He swatted me with his shield, hitting me with the force of an avalanche. I found myself face down on the road. Buy time. Instinctively, I rolled out of the way, expecting him to come at me with the rod, and struggled to my feet.

The sizzling crack of a gun fired, and at the same instant, a punch hit me in my back. It didn't feel like a big hit, not like getting shield-bashed by Jak. Even so, a force whirled my body around, and I flopped helplessly onto my back.

I tried to get up, but it seemed the weight of the Shandong Mountains themselves pushed me down, and I could not feel my right arm. I needed a moment's rest to get my breathing under control. The night sky filled my vision. Could I see Terosuno from here? Ah, there it was at the tail of Aaron's Cross. The light from that star began its journey before the Founders were even born, and here it is reaching me now, thousands of years after they had died. Such a wonder, this universe.

I was having trouble catching my breath. My brain caught up with events. I'd been shot.

Pulling my eyes from the heavens, I rolled my head to see who shot me. It was Mihaelo, clad in the splendor of the kapo's kiraso. Founders, no, not Mihaelo. I knew the deep, festering pain of cleansing a falchilo, and to know my mentor would carry that with him weighed my spirit. He held his gun still pointing at me. It was called the Rava, named after the first falchilo recorded to own it, and it was the personal weapon of the kapo.

Buy time. I tried to speak but didn't have enough breath to give life to my voice. Mihaelo came over, his helmet down, and he kneeled at my side, Jak looming behind him, arms crossed. Mihaelo wore heartbreak on his face as he manually withdrew my helmet so he could look me in the eye. A vision of Aprila in the mud came to me, and I supposed I would see her soon. Mihaelo only knew what he knew and could only base his actions on that. My mouth moved as I tried to tell him that I forgave him, that I understood, but all that came out of my mouth was a wheezing, wet gasp. I put the sentiment in my eyes instead.

He cupped my head in his hand as he told me in a hoarse whisper, "Tonight, you dine with the Founders, Kredo. And your mother, and Talia." Oh, Talia. Tonight, she and I will dance. I will beg her forgiveness, and then we will dance and dance.

"It's a shame about the kiraso," Jak said.

The right side of my torso began to throb like someone was jabbing a red-hot poker into my chest with each breath. My vision began to narrow, and I fought for consciousness. I felt my mother's hand in mind. It was cold, but I held it tight as pain stabbed me.

The soldiers returned, their leader approaching Jak.

"What'd you find?" Jak asked.

Founders, keep Esper safe, I prayed.

"Nothing, Falchilo. There is no sign of anyone. It's night, though. Easy enough for a contaminant in a black kiraso to hide."

Thank Donna, Aaron, Jinjing, Dorian, Sabine, and all the Founders.

"It's out there," Mihaelo said, rising to stand. "Get all the soldiers and falchilo you can and scour these woods."

I allowed myself to believe. I believed Esper would make it and that she'd save Duatero. The troops ran off to obey, and I imagined her moving through the forest, evading them and the falchilo who would follow. I saw her find a pass through the mountains to the mainland and envisioned her planting her contaminant-repelling fungus around towns and homesteads.

"Shall I cleanse it?" Jak asked.

"No," Mihaelo said, taking the flamjetilo from Jak. "It should be me."

I imagined Esper planting her grain, and I saw it flourish in the summer sun. I had a vision of my brother Fondo eating, and his children growing up strong and having children of their own, and I saw Gaja laughing as she held a grandchild in her arms, singing a song our mother sang to us. Hope. Such a small, subtle thing. Yet on its foundation, we reach up, touch heaven, and bring some of its grace back with us.

"To Kredo, whose body this once was, your torment is at its end. Tonight, you dine with the Founders."

Time slowed as I finally held onto that eternity between falling grains of sand. My vision faded, and I could no longer see the stars. Instead, laughter rang in my ears while music played, and plates and cutlery clattered on a table nearby. Voices beckoned me, growing louder. Where were they? They were near and getting closer. Somewhere far off in the distance, there came another voice, but it was thin and fading away, like a breeze blowing through a field at summer's end. "To Malamiko who stole this body—*burn*."

We are blind, but we'll find our way.

Tiel estu.

ACKNOWLEDGMENTS

Many years ago, when I still worked in the biotech industry, I was at an event where one of the speakers dropped this wisdom bomb: "If the only prayer you know is 'thank you,' then that is enough." There are many to whom I wish to express my gratitude. I am blessed with a couple of phenomenal editors and beta readers. Adria Laycraft did a fantastic job editing an early version of this novel and helped me turn it from something that was initially quite dark into a story with glimmers of redemption and hope. Over the years, Sarah Johnson at the Alexandra Writers' Centre Society has taught me much about the craft of writing through her insightful reviews of the stories I have written. I owe a large debt of gratitude to Edward Willett at Shadowpaw Press for giving Duatero life after its original publisher retired. My mother and father, Hilda and Ed Anderson, and my wife, Joelle Bradley, continue to be my biggest cheerleaders. They have been excited by my writing since the beginning and spread the word I was an "author" long before I felt the epithet applied to me.

Creating the world of *Duatero* was an enormous task combining equal parts of imagination and research. I had a theme I wanted to explore with my readers, and I felt the best way to allow my readers to engage with that theme was to create a setting that was familiar enough they could relate to it yet different enough that their personal beliefs and attitudes did not influence their interpretation of the story. Achieving that, in part, required the construction of the Founder-worship religion. To this end, I found Dr. John R. Hale's video series, *Exploring the Roots of Religion*, an invaluable resource. To create an alien planet that, though it teemed with life, was unable to support human habitation, I had to speculate on the biochemistry of alien plants and animals. To all the budding xenobiochemists out there, I found the "Alternative Biochemistry" webpage on the *Speculative Evolution Wiki* a useful primer on alternative metabolic pathways that extraterrestrial life might possess. For those who felt the pathology of the contamination that terrorized the people of Duatero was too fantastical or little more than a writer's flight of fancy, you might want to research the impact of the fungus *Ophiocordyceps unilateralis* on ant colonies before you judge my artistic liberties too harshly (or maybe not, if you enjoy sleeping at night).

Finally, I wish to thank you, the reader. It is my sincere desire that this story has touched your life and added value in some way. I hope you found within these pages ideas worth talking about and debating. I believe we can become wiser. We draw on wisdom to navigate a complex world where there are no clear answers to our problems. Through exploring the lives of Kredo, Esperanta, Talia, and Jak, let us together learn how to act wisely in a turbulent world.

ABOUT THE AUTHOR

BRAD C. ANDERSON lives with his wife and puppy in Vancouver, Canada. He teaches undergraduate business courses at a local university and researches organizational wisdom in blithe defiance of the fact most people do not think you can put those two words in the same sentence without irony. Previously, he worked in the biotech sector, where he made drugs for a living (legally!).

His stories have appeared in a variety of publications. His short story "Naïve Gods" was longlisted for a 2017 Sunburst Award for Excellence in Canadian Literature of the Fantastic. It was published in the anthology *Lazarus Risen*, which was itself nominated for an Aurora Award.